THE ALEXANDER SECRET

Book 1 of The Mahabharata Quest Series

Christopher C. Doyle is an author who transports the reader into a fascinating world where ancient secrets buried in legends blend with science and history to create a gripping story.

His debut novel, *The Mahabharata Secret,* featured among the top ten books of 2013 and was nominated for the Raymond Crossword Book Award, 2014. He followed it up with the bestselling The Mahabharata Quest series, featuring *The Alexander Secret* and *The Secret of the Druids* and the bestselling The Pataala Prophecy series featuring *Son of Bhrigu* and *The Mists of Brahma,* all of which have won rave reviews from readers.

Christopher can be contacted at:

Website: www.authorchristophercdoyle.com

Email: contact@christophercdoyle.com

Facebook: www.facebook.com/authorchristophercdoyle

The Quest Club: www.authorchristophercdoyle.com/the-quest-club

Other books by Christopher C. Doyle

The Mahabharata Quest Series

The Secret of the Druids

The Khandavaprastha Conspiracy

The Pataala Prophecy

Son of Bhrigu

The Mists of Brahma

BOOK 1

THE MAHABHARATA QUEST

THE ALEXANDER SECRET

CHRISTOPHER C. DOYLE

First published by westland ltd in 2014

Published by Westland Publications Private Limited in 2017

Published by Westland Books, a division of Nasadiya Technologies Private Limited, in 2022

No. 269/2B, First Floor, 'Irai Arul', Vimalraj Street, Nethaji Nagar, Alapakkam Main Road, Maduravoyal, Chennai 600095

Westland and the Westland logo are the trademarks of Nasadiya Technologies Private Limited, or its affiliates.

ISBN: 9789395767255

10 9 8 7 6 5 4 3

Typeset by PrePSol Enterprises Pvt. Ltd

Printed at Thomson Press India Private Limited

The jewel, the illuminator, shone in his hand;
Khizr looked down; what he sought, he found.
That fountain appeared like silver,
Like a silver stream which strains from the middle of the rock.
Not a fountain,—which is far from this speech;
But if, verily, it were,—it was a fountain of light.
How is the star in the morning-time?
As the morning star is in the morning,—even so it was.
How is the undiminished moon at night?
So it was that it was greater than the moon.

CANTO LXIX - ESKANDAR NAMA

For

Ajay Mago and Dipa Chaudhuri

For their faith in my writing

Their guidance while writing my first book

And for giving me my first break as an author.

ACKNOWLEDGEMENTS

This book owes its existence to many people. I am grateful to each person for their contribution towards its writing.

First and foremost, my wife, Sharmila and my daughter Shaynaya, who put up with my long absences while I wrote the book and researched it for well over a year. I could never have written it without their support and understanding. Shaynaya also helped me with the research for this book, as she did for my last book, especially with the mythology and history.

Artika Bakshi, Asha Michigan, and my wife, Sharmila, who read the final draft of the book and gave me valuable inputs that ensured the book stayed true to its promise.

Dr Rajesh Bhatia, Director — Department for Communicable Diseases at the WHO Regional Office for South East Asia, who patiently put up with all my queries and theories around the science that is presented in this book. By critically reading the draft and straightening out errors in my understanding, his support was invaluable in ensuring the accuracy of the scientific and medical facts, concepts and evidence presented. His aid, while ensuring the final hypothesis and speculation is plausible and supported by scientific evidence, in no way implies that he agrees with any or all of the theories, hypothesis or interpretations that I have presented in this book.

Mrs Jyoti Trivedi and Mrs Asha Michigan who not only provided help and expertise with the Sanskrit language, but also patiently answered all my questions on the interpretation of the original Sanskrit shlokas and verified that the meanings I attributed to some of the Sanskrit words were correct.

Anand Prakash, who designed the brilliant cover of this book and made the story within these pages spring to life.

My thanks go out to Gerald Nordley, Jacqueline Schumann, Phyllis Irene Radford, Kevin Andrew Murphy, Christy Marx, Pat MacEwen, Barritt Firth and Dave Trowbridge, fellow scribes in my writers' research group, who answered all my questions on topics that were hard to research, to ensure accuracy in the book.

Mayank Mehta for creating the maps in this book that depict the route that Alexander took over two thousand years ago, and the locations featured in this book. Priyankar Gupta for the brilliant illustrations that brought my descriptions to life.

A big thank you to all the people at Westland, especially Gautam Padmanabhan, who also read the final draft and provided valuable inputs on the plot and story. And to Sanghamitra Biswas, my editor, who has done such a wonderful job of polishing my writing and keeping the narrative true to the plot.

While the books, articles, blogs and videos that I researched are too numerous to be listed here, as they would make up a book by themselves, I must acknowledge every reference that I researched while writing this book. Without the wealth of information about the history and the science behind the speculation I have presented in the book, it would have been very difficult to propose theories backed by evidence and research, which made my job so much easier.

Finally, while I acknowledge the contribution of everyone who has supported me, I take full responsibility for all errors and omissions of fact or detail in this book.

PROLOGUE

316 BC

Gabiene, Persia, present day Iran

Eumenes lay on the bed in his prison tent and brooded on his fate. He knew he was doomed. He was a prisoner of Antigonus, the One-Eyed, with whom he had crossed swords before. This time he had been betrayed in the final battle. His own satraps had handed him over to the one-eyed general, in exchange for their baggage train which had been seized by Antigonus.

The capture of Eumenes had been celebrated publicly by Antigonus as the end of a long, bitter rivalry. But later that day, as the sun set, Antigonus had paid Eumenes a private visit.

It was then that Eumenes realised that Antigonus knew the true reason behind Alexander's determination to march to the land of the great Indus; about what Alexander had found there. And he knew what had led the great conqueror to his death just two years later.

Eumenes had first served Philip, Alexander's father, as a friend and secretary. After Philip's assassination he had been Alexander's chief secretary. It was Eumenes who had maintained the King's Journals—the royal diaries, keeping daily records of the State. But it was what Eumenes had left *out* of the journals that was more important: a record of Alexander's true ambitions and the great secret that had made him a god.

Sixteen years earlier, Eumenes had accompanied the conqueror to the Temple of Zeus-Ammon in the Siwa Oasis, where Alexander had been told that he was the son of Zeus-Ammon. And, therefore, a God himself.

Alexander had lost no time in proclaiming his divinity and began his march further east, towards the Indus River, to the ultimate goal that would truly make him a god. The stories he had heard about the great secret that would enable him to achieve that goal drove him relentlessly forward, even as his soldiers yearned for their homes.

Eumenes had stood with Alexander outside the underground cave where the secret of the gods was hidden. But Alexander had entered the cavern alone. When he returned, his face was flushed with triumph. He had found what he came for.

Proof of Alexander's success in his secret mission came during the siege of the Mallis, during the journey back home along the Indus. Alexander had led the attack, scaling the wall using a ladder which broke and left him among the barbarians and separated from his army. So radiant was his face and so bright his armour that the barbarians had, at first, fled in fright, thinking a god had arrived in their midst! They had, however, recovered fast and charged. But Alexander had fought on with two guards by his side. Despite being struck by an arrow that lodged in his ribs, he put up a valiant stand, until the Macedonians made their way in and rescued their king.

But while the operation to extricate the arrow was under way, stories had spread in the camp that the conqueror was dead. Eumenes had waited anxiously for days outside Alexander's cabin on his boat, for news of the conqueror's health until, at last, Alexander emerged on deck, weak but alive. Whispers reached Eumenes' ears about the miracle that had saved Alexander. The wound should have been fatal; a lot of blood had been lost. The physicians had given up – there was nothing they could do to heal the internal wounds or stem the blood loss.

But, even as they sat by helplessly, awaiting their king's death, Alexander's wound had begun to heal. The healing process was slow but it had started spontaneously. Observing Alexander's recovery, the physicians had promptly tended to him in an attempt to accelerate the healing. And in a matter of days, the conqueror had recovered, his wounds healed, and he had insisted on showing himself to his men despite his weakened state.

Eumenes did not know what to think of the rumours. But on that day, like the rest of the army, he, too, believed that Alexander was a god. Immortal. Impervious to any weapon known to man. And Eumenes knew that Alexander's visit to the cavern of the gods had a role to play in this transformation.

But now he was also convinced that, whatever the great secret that had lain in the cavern, whatever Alexander had done that night when he entered the cavern alone, it had something to do with the affliction which had left the conqueror delirious with fever, hoarse with thirst and unable to speak during his final days in Babylon. Alexander's ambition to become a god had been achieved, but ironically at the cost of his life.

Eumenes also knew that it was this secret of Alexander's that had been the reason the conqueror's body lay in death for six days without decomposing, as fresh and white as if Alexander was alive and merely sleeping.

And, now, here he was, a prisoner to one of Alexander's generals, who would surely execute him.

His only consolation was that Alexander's great secret was safe. Eumenes had faithfully recorded all of the information from Callisthenes' book, *Deeds of Alexander.* But he had removed from the official journals the portions of the book that referred to the secret mission that Callisthenes had undertaken on behalf of Alexander, in the land of the Sogdians, before the conqueror executed the historian. He had, instead, recorded his personal account of his experience with Alexander, along with Callisthenes' mission, in his own secret journal, which he kept concealed in his tent as he campaigned.

He had also destroyed all his papers and documents before the great battle with Antigonus, denouncing his satraps as a "herd of wild beasts". The secret journal had been despatched through a trusted courier to Olympias, Alexander's mother, who was busy protecting the Macedonian throne from the ambitions of Cassander.

Antigonus would get nothing.

He drew a satisfied breath. He had done his duty by his conqueror. Antigonus, Ptolemy, Cassander – the men who were carving out Alexander's empire amongst themselves – would never know Alexander's great secret from the land of the Indus.

And neither would the rest of the world.

391 AD

Burial of a Secret

The empty wagon trundled along the lonely country road, its journey illuminated by the weak light of a half-moon. The horse trotted along, seemingly in no hurry, as if it knew that its mission was over and there was no longer any need for urgency. For the wagon had, until three days ago, carried something precious. Something valuable. Something that the world had worshipped for the last 500 years.

It was no longer safe. The new religion that had arisen in the Middle East was spreading rapidly across the world. Based on the life and death of a man called The Christ, it had reached

Egypt, where the relic had lain for over 500 years. The new converts, who called themselves Christians, after their leader whom they believed to be the Son of God, were questioning the old gods. Statues were being torn down, temples were being destroyed, and images were being defaced.

It would have been a matter of time before the tide reached the sacred spot in Alexandria where the object of worship had lain buried, undisturbed for five centuries.

It had to be protected. And the Order had taken it upon itself to discharge this responsibility. The contents of the now empty wagon had been transported from its resting place in Alexandria, across rivers and oceans — borne in boats, ships, carts and wagons that bore the symbol of the Order.

A single serpent with five heads raised as if to strike.

It had been this symbol that had kept curious eyes and inquisitive minds away from the treasure on its journey. For the symbol was feared by all who saw it. The Order was secret — no one really knew what the Order was or who its members were; or even what its origins were—but its deeds were not.

Finally, its duty complete, the wagon and its driver were making their way towards the desert. The driver, Karmal, had one last stop to make.

The wagon passed through a village, hushed and silent. Asleep. Though the silence could have equally been on account of the serpent symbol painted on the sides of the wagon.

Presently, it reached the boundary wall of a large house and entered the gates, which were open, as if Karmal's arrival were expected. At the end of the driveway stood the house, a multi-storeyed structure, built of stone and brick.

The wagon stopped before the main door of the house and Karmal dismounted. He didn't have to wait long as the door opened and a tall figure emerged, hooded and cloaked.

'Is it done?' the hooded stranger asked in deep tones.

Karmal nodded wearily. It had been a long journey and he was tired.

'Good. Then you know what you must do.' The man turned to go.

'Wait,' Karmal held out his hand.

The figure spun around, clearly surprised. 'What is it?'

'Keep this.' Karmal placed something in the man's hand and resumed his seat on the wagon. He had one final task to complete.

The man stared after Karmal as the wagon exited the gate and disappeared from view, his hand clenched tight around the metal object Karmal had handed him. Then, he hurried into the house and threw off the hood, revealing a lean face with deep-set eyes and thin lips.

He unclenched his fist and stared at the small copper capsule that lay in his palm. Then, closing his fist around it once more, he bounded up the stairs and entered a study on the first floor.

After latching the door of the study, he sat down at the desk. His face was pale and he found his hands trembling.

What had that fool Karmal done?

He knew that Karmal would not fail the Order. He would faithfully drive the wagon for a few miles and then abandon the horse to trudge deep into the desert where he would slit his own throat. For no one should know the location of the relic. The Order had decreed that, to protect it, the relic should disappear forever.

Using a knife, he carefully prised open the cap that covered one end of the capsule, and shook it over the desk.

A thin strip of vellum fell out. He groaned. Even without looking at it, he knew.

It was a map!

He quickly rolled it up and stuffed it back into the copper capsule. The Order should never get to know about the existence of this map. It was the only clue to a location that was supposed to have been secret; hidden away forever.

He contemplated destroying the map then decided against it. He was the only one who knew of its existence. It could come in useful later, if he was ever in trouble with the Order.

But the map would have to be artfully concealed in a place and manner that only he knew of. And after him, the location would stay secret.

And he knew just the place to hide the capsule away.

June 1990

St. James College, Philadelphia, USA

Mike Ashford gritted his teeth as he willed the photocopier to work faster. It was brand new, one of the latest models which could photocopy using plain paper rather than the electrostatic copiers or the wet-type plain paper machines that were in vogue earlier. Yet, it was not fast enough for his purpose.

Sweat beaded his brow as he thought back to the telephone call that he had answered two hours ago.

'Mike Ashford?' the voice on the other end of the line enquired.

'Yes. Who is this?'

'Never mind. That isn't important. Listen very carefully. I need something that you have. The papyrus documents that you discovered yesterday.'

Ashford was puzzled. He had told no one about the papyrus journals that he had found in a box in the basement of the library, apart from the faculty at the Classics Department. Had someone from the department leaked the news? That would be unlikely. Then, again, this unknown caller knew.

'What documents?' he ventured, testing the waters.

The voice grew hard. 'Don't play games with me, Ashford. I want the documents delivered to the address I will give you now. The journals should be in a sealed envelope. I don't want the papyrus falling apart. Even if they are in relatively good condition.' The caller proceeded to dictate an address in downtown Philadelphia.

Ashford was stunned. The caller had detailed knowledge about the journals, even down to the condition of the papyri!

'And if I refuse?' he countered. 'These journals are the property of the college. As the librarian, it is my responsibility to protect them, not pass them around to anyone who calls.'

A note of impatience entered the voice of the caller. 'Fine, then. You had your chance. You didn't take it.'

The call was abruptly disconnected, leaving Ashford listening to an engaged tone.

He would have dismissed it as a crank call had it not been for the shocking news that he received just forty-five minutes later. Carl Dunn, the faculty member from the Classics Department whom he had first spoken to about the papyrus journals, had been hit by a car as he was crossing the street in front of his house. Dunn had died on the spot. The car that mowed him down had vanished. There were no eyewitnesses so the car would remain untraceable.

An uneasy feeling took hold of Ashford as he received the news. Dunn was a good man. A deeply religious Catholic, he had fitted well into this Jesuit liberal arts college. Was his shadowy caller behind this accident? It seemed too much of a coincidence.

He now recalled the mysterious circumstances that surrounded the disappearance, two weeks ago, of Lawrence Fuller, a former Professor of Classics and Dean at the college. Fuller was returning from attending a seminar at the Oriental Institute of the University of Chicago. He had checked out of his hotel and then vanished into thin air. The doorman at his hotel and the bell boy had reported seeing him into a cab but he never made it to the airport. The college had, under the terms of Fuller's employment contract, taken custody of his letters and journals. These had been stuffed in boxes and buried in the basement without cataloguing them at the time. It was in one of these boxes that Ashford had found the papyri, while he was doing an inventory of Fuller's possessions.

Where did that leave him then? Ashford had been obstinate, turned down the caller's request. Would he be next?

Thinking swiftly, he made up his mind. He had one advantage over the caller. No one knew about the two journals he had found along with the papyri. He hadn't told Dunn or anyone else about it. Both journals were in English and one was a translation of the contents of the papyri, a fact that had been emblazoned across the first page of the journal in Fuller's handwriting. If the translation had surprised him, the second journal had left him dumbfounded. Dazed.

If the two journals together meant what he thought they did, then this discovery was more than just unearthing meaningless documents that were thousands of years old.

The future of the world could be at stake.

The copier spat out the last copy. Ashford hurriedly gathered up the papers and stapled them together. Gathering the two sets of photocopies, he stuffed them into an envelope and scrawled the recipient's address with shaking hands that revealed his state of mind. For a few moments he stared at the sealed envelope as if reconsidering his course of action.

He called his colleague, from the architecture department, who had offered to drop off the package at the FedEx office downtown. Five minutes later, the package was safely on its way to its destination.

After his colleague left with the package, Ashford slumped in his chair. He had done everything he could to ensure that he was not the only one who knew what the journals contained. He was a simple man with a strong sense of duty. Even in this situation, the thought that the journals themselves could have been despatched to his friend had not crossed his mind. They were the property of the college and had to stay here. Like the papyrus texts. His solution had been to photocopy the journals and send them off instead.

Ashford knew what was in store for him. His mysterious caller didn't sound like the kind of person who liked being trifled with. He had no idea what to do next to protect himself. He had thought of making a run for it, but where could he go? This college had been his life for the last thirty-five years and he had not stepped out of the campus in all that time, except for the one occasion when he had attended a conference in Washington DC, in 1983. That was the time he had made his only friend outside the college, a historian from India who was speaking at the conference on the subject of preserving ancient documents. They had hit it off, surprisingly, and stayed in touch over the years. It was this friend whom he had now sent the photocopies to.

Resigned to what was to come, he closed his eyes and began praying. A devout Catholic, this was his only succour when he had problems.

The sound of footsteps approaching his office made him open his eyes. Five men entered and fanned out along the walls. He could see the bulge in their jackets indicating shoulder holsters. They were armed. Except for the one in the centre, a tall man with coal-black eyes and an intense look on his face as if he was perpetually in deep philosophical thought. He was clearly the leader of this pack.

The unarmed man's eyes alighted on the papyrus documents on Ashford's desk. 'Ah, I see you've kept them ready for me.' He made it sound as if he was appreciative, but the menacing look on his face never changed. At a gesture, one of his men picked up the papyri and carefully eased them into a leather briefcase he was carrying.

Ashford stared at them defiantly. He still had an ace up his sleeve. The two journals he had photocopied, which were now safely in a drawer in his desk.

'You have something more for me, don't you?' the leader said.

'What do you mean? I've given you the papyrus documents.' Ashford hoped he could carry this off without betraying himself. He had always been useless at lying.

'The two journals in English that you found with these documents.' His voice was hard, 'You weren't meaning to tell me about them, were you? You thought we didn't know.'

Ashford's jaw dropped open. *How did they know?* He hadn't told anyone about them.

The leader of the pack nodded and one of the men lashed out with a clenched fist. Ashford cried out in pain, as the goon's fist connected with his nose, breaking it. Blood streamed down his face.

'Search his desk.' The leader commanded. Three men swiftly rifled through the drawers. One of them found the journals and held them aloft before slipping them into the briefcase with the papyri.

The leader then leaned forward and fixed Ashford with a stare. 'You know, I was going to kill you after taking the documents. But you've just made me change my mind. I'm going to take you with us. You're going to disappear. Like old Fuller. And you're going to wish I had killed you instead.'

1

PRESENT DAY

DAY ONE

North of Korinos and south of Markigialos, Greece

Alice held her cellphone to her ear as she listened to the endless ring at the other end of the line. Her face betrayed her frustration and hinted at the seeds of anger being sowed as a result of multiple calls all ending with the same result.

No response.

She clicked her tongue in exasperation as the call disconnected yet again. She knew by now that she wouldn't get a call back.

Why do I even bother calling?

She stared glumly at her phone for a few moments before stuffing it into her pocket. It wasn't easy managing a relationship long distance. She had been camping here for the better part of the last twelve months as part of an international team put together by the Greek-American Archaeological Mission of Pydna. The mission was on the cusp of revealing to the world one of ancient Greece's most puzzling secrets. The long months apart had taken a toll on her relationship, culminating in an acrimonious slanging match that had taken place two weeks ago. Her boyfriend hadn't called back since then. And he hadn't picked up any of her calls either.

Bloody idiot. If he didn't have the courtesy to apologise, the least he could do was take her call so she could try and patch the relationship back together again. Unless...she pushed the unpleasant thought away with a shake of her head.

Her brooding was interrupted by an excited student, breathless from his dash through the tunnel that led to what was expected to be the discovery of the century – a tomb that had not been opened for over 2000 years. A tomb that had been the subject of much speculation for the last 150 years. The excavation team had been assisted by a contingent of over fifty students and an army of local workers, while the two co-directors of the project, a Greek and an American, were based in Thessaloniki, around 50 kilometres away via the E75 toll road.

'Alice, we've broken through to the tomb entrance!' The excitement in his voice was palpable and infectious. 'C'mon, hurry up!' The words were hardly out of his mouth than he was retracing his steps to the opening of the shaft that led to the tunnel deep below the earth.

All concerns of her boyfriend banished from her mind, Alice adjusted her backpack and turned to follow the student, her thoughts flitting back to the moment, eighteen months ago, when she had been approached to join the team.

It was ironic that she had just met her boyfriend at the time the invitation came. She had been wallowing in the wake of the incident which she never spoke of anymore. At that time, she was struggling to put it behind her, and she had finally managed to bury it deep in the recesses of her mind like a centuries-old secret. He had been such a support to her then, and she had been grateful to him for it. After dating for a couple of months, she had moved in with him – until she had been called away for this excavation. And today, when she was about to unveil one of the last great secrets of ancient Greece, it looked like he wasn't there for her anymore.

As she followed the student to the tomb, she recalled her meeting with Kurt Wallace, the billionaire philanthropist. Wallace was funding this excavation through his Wallace Archaeological Trust, an organization devoted to archaeology and the study of ancient civilisations. He was also the man behind the "Forgotten Roots" movement: a counter-evolutionary initiative of the Trust based on the five books he had authored. The common theme of the books was the hypothesis that humanity had forgotten its roots and turned to an erroneous theory based on the concept of evolution, when the true origins of humankind were hidden deep in the ancient myths of cultures across the world.

Alice had heard and read about Wallace but had never really given much thought to what her opinion was about him and his theories. But she had been blown away by the man's intellectual capacity and his genteel, refined manner. And, of course, by the ornate trappings of his stately mansion where she had been summoned to meet him.

The meeting had lasted precisely ten minutes, and Wallace had opened the conversation by getting to the point.

'The reason I have requested your presence on the team is because of your rich expertise, among other things, concerning the era of Alexander the Great and the years prior to and after his death,' he began, after the formalities of greetings and asking her if she wished to be served any refreshments.

This opening remark had ignited her curiosity and she stared back at the tall figure of Wallace, standing by the window of his study, the portrait of an aristocrat with his finely cut suit, silk tie, rugged face and salt and pepper hair.

Wallace smiled at her, knowing that she'd taken the bait. 'You see, my research team at the Trust has unearthed a clue to one of ancient Greece's most enduring mysteries. And it has everything to do with Alexander the Great.'

He had gone on to explain the nature and purpose of the mission and the composition of the team. By the time he finished, she would have paid to sign on for this project.

'Watch your step here,' the voice of the student intruded once more on her thoughts. 'The roof of the tunnel is lower from here on.' They had scrambled down the shaft and made their way through the tunnel, aiming for the light from the portable lamps that grew stronger as they advanced.

They hurried through the tunnel as fast as they could in the beam of the student's torchlight and finally emerged in a cube shaped chamber with smooth stone walls.

Two portable LED pole lights stood in diagonally opposite corners, lighting up the little space.

'Thank you, Marco,' Alice smiled at the student, as he switched off his flashlight.

'The mother-lode, quite literally.' Damon, the other archaeologist on the team, a pudgy, black-haired man in his late forties, pointed to the entrance to the tomb that they had painstakingly excavated over the last twelve months.

Alice saw stacks of containers in the chamber. These were padded containers used to gather artefacts from excavation sites to transport them safely to labs where they could be tested, dated and examined more thoroughly. 'We're picking up stuff from here?' She was a bit taken aback. This was against standard archaeological procedure, where every artefact has to be photographed, tagged, mapped and measured to the last detail before being removed from the site.

'Orders from HQ. Our directors gave me specific instructions to remove every moveable artefact and secure them all in the dig hut,' Damon replied, studying her curiously. 'Where have you been?'

Alice shook her head, trying to keep her emotions at bay. 'I noticed that you sent everyone else away.' On their way to the shaft entrance, they had passed the other students and workers heading the other way and she had realised that Damon was planning a private preview of the tomb.

'I sent them off,' he replied, grinning at her. 'I thought you and I should have the privilege of opening this tomb by ourselves.' He glanced at the student. 'With a little help from Marco, of course. Lucky guy.' He winked at Marco, who grinned back.

'There's no door here,' Alice frowned. 'All the Hellenistic tombs have doors.'

Damon shrugged. 'Let's find out, shall we?' His face betrayed his anxiety. Had they laboured so hard for so many months only to be disappointed?

Alice took a deep breath. This was the moment of truth. She nodded to Damon who beckoned to Marco. The student hefted one of the pole lights and carried it through the open doorway, into the tomb. As Alice and Damon entered the tomb, he returned for the other lamp, his eyes glistening with excitement.

'There are two chambers,' Damon whispered. 'Just like the other Macedonian tombs. Barrel vaulted. It's Hellenistic alright.'

Alice found herself standing in a small antechamber, the walls covered with murals of a woman in colourful robes, commanding armies, instructing men and generally assuming the pose of a leader in charge.

She looked at Damon and saw the excitement on his face as well. They had been right about this.

'The tomb of a queen,' Damon breathed. 'At last the world will see her resting place.'

Alice moved through the doorway separating the antechamber from the burial chamber within, Damon following her.

As she entered the chamber, Alice gasped. She had been prepared to find a sarcophagus, a larnax, or even a mummy. But the sight that greeted her eyes was something that made her hair stand on end.

2

R.K. Puram, New Delhi

Imran Kidwai, Special Director at the Indian Intelligence Bureau, contemplated the day's events as he was being driven home.

Six months ago, after the dust raised by a terror threat to the G20 nations and the discovery of an ancient secret from the Mahabharata had died down, the governments of the US and India had decided to set up a joint task force to monitor and investigate leads to technology based terrorism. The idea had stemmed from the attempt by a shadowy global group to partner with terrorists to use cutting edge technology based on the secret from the Mahabharata with the objective of global political and economic domination. The plot had been foiled but the enemy still existed. And the entire episode had demonstrated that there were enough people out there who would not have any scruples about using technology to achieve their ends.

Imran had willingly embraced the idea of a task force that was supported politically and had the authority and responsibility to investigate potential leads for techno-terrorism. But he had met the leader of the task force for the first time only today. And he didn't like what he saw. What was worse was, having backed the idea to the hilt initially, there was no way for him to withdraw from the task force. It was a difficult situation.

The email alert from his Blackberry intruded on his thoughts. *Not tonight.* Normally, he welcomed the challenge of an after office hours email. It usually meant there was a problem to be solved. And Imran was nothing if not a problem solver. A true Gemini, he loved nothing more than the novelty of a new crisis rearing its ugly head. It gave him the variety his nature sought as a natural diversion from his routine work.

He glanced at his email inbox. What he saw there made him sit up immediately. It was an email from a ghost.

The tomb of a Queen

As Damon and Alice entered the inner chamber an eerie sight greeted them in the diffused light that filtered through the doorway from the lone lamp in the outer chamber.

In the centre of the room lay a stone larnax, plain and unadorned. There was no other object in the room. But it was not the emptiness of the chamber or the simplicity of the larnax that stood out.

On the wall of the chamber facing the doorway, an immense stone snake seemed to emerge from the floor of the tomb. The massive coils of the snake's body wound from the floor, across the length of the far wall, up to the roof of the chamber, terminating in a massive five-headed hood, which protruded from the wall for around three feet over the stone larnax on the floor below. Its enormous jaws gaped open and its fangs were bared, as if expressing displeasure at an unwelcome intrusion.

Like a protective shelter for the larnax. Alice couldn't help the thought flashing through her head. As it was in life, so it was in death for this queen.

Adding to this surreal vision were the carvings on the remaining walls of the chamber. There were serpents carved in bold relief, coiled, hissing, and stretched out. In the dim light, they looked like stone shadows about to leap off the wall.

Marco staggered in with both the pole lights and stopped short as he saw the strange decoration in the tomb.

'What on earth is this?' he whispered, overawed.

Alice looked at her two companions excitedly. 'It *is* her tomb!' Her voice trembled with the thrill of the discovery. For the last twelve months they had been hoping that their guess about the occupant of the tomb had been correct. Now, all doubts were laid to rest.

'Um... you'll want to see this.' Marco had been walking around the chamber, studying the carvings. The chamber was fairly large, at least fifty feet in length. Marco was now standing in the far corner of the chamber opposite the entrance, just below one of the massive coils of the snake that towered over them.

Alice and Damon hurried up to see what he had found. Hidden behind the bulk of the snake, as it reared off the wall, was an opening. They looked at each other. Was there a third chamber? This was unusual for a Hellenistic tomb.

Marco didn't need to be told. He was already carrying one of the lamps to illuminate the hidden doorway, revealing a small chamber lined with two rows of shelves which bore stone statues and stone slabs of different sizes.

Alice and Damon proceeded to examine the contents of the shelves.

'She certainly had a fascination for snakes,' Damon remarked, studying a five-inch-tall statuette carved from stone which depicted a beautiful, young woman trapped in the coils of an enormous serpent which was wrapped around her from head to toe.

Alice nodded. 'Remember that Alexander III was said to have been fathered by a serpent. I guess the stories about her fascination for snakes were true after all.'

'This is amazing,' Damon remarked as he read the inscriptions on a square tablet, which was around ten inches long. 'These texts can fill in many of the gaps about what actually happened after Alexander the Great died.'

Alice nodded, as she studied the tablets and statuettes on the shelves.

Damon looked at his watch. 'We should inform HQ. They're waiting for us. They'll want to leave right away to see this for themselves.'

'Mmm. Why don't you carry on to the hotel and wait for them? I'll finish photographing the tomb.' Alice was already pulling out the camera from her bag. 'I'll also tag the artefacts and pack them in the containers.'

'Thanks. I'll send Marco back for you.' Damon smiled at her and left, followed by Marco.

Alice looked around as an enormous sigh escaped her. This was the high point of her career as an archaeologist. She busied herself clicking photographs of the chambers, the larnax and the murals.

After she had finished, she turned her attention to the artefacts in the hidden chamber, carefully photographing each one before she packed them in the padded containers.

'Hey, what's this?' she muttered to herself as she picked up the final artefact, a yellowing cube with inscriptions on five sides. It had been hidden until now behind the statuettes and clay tablets. At first she thought it was made from ancient bone which had discoloured over the centuries. But, as she turned it over in her hands and studied it in the light of the lamps, she realised that it was actually carved from ivory. The "cross-hatch" or wavy pattern that is so distinctive in ivory was clearly visible in the strong light of the lamps.

'Ivory in Madeconia two thousand four hundred years ago?' she muttered to herself. 'That's strange. There weren't elephants in these parts.'

'You done?'

Alice jumped and almost dropped the cube. She turned to see Marco grinning at her.

'You startled me,' she complained light-heartedly. 'Don't go doing that to folks who are alone in dark ancient tombs.'

'Sorry,' Marco grinned back, his voice betraying his excitement. It wasn't every day that a student got to be a part of a discovery like this. 'But you were talking to yourself, so I couldn't resist it. Damon's spoken to HQ. They're on their way. Oh, by the way, Damon asked you to get the cube with you. Apparently the directors want to see it.' He indicated the ivory cube that Alice was still holding.

'Sure. I just need to photograph and tag it.' She photographed all the sides of the cube, placed it in a container like the other artefacts and then dumped the container in her backpack along with the camera.

'Great. I'm done here. Let's get these to the dig hut.' Alice led the way out of the tomb. Together, they lugged the containers containing the artefacts to the dig hut, and carefully laid them out on the central table. Alice was sure the two directors would want to see these immediately, since they had specifically asked for them to be removed from the tomb.

'Done.' Marco slipped off his white gloves and looked at her expectantly.

Alice nodded. 'Let's go.' They locked the door of the dig hut. There were two guards posted at the site and it was miles from anywhere, so it was unlikely that anyone would steal the artefacts. But this was the discovery of the millennium, so one couldn't take chances.

Back at the hotel, which was little more than a cluster of rustic villas, Alice made her way to her room while Marco parked the car and left to find Damon. 'I'll join you guys in five minutes,' she told Marco. She knew that she was just trying to postpone the inevitable. All through the excavations, she had avoided interacting with the two directors as far as possible, leaving Damon to brief them, report to them and take instructions where required. But tonight there was no escape. She would have to accompany Stavros and Peter, the two co-directors of the mission, to the tomb. She wasn't very fond of either of them and she was aware that the sentiment was reciprocated by both of them. But, as one of the lead archaeologists on this mission, there was no getting away from them tonight. And, as the team's expert on the period in which the tomb had been built, she knew the two directors would want to hear her views on the bizarre discoveries within the tomb.

As she contemplated this unwelcome thought, a staccato chopping sound filled the night. A helicopter, passing by overhead, very low. The sound of the chopper continued for a while and then suddenly died down, almost as if the machine had landed somewhere nearby.

Alice was still focused on the unpleasant task ahead of her. Sighing, she took out her laptop and camera and placed them on the desk in the room. She slipped her mobile phone and the memory stick from the camera into her waist pouch and rose to make her way to Damon's villa.

As she placed her hand on the doorknob, an insistent tap came from the window that overlooked the garden. It was unbarred and the shade was up, so she could see Marco's frightened face pressed against the window pane very clearly. It was white with fear, as if the blood had all been drained away from his face. He tapped again, with greater urgency, indicating that she should open the window.

Alice retraced her steps and let Marco in through the window. 'What...' she began, wondering what had terrified Marco, but stopped short as Marco burst into tears.

3

Out of the frying pan…

'They killed Damon,' Marco blubbered, collapsing into a heap on the floor. 'Peter shot him. Just like that.'

Alice couldn't comprehend what Marco was saying for a few moments. What was he babbling about? He wasn't making any sense. Why would Peter shoot Damon?

She knelt down beside the weeping boy and put her hand on his shoulder reassuringly. 'Tell me what happened,' she said gently. 'I'm sure it is all a misunderstanding.'

'I saw it with my own eyes!' Marco wailed. 'Stavros was shouting at Damon. He was angry with Damon for leaving you alone in the tomb and for letting you photograph the artefacts. He said that Damon should have brought the cube to show them.' A fresh flood of tears welled up in his eyes and he choked on his words.

Alice waited patiently, offering him a box of tissues. Suddenly she felt she was in a dream. A very unpleasant dream. She wished to be woken up right now.

Marco blew his nose loudly and continued. 'Then Peter took out a gun. He told Damon that he was a liability since he didn't follow instructions.' He paused as he recollected the scene he had witnessed through the open windows of Damon's villa. 'Damon was terrified. He pleaded, begged for Peter to give him another chance. He was crying. But Peter wouldn't listen. He just shot him.' Marco's sobbing renewed.

Alice stood up as she heard the sound of people racing down the corridor leading to her villa. Was it Stavros and Peter? The reality of her situation suddenly hit her like a cold shower on a snowy winter's day, shocking her into action.

She sprinted for the door and double bolted it. That would buy them some time. If Damon had been killed, there was no doubt about what would happen to Marco and her.

'We have to get out of here,' she voiced her thoughts to Marco. 'Come on.'

She hefted her backpack and slid out through the window just as someone tried the door.

'It's locked!' That was Peter.

'Break it open!' That was Stavros.

The sound of an assault on the door came to them. The latch shook with the impact but stayed fast.

Alice looked at the door and then glanced at Marco, who was frozen where he sat, staring at the door like a deer caught in the headlights of a car on a forest path. She knew it wouldn't be long before they broke through.

'Marco!' she hissed, not daring to shout. If Peter knew that she was aware of what had happened, they would guess that she was trying to flee and would take action to pre-empt her. 'Get the hell out of there!'

Her voice seemed to jolt Marco back to reality. He stood up shakily and tottered to the window, sliding out and onto the grassy lawn just as the latch gave way and Peter burst into the room.

'On the lawn!' Peter yelled, as he dashed to the window.

Alice didn't wait to see what was happening behind her but grabbed Marco's hand and sprinted away from the villa. She didn't know if the two co-directors were accompanied by anyone but she was guessing they weren't by themselves.

Two soft coughs sounded and bullets whistled past their ears.

Alice realised that someone was shooting at them and the gun was fitted with a sound suppressor.

She raced across the lawn, dragging Marco behind her, to where the Land Cruiser, which was their official transport, stood.

As she ran, Marco suddenly seemed to grow heavier. One moment she was pulling him forward, the next he was an immovable object, as if set in stone.

Alice glanced back at Marco as he slumped to the ground. His face was a mask of red and his hair was drenched in blood. The bullets had found their mark.

For a precious moment, she hesitated, tears welling in her eyes. She was torn between her own safety and the tragedy she was witnessing now. A young boy, his life brutally cut short. And for what?

More coughs rang out and her instinct took over. Reluctantly, she let go of Marco's hand and slid swiftly into the driver's seat.

The key was in the ignition. Marco must have left it there, in anticipation of driving the co-directors to the tomb site. The engine complained and then revved up as she accelerated, heading out onto the dirt road that led to the tomb.

As she raced down the dirt track, she heard shouts behind her. The coughs rang out once again, and bullets thudded into the Land Cruiser as she pressed the accelerator to the floor. *She had to get to the tomb.* There were two armed guards at the tomb site and they would protect her from the madness that suddenly seemed to have broken loose here.

It didn't take long for her to arrive at the excavation site. To Alice's surprise, it was dark and silent. The floodlights which had been fitted to light up the excavation were off and so were the generators powering them.

Where were the guards?

She jumped out of the vehicle and stumbled across the uneven ground. Though she knew her way around, she had never been here after dark, aided only by the light of the stars.

Abruptly, she tripped over something heavy on the ground and just about managed to regain her balance.

Shocked, she realised that it was Geordi, one of the guards. She bent down to check on him but there was no pulse. He was dead.

She stood up warily, confused; caught between the need to understand what was happening here, and her instinct, which was telling her to flee.

Even as she struggled with her thoughts, a dark shadow clambered out of the shaft that led to the underground tomb.

Alice froze. Only now did she see the helicopter, an immense shadow off to one side.

Her mind was a whirl of confused thoughts of which one stood out clearly. *She was trapped.*

4

A call for help

Anwar!

Imran stared at the email he had just received, unable to believe his eyes.

Anwar and Imran had grown up together in Meerut before Anwar moved to Lucknow to stay with his uncle, after losing both his parents. That was years ago, but the two boys had kept in touch as they grew up. While Imran had joined the IPS, Anwar had started a small business in Lucknow that hadn't done too well over the years. But the two had remained good friends.

Until five years ago when Anwar had suddenly vanished without a trace.

And now, he had turned up out of nowhere. A ghost from the past.

A surge of anticipation coursed through Imran's being as he felt the exuberance of connecting once more with his old friend. He opened the email. And felt like someone had punched him in the face.

It contained two words.

Help Anwar

... and into the fire

Alice stood, immobilised, as the shadow emerged from the shaft and advanced towards her. She saw it move one hand to its hip and realised it was reaching for a weapon.

Abandoning all thoughts of trying to find out what was happening, she turned and sprinted back towards the car, opening the driver's door and sliding into the seat in one motion, as shots rang out, shattering the silence of the night. This gun had no silencer. There was no need for stealth here.

Bullets smacked into the windows, shattering them, as she struggled to start the car.

A bullet whizzed past her face and embedded itself in the passenger seat next to her.

The Land Cruiser's powerful engine roared to life and the tyres skidded on the gravel as she reversed at top speed. Alice threw the vehicle into forward gear and raced away from the tomb. Another bullet thudded into the stereo system and she bent low over the wheel, hysterical with fear, trying to control her panic, one thought racing through her head.

She had to get away.

Behind her, she heard the helicopter start up and she knew that the intruders were going to hunt her down and kill her.

Who were these people and what did they want?

Sobbing and shaking with fear, she sped towards the E75, the toll road that led to Thessaloniki. It was the only thing she could think of at the moment.

The sound of the helicopter pursuing her followed in her wake. She pressed hard on the steering wheel of the Land Cruiser as if that would make the vehicle go faster.

But she knew that the helicopter would overtake her. It was just a matter of time.

Searching for Anwar

'Back to the office,' Imran barked to his driver. 'Use the beacon!'

The driver obediently turned back, switching on the beacon, and speeded up. Imran knew he was stretching his official privileges. It was something he never did, but right now he didn't care. He knew one thing for sure from the message he had received. His friend was in trouble.

And Imran was going to do everything he could to help.

As they raced back towards IB headquarters Imran barked orders into his phone. The red beacon ensured that traffic made way for them. It was as if the traffic jams miraculously melted away, like snow under a deluge of salt.

Back in his office, Imran summoned his team.

'Okay, so what do we have?' His voice was surprisingly calm. His anger was on a tight leash, his apparent calmness a thin veneer disguising his worry that he might be too late to help his friend. He was sure that Anwar had been interrupted while typing the message which had prevented him from providing more details.

'We have a trace on the IP address,' one of his men reported. 'It's a server in Delhi. We have an approximate location,' he showed Imran a printout of a map with a dot in red marking the location, 'but it could be anywhere within 50 kilometres of this spot.'

Imran looked at him. 'I want an exact location. I want the physical address.'

'Sir, you know that needs a court order. I can call the ISP...'

'We can't wait for a court order,' Imran interrupted him. Every second was valuable. They didn't have the luxury of affording discussions. 'We don't have time to explain to the ISP. This is an emergency.'

His agent stared back at him. 'You want us to hack into the ISP's database?'

'Do it. I'm authorising it.' Imran was conscious that this was a gross misuse of his authority. But he was convinced his friend was in dire trouble. Tonight was the night he would break rules if necessary, even though he had never done it in his long career with the IPS.

The men scurried out, looking at each other in bewilderment. Imran leaned back in his chair and exhaled.He could only hope they figured it out in time.

5

Hunted

The roar of the explosion came to Alice seconds after the blast of the shockwave that rocked the Land Cruiser as it sped towards the asphalt road that would take her off the dirt road and onto the highway. She screamed involuntarily.

In the rear view mirror, through her tears, she saw the ball of fire rise above the excavation site. She couldn't believe it. *They had destroyed the tomb!* Fortunately, she had photographed the find. She still had the memory stick from the camera with her. She consoled herself with the thought that, though the destruction of the tomb was an irretrievable loss to history and archaeology, she still had something that could be salvaged.

Then it struck her. If these people, whoever they were, could blow up the tomb, then they clearly didn't want to leave any trace of what had been found within it.

And she was a living testimonial to the discovery within the tomb. They would not rest until she was dead.

There was a sudden bump on the roof of the Land Cruiser. The pilot was battering the roof of the vehicle using the struts of the helicopter. Alice jumped in her seat and screamed again, her nerves on edge with the trauma of the evening and the realisation that she would be relentlessly hunted down.

She shifted gears and accelerated again. Whatever happened tonight, she was not going to give up so easily. They may get her in the end, but she would not meekly surrender.

Apparently the helicopter pilot realised that, and, with a sudden burst of speed, the chopper veered off to the right, racing ahead of her and then arcing back towards her, descending as it approached the SUV.

Alice stared in horror at the sight of the helicopter heading straight at her. She instinctively realised what the pilot was trying to do. While it was evident that he planned to land on the motorway and block her path, he was also trying to add to her terror by playing with her mind, making her believe that he was going to ram the SUV head on.

Alice struggled to get a hold of herself. The thought of someone thinking that she was so helpless that she would allow herself to be toyed with helped her centre herself.

'Okay, pal,' she said grimly. 'Two can play at this game. You want a game of roulette, you got it.' She shifted gears and slowed down for a brief instant before speeding up again, heading directly at the helicopter which was now just a few metres above ground level. 'Let's see who blinks first.'

For a few moments, the helicopter and the SUV roared towards each other, both apparently bent on a collision.

Then, the pilot seemed to think the better of it and settled the helicopter down on the motorway, straight in the path of the oncoming Land Cruiser. He had given up the psychological tactics and was now banking on a physical rather than a mental obstacle.

A lone figure emerged from the helicopter as its rotors died down and Alice realised that there was no one accompanying the pilot in the helicopter. The man stood to one side, waiting like a spider in its web watching the approach of a fly, secure in the knowledge that the fly would be trapped in its silken snare.

Alice looked wildly around, desperately searching for a way out. She struggled to fight the wave of panic flooding her mind as the helicopter's bulk filled her vision, blocking out the highway beyond it. If there was a way out of her predicament, she knew she would never find it if she allowed herself to succumb to the terror that was threatening to overcome her.

Blinking back her tears, she forced herself to focus on the scene ahead of her, even as her instincts goaded her against it.

Then she saw it. A chance, however slim, but it offered her hope. She knew the odds were stacked against her but she wouldn't give up without trying.

Alice slowed down again and did some quick mental calculations. It might just work.

The pilot, interpreting her slowing down as an indication that she was going to stop, began advancing towards her.

Jaungarh Fort, 130 km from New Delhi, India

'I can't say that I'm happy about this development,' Colin grumbled.

He and Vijay were sitting on a balcony of Vijay's ancestral fort, enjoying the pleasant weather. Winter hadn't set in yet and the nights were cool, especially at the fort which was built upon a hill that towered over the farmland around, with its own little village nestled at the base. The fort had belonged to Vijay's uncle, a retired nuclear scientist, who was brutally murdered a year ago.

Vijay grinned at Colin. 'You don't like the guy? I thought he was all charm.'

Colin frowned at Vijay. 'You're damned right I don't like the guy. You know, when our friend Kidwai first told us that the US and Indian governments planned to set up this joint task force, I thought it was a great idea.'

'It certainly is,' Vijay agreed. 'Putting together a team of scientists and engineers, specialists in their fields, to anticipate and investigate technology based terrorism, supported by both governments – it is an idea whose time has come.'

'Yeah. But now I know how Red Riding Hood felt when she went walking in the woods. It was a great walk until the wolf jumped out at her.'

Vijay chuckled. Just this morning they had both been summoned to the headquarters of the Intelligence Bureau to meet with Michael Blake, the CIA operative who had worked with the IB on their adventure last year. Blake was accompanied by the American who had been appointed by the US President to head the joint task force. It was for this meeting that Colin had flown down from the US a few days earlier.

Bill Patterson was 6 feet 3 inches, all muscle, and evidently all brain too, given his credentials as a PhD in molecular biology as well as chemical biology. A former US Navy Seal, the African American had a brusque manner, leaving no one in doubt that he was in command.

Colin, a natural rebel, had disliked him from the moment he laid eyes on Patterson. His instinctive feeling of repulsion had led to an acrimonious debate over how much devolution of decision making would take place, with Colin ending up at the losing end of the argument. He was still smarting at the encounter.

'Listen, if the President of the US thinks he's good enough, I'm fine with that. And you should be, too.'

'I just don't like having to go back to him every time we need to do something,' Colin glared at Vijay.

'Hey, don't bite my head off! And we don't need to ask him for permission for everything we do. Only if there is military action or anything that requires specialist training. Our job as part of this task force is to investigate and test hypotheses. If there is any action, it should be left to the guys who are trained for the job.'

Colin grunted. He knew Vijay was correct but didn't want

to admit it. He looked at his watch instead. 'Time to turn in,' he said, still scowling. 'I just hope I don't have nightmares with Patterson playing a ghoul. That's all I need at this moment.'

6

Calling for help

As the helicopter pilot moved into the middle of the carriageway, Alice swerved hard to the right and accelerated. She was aiming for the narrow gap between the helicopter's nose and the shoulder of the highway, gaining speed as she approached the edge of the road.

She whizzed past the surprised pilot who began running after the speeding SUV. Alice prayed fervently that her gamble would pay off. Was the gap wide enough?

The next instant, the Land Cruiser was scraping metal on both sides and the sound of metal crumpling and tearing shattered the silence of the night, as the vehicle squeezed past the helicopter on one side and the metal railing at the shoulder of the highway, on the other side.

For a long moment, time seemed to slow down. It seemed to Alice that the helicopter and the railing were both converging on the SUV, crushing it, shattering the remaining windows that had not been shot out earlier that night.

Alice closed her eyes and willed the SUV to force its way through as the harsh grinding of the metal seemed to pierce right through her brain.

Suddenly, the Land Cruiser seemed to leap forward, freed of the crushing restraints it had endured. With a start, Alice realised that the vehicle had made it through the gap and she could see the highway stretching ahead of her.

A new burst of energy surged through her and her hopes lifted. She forced the accelerator to the floor trying to put as much distance between the SUV and the helicopter, before the pilot could recover and take to the skies once more.

Behind her, through the glassless windows of the SUV, she heard the pilot shout curses and hunched down in her seat in anticipation of the shooting which she was sure would follow. Bullets began whizzing past her head once again. The front windscreen metamorphosed into a spider web of silvery cracks as a bullet tore through it.

Somehow, she was able to keep driving but she knew that she couldn't drive as fast with the windscreen blurring the view ahead of her. Her hopes sank again, as she slowed to a pace that allowed her to focus on the road ahead.

She kept listening for the sound of the helicopter's continued pursuit. But minutes ticked by and she heard nothing apart from the sound of the wind rushing through the cabin of the SUV, through the shattered windows, and the roar of its engine. She wondered if the helicopter had been damaged by her daring getaway or whether the pilot had decided to give up the chase.

The mystery behind the night's events reared its head again. Initially, she had thought that the antiquities mafia was behind this. That would certainly explain the furore over photographing the tomb. If photographs of any artefacts within the tomb were leaked to the world, it would become very difficult to hawk them on the antiquities black market, especially for a tomb that was as famous as this one.

But that theory was blown to bits along with the tomb itself. There seemed to be no logical explanation. *What could anyone gain from the destruction of a two-thousand-year-old tomb?*

And why go to the trouble of excavating the tomb for over a year only to destroy it? There seemed to be no answers forthcoming.

She was now driving over the Loudias river and she knew it would not be long before she reached Thessaloniki. With an effort, she pushed away the thoughts about what had happened so far and tried to focus on what lay ahead of her.

It was extremely likely that the pilot, if he was linked to Stavros and Peter as it seemed, also had accomplices in Thessaloniki. Rather than pursue her, it would have been easier to call ahead and have people waiting for her to enter Thessaloniki. She realised that she was not out of the woods yet.

Alice stopped the SUV, and got out, forcing back her tears. She had to take control of herself. Marco was dead. And so was Damon. But she wanted to get out of this alive. She stood at the rail of the bridge and pounded against it with her fists until they hurt, trying to vent her frustration. She thought of Marco and his unnecessary death. Why did his luck have to run out so soon?

She turned her tear-stained face to the sky which was speckled with stars, but found no solace there.

Gripping the rails of the bridge, she forced herself to think. There was a US consulate in Thessaloniki. She had to get there. It was the only place where she thought she could be truly safe. Though she had left her passport back at the hotel, she still had her driver's licence on her. That would suffice to establish her identity and seek asylum in the consulate.

She whipped out her mobile phone and looked up the address of the consulate. 43 Tsimiski Street. That was a start.

Next, she figured she should call someone and ask for help.

Her boyfriend. For a moment, she hesitated. Was he even her boyfriend any longer? She had no idea. But he was all that she had. Apart from her few friends, none of whom were close enough for her to rely on.

Alice dialled his number. It rang a few times and was abruptly disconnected. She looked at the time. It was early morning back in the States. She tried again with the same response. A few rings and then a busy tone. Disheartened, she looked at the phone screen which displayed a message informing her that the number she was trying to call was busy.

He was awake. The thought that he was deliberately not taking her calls hurt even more tonight. The one person who should have been there for her at a time like this, when she was so delicately balanced between life and death, was suddenly missing from her life. Another surge of tears threatened to well up and she forced them back.

She had to be strong if she wanted to make it.

Another name swam into her thoughts, and she punched in a number. This time it was not a mobile but a landline number. She wasn't privy to Kurt Wallace's personal cellphone number.

A female voice answered the phone after two rings.

'Mr Wallace's office. How may I help you?' It was Clara, Wallace's assistant.

Alice found her voice shaking with the trauma of her experience. 'I need to speak to Mr Wallace, please. It is urgent.'

'Mr Wallace is in a meeting and cannot be disturbed at the moment.'

'It's a matter of life and death. Literally! Please, you have to connect me to him,' Alice pleaded, a cold fear gripping her as the last straw slipped through her hands.

'Please leave your name and phone number with me and I will ask Mr Wallace to call you back the moment he gets free. I'm really sorry but I don't have access to him right now.'

The words struck her like a sledgehammer. She was on her own. There was no help at hand.

7

On the E75, near Thessaloniki, Greece

For a few moments, Alice stood stunned, numb with shock at Clara's words. With an effort, she pulled herself together. Perhaps if she explained…?

'My name is Alice Turner. I'm part of the mission Mr Wallace has funded in Greece. Please...please tell him that the tomb has been destroyed, two team members are dead and someone is after me as well. I… I'm scared.' Alice found herself sobbing as the words tumbled out.

Clara's voice softened. 'Ms Turner, I'm really sorry to hear about your predicament. I will have a message sent to Mr Wallace right away. Unfortunately, he does not believe in carrying a personal mobile phone, so it may take a while before I can reach him. My only request to you is to ensure that you keep checking to see that your mobile phone is accessible to incoming calls.'

Alice nodded and thanked Clara, then slid into the driver's seat, wiping away her tears. She was on her own. Hopefully, Wallace would call back soon and help would be at hand.

But until then she had to get by on her wits. And panicking wouldn't help. She tried to clear her mind, trying to define a goal that she could work towards.

The US consulate. She had to reach the consulate.

She keyed in the coordinates of the consulate into the Land Cruiser's GPS system and forced herself to concentrate on working out her next steps.

'Interesting,' she murmured to herself as she gazed at the route that had materialised on the GPS. The A2 motorway, which had merged with the E75 a short distance back, delinked from the E75 at the Axios Interchange which lay a short distance ahead, and then carried on towards Thessaloniki. A few miles after the Galikos bridge, the A2 merged into the Nea Dytiki Isodos which eventually led to the Navarchou Kountouriotou from where, after a short distance, she could turn left for Tsimiski. This was the route outlined by the GPS.

What had caught her interest were two alternate routes that she could see on the screen. The first alternate route entailed branching off the Nea Dytiki Isodos and onto 26 Oktovriou which curved back to rejoin it at the junction where she would turn into the Navarchou Kountouriotou.

Neither of these routes would help her, she realised, since there were sure to be men lying in wait for her at the junction that both routes led to.

The second alternate route seemed more promising. Instead of turning into 26 Oktovriou, she could take the next exit which would lead her under the motorway and onto 28 Oktovriou and then, after a while, turn onto Monastiriou which eventually led to Egnatia, from where a right turn would bring her to Tsimiski.

It was this route that she decided to take. It was still a gamble, because there was no guarantee that they wouldn't be watching this route, but she didn't have much of a choice.

As she walked towards the car, another name occurred to her. Someone she could trust and rely on. At least she thought so. Her boyfriend at college. It had been one of her best relationships, while it lasted. But she hadn't kept in touch over the years, though he had called her a few times and sent her emails which she had chosen not to respond to. Eventually he had stopped trying, realising that there was no point. Part

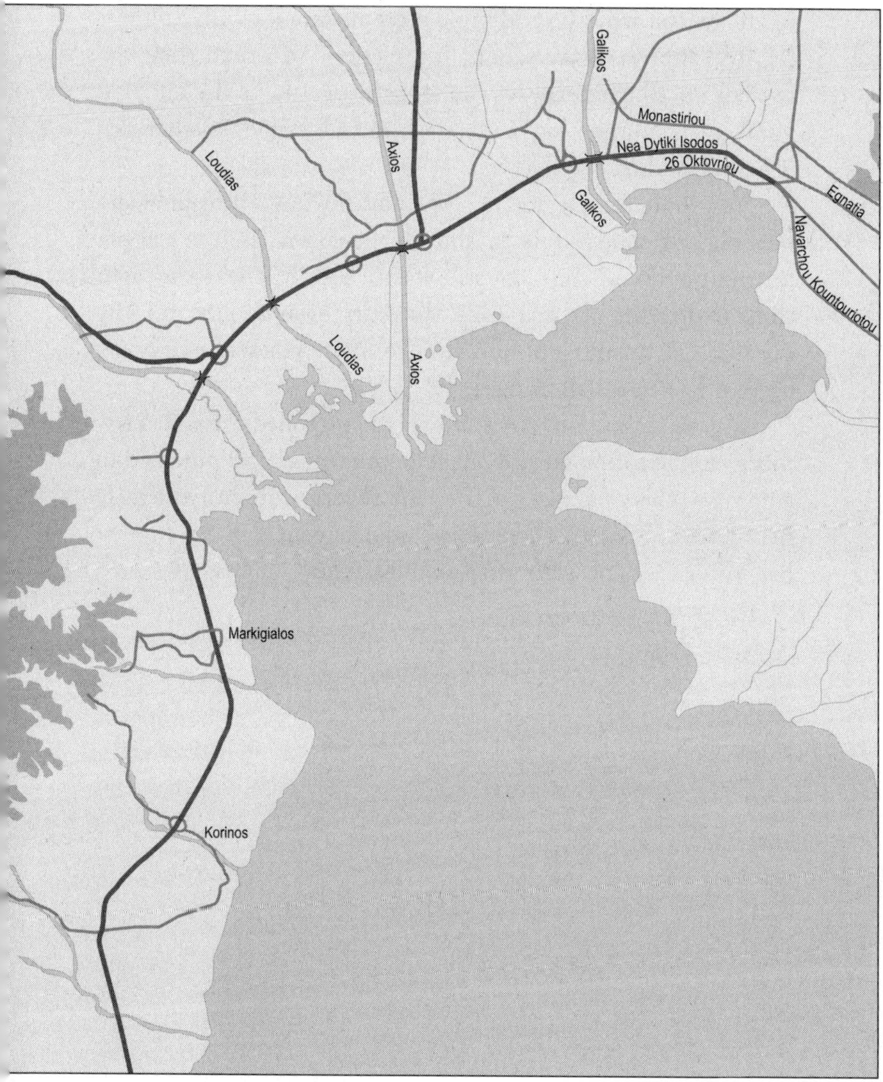

Galikos
Monastiriou
Nea Dytiki Isodos
26 Oktovriou
Loudias
Axios
Galikos
Egnatia
Navarchou Kountouriotou
Loudias
Axios
Markigialos
Korinos

of the reason why she had broken off all contact with him was because she was bitter about the manner in which they had broken up. She had always thought this would be the one that would last, culminating in marriage and a lifetime together. But it hadn't worked out that way.

For some reason, today, alone and hurting, in trouble and needing someone to talk to, she felt the compulsion to call her former boyfriend. But she still wasn't sure if it was the right thing to do after all these years. She didn't even understand why she was still thinking of him after so many years, after a break up that had burnt all bridges.

She thought for a few moments then scrolled through a few more contacts. She quickly made up her mind and punched in a number. *Come on, pick up!* It wasn't that he wouldn't recognise her number. Unless, of course, he had deleted it from his contact list. Which was possible after all these years.

8

Jaungarh Fort

Colin sat in his room and stared at his mobile phone. Eleven years without any news from her. She hadn't replied to his emails after the breakup. Though he hadn't been surprised when his efforts met with no success; she had walked out swearing that she would never have anything to do with her ex-boyfriend. And now, she was calling him. What had happened after such a long time to make her change her mind?

His first instinct on seeing her number was to take the call. But he hesitated, unsure, perhaps even afraid, especially with things the way they were. If she was trying to get back together, that would really complicate the situation.

He took a deep breath and accepted the call, not knowing what to expect.

Light at the end of the tunnel

'Alice?' Colin's voice never sounded better to her, despite the yawning chasm of the years.

'Colin! I...I didn't know who else to call.' Her voice was still shaking, but this time there was a measure of relief in it, even though she knew that Colin was miles away in the US and was of absolutely no help at this moment.

'Hey, what's wrong?' Colin sounded concerned, even troubled. He had noticed the tremor in her voice. 'Are you okay?'

Racked by guilt and terror, Alice spilled out the story of what she had gone through in the last one hour, starting with her entering the tomb and ending with her current position on the highway.

There was silence when she had finished. Finally, Colin spoke. 'Is there no one from the mission in Thessaloniki who can help you?'

'I don't know who to trust anymore, Colin. If Stavros and Peter are behind all this, who knows about the others? And I think Damon was part of it, too. He was killed for not following "instructions". That's what Peter said.'

'Okay. I think your plan to enter Thessaloniki using the alternate route is a good one. They won't be expecting you to do that. You head for the consulate. I'm in India right now, but I'll make a few calls to the US and we'll find a way out of this for you.'

'What are you doing in India?'

Colin told her about Vijay inheriting the fort from his uncle, without going into too many details.

'I see. Thanks. I really appreciate this, Colin. After everything...'

'Don't bother. That's what friends are for. Even if they haven't been in touch.' Colin seemed to hesitate. 'Should I tell Vijay?'

'Umm... not yet. I'm not sure how he'll react.'

'Take care. Talk to you soon.'

Alice disconnected the call.

Her mind made up, she started the engine and moved forward again. But she had barely gone a kilometre when her phone began ringing.

She grabbed it and looked at the screen. Was it Wallace?

'Alice?'

'Mr Wallace!' Her relief knew no bounds.

'I was informed that you are in need of urgent help.' Wallace sounded deeply concerned.

Alice poured out her heart to Wallace. She could hardly believe that barely an hour had passed since she had entered the tomb and so much had happened since then.

There was a moment's silence when she finished. Then Wallace spoke, his voice decisive and authoritative. 'You say your GPS shows that you are not more than half an hour from the US Consulate? That gives us enough time to sort things out.' His voice took on a kindly tone. In other circumstances, she may have found his tone almost patronising. But he seemed to be her best option to get out of here alive. 'Don't worry, my dear. You're going to be fine. You have my word. Just carry on driving. Someone will contact you within the next ten minutes. Call me when you reach the consulate. I must go now.'

Alice murmured her thanks as Wallace disconnected the call, and resumed the drive. For the first time tonight, she realised that there was no one else on the highway. She had passed no cars going in either direction. That was unnatural. And more than a bit eerie.

She drove steadily now, her mind calmed by the conversation with Wallace. As she passed over the Axios river, her phone rang again.

'Ms Turner? I'm calling from the General Police Directorate of Thessaloniki,' a deep voice with a heavy Greek accent spoke into her ear as she connected the call.

Her heart skipped a beat. Was she really hearing this? Wallace had contacted the local police?

'Yes,' she stammered, trying to hide her surprise.

The police officer on the line swiftly outlined the plan. An escort of three motorcycle borne policemen would meet her at the intersection on the Nea Dytiki Isodos and accompany her, not to the American consulate, which was closed at this hour, but to a hotel where armed guards would be stationed outside her room and in the lobby for her protection. The consulate would be in touch with her directly to arrange her papers for departure from Thessaloniki to the US.

Alice didn't know how to react. The terror of the last one hour had numbed her and this news was like a monsoon shower after a drought. She thanked the police officer profusely before hanging up. Then she stopped the car and stepped out onto the road, collapsing to her knees and allowed her pent up emotions to overwhelm her, as she burst into tears of relief, her body trembling – this time not with fear but with the joy of knowing that she was finally going to be safe.

Intelligence Bureau Headquarters, New Delhi

Imran looked up as one of his men hurried into the room. He raised one eyebrow enquiringly.

He glanced at the sheet of paper the man placed on his desk. 'Okay, let's go.' He strode towards the door. 'Alert the commandos.' He had already asked for a team of commandos to be kept on standby. Within minutes the IB team with Imran was rushing to the address provided by the ISP's database.

One of his agents received a call. He listened to the caller, then turned to Imran. 'Sir, the Fire Department has just reported a major fire at the medical facility that's our target.'

Imran gritted his teeth and prayed they would reach in time.

9

Thessaloniki, Greece

Alice sank onto her bed, exhausted and glad to be alive. The police escort had met her as promised and accompanied her to a hotel where she had been checked in under an assumed name. She didn't know what they had been told about her situation, but it was obvious that they had instructions to ensure that her true identity was not revealed to anyone.

The police would open a case file and investigations would commence immediately with a manhunt to apprehend Stavros and Peter. Though, somehow, she had a feeling they wouldn't be caught.

The consulate had called to say that the documents that would help her leave the country would be ready before noon the next day. They had reassured her that she was under their protection and would be completely safe now. Wallace had certainly pulled a whole lot of strings and she was grateful for his help.

Only one thing remained now. She needed to book her ticket out of here. She would do that tomorrow. But she wouldn't go back home to the US. It wasn't a good idea anymore. Stavros and Peter knew where she was from and probably had her home address as well. While she felt safe and protected here, who would protect her in the US? She couldn't possibly keep going back to Wallace for help. He had done his bit and more in getting her out of this mess.

Where could she go? She had pondered over this question as she showered. Now, even as she relaxed with a glass of Chardonnay, she didn't have any answers.

She switched on the television. It was a local channel, in Greek, but she didn't have to know the language to understand the images accompanying the headlines which announced that two freak accidents had occurred on both carriageways of the highway to Thessaloniki, blocking off traffic. The accidents had been reported by anonymous callers and no one was on the scene when the police had arrived in both cases. The people involved had, apparently, deserted the accident scenes.

A cold fear gripped her as she heard the news.

What had she got herself into?

This was no ordinary conspiracy. Whatever was going on, it was big. If they could plan on something as crazy as blocking off the highway for a few hours just to ensure that no one from the excavation site made it out alive, there was something really big at stake here.

But what was it? She racked her brains but could come up with no explanation that made sense.

Her phone rang, interrupting her thoughts.

'Alice?' Wallace's polished accent came over the line.

'Mr Wallace, I don't know how to thank you.' Alice was overcome with gratitude. 'I'm in a hotel in Thessaloniki.'

'Yes, I know,' Wallace replied. 'I was told. And, by the way, I do think that I have asked you before to call me Kurt. Anyway, I'm just glad you're safe.'

'I'm glad to be safe,' Alice responded. 'But I'm still scared.' She told him about the accidents on the highway being reported on television. 'I'm going to book my ticket first thing in the morning. I think I need to get out of here really fast.'

'Ah, that's why I called. I didn't want to promise anything until I was sure. I don't think you will be able to get a seat on any commercial airline out of Greece for at least a week. But I've managed to speak to a few people I know and you will have a private jet ready by noon tomorrow to bring you back to the US.'

Alice's mouth fell open. A private jet? Kurt Wallace definitely had friends in high places. She pulled herself together as she realised that he was planning to ship her back home.

'I've been thinking about that, Kurt.' Alice suddenly knew exactly where she wanted to go. She explained to Wallace her apprehensions about returning to the US, gently and politely but firmly brushing aside his offer to help her find a safe place to stay there.

'Are you sure about this?' Wallace finally asked, after hearing her out and learning about her desired destination.

'Absolutely.' Alice had no doubts in her mind that this was what she wanted. 'And I have a request, if that's possible.' She told him what she needed him to do for her.

'Fine, then. It will be organised. Expect a call around 10 am. Have a safe flight and do let me know if there's anything else you need.'

'I will.'

As she disconnected, a pang of doubt suddenly surfaced in her mind. Was she doing the right thing?

Alice firmly pushed the thought away. She had to confront her demons. She had run from them for too long.

10

Aryan Laboratories, New Delhi

Imran stood with the firemen and the commandos, his shoulders hunched, weighed down with grief.

They had arrived three hours ago at the medical centre, only to find the firemen battling a fierce blaze that had consumed most of the top three floors of the facility, a four storeyed building.

Fifteen fire tenders had battled the fire for four hours before it was brought under control. Imran, the IB team and the commandos had stood by helplessly, watching, unable to contribute to the operation, as the firemen went about their job.

As soon as he received permission to enter the building, Imran had rushed in, shouting instructions to the commandos, the firemen and his team. While the upper storeys were ravaged, the ground floor seemed to be intact.

'What's this place supposed to be?' Imran asked his deputy, Arjun, as they entered the building.

'It's a clinical laboratory. They conduct research into pathological diseases for Titan Pharmaceuticals Inc., based in Seattle, Washington.'

Imran frowned. 'A US multinational pharma company?'

'Yes. We're contacting them as we speak to get further information. But it seems that this was a centre where they conducted clinical trials for their research programs. Apparently, they are working on developing a few molecules which are touted to be the next big thing in medicine.'

Imran's walkie talkie came to life. 'Sir, you need to come up here. Fourth floor.' It was one of his agents.

A cold dread took hold of Imran as he sprinted up the stairs. Though he was in his mid-forties, he was still very fit, working out regularly, and he took the stairs two at a time.

As he entered the fourth floor from the stairwell, he recoiled in shock. The entire floor was charred. What was not destroyed by the fire had been devastated by the water from the fire tenders.

He sloshed through the puddles on the floor and entered what looked like it had been an IT lab, now lit up by torches and the head lamps of the firemen. Charred furniture and blackened computer terminals greeted his eyes.

And his worst fears seemed to come true. On one of the chairs, seated before a computer terminal, was a charred body.

'Anwar?' Imran could barely get the name out of his mouth.

'I'm sorry, sir. No positive identification is possible right now. The body is charred beyond recognition.'

Imran was silent for a moment. Then he pulled himself together. 'Arjun,' he addressed an agent. 'I want a complete investigation. Who owns this place? What were they doing here? What caused the fire?' He looked at the charred body. 'And I want this body identified.'

His walkie talkie crackled again. 'Sir, you'd better come to the ground floor. We've found something.'

Imran rushed downstairs, followed by Arjun. One of his men had been checking out the elevator shaft and discovered that it didn't end at the ground level. It seemed to extend downwards for quite a distance, as if accessing the basement levels of the building.

Sensing something odd, Varun Jha, the agent had forced the elevator open. The panel for choosing floors was an electronic touch panel rather than the more commonplace buttons.

Nothing seemed to be out of place except for the fact that there were no basements mentioned on the panel.

Jha noticed that there was a second, smaller panel almost hidden below the main one. It was blank, but he had a suspicion that if someone were to swipe a card with the correct authentication, the panel would show up more floors. Going down.

The resourceful agent had then spoken to the firefighters, on the assumption that, if there were hidden basements below the building, there should also be a staircase to access them as a backup to the lift.

The firefighters had stormed into the stairwell and discovered that the stairs led to a small square room which was bare. A dead end. Jha had instructed the firefighters to demolish sections of the three walls surrounding the stairwell. It had paid off. The wall directly in front of the stairs had an empty space beyond it.

It was then that Jha had called Imran, who now hurried into the chamber at the foot of the stairs and watched the firemen break the wall down. As the wall was being flattened, cables and ducting broke free and flapped around aimlessly. Clearly there was some sort of electronic rigging that probably operated a hidden doorway in the wall.

When they had finished, a landing was revealed which led to stairs going down to the lower levels of the building.

Imran was afraid of what they might find. If someone had gone to such lengths to keep the basement hidden, there must have been something important to conceal.

Torches were organised and the IB agents, with the firemen, cautiously made their way down the stairs. It was obvious that the people in charge had fled, but there could be people trapped down there who needed to be rescued.

But the rescuers were not prepared for what they found.

The basement had three levels. The two lowest levels seemed to have been some kind of accommodation, with small cubicles lining long, narrow corridors. Only this was no hotel or dormitory. The cells were all locked from the outside, using electronic locks.

And the occupants of the cells were dead. Not from asphyxiation. It didn't need a forensic expert to reach that conclusion. The bodies were riddled with bullets. While the fire had left these levels untouched, not one soul was alive.

Imran turned to Arjun. 'An American multinational, huh? Well, let's find out what they know about over one hundred corpses of people shot dead in their facility. I'll handle this personally. In the meantime, I want a meeting set up with their CEO as well as their Chief Medical Officer. And get me all the data you can about their operations in India, their history, the trials they are conducting. I want to know everything about them before I meet these guys.'

Arjun nodded. 'You'll have a report by tomorrow evening.'

Imran beckoned to Arjun and the two men moved away from the others. 'Two more things,' Imran whispered. Arjun waited.

When Imran had finished, Arjun looked surprised. But he didn't object. 'I'll get it organized right away,' he promised, and left to carry out Imran's instructions.

Imran gazed around at the bodies and the cells. Hidden basements. Bullet ridden corpses. What was happening here? Someone had gone to great lengths to destroy this building. Were they trying to destroy evidence? In which case, what would that evidence point to? What had happened to Anwar? And what was he doing in a facility that conducted clinical trials?

There were too many questions. An unsettling feeling nagged at him. He knew the feeling well. He had a hunch. Something told him that this was a massive cover-up for a deeper, darker purpose.

He set his jaw as he contemplated his next steps. Whatever it took, he would get to the bottom of this mystery.

Jaungarh Fort

Vijay stroked his chin thoughtfully as he stood at the centre of the room which he had discovered just last week. The fort was fairly large, built in five levels with over fifty rooms, and Vijay had not had either the time or the inclination to immediately explore all the rooms after he had inherited the fort a year ago. He had stayed largely confined to the study on the first floor and his own room on the second floor.

While he was familiar with some of the rooms in the fort, there were many which he had never set eyes on. Over the last six months, he had finally started on the task of getting to know the fort better. It was during this exploration that he had discovered several interesting rooms which had given him insights into his uncle's tastes and predelictions.

Two weeks ago, however, he discovered something totally unexpected. He had come upon a room on the fifth level of the fort, just below the terrace. The room itself was unremarkable and seemed to have been used as a storeroom, judging from the cartons stacked in there along with large, bulky packages wrapped in brown packing paper.

Curiosity had driven Vijay to check the contents of some of the cartons and he had not been prepared for what he found.

Apparently, at least some of the contents of the room belonged to his parents, who had both died in a car accident when Vijay was just fifteen years old. He had heard from his uncle about the truck that had driven, head on at high speed, into the car his parents were in. Both of them had died on the spot. Vijay had not been with them in the car only because, at the last minute, he had to stay behind for some reason that he had now forgotten. But it had saved his life.

He had realised, after examining some of the cartons, that his uncle had arranged for his parents' personal possessions to be packed and transported to the fort, where they had been stored in this room for all these years.

Suddenly, on seeing his father's papers and his mother's journals, he realised just how much he missed them. His uncle had taken good care of him, sending him to MIT for his higher studies, and never allowing him to feel like an orphan. And Vijay had immersed himself first in his studies and later in work, keeping all thoughts of that tragedy out of his mind.

It was only when he came face to face with the physical memories of his parents that the loss really hit home, especially since his uncle, too, was no more.

Vijay had, in that moment, determined that he would sift through the cartons and cherish every memory of his parents that would be churned up. He had barely known his parents, having lost them just as he was growing up and getting to understand them better. He knew that both his parents had been academic historians and researchers, working with the Archaeological Survey of India, but he didn't remember much more than that. He had missed out on that precious relationship that grows through love and conflict during adolescence and he now thought that, perhaps, something in that room would help him get closer to his parents, even after their death.

Every night since then, he would spend an hour or two in the room, sorting the contents of the cartons, reading through papers and journals, seeking insights about his parents that he had never bothered about during his teenage years.

He switched on the desk lamp perched on the desk that

he had stationed in the room for this purpose, and began working his way through the papers stacked on the desk.

Would tonight bring some revelations that the previous nights had failed to provide?

11

DAY TWO

Intelligence Bureau Headquarters, New Delhi

Imran stared into the video camera and adjusted the angle as he waited for Patterson to join the video conference. The leader of the special task force had sounded irritated and doubtful when Imran had called him a few hours ago. It hadn't helped that it was early morning in Washington and Imran had woken him up. But the IB officer didn't think this could wait. He wanted to get moving on the leads he had gathered so far. And if it meant waking the leader of the Indo-US task force in the middle of the night that was fine by him.

But Patterson had changed his mind when he saw the email Imran had sent him. Within an hour of receiving that email, Patterson had confirmed the video conference.

The television screen flickered to life and Patterson's stern visage appeared in a box that filled up half the screen. The other half was filled by the face of a thin, pale man with thinning grey hair. Imran knew who he was. Dr Hank Royson, from the Washington office of the Centres for Disease Control and Prevention. In his email confirming the conference, Patterson had indicated that Royson would be joining them.

'Morning,' Imran greeted the two Americans.

'Morning,' came the chorused response.

'Dr Royson, I appreciate your joining us at short notice,' Patterson got straight to the point. 'Please let us have your views on the reports, which Kidwai sent us.'

'Well,' Royson cleared his throat and began, 'you have to understand, first, that the reports are very preliminary and definitely not conclusive. The detailed toxicology reports and DNA sequencing will take some time, obviously. What we have here, are the preliminary toxicology reports and the result of Polymerase Chain Reaction testing, or PCR testing, which amplifies the DNA target sequence.'

'We know what PCR testing is,' Patterson cut in abruptly. 'Your views on the reports we were sent are what we're looking for.'

Royson stared resentfully into the camera. 'I wasn't sure if Mr Kidwai was familiar with the jargon.'

'Well, I'd figured out some of it by looking at the reports, and I also spent some time on Google,' Imran smiled. 'But thank you for being so thoughtful.' He felt like he just had to soften Patterson's asperity.

Royson sniffed. 'So here it is. It's complex. We have — speculatively speaking of course — a previously unidentified bacterium and an unknown retrovirus. Both present in all the samples.' He stared at the camera again. 'CDC will be conducting our own tests on the samples you had airlifted to us and we'll validate these results. But I'm quite sure there's no major error here.' He looked down, apparently scanning the reports, and then looked back into the camera.

'It is odd, really. The bacteria have formed robust biofilms, in which the cells are surrounded by large expanses of matrix material, protecting them from immune responses. The preliminary toxicology reports indicate that the bacteria were spewing out multiple toxins which would definitely lead to death.' He now addressed Imran. 'Mr Kidwai, just where did you get these samples from?'

Imran narrated the events of the previous night. 'The samples were from a random selection of some of the bodies we found at the facility,' he concluded. 'And, the data we were able to recover from the hard disks, which I suppose you've seen, contained medical histories, which have the same information as these reports.'

Royson nodded. 'Yes, indeed. The medical histories you shared with us correlate with the conclusions of these reports you sent us. And some of the medical files belong to people who died as a result of the infections. The interesting thing is that, according to the medical files, death in all cases occurred four to five years after the initial bacterial infection. It would seem that, after the bacteria infected the patients, they went dormant, possibly as a result of a cell mediated immune response which contained the infection but did not eradicate it, owing to the biofilms. Clearly, the bacteria seemed to have had the ability to bind to or modify naturally occurring human proteins, enabling them to persist chronically but without apparent clinical or symptomatic effects, due to the CMI.'

'Let me understand this,' Imran said slowly. 'You're saying that these people were infected four to five years ago by these bacteria. The bacteria somehow bound to human proteins, which enabled them to persist for a long period of time. At the same time, they formed these biofilms which protected them from the cell mediated immune response or CMI, whatever it is, and so they didn't display any symptoms of the infection.'

'Correct.' Royson smiled for the first time, showing a row of teeth stained by heavy smoking. 'And then, suddenly, something, maybe a weakening of the CMI or some other trigger factor, activated the pathogenicity of the bacteria, releasing their toxins which produced symptoms like high fever and chills, excessive thirst and diaphoresis, acute abdominal pain, increased weakness leading to prostration with intermittent periods of energy, delirium, aphonia and terminal flaccid paralysis. They usually died within a few days of displaying these symptoms.'

Imran took a few seconds to digest this information.

Patterson spoke up. 'It seems you were right, Kidwai,' he conceded. 'It is possible that the clinical trials being conducted on these poor SOBs were tests to see the effects of the bacterium and how long it stayed dormant before expressing itself.'

'Bioterrorism,' Imran breathed, hardly able to believe that anyone could use human subjects in such a callous manner.

'Er... let's not jump to conclusions, shall we?' Royson interjected, holding up one finger. 'DNA sequencing and checking the gene banks of existing pathogens need to be carried out to check if this is really a new strain of bacteria or whether there is any relation to an existing species. More tests need to be carried out to determine the vectors that carry and spread the infection.'

Patterson nodded dismissively. 'Sure, sure. But we have enough to go on to make this a priority for the task force. This is what the team was put together for.'

'What about the virus?' Imran asked, suddenly remembering that Royson had also mentioned a virus.

Royson scratched his head. 'Now that's another strange thing.' He paused to scan his papers once again. 'We don't know much about the retrovirus. There don't seem to be any adverse effects of the viral infection, surprisingly. There is nothing in the medical files on the hard drives about the virus either. We will need to await the detailed tests before we can say anything conclusive.'

'Okay,' Imran collected his own papers and stacked them neatly. As far as he was concerned, this conference was over. He had work to do. 'Guys, let me have the CDC's conclusions as soon as they're out. In the meantime, we've spoken to Titan in Seattle and they claim no knowledge of anything other than legitimate clinical trials to support the research they've been conducting on the new molecules. And the owner of the building says he only leased it out to Titan and had nothing to do with the operations in the building. It seems someone was running a private operation there.'

Patterson looked thoughtful. Royson looked a bit bewildered. 'I'll get some people here to work the Seattle angle,' Patterson promised. 'If there's a connection, we're going to find it.'

Imran nodded, his face grim. 'We will. Good day, gentlemen.'

The two Americans nodded and the television screen went blank again.

Imran leaned back in his chair. Wheels were spinning in his mind as he plotted the course he was going to follow. This was one of the toughest cases he had come across. But one thing seemed to be obvious.

There were bioterrorists out there.

In India.

On his watch.

And he didn't know where to start looking for them.

Jaungarh Fort

Vijay sat, puzzling over the file he had picked up ten minutes ago. The label on the spine of the file had aroused his curiosity. All it said was: "???"

It was but natural for him to select that file out of all the others in the carton and start leafing through the documents filed in it. All the papers were either notes in his father's handwriting or clippings of newspaper articles, that referred to various archaeological digs all over the country along with notes and diagrams. There was no context for the records in this file; just data. It was almost as if his father had googled all the data on these excavations or searched Wikipedia and then recorded the facts he had researched. Only, when this file had been created, Wikipedia hadn't been invented, and Page and Brin were still working out of a garage in California.

So what had his father been thinking when he filed these pages? Clearly a lot of work had gone into research to obtain all this information.

Vijay had no idea. He began studying the papers, trying to find clues to his father's thought process, attempting to understand why this information had been important enough for him to record in this manner.

The more he studied the file, the more puzzled he grew. There had to be something behind this enormous effort.

But what was it?

12

DAY THREE

Jaungarh Fort

Vijay sat and pored over the strange file he had discovered a few hours ago. The contents of the file were mind-boggling. There didn't seem to be any connection between the documents, but then he probably wouldn't see the connection unless he knew why the file had been created in the first place.

Suddenly, his mobile phone rang and he jumped. The clock showed 3 am. What was Colin calling him at this unearthly hour for? Especially since Colin was in the fort!

'You startled me,' he reprimanded Colin.

'Thank heavens. I'd have been worried if you were expecting my call at this hour.' Colin's repartee was swift.

Vijay smiled. 'And just why are you calling me at this hour?'

There was a pause. Then, 'I think you need to come downstairs and see for yourself.'

'In the living room?'

'Yup. Don't dawdle.'

Vijay sighed as he shut the file and locked the door of the room. Since his discovery of this room, he had kept the key to himself, even making a duplicate which was hidden away in a safe place known only to him. He had been thrown a lifeline, a means of communicating with his parents, and he wasn't going to lose this opportunity.

Sometimes you never know what you have until you lose it.

This was a night for surprises. As he entered the living room, he froze. It was like he had seen a ghost. He couldn't believe his eyes.

Slowly, he regained his composure and walked into the room. But he was still unsure of how to react to this situation.

Colin read his friend's face and said nothing.

'Hi, Vijay,' Alice ventured timidly from the white leather sofa, where she sat with Colin. She, too, was apprehensive.

Vijay didn't respond. His jaw was clenched, his brow furrowed. This was the last thing he had expected. He had forced the memories of the past deep down into hidden recesses of his mind and had thought that they would never resurface. Yet, today, they were bubbling up, as fresh as they were eleven years ago. And the emotions they brought with them disturbed him. This was one memory lane he had never wanted to walk down. Ever. And he was doing exactly that now.

Finally, he found his voice. 'It is 3 am in the morning.' He tried to sound nonchalant. 'Why are you here? You had said that you never ever wanted to have anything to do with me. What changed now?'

'She's in trouble,' Colin interjected, before Alice could reply. 'She needs our help.'

Cold silence greeted this explanation.

'Vijay, her life is in danger. We have to help her,' Colin tried again.

With an effort, Vijay suppressed his emotions. 'It is a long way from the US,' he said slowly. 'If you are here and you need help, you must be desperate.'

Alice gazed back at him. The old wounds were hurting once again. A reminder that, though she had tried to forget them, they still existed below the surface. 'I know how you feel, Vijay,' she began. 'And I swear I wouldn't have come here if I had a choice. But I don't.'

Vijay forced himself to keep his voice even. 'What happened?'

Alice recounted the trauma she had experienced in Greece. Her voice shook as she described Damon's murder, Marco's death and her escape on the highway. 'I couldn't go back to the US,' she finished. 'No matter where I would go, they would have found me. I had to go someplace else. But I don't know anyone else outside the US whom I could trust. Kurt Wallace had some people in Delhi provide me with a car to get here from the airport. He said it was the only way to ensure that no one was able to track me from Greece. Private jet. Private car. No paper or electronic trail.'

She stared at Vijay, trying to discern his reaction. It was obvious that he was affected by her story.

'C'mon, Vijay,' Colin broke in. 'The girl needs a place to stay. Her life's in danger. You have, what, fifty rooms here in the fort? Can't she stay here for a couple of nights till this blows over?'

Vijay looked at him then turned to Alice. 'You have to understand one thing,' he said, his voice serious. 'I want both of us to be clear about this. I've moved on. I'm engaged. You and me – that's in the past. I don't want that to come between me and Radha.'

'Radha's his fiancée,' Colin explained to Alice, helpfully.

Alice nodded. She hadn't expected any more than this. Somehow, she felt safe here. Even though she had never been to India, she knew she was among friends.

'We have a security system protecting the fort,' Vijay continued. 'As long as you stay here and don't venture out, no one is going to get to you.' As he spoke, he remembered his uncle's fate the previous year, but dismissed the thought from his mind. The system had been upgraded since then.

'Thank you, Vijay,' Alice responded. 'I really appreciate your helping me out.'

Vijay forced a smile. He was consciously trying to push his emotions away. 'Sure. Always happy to help. Colin, will you show Alice to one of the guest rooms. Choose any one. Okay, guys, I need to sleep. Radha's coming here tomorrow and I don't want to be sleeping in when she gets here.' He looked at Colin. 'And we have our meeting with Imran in the morning.'

Colin nodded as Vijay left the room.

He then turned to look at Alice. 'Well, that didn't go so badly, did it?'

'So tell me more about Radha?' Alice asked. 'What's she like?'

Colin frowned. This was not going to be as easy as he had thought.

13

Jaungarh Fort

'Morning,' Vijay frowned as he walked into the dining room of the fort. Colin and Alice were finishing breakfast. Bad timing. Radha would be here any moment now.

Colin grinned up at him like the Cheshire Cat, which Vijay was accustomed to by now. But Alice smiling up at him at the breakfast table; he had to calm himself down all over again.

'Did you sleep well?' he enquired of Alice, more out of politeness than genuine concern. Though there had been something that had stayed on his mind from the conversation last night.

Alice nodded. 'Umm hmm. I did, thanks. Did you?'

Vijay didn't respond. His mind was now ticking away, focused on what Alice had mentioned last night.

'You said that you found an ivory cube in the tomb,' he said finally, between mouthfuls of masala omelette and *parantha*.

Alice looked at him, surprised. She hadn't thought that anything about her experience in Greece had registered with Vijay, considering the background of their conversation last night.

'Yes,' she replied. 'It had inscriptions carved on it.'

'And when Marco came back for you, he told you that Damon had asked you to carry the cube back to the hotel.'

'That's right.' Alice wondered where Vijay was going with this line of thought.

'And what did you do with the cube?'

'I put it in my backpack.' The realisation struck Alice hard. In her panic and wild attempts to get away, she had forgotten that she still carried the cube, safe in its container inside her backpack, which she had brought with her to India.

'So that's what they wanted,' Vijay murmured. 'The cube.'

Alice shook her head. The images from two nights ago were burned into her mind as if they had been seared by a red hot branding iron. 'They were after me because I had seen the tomb. Marco had nothing with him. But he was in the tomb with us. So they killed him, too. They just wanted to kill everyone who was there that evening.'

Vijay looked thoughtful. 'What did you do with your laptop and camera?'

'Left them both in my room at the hotel.'

'So they would have the photographs of all the artefacts with them.' Vijay looked puzzled. 'That doesn't explain anything.'

Alice's eyes widened. 'No, they wouldn't,' she said. 'I didn't have time to upload the photographs to the laptop. I thought I'd do it later so I took out the memory stick and put it in my waist pouch. I still have it with me.'

Vijay slapped his thigh. 'It has to be the cube,' he persisted. 'Two good reasons why. First, the cube is the only artefact that is missing from the collection. And since they don't have the photographs either, they need the original. Right?'

'Right,' Alice murmured, still doubtful.

'Second, you mentioned that you discovered the cube right at the end since it was hidden behind the tablets and statues and Damon had left the tomb by then.'

'That's right.' Alice realised what Vijay was leading up to. 'So you're wondering how Damon could have known it was there when he hadn't seen it. It is possible that he saw it while he was examining the artefacts in the hidden chamber.'

Vijay shook his head. 'That's not it. What I'm wondering is this. The co-directors had given instructions to remove all artefacts and place them in the dig hut. Correct?'

'Right.'

'So why did Damon ask you to bring only the cube with you to the hotel? Why was the cube so significant? And, more importantly, Marco told you that Stavros was reprimanding Damon for asking you to bring the cube to the hotel. According to Stavros, Damon should have brought it himself. Which *could* mean that Damon had been told that the cube was significant in some way and should be brought back to the hotel. Which begs the question: how did Stavros or Peter, or anyone for that matter, know that the cube was down in that tomb when they weren't there to see it?'

Alice mulled this over. 'It is possible,' she said slowly, thinking aloud, 'that Damon told them about the cube and they asked him to get it to the hotel.'

'I don't think so,' Vijay argued, 'there are too many coincidences for your explanation to be acceptable. First, Damon would have needed to have seen the cube before you discovered it. Unlikely. And then, it is also very unlikely that Damon would have told Stavros about it and would be asked to bring only that particular artefact to the hotel without there being any particular significance attached to it. And, why did they want to see only the cube? Why not any of the other artefacts from the tomb? Finally, the cube is the only artefact not in their possession and they don't have a photograph of it either. So it has to be the cube that they are after.'

'I don't know,' Alice replied. 'You could be right. Your logic certainly makes sense. The cube was intriguing. But there was nothing special about it. Other than the fact that it was made from ivory and it had unintelligible inscriptions on it.'

'Why would an old ivory cube in a tomb drive people to kill?' Colin wondered. 'Whose tomb was it anyway?'

Alice smiled at him. 'Maybe I should give you a background of this excavation, so you can get an idea of what we were looking for.'

'Guys,' Colin interjected. 'If we're going to be discussing archaeological ruins and tombs and such like stuff, can we please move to somewhere more comfortable? I know how these discussions can get and I don't want to be in the middle of one at the dining table.'

Vijay smiled. 'Sure,' he replied. 'Study?'

'Great idea,' Colin responded. He loved the study that Vijay's uncle had created for himself in the fort. 'The sun's up today so hopefully it will be nice and sunlit.'

They headed up to the study and sat around the glass coffee table that occupied one corner next to a wall mounted LCD television.

'I was approached eighteen months ago,' Alice began, 'by the Wallace Archaeological Trust, to be a leading member of the team for this excavation.' She looked at both men. 'How familiar are you with the history of Alexander III of Macedon?'

'Who's that?' Colin asked, leaning comfortably against the white leather cushions. 'Any relation to Alexander the Great?'

Alice sighed. 'Alexander III *was* Alexander the Great.'

Colin smiled sheepishly. 'Oh. Sorry. History has never been my strong point.'

'Anyway,' Alice continued, 'Kurt Wallace personally wanted me on this mission for some reason. And since Hellenistic history is one of my areas of interest, I agreed to sign on.'

'There must have been something that drew you to this mission,' Vijay said. 'I know you. You wouldn't get involved in something unless you were passionate about it.'

Alice smiled. This was why she had fallen in love with Vijay. Somehow he knew her so well. Why couldn't it have lasted?

She opened her mouth to respond, but Shivjeet the butler appeared. 'Hukum, Radha ma'am is here with Dr Shukla.'

Radha entered the room, smiling, followed by Shukla. 'Shivjeet,' she remonstrated, 'you don't have to announce us!' She stopped short as she saw Alice and her smile faded.

Colin quickly did the introductions. He knew how possessive Radha was about Vijay so he was careful not to introduce Alice as Vijay's ex-girlfriend. Vijay would have to do that himself at a time of his choosing.

Vijay got up and greeted Shukla with a warm embrace. 'I'm glad you came, too,' he told the linguist.

'I thought I'd come along and spend some time with you guys,' Shukla smiled. 'I haven't seen Colin since last year!'

Vijay turned to Radha and kissed her. 'Hey,' he beamed at her. 'I couldn't wait for you to get here.'

Radha smiled back. 'Me too.'

They sat down together on a sofa as Shukla took a seat next to Colin. 'Alice had a terrible experience in Greece,' Vijay explained. 'She was just telling us about it.'

'Go on, Alice,' Radha smiled. 'I'm sorry to hear that, but I'm also curious.'

Alice smiled back at Radha and continued. 'Kurt Wallace told me about a clue that his team had unearthed which could lead us to solving one of ancient Greece's most enduring mysteries.'

'Kurt Wallace is a billionaire who funded her excavation,' Colin enlightened Radha, who nodded her understanding.

'And what was that mystery?' Shukla looked interested.

'The tomb of Olympias, the wife of Philip II, and the mother of Alexander the Great. Her tomb has been the subject of much speculation but there was never any evidence that it even existed, leave alone its location. Until now.'

Something tickled Vijay's memory. That name. Olympias. Where had he encountered it before? And fairly recently, too, maybe in the last month or so. But the answer to that question eluded him. So he just said, 'Wow, that sounds big.'

Alice smiled at him. 'I don't know how much you guys know about Greek history, but Olympias had a tumultuous tenure as Queen. After Alexander died, she indulged in power politics with the aim of securing the throne for Alexander IV, the son of Alexander the Great. She allied with Perdiccas at first and then with Polyperchon, both Macedonian generals with ambitions of their own. After shuttling between Epirus and Macedonia, she was finally besieged at Pydna in 316 BC by Cassander, the son of Antipater who was Alexander's viceroy in Macedonia during his Asian campaign. She was then executed by the relatives of Macedonians whom she had put to death and who were instigated by Cassander, who didn't want to do the deed himself. Cassander hated Olympias and refused to have her body buried, decreeing that it should be cast away in the open. However, apparently, there was a surreptitious burial, and a tomb was subsequently constructed, possibly during the reign of Pyrrhus of Epirus, who was, like Olympias, an Aeacid.'

She looked around. 'Go on,' Shukla encouraged her. 'This is really interesting.'

'We found the tomb.' She was surprised that she could summarise the momentous discovery in four words.

'How do you know it was the tomb of Olympias?' Radha wanted to know. She hadn't liked the way Alice had smiled at Vijay when he had complimented her on her discovery. Who was this woman? Vijay had never mentioned her to Radha.

'Well, to start with, there have been references to Olympias' tomb on inscriptions discovered in the early 20th century in the village of Makrigialos. There has even been speculation that Makrigialos is the site of ancient Pydna. And Kurt's research team unearthed an obscure news item relating to a stele that was half eroded. They were able to locate it and purchase it. The inscription on the stele had a direct reference to the tomb, indicating that it was nearer to Korinos than Makrigialos. So we began excavating on the site that was mentioned in the inscription after satellite remote sensing showed evidence of a tomb-like structure buried deep within a mound. Though, we still weren't sure about the occupant when we entered the tomb,' Alice admitted. 'But when we saw the sculptures on the walls...' She paused, thinking about the snakes all over the burial chamber. 'You see, according to legend, Alexander was not begotten by Philip. Olympias had told Alexander that he was the son of Zeus, who had come to her in the form of a serpent. Legend also says that she had a strange fascination for snakes – she even used to sleep with them. That's also, perhaps, how the legend of Alexander's birth was perpetuated.' She described the paintings on the walls of the ante-chamber depicting a queen, the snakes on the walls of the burial chamber and the discovery of the third, hidden chamber, with the statues and tablets.

'And the cube?' Vijay pressed, his curiosity getting the better of him. 'Can we see it?'

14

A riddle in ivory

Alice excused herself to fetch the cube from her room. While she was gone, Vijay updated Radha and Shukla on her traumatic night in Greece and their discussion regarding the cube just before she arrived.

'So, she didn't go back to the US,' Radha remarked. 'She came here.'

'She called me when she was trying to get away,' Colin said quickly, detecting an acerbic note in Radha's voice. 'Maybe she thought she would be welcome here.'

'And she is, isn't she?' Radha observed.

Just then, Alice returned with the container and opened it, placing it on the coffee table for everyone to see. Four heads bent over the cube, studying the face that was visible.

'What does the text say? Can you read this?' Radha looked at Alice.

Alice shook her head. 'The script is unknown to me. But the inscriptions look like verses. I could be wrong, though.'

'This is the Brahmi script,' Shukla announced. He had been studying the cube intently. 'The language is, strangely, Sanskrit. Which is odd, since Brahmi was not often used as a script for Sanskrit. This cube could have originated in India.'

Alice, Colin and Vijay exchanged glances. 'What's a cube from India doing in an ancient Greek tomb?' Alice wondered. 'That's a long way for a cube to travel. I wonder how it got to Greece in the first place.'

Shukla looked up at Alice. 'Do you mind if I take it out of the container and examine it more closely?'

'Sure.' Alice nodded. She was as eager as the others to learn what the inscriptions said.

Shukla turned the cube over and studied all six faces. 'Interesting,' he observed.

'Go on, Papa,' Radha pressed him. 'Read us the inscriptions.'

Shukla peered at the face of the cube. 'One face of the cube is blank. The others are inscribed – five verses in all. This one says:

Above the river on the ridge
Where day and night together meet
And Sukra points to Shiva's staff
The herald to the mighty snake
Five crowned, eternal guardian of
The portal that will give you life.'

Radha's eyes were shining with the anticipation of the challenge of interpreting this riddle. 'We might be able to decipher these riddles. The allusions are Indian in nature. Shiva's staff, for example, could be his trident.'

Alice shrugged. 'I have no clue. You guys would know best. But it is intriguing how an ivory cube with inscriptions connected to India ended up in a Greek tomb.'

'It has to be Indian in origin,' Shukla said. 'The allusion to Sukra is also from Indian mythology. Sukra was the son of the rishi Bhrigu. According to the Mahabharata, he was the chief priest of the Asuras and was learned in the science of revivification. The Danavas who were killed by the Devas were revived by Sukra using this science.'

'What do the other faces say?' Vijay wanted to know.

Shukla turned the cube over. 'This is further proof that the cube is Indian in origin. The inscription on this face says:

Across the swiftly flowing eye
Beside the deep and saltless sea,
Three brothers cast their shadow on
The arrowhead that shows the way
To enter the embrace of Pataal.
Dig deep beyond the serpent's seal
And find the kernel of your quest.'

He looked up from the cube. '*Pataal* in Indian mythology refers to the netherworld or the underworld. Technically, it is one of the seven regions of the netherworld.'

'You mean, like, hell?' Colin asked.

'Not really,' Shukla clarified. 'Hell is a western concept, invented to keep people to a path of righteousness out of fear. There is no concept of hell in Hindu philosophy or mythology. It is truly a netherworld, a world that exists below the surface of our world.'

Alice looked around. 'Any ideas? Doesn't make sense to me. Except it seems to be some sort of instruction for a quest that needs to be undertaken.'

'The only thing that I can see,' Colin said, 'is that this verse is urging people to enter the netherworld. I don't see the connect with reality here. Isn't the netherworld a myth?'

'Perhaps we'll get a better idea once we translate them all,' Radha pitched in. 'Go on, Papa,' she urged. 'Let's see what the other verses say.'

15

More riddles

'Okay, here's the next one.' Shukla turned the cube over once again.

'And from the lands around the rock
Pluck the fruit and leaf and bark
The first with many stems and fruit
Dark purple, clothed in grey and white
And green or brown. The next is smooth
Of texture, bearing violet fruit
Beware for burns will greet the touch.'

'Pretty clear instructions,' Colin remarked sarcastically, 'if you knew what you were looking for.

'But it does seem to confirm what Alice said just now,' Radha countered. 'This cube could be a secret guide to a quest. The only problem is we don't know what the objective of that quest is.'

Shukla read out the next inscription.

'Remember, adventurer, bold as you are
Ignore the warnings at your peril
The elements must come together
Protected by the fiery gaze
Of the serpent – disregard
And forfeit your most precious gift.'

'Okay,' Colin interjected. 'I can decipher at least one line of this riddle.' He grinned at the others. 'This is what we would call a disclaimer today. What this one is saying is that if you don't follow the instructions and ignore the warnings – whatever they are – you will lose your life. That's the "most precious gift". It can't be anything else.'

'You could be right,' Radha said thoughtfully. 'But it still doesn't tell us what the instructions will lead us to. And there is such a mix of imagery – we have Shiva, a serpent, fruits to be plucked, a swiftly flowing eye – how does one figure this out?'

'Wait till you see the last one.' Shukla had been studying the final inscription while they were talking. 'It says:

Then enter you the portal to
The valleys parting east and west
Choose wisely here, remember where
You march and where Surya lies.'

'Oh great,' Colin groaned. 'Another portal and Surya now. This is crazy. Who is Surya?'

'Not really,' Radha frowned, thinking hard. 'Surya is the Indian sun god. So Surya rises in the east. Which means that this riddle is talking about two valleys and the instruction is to choose the valley in the east.'

'That's a good point. But what valley? And the sun moves from east to west, so Surya could lie in the west, depending on the time of day,' Vijay pointed out.

The gleam in Radha's eyes faded. 'We don't have a reference point to try and solve this riddle,' she shrugged, a note of disappointment in her voice. 'We need either a starting point so we know which face needs to be read first. Or we need to know the purpose for which the cube was created. Without either, we can't decipher the cube.'

'True,' Alice agreed. 'The cube was definitely created for a purpose. But there's no way of knowing why it was made.' She placed it back in the padded container.

'Okay, that settles it. Why don't we go outside and take a walk around the fort? It's a beautiful day. We can't solve these riddles anyway. God knows I'm glad about that. I don't want to have anything to do with fiery serpents. And my life is my most precious gift and I don't intend losing it by getting involved with any kind of quest. These quests were made for Greek heroes; Hercules and his ilk. Not for twentieth century guys like me.' Colin rose and extended a hand to Alice. She smiled at him and allowed him to help her up.

'Don't worry,' Vijay laughed. 'We weren't about to set off on a trip chasing those riddles anyway. Greece is too far away for us to hunt for answers to these riddles there. And, in any case, there's no reason for us to do that. It was more an intellectual challenge, which I think we've all agreed is pointless.'

'I think I need some fresh air too.' Shukla arose and accompanied Colin and Alice out of the room. Radha hung back with Vijay as the others departed.

Vijay eyed her quizzically.

'So,' Radha began. 'Just who is she? A hot blonde, built like Barbie, arriving in the middle of the night, and pally enough with both of you. What's she doing here? What's the story?'

While Radha sounded cheerful enough, Vijay realised that she needed to know. He explained his past relationship with Alice. 'But don't worry,' he assured her. 'It's all in the past. I got over her a long time ago. When you and I met the only relationship I had was with my work.'

Radha nodded and smiled. But in her heart, she had misgivings. She wasn't worried about Vijay; she trusted him implicitly. And somewhere, her intuition told her that the relationship between Vijay and Alice had been stronger on her side than his. But she had observed the way Alice kept looking at Vijay. She suspected that Alice still harboured feelings for him, despite the breakup, despite the intervening years.

She decided to not worry and handle things as they came. 'What time is Imran going to be here?' she asked.

Vijay looked at his watch. 'He said around noon. We've got time to kill.' A thought struck him. 'Hey, since we have time, I want to show you something really weird. We'll need to go to one of the rooms on the top floor.'

'What did Imran want to meet about?' Radha enquired, as they climbed the stone staircase to the fifth floor.

'He didn't specify. All he would say was that the task force has its first case and he needs to brief us. But he didn't sound too happy about it.'

16

Jaungarh Fort

'This is really mysterious,' Radha mused, as she leafed through the file that had perplexed Vijay. 'There must have been a good reason why your dad put this file together.'

Vijay shrugged. 'I keep thinking that. But I haven't the foggiest what that reason could be.'

'What's this?' Radha indicated a single A4 size sheet of paper with symbols on it. She peered closely at the symbols. 'They look like runes of some kind. And they're handwritten. Is this your dad's handwriting?'

'I don't know,' Vijay admitted. 'I don't remember his handwriting. Come to think of it, I don't remember much about him.' He shook his head. 'I never spent enough time with him. I guess I just felt that he would always be there and there would be enough time to hang out together. So I spent my time playing football and cricket with my friends in the neighbourhood parks. And, as it turned out, there never was enough time.' He fell silent and Radha slipped her hand into his. He pressed her hand in response, grateful that she was there.

'There's a list of some kind here,' Radha observed, studying one of the papers. 'Looks like an index.'

Vijay peered down at the file at the sheet of paper Radha was examining. 'Tell you what,' he said. 'Let's see if there's any correlation between this list and what's in the file, shall we?'

Radha nodded. This was intriguing. It probably amounted to nothing significant but she understood Vijay's need to know. She slipped the sheet with the index out of the file. Vijay began listing the papers in the file as she checked for their presence on the list.

It was tough going. There were few exact matches. While they were able to identify papers listed in the index in most cases, a few could be matched only through guesswork and approximation.

'There are three items on this list which don't seem to be in that file,' Radha said finally, after they had gone through its contents. She pointed them out. 'KS-1, KS-2,' she read out the names on the list. 'And this third one.' She tried to make out the name, which was a single symbol. 'What is this – a "W"?'

Vijay strained to make out the symbol. 'Looks like a "W",' he said. 'But it is too wavy to be a "W". See here, there are no straight lines.' Something stirred in his memory and he stiffened.

'What happened?' Radha noticed the change in his posture.

'I think I came across one of the missing documents earlier,' Vijay narrowed his eyes as he tried to remember. 'I remember seeing "KS" somewhere.' He got up and started studying the cartons which he had already gone through over the last two weeks. 'I'll have to go through them again,' he mused.

'Here, let me give you a hand.' Radha pulled one carton towards her and began pulling out its contents.

Vijay smiled at her and chose another carton to examine. This was what he loved about Radha. He knew that, despite her nonchalant demeanour, she was troubled by Alice's presence. But she had shrugged that off and was, as always, ready to help out. It was something he admired in her in addition to her inner strength and confidence. She was always there for her friends and family, pushing her own needs and priorities aside at a moment's notice. He wished that he could be like that. He was too much of an introvert, caught up in his own world. Abruptly, his thoughts moved to Alice. He knew why Alice had broken up with him, when they were both at MIT. He had agonised over it after their break up, trying to work out what had gone wrong. And he had finally understood. He had never been able to open up to her. While he had always been serious and reserved, ever since his parents died he had drawn even further into his shell. It was his way of trying to forget the tragedy that had befallen him. He had built mighty walls around himself. And the project that had been his dream always meant more than anything else. When he met Alice, it seemed that things might change. But he had never been able to raze the walls that always stood between them.

For a long time, he had been unable to forgive her for the manner in which she had walked out on him. No discussion, no explanation, no chance for him to redeem himself. Or even realise the mistakes that he had made. He had been bitter. Angry with her. It was much later that he realised that it wouldn't have made a difference at that time even if she had explained where he had gone wrong. He had just not been ready. It had taken him two years to come to terms with the break up. After that, he had been wary of getting into another relationship. Partly because his work kept him busy, and partly because he felt that he couldn't really give himself completely to any relationship. Then he had met Radha. Their friendship had blossomed into love a year ago, during their adventures following the murder of Vijay's uncle. Somehow, things had worked out and he was happy now. Contented. He couldn't have asked for a better person than Radha to be in a relationship with.

'Here it is!' Radha's voice seemed to float on the surface of the ocean of his thoughts. Vijay emerged to see what she had found.

Radha was holding a slim cardboard file in which a sheaf of papers was bound with a ribbon. It looked well thumbed and worn. 'KS-1,' she announced.

Vijay beamed. 'Great. Let's find out what's inside.'

'Looks like a photocopy of a handwritten journal,' Radha remarked as she opened the file and began scanning the contents. 'This is interesting. Your father was a historian wasn't he?'

Vijay nodded.

'He must have been pretty passionate about his work to collect stuff like this. This journal is the translated copy of a journal that dates back to the time of Alexander the Great.'

Vijay's mobile phone rang. It was Colin. Imran had arrived.

'Is it noon already?' Radha looked at her watch and grinned at Vijay. 'Times flies when you're having fun.' She waved the journal at Vijay. 'This is interesting stuff. According to the first page, it is a translation of a much older journal belonging to a guy called…' She looked at the journal to check the name. 'Right. Eumenes. He's the guy who wrote the original journal which some guy called Lawrence Fuller has translated into English.'

Vijay took the journal from her and flipped through it. His father had taken pains to keep this safe. He had to know why. His attention was attracted by the mention of a name in the journal. He showed it to Radha, who took the journal from him, her eyes glistening with excitement.

17

The Task Force meets

They made their way downstairs with Radha clutching the journal they had just found. She planned to go through it with Vijay after Imran had left.

Ten minutes later, Vijay, Radha and Colin were seated in the study around the glass-topped coffee table. Imran wore a serious look on his face as he double-locked the door of the study and joined them. Even his greetings when they had met were unusually subdued.

'Right,' Imran began. 'The task force has its first case and as members of the think tank, you need to be briefed. That's why I'm here. I've been in touch with Patterson who will brief the team members in the US.'

He paused. 'We have a potential case of bioterrorism on our hands. Two nights ago, I got an email from a childhood friend, Anwar, requesting help. I didn't know it at the time but it seems that he had enrolled, five years ago, as a volunteer for clinical trials being sponsored by Titan Pharmaceuticals, a US multinational with research centres in India.' He described the events of that night leading to the discovery of the corpses in the centre run by Aryan Laboratories.

'The body in the IT lab was Anwar's,' he continued. 'It was charred beyond recognition but we identified it using DNA analysis.' He paused for a while. The death of his friend had affected him deeply. 'We can only conjecture but it seems that Anwar somehow managed to sneak into the IT lab and send out that email. Apparently, he was discovered and killed. The autopsy confirmed that the cause of death was a bullet through his head. At point blank range. It seems that when they realised that the email had been sent to an IB officer, they decided to kill all the inmates and burn the place down to destroy any evidence that might fall into our hands.'

'So these clinical trials were being conducted to test a new bioweapon?' Radha asked. 'What does Titan have to say about this?'

'That's what we suspect,' Imran replied. 'But Titan claims that all trials they sponsored were legitimate and approved by the Drug Controller General of India. And we checked with the Clinical Trials Registry – India, where Titan had registered several clinical trials. Patterson and his team have spoken to the senior management of Titan in the US, and even to the Chairman of the Board, Kurt Wallace, who is also a majority shareholder in Titan.'

The name registered immediately.

'The guy who funded Alice's expedition,' Vijay said, looking surprised.

'Who's Alice?' Imran asked immediately. 'And what's her connection here?'

'A friend of mine from the US who turned up suddenly early this morning.' He swiftly sketched out Alice's story, including the details about Wallace that Alice had mentioned.

Imran pursed his lips when Vijay had finished. 'Your friend certainly had a tough time. I'm glad she managed to get away from there. Though it certainly is an interesting coincidence that Kurt Wallace is the common factor in both cases. And it is also an interesting coincidence that your friend turned up here at the same time that we're investigating a possible case of bioterrorism.'

Vijay realised what Imran was thinking. 'I can vouch for her,' he remonstrated. 'I've known her...' he faltered as he struggled to describe his relationship with Alice without getting Radha upset. 'I know her well,' he finished.

Imran looked pointedly at Vijay. 'Maybe you do. But it is curious that the timing of her visit and the fact that she is connected to Kurt Wallace coincides so well with the facts of our case. Maybe it is nothing but sheer coincidence. But I'm not ruling out anything until we're sure.'

Vijay subsided, trying to conceal his dismay.

Imran resumed the briefing. 'Wallace and the entire senior management of Titan have pointed to the owner of Aryan, Suman Pahwa, who seems to have disappeared after the fire. We've tracked down all the possible places we could have found him but he's vanished. We've reached a dead end with Pahwa. But there was something going on there. The hard drives were badly damaged by the fire, but we have a pretty sophisticated IT lab where we were able to recover a lot of the data. There were medical files with histories on the subjects of the clinical trials. This gave us a lot of information. We also conducted an autopsy on the bodies we found and sent samples to the National Centre for Disease Control, New Delhi and the National Institute of Virology in Pune. Their findings were corroborated by tests conducted by the CDC in Washington – I got their reports just this morning.'

He briefed them on the conversation he had had with Patterson and Royson the previous evening. 'So our guess is that this Pahwa guy was running this covert clinical trial operation in the centre. We haven't ruled out the involvement of anyone from the US, of course. Even Wallace himself. But there's no evidence to support that.'

There was silence when he concluded.

'So, what are the next steps?' Colin asked.

'And how can we help?' Vijay chipped in.

'We don't have a lot to go on right now,' Imran conceded. 'I wanted you guys to have all the facts in case you could think of a new angle, something that we could work on. For now, the field agents assigned to the task force are hunting for Pahwa and trying to get any other leads on the clinical trials. They're scouring newspaper advertisements for clinical trials from four to five years ago and talking to people in the industry. I am going to visit the CEO of Titan in India, Dr Swaroop Varma. And I will also meet the Chief Medical Officer of Titan, Dr Varun Saxena.'

'We could help you with that,' Radha offered. 'I don't mind meeting the CMO, if you'd like.'

'Thanks,' Imran smiled, 'but that's a field job. I know you guys have undergone field training after the task force was set up, but you have no field experience. This could be dangerous if we happen to meet someone who is actually involved in the bioterrorism operation.'

'So we're never going to gain field experience if we don't start somewhere,' Radha persisted. 'What if I come with you when you're meeting the CEO, so that you're around in case anything goes wrong?'

'You may as well agree, Imran,' Vijay grinned. 'She's like a bulldog. She won't back down now.'

Radha slapped his back lightly and made a face. 'I think this will be interesting. Come on Imran. Let's do it.'

'Oh, okay,' Imran held out his hands. 'Fine. What could go wrong with an interview? I have the meeting scheduled with the CEO at 4.30 pm. I'll get my guys to organise the meeting with the CMO at the same time.'

As he reached for his phone, it rang. Imran listened intently to the caller and his face clouded.

'Bad news?' Vijay guessed.

'We just found Pahwa's body. Car crash on the Agra

expressway. Apparently his brakes had been tampered with and they gave way. He must have been zipping on that road so he didn't have a chance.' He sighed. 'That's our last live lead gone. And that also means that he was probably just a pawn in the game. There's someone in Titan who is running the show. Only, we now have no way of finding out who that is.'

18

Gurgaon

Peter Cooper sat in an armchair and stared at the flat screen monitors in the Presidential suite at The Westin, Gurgaon. In one corner of the room, a rack stacked with equipment stood with bundles of cables snaking out of them, connecting to a row of servers.

Cooper didn't understand computers at all. In all of his fifty-two years, he had never felt comfortable with technology. He had joined the Order at twenty-one, a hired gun with an amazing ability to hit a moving target at any distance that was visible through a gun's telescopic sight. He was also blessed with an eidetic memory. Both abilities had combined to make him a fearsome assassin, which was only enhanced by his ability to kill with no compunctions.

He had never kept count of the number of people he had murdered: men, women and children. For him, they were not statistics. They were not even people. They were simply targets that had to be eliminated. And he did his job with precision. He prided himself on his consistency. He had never missed a target. And never once had he hesitated, his finger hovering over the trigger.

Over the years, he had moved up in status within the Order. Now, his job was less tactical and more strategic. Which meant fewer assassination assignments, even though his eyesight hadn't weakened with age. And even though technology's importance as a contributor to his success had increased over the years as his role changed, he had never taken to it. For him, the strategist's ultimate weapon, the highest level of technology, was within his head. That was all he required. Everything else was superfluous.

'What's the status?' he asked the man sitting at the console, a dark, balding man with a moustache who ran the local technology team. His name was Krishnan and, despite his unassuming appearance, he was a whiz with IT, as Cooper had discovered.

After the police had got involved in Thessaloniki, Cooper had decided to play a more passive role and track Alice rather than pursue her. This was a covert mission and he didn't want any attention drawn to it. Stavros was taking care of ensuring that news about the events at the excavation site didn't leak to the media. No one would know the truth about what had happened there. And the mission would remain a secret.

That left Alice. Not only was she a witness to what had happened, she also possessed the one thing that his entire mission revolved around. And he had to retrieve it. Without drawing attention to himself or the mission.

When Alice disappeared in Thessaloniki, he had searched for her but soon realised that she had left the country. But he wasn't one to give up. Not so soon, especially when he knew that her passport was lying in her room at the site hotel. Using his network, he found a contact in the American consulate in Thessaloniki. A Greek single mother, she had refused to cooperate at first, but Cooper had had her five-year-old daughter picked up. It was amazing, he thought, how fast she was able to feed him with information after that. He learnt that special orders had come from Washington and Alice's passport had been issued with unusual speed. The mother and daughter duly featured in the newspapers the next morning as photographed corpses, their throats slit. It wasn't his style, but his new deputy had carried out the hits and he was better with blades than with guns.

His next stop was Greek immigration where he had a network of paid contacts. From them, he learned that Alice had boarded a private jet to New Delhi, India.

Leaving Stavros to mop up in Greece, Cooper had immediately flown to New Delhi in his own private jet, provided by the Order. Once in India, he had contacted the local cell and set up his headquarters in Gurgaon. Now, all he needed to know was where Alice was hiding and whom she was with. It was just a matter of time before he had what he wanted and his mission could continue undisturbed. Alice had been a minor irritant, an ant who had crashed the picnic. It was time for the ant to be squashed.

Krishnan swivelled around in his chair to face Cooper. 'She is in a fort at a place called Jaungarh, which is 130 kilometres from New Delhi. We've identified the other people with her.' He paused. 'Not good news.'

Cooper raised his eyebrows.

'Two American citizens are with her. One is of Indian origin. Vijay Singh. The other is Colin Baker. There's also a woman who works with the Indian Department of Atomic Energy – a nuclear physicist called Radha Shukla. And, there's also a Special Director from the Indian Intelligence Bureau. Imran Kidwai.'

Cooper frowned. This was a bit more than a minor irritant. The Indian intelligence agencies were involved. Krishnan was right. This was bad news.

'What's the IB guy doing there?' he asked. 'Can we get some intel on their conversation?'

'Our team is in position. But they're in a room that's wired to keep surveillance out. We have no audio contact. And there's no vantage point that can provide us with visual contact either. We're blind here.' He held Cooper's gaze. 'We should have got the Stingray. That would have enabled us to track their calls and get a whole lot of data that we could have used to figure out what they're upto.'

Cooper frowned at him. 'We're trying to keep a low profile on this mission. Do you know what is involved in getting a Stingray into a country? It is possible, but it would put us at risk. You're supposed to be a genius. Work with what you have.'

He considered the options. If the targets were holed up in a fort, it would not be easy to storm the place without heavy firepower. And that would attract attention.

'Keep all our teams on alert,' he ordered. 'I want every person in that fort tracked. I want to know where they are and what they are doing.'

He settled back and closed his eyes. Years of waiting for the right opportunity to pull the trigger had trained him to be patient. He would wait. Until the right moment presented itself.

And he knew it would happen before long. It always worked out that way.

19

An interesting discovery

Vijay sat in his study on the first floor of the fort and studied his laptop's screen. Ever since Imran and Radha had left for their meetings at Titan Pharmaceuticals, he had his nose glued to the pages of the journal Radha had found. From time to time he would make notes on a notepad.

He had spent the last half an hour, after he had read the journal, searching the internet, referring to his notes as he worked. The only break he took was when he left the study to run up to the fifth-floor room which contained the possessions of his parents. He picked up the file which Radha and he had been perusing earlier and dashed back to the study.

There was a knock on the door. 'Hey, have you taken root there or what?' Colin opened the door and walked in.

Vijay grinned. He knew that Colin would have been eaten up with curiosity. It was surprising that he had waited so long to find out what Vijay was up to.

Colin scowled at him. 'Alice is a bit miffed that you didn't even bother to ask her about Imran's meeting with her.' After the briefing, Imran had asked to see Alice and had spent half an hour closeted with her in the study. But Vijay had the journal on his mind and, the moment Imran and Radha departed, he had occupied the study to read the journal.

'She's an adult,' Vijay grinned back. 'What's to ask? And Imran's a nice guy. Even if he is an Intelligence man. I'm sure it went well.'

Colin nodded. 'He asked her loads of questions about the excavation, Wallace, his Trust and about what happened to her the night before last. He even asked her to Whatsapp him a photograph of Stavros and Peter. Apparently he wants to see if he can dig up any information about them.'

He looked curiously at the journal and Vijay's notes. 'Just what have you been up to?'

'I was going to call you guys. I discovered something really interesting. And Alice is going to freak out when she sees this. We're going to solve an ancient mystery.'

Colin's scowl grew deeper. 'I knew it was a mistake coming up here,' he grumbled. 'I should have left you alone.' Nevertheless, there was a gleam in his eye. 'Hang on; I'll get Alice and Dr Shukla up here.'

While he waited for them, Vijay placed the journal and his laptop on the centre table, with the file from the fifth floor room. He had also taken out the container with the ivory cube from the safe in the study, where he had earlier kept it for safekeeping, and placed that on the table as well.

Alice looked enquiringly at him as she walked in with Colin and Shukla.

'Alice,' Vijay began. 'You're not going to believe this. But you're going to love it. When you mentioned Olympias earlier this morning, I knew I had heard the name before but I couldn't remember where. It turns out that I had read it quite recently. In this.' He picked up the journal. 'This is the secret journal of Eumenes of Macedonia.' He looked expectantly at her.

Alice stared back. She wasn't sure if Vijay was joking or not. 'A secret journal? Belonging to Eumenes?' She couldn't keep the disbelief out of her voice. 'You can't be serious.'

Vijay grinned. After reading the journal and referencing the internet, he had learned enough about Greek history to expect exactly this reaction from her.

'Fine,' he said, looking at his notes for reference. 'Here's something that will show you that I'm serious: this journal talks about a secret journey that Callisthenes made in Bactria, near the Sogdian rock, on behalf of Alexander. It also talks about another secret mission that Alexander and Eumenes undertook during Alexander's invasion of India.'

Alice gave him a puzzled look. While Vijay was mentioning all the right names, it still seemed highly improbable to her that there could have been a secret journal written by Eumenes. And that it was right in front of her.

'Can I take a look?' she asked immediately and Vijay handed over the journal.

'Wait a minute,' Colin held up his hand. 'Who is Eumenes? And who is Callisthenes? Sounds suspiciously like the guy who may have invented callisthenics.'

'Callisthenes was a Greek historian during the time of Alexander the Great.' Alice momentarily diverted her attention from the journal to answer Colin's query. 'He was the author of an extensive history of Greece and the Phocian war. But he is probably best known for writing *The Deeds of Alexander*, a history of Alexander's conquests, in which he deified Alexander. It is widely believed that he was the originator of the legend about Alexander's divine birth, as the son of Zeus. He was also responsible for spreading stories around the Greek world about Alexander's visit to the Oracle at Siwa, who proclaimed Alexander to be the son of Zeus-Ammon in 332 BC, and about the sea parting in Pamphylia to let Alexander through. It is ironic that, even as he built up Alexander as a god, it was his rebuke to Alexander's proclamation of himself as a god that led to his death.'

'Wow! You mean Alexander actually thought himself a god?' Colin was genuinely surprised.

'Yes,' Alice smiled at his amazement. 'In 328 BC, after Alexander's victory over the people of Central Asia, he camped in the town of Balkh and announced that he wished to be worshipped as a god. His victories in Persia and Central Asia and the proclamation of the Oracle at Siwa, aided by Callisthenes' eulogistic accounts of his conquests, would have spurred him to believe that he was, indeed, a god.'

'While Callisthenes refused to accept him as a god,' Vijay murmured, recalling his own research in the last half hour.

Alice nodded. 'Correct. And he didn't just refuse. He is said to have quoted a line from the *Illiad* to Alexander: "A better man than you by far was Patroclus but still death did not spare him."'

'That's some taunt,' Colin remarked. 'I mean he could have been a bit more circumspect. There are better ways of telling a guy that he's not a god. Especially if that guy has a sword.'

'That's why Alexander had him executed. By this time, Alexander had become rather intolerant of anyone who did not agree with his views. There had been a page boy conspiracy to assassinate Alexander around that time. Callisthenes was falsely accused of being part of the conspiracy and put to death for treason. Alexander had him crucified.'

Colin shuddered. 'That's awful. And pretty ungrateful of Alexander after all that Callisthenes did for him. What about this Eumenes of Macedonia?'

Alice looked at Vijay. 'Since Vijay has clearly been doing some secret research of his own, maybe he'll tell us,' she smiled.

20

334 BC

Macedonia, Greece

Olympias, wife of Philip II, King of Macedonia, stared at the man who stood before her. Brown skinned, dark haired and dark eyed, clad in loose white garments the like of which she had never seen before, he seemed the unlikeliest person to harbour the knowledge that she had been told about. If the information had not come from the highest echelons of the Order, she would have dismissed him without a second thought.

'I hear that you know much about the secrets of the gods,' she said finally, fixing the man with a piercing gaze.

The man nodded. 'I do. But these are not your Gods. They are the Gods of the East. The Gods of my people.' His accent was strange and he spoke slowly, as someone would who was speaking in a language that was alien to him.

Olympias frowned. The man's nonchalance and his absolute disregard for her royal status were irritating. But she needed his information. Badly. So she suppressed her anger and continued. Once she had what she wanted she would decide his fate.

'I am aware of that. It does not matter. I care little about whose Gods they are. What matters to me is the truth about the myth. Do you verify that?'

The brown skinned man was unperturbed. 'The myth is true. I can vouch for it.'

'How do I know you speak the truth?' she demanded.

The man returned her gaze. 'Do you doubt me, O Queen?' As Olympias hesitated, clearly thrown off balance by his straightforward question, he smiled. 'So proud. So ambitious. You did not arrange for my travel across the rivers and oceans if you did not believe in my word. Yet, you may be forgiven for being suspicious. The myth is beyond understanding or belief for those who do not know.'

He paused for effect then continued. 'O Queen, how old do you think I am?'

Olympias frowned again. How did this man's age matter? What she really wanted was his knowledge about the myth. She shrugged lightly. 'How would I know?'

'I have walked this earth for 600 years and more. I have stopped counting the individual years, and mark only the decades.'

Olympias was now alert and her attention fully focused on this man. This was different. He didn't look older than forty years. If what he claimed was true...

Olympias considered his words. 'Tell me where the secret of the gods is hidden.' She leaned forward, her eyes shining with anticipation.

'It is far from here, O Queen,' the man replied. 'In the land of the Indus, in a secret location. Hidden away where none can find it unless they have the means.'

'The ends of the earth,' Olympias whispered, anticipation making her face glow.

'For a race as advanced as the Greeks are, it is amazing how little you know about the world we live in,' the philosopher smirked.

Olympias glared at him. He was really quite insolent. She raised one eyebrow enquiringly.

'Is that what your philosophers teach you? That the ends of the earth lie beyond the Indus? Then your son will spend the rest of his life marching to the ends of the earth and will find himself none the wiser when he returns to Macedonia.' The philosopher lowered his voice. 'Let it be known to you, O Queen, that the earth spreads vastly beyond the Indus, across rivers fierce and broad. The kingdoms that rule there are mighty, with weapons that you know naught of. It is that land where our Gods once held sway. Once your son has what he needs, he must return. Let not your ambition, and his, drive Macedonia to ruin.'

Olympias was speechless at the man's impudence. But she held her peace. She still did not have what she wanted. 'And what have you to offer me?' she asked instead.

He drew out two objects from a pocket hidden within his loose fitting clothes, and handed them to her. 'This is what my ancestors made for us. But you will not understand what is inscribed on them. For you know nothing of our gods.' He slipped out a parchment from his robes and gave it to her. 'I prepared this for you on the journey here. The inscriptions are in Greek. I will explain them to you. You will not understand otherwise. And this,' he indicated one of the objects, 'must be returned to our lands. When your son crosses the Indus, he must bury this, deep, where it will never be found.' He paused before resuming, his face serious now. 'But be warned. This is a dangerous enterprise. If the instructions are not followed well, only death lies ahead.'

Olympias took the two objects, her hands trembling with excitement. The first was a cube made of what appeared to be bone. It was yellowed with age, quite ancient, going by its appearance. The surfaces of the cube were inscribed in a script that was alien to her. The second object was a black metallic plate with inscriptions upon it. The philosopher began speaking, explaining the inscriptions on the parchment, giving her instructions on what needed to be done.

The philosopher indicated a spot on the vellum. 'This is where your son must stop. He must go no further. He must return home or not return at all.'

Olympias paid him scant attention. As her eyes skimmed the surface of the vellum, her excitement grew. This was going to be the culmination of her plans for her son, Alexander. Already, she knew that he was chafing at the bit, driven by a hunger to extend his empire beyond the boundaries that had been drawn by Philip, who had been a zealous conqueror himself. With the secret of the gods in her grasp, she was going to ensure that her son would rule the world. But not as a man. As a God.

21

PRESENT DAY

DAY THREE
A strange interview

Radha studied the spacious lobby of the India headquarters of Titan Pharmaceuticals, as she waited for her meeting with the CMO. She consciously avoided looking at Imran, who sat a few feet away on another leather sofa. They had arrived at the same time, but in separate cars. Radha had been assigned a field agent from the IB to drive her here and back.

The building itself was a nondescript six-storey structure, much like many corporate offices in Gurgaon, all steel and glass. The interiors were well appointed with marble floors, a granite counter for the reception and a fountain in the centre of the lobby. It was clearly a profitable and flourishing business.

She sat up as a tall, gaunt man with salt and pepper hair approached. He was wearing a laboratory coat and his air of authority indicated that he was Dr Varun Saxena. Radha was impressed. She hadn't expected him to personally greet her in the lobby and escort her upstairs. But then, he had been told that she was a journalist covering the recent fire at their medical facility and she guessed that the company was keen to avoid any bad press. That also explained the alacrity with which he had responded to and confirmed the meeting.

'Hello, Seema,' the gaunt man greeted her using her assumed name. He wore a smile that was perceptibly forced. Clearly, he wasn't too happy about this meeting and was conscious that he didn't have a choice. 'I'm Dr Varun Saxena.'

She greeted him in return. 'Thank you for meeting me at short notice,' she added. 'We'd like to run this story tomorrow, if there is anything of substance in it.'

Saxena grasped at the opening she had provided him with. 'Oh, I'm sure you'll see that there isn't much to talk about. I'll be happy to provide you with all the information you need, but I don't think you'll have enough masala for a story.' He made a show of smiling at his attempt at making light of the situation. 'Shall we go upstairs and talk?'

Radha nodded and they made the trip to the fourth floor in silence. When they were seated in the meeting room and Saxena had ordered coffee for them, Radha decided to get straight to the point.

'I've heard rumours regarding the fire at your facility in East Delhi,' she began, 'and I thought the best way to clear them up was to speak with you.'

'Oh, absolutely,' Saxena flashed a toothy grin at her. 'That's a very good idea. So, what rumours have you heard?'

'Well,' Radha paused as if deliberating what she should say, 'I've heard that some of the clinical trials were not approved by the DCGI. That people were being experimented upon using deadly microbes.'

Saxena emitted a forced, nervous laugh, as if he had been expecting and dreading this question. 'Wherever did you hear that? It is absolutely untrue. All the clinical trials Titan was conducting at that facility are above board. All approved by the DCGI. I can provide you with papers supporting my statement. And using deadly microbes is out of the question. That's not the way clinical trials work, you know. And, at Titan, we have a rigorous work ethic which we're proud of. As a virologist, I would immediately get to know if there was any hanky panky going on.'

'And the bodies found in the facility? How do you explain them?' Radha knew that Imran had decided not to make the discovery of the corpses public yet, since the media glare and publicity might hamper investigations. She was sure that Saxena believed that no one from the media knew about them and wanted to catch him off guard.

Saxena looked surprised. Clearly, he hadn't been expecting this question. His eyes narrowed. 'Where did you get that from?' he asked. 'That's just not true. No one was killed in the fire. There was a lot of damage to the property and equipment, but there were no casualties.'

Radha took a deep breath. 'Dr Saxena, I'm sure you know that we journalists have sources in different places. Even in the police. What I've heard doesn't match what you're saying. According to my sources, there was no one in the building when the fire tenders reached. No staff, no lab technicians, no researchers. Everyone had vanished. Except for the bodies which were found in a hidden basement, in hi-tech cells, locked from the outside. And I've also heard that those poor people had been shot dead. They didn't die in the fire. I guess that's the only thing you were right about.'

Saxena's shoulders slumped and a look of dismay crossed his face. But it was momentary and he recovered his composure almost immediately. Apparently he was either very well trained or had tremendous experience in handling difficult situations like this one.

'Okay, fine,' he smiled at her. 'I thought no one knew about that. I'm sorry I lied to you. But I'm sure that you also realise the enormity of this situation and the impact it can have on our firm.' He shook his head. 'We have no idea how those bodies came to be there or why they were there. Believe me, Titan is a company with firm values and principles. Our founder and Chairman, Kurt Wallace, is a highly principled and respected man not just in the US but across the world. I'm not saying that we don't stray. We do make mistakes. But this was no mistake. Our theory is that the owner of the facility, Suman Pahwa, was running a clandestine operation. If you want to know why, it is best that you speak to him. When the police find him, that is. I'm sure your sources can help you with that.' He emphasised his last words.

So he doesn't know that Pahwa's body was found today. Radha decided not to enlighten him.

'But the centre was exclusively running Titan's trials.' Radha wasn't giving up.

'Oh yes, absolutely. I don't deny that at all.'

'Why would you need cells in a facility that conducts clinical trials?'

Saxena sighed. 'You're looking for dirt where there isn't any. As I just told you, these clinical trials, like most trials, were outsourced. The lab carrying out the research was Aryan, who owned the facility. While we did send a representative to check the facility before we signed on the dotted line agreeing to sponsor the research, there was no way we could have known about the concealed basements. One doesn't go looking for hidden rooms when one is doing a site inspection, you know. You're asking the wrong man the wrong questions. I'll say this again. Ask Pahwa. He's the guy you should be digging up dirt on, not Titan. We're as shocked as you are about what was discovered at the facility.'

'The other strange thing,' Radha responded, almost ignoring Saxena's words, 'was that only three storeys of the facility were gutted. Coincidentally, these were the three floors housing the IT centre and all medical records for the facility. Don't you think it is a bit odd that only those floors were burnt down? It certainly seems that there was a deliberate attempt to destroy all records and stored data on the trials being conducted in the facility.'

'My answer is the same.' Saxena's tone was curt now. 'We have no idea who or what caused the fire. An inquiry has begun and, doubtless, we shall have more information when it is completed. All we can do for now is conjecture; and our opinion is that Suman Pahwa was behind this.'

Radha nodded. It was time to go out on a limb. 'I also heard that the bodies found in the facility were infected with an unknown bacterium and virus. How do you suppose Pahwa, if he is the one responsible, got his hands on not one but two new microbes and conducted clinical trials on over one hundred people in your medical centre without anyone knowing about it?'

Saxena's face hardened. Clearly, this question had struck a nerve. 'I'd really like to know who your sources are,' he said grimly, now making no effort to appear pleasant. 'You certainly seem to know a lot of unsubstantiated things. You are levying serious allegations against Titan, which are unsupported by any evidence. Unfortunately, what this tragic episode proves is that somewhere our controls failed. The staff at the centre were only carrying out their duties, conducting tests and taking samples and so on, in the mistaken belief that they were officially approved. We are looking into our internal systems and will implement a failsafe process to ensure that this is not repeated. Of that, I will personally assure you.'

He leaned towards her, his face stony and dark with suppressed fury. 'And I know you will not run this story, Seema. Do you know why?'

Radha said nothing. Something in his tone was unnerving. Had she gone too far?

'Because,' Saxena continued, 'you have no evidence. If you run a story like this, slandering Titan Pharmaceuticals, we will sue your newspaper for every rupee it has. And I'm sure your editor is not going to take that risk.'

Radha found her voice. 'What if we do find the evidence?' She gazed back at the CMO defiantly, even though her heart was in her mouth.

Saxena smiled unpleasantly at her. 'You won't. And I will suggest that you don't even try. It could be dangerous.'

'That sounds like a threat to me, Dr Saxena,' Radha fought to control herself. Her lower lip quivered slightly.

Saxena's tone changed immediately. The mask of pleasantness was back. 'Oh no, not at all,' the forced smile returned to his face. 'All I am saying is that if someone was using our premises to run illegal clinical trials, and they were able to hide it from us for so long, they may not stop at anything to ensure that they and their nefarious plans remain concealed. They may not take too kindly to a reporter sniffing around, trying to unearth their secrets.' He stood up, indicating the meeting was over. 'You're a nice young lady,' he concluded. 'I would hate to see anything happen to you. So please do be careful.'

Radha nodded, dumbfounded. She had no illusions about what she was hearing. She quickly shook hands with Saxena and left.

After she had gone, Saxena sat back in his chair and studied the ceiling lights for a few moments. Then he sighed and pulled out his mobile phone.

'Saxena here,' he said when the call had connected. 'There's something you need to know.'

22

The secret journal

'Sure,' Vijay cleared his throat. 'Let's see. It is a bit confusing. Different sources say different things about Eumenes. But from what I could glean it seems that he was one of Alexander's generals who got caught up in the civil war that followed Alexander's death. He also supported Olympias in her efforts to retain the Macedonian throne for her grandson, eventually losing his life in the process. It also appears that he was a scholar and maintained the royal diaries for Alexander on his Asia expedition.'

'That's a pretty good summary considering you didn't have a lot of time to research both Callisthenes and Eumenes,' Alice observed. 'Eumenes had also been the secretary for Alexander's father, Philip II. And, after Philip died, Eumenes became the chief secretary for Alexander, in addition to being one of his key generals. After Alexander's death, his generals fought bitterly over the division of the kingdom. Eumenes has been acknowledged by most sources to have been a very able general, but it seems luck was never on his side. It's a long story but I'll give you a quick synopsis. He escaped death once, having been sentenced to be executed by the generals who rebelled against Perdiccas, who was Alexander's chosen successor. But death pursued him in his battle with Antigonus, another general of Alexander. Despite defeating Antigonus, Eumenes was betrayed by his own satraps and was executed by Antigonus in 316 BC. It is said that he destroyed all his documents and journals before the battle with Antigonus.

There's no mention of a secret journal in any historical record available, though.'

'You think this is a fake?' Vijay asked, a bit fiercely. Colin raised an eyebrow at the note of aggression in his tone.

Alice was studying the journal now. She didn't seem to have noticed. 'Doesn't seem like it,' she muttered, half to herself. 'According to the introductory note by the translator, Lawrence Fuller, he acquired a set of papyrus documents in pretty good condition from an antiquities dealer in Egypt in 1954 when he was part of a team involved in an excavation near Cairo. Fuller has also added extensive notes and annotations. But I don't understand how or why this journal would end up in Egypt. Eumenes died in modern day Iran.' She looked up at Vijay. 'Where did you get this from?'

Vijay explained how he and Radha had unearthed the journal earlier that day. 'My parents were historians,' he concluded, 'working with the Archaeological Survey of India.'

'Fascinating,' Alice murmured, turning her attention back to the journal. 'It seems that the papyrus documents were in pretty good condition but there were fragments missing. Fuller, whoever he was, has done his best to translate in a manner that the meaning is not lost, but it makes for difficult reading with all the missing words.'

'I wonder how your parents came by this journal,' Colin wondered aloud. 'They must have known this Fuller guy.'

Vijay shrugged. 'I was too young,' he admitted, 'and, unfortunately, not too interested in their work at that time. I have no idea who their friends were or if Fuller was one of them. I wish I knew, though. It would have been nice to be able to contact him and talk to him about my parents.' A wistful note entered his voice.

'Okay, I don't have the patience to go through the entire journal right now,' Alice concluded, her voice betraying her excitement. 'Tell me the gist of it.'

'According to Fuller, the journal is actually in two parts and there's a letter as well in there,' Vijay began. 'The part about Callisthenes seems to be written by Callisthenes himself, but was apparently excised from *The Deeds of Alexander* by Eumenes, who then made it part of his own journal. According to Callisthenes, Alexander had sent him on a secret mission during the expedition to the Sogdian rock. There's a lot missing in this story because this part of the journal was pretty badly damaged. So it isn't very clear exactly what the objectives of his mission were. But there is quite a bit about his wandering through the forests of Bactria, examining trees and leaves. It didn't make any sense at all.'

'That's it?' Alice thought this was a bit anti-climactic.

'That's all there is to that story. Callisthenes returned, his mission successful, and Alexander professed his undying gratitude for his service.'

'And then he executed him shortly thereafter,' Colin chuckled. 'Talk about mood swings.'

'Does the journal say exactly what Callisthenes found in Bactria?' Shukla spoke up softly. He had been sitting quietly all this while, studying the ivory cube and listening to them talk.

Vijay referred to his notes and shook his head. 'There's nothing here in Fuller's translation. Unless it was in the original papyrus documents and that part was damaged.'

'That does sound plausible,' Alice remarked. 'Callisthenes did go on several scientific missions during the invasion of Asia by Alexander. But it is surprising that there isn't more to this story. What he was doing in the forests of Bactria, for example.'

'The Eumenes story is a bit more interesting. Brace yourselves.' There was a twinkle in Vijay's eyes. 'According to Eumenes, Alexander had been given a parchment with six verses, by his mother, which would help them find what he calls "the secret of the gods". Eumenes doesn't disclose what the secret is, but he says that the verses on the parchment were instructions to help Alexander locate the secret. The two of them left the army one night, carrying a small leather pouch and an oilskin bag, the contents of which Eumenes was not privy to. They found the secret location, which was inside a rock shaped like a serpent with five heads. Alexander left Eumenes behind and was gone for quite a while. When he returned, his breastplate and the leather armour were wet, as if he had been splashing around in a pool. Eumenes didn't know what happened that night, but he ends by saying that Alexander had found the secret of the gods and from that night onwards, he, too, had become a god.'

There was silence when Vijay finished.

'That's some story,' Alice spoke up finally. 'It certainly ties into what the historical record says about Alexander proclaiming himself a god and wanting to be worshipped. But the story itself sounds a bit like something out of the Alexander Romances.'

'I've heard about those,' Colin said. 'See, I'm not quite ignorant about Greek history. Isn't that a collection of stories about Alexander?'

'Well, I wouldn't quite call it Greek history, Colin,' Alice smiled at him. 'The Greek Alexander Romance was written by an unknown Greek author who is today referred to as Pseudo-Callisthenes. The Romances survive in three versions, each more fantastic than the other and the earliest manuscript dates from the 3rd century AD. They contain stories about Alexander that are too fantastic to be believed. More fantasy than history, actually.'

Colin grinned. 'Of course I knew that,' he protested. 'Seriously.'

Alice was mulling over what Vijay had just told them. 'The only quest that Alexander embarked on was conquering the world. That's pretty well established in history.' She was still unmoved. 'And even if we assume, for a moment, that he was on some mysterious quest to find this "secret of the gods", Eumenes doesn't describe anything valuable that was found. All he says was that Alexander went into the rock alone and came back with his armour wet.'

'Maybe he found the swimming pool of the gods,' Colin grinned. 'That would be pretty exclusive, no?'

Alice made a face at him. 'That's funny, Colin. But seriously, this really sounds like the farfetched tales in the Alexander Romances. Painting Alexander as a god was commonplace in all versions of the Romances. Maybe that's why Eumenes didn't include this narrative in his official records. It was just too fantastic to be true.'

Shukla cleared his throat and addressed Vijay. 'Does Eumenes say what the six verses were about?' he enquired softly.

'I thought you'd never ask,' Vijay's expression revealed that he was about to disclose something momentous. 'He's actually recorded each verse in the journal and Fuller kindly translated each one. Some of the words are missing, but you'll get the gist of each verse anyway. Here goes.'

He turned a page in his notebook and began reading.

23

A threat looms

Cooper sat in the bedroom of the presidential suite, at the personal workstation and stared at the face of Christian Van Klueck. He had just finished updating Van Klueck on the progress of the mission. Van Klueck had been nodding during the entire account, quite clearly eager to end the call quickly.

When Cooper mentioned the people who Alice was with, however, he had the Austrian businessman's full attention. His eagle sharp eyes bored into Cooper across the distance of place and time.

'I recognise those names.' Van Klueck's tone was sharp. He hadn't forgotten the people who had thwarted the Order's efforts the previous year to get their hands on a secret from the Mahabharata which had been hidden away for over two thousand years. 'They are a pain in the arse. We lost an important member of the Order last year because of them.' He quickly briefed Cooper on the events of that misadventure.

'Why didn't we eliminate them?' Cooper was surprised that the Order had let these people off so lightly. The fact that they were still alive didn't fit in with the way they worked. "No survivors, no witnesses" was the guiding principle of the Order. Everyone who worked with the Order had been indoctrinated with this principle. There could be no exceptions. He couldn't understand the deviation from this principle in this case.

Van Klueck realised that Cooper wouldn't understand. He was not really a member of the Order; just an employee. 'The Order has been around for as far as anyone can remember; right from the dawn of history. It is bigger than personal vendettas. No one knows what the Order exists for. That is only known to members of the Order. But enough people who matter, know what we can do. And that has been achieved by lying low, operating behind the scenes, manipulating politics, war, economies, trade and the financial markets. That's why your mission is so important.'

'That's going to pose a problem,' Cooper rubbed his chin thoughtfully. 'It's going to be more difficult to achieve anything with the Indian intelligence involved.'

Van Klueck allowed himself the shadow of a smile. I know you. You'll cover your tracks. These people are of no importance to us. And we do have an axe to grind. So, if anyone gets in your way, do what you have to. No survivors. No witnesses. You know the rule.'

Cooper nodded and the line went dead.

There was a knock on the bedroom door. It was Krishnan. He looked perturbed.

'Trouble?' Cooper queried.

'The IB officer and Radha Shukla are both at Titan Pharmaceuticals.'

Cooper was in the living room of the suite in a flash. 'It can't be.'

Krishnan pointed to one of the monitors where two red lights were blinking. 'That's Titan. And those are the two targets.'

Cooper couldn't believe his eyes. Had the Indian intelligence agencies got wind of their plans? It just wasn't possible. No one knew. Even he didn't know the complete details. All he knew was that this was a mission that had begun over twenty-five years ago. He had been given a brief to enlist Stavros and co-head the excavation at the tomb of Olympias. He had been told what needed to be recovered from the tomb. And he had been instructed in what he needed to do once the artefact had been recovered. He knew nothing more than that.

What did the IB know that he didn't?

Nevertheless, he had to act. He immediately decided on a course of action. First, he had to make a call. And then he had to eliminate his targets. They were getting too close to the truth.

And he couldn't allow that to happen.

24

A missing link

Vijay read out the six verses, pausing only to prefix each verse with a number and skipping over the missing words.

'Verse 1,' he began. 'This is the most complete verse of the lot.

Then... birthplace of the ruse
Born of death, sworn vengeance
That felled the line of a mighty king
Adventurer... roll the dice!
And... fortune guides you!

'Verse 2 onwards have many more words missing,' he added before reading on.

'Across... swiftly...eye
Beside the...saltless sea,
Three brothers...on
The arrowhead that...way
To enter...of Hades.
Dig...the serpent's seal
And find...quest.

'Verse 3,' he continued.

'And … the … rock
Pluck the … and … and bark
The first with … and fruit
Dark … clothed … white
And … or … next is smooth
Of … fruit
Beware … burns will … the touch.

'Verse 4:

Then enter … the portal …
The valleys … east …
Choose … here, remember where
You … Apollo lies.

'Verse 5 is:

Above the … the ridge
Where …and night…meet
And… Poseidon's staff
The … to the … snake
Five … guardian
The portal … will give…life.

'And, finally, here's verse 6:

'Remember … bold as … are
Ignore the … at your peril
The elements … together

Protected by ... gaze
Of the ... disregard
And forfeit ... most precious gift.'

Vijay looked up from his notes. Silence greeted him.

'So there's a connection between the parchment that Alexander carried with him and the ivory cube Alice found in the tomb of his mother.' Colin was the first to speak. 'Apart from the first verse, all the others seem to be identical to the ones on the cube. You can see that even with some of the words missing.'

Shukla nodded. 'I had a feeling this was the case,' he confessed. 'When you described the mission that Callisthenes undertook in the woods of Bactria, my mind immediately recalled the verse about the leaf and bark and the detailed description of the plants in one of the verses. And when you mentioned that Alexander's quest ended with a snake with five heads, it seemed to reinforce my conclusion. One of the verses on the cube talks about a five-crowned snake being the guardian of the portal, which could be interpreted as a five-headed snake. But I wasn't sure if I was merely making a big leap to connect the dots and establish a connection that didn't really exist.'

'This is interesting,' Alice said slowly. She seemed to be thinking as she spoke. 'The cube mentions Indian gods and is written in an ancient Indian script, using an ancient Indian language. The parchment that Alexander had, on the other hand, replaces the Indian gods with Greek gods. Apollo replaces Surya. Poseidon replaces Shiva. And not just the gods — Hades replaces *Pataal*. The parchment was most probably written in Greek. Which means that the cube probably originated in India and was translated by someone into Greek. This would make the verses more relevant and more easily understood by Alexander than the original Sanskrit verses.'

'This only raises more questions,' Vijay admitted. 'Where did the cube come from, for one? And who translated the original Sanskrit verses into Greek? It would have to be someone who knew both Sanskrit and Greek. Then, what was the quest that the parchment led to? It must have been really important for Alexander to have undertaken the quest all the way from Greece until India. According to Eumenes, the quest was to find the secret of the gods. But that doesn't explain anything.'

'What about the letter?' Alice asked Vijay. 'You said there was a letter along with the journal.'

Vijay nodded. 'According to Fuller, the letter seems to be a kind of a covering letter for the journal. It was written by Eumenes and addressed to Olympias. Fuller believes that this letter, along with the journal, was despatched by Eumenes to Olympias. Perhaps he sent it off to Olympias shortly before he died?'

Alice frowned. 'Eumenes died in 316 BC. So did Olympias. She may never have received the letter. Perhaps Fuller's hypothesis is correct. And somehow, the entire set of documents found their way to Egypt.' She shrugged. 'This is all conjecture. We don't have any facts or evidence to go on.'

Vijay smiled. The archaeologist in Alice was coming to the fore, unwilling to accept any explanation for deviations from the historical record without archaeological or archival evidence.

'Anyway,' he continued, 'the letter informs Olympias that Alexander's mission to the land of the Indus was successful. The letter also tells her that the circular metal plate she had given Alexander was buried, in accordance with her instructions, under an altar to Zeus, Alexander's divine father. It was one of the twelve altars Alexander constructed on the banks of the Hyphasis river before retracing his steps back to Babylon. And Eumenes refers to the metal plate as being the key to finding the secret of the gods.'

'So you think that this metal plate may be the means to work out what the verses on the cube mean?' Colin guessed what his friend was thinking.

'It could be possible,' Shukla agreed. 'The verses on the cube make no sense at all unless, as Radha said earlier, we have a reference point to understand what they mean. Perhaps this plate could provide the reference point. And if it is, indeed, a key, then it makes sense that Olympias asked for the key to be buried. After all, she wouldn't want anyone else finding the secret of the gods after gifting it to her son.'

'What I still don't understand is where Olympias got possession of the cube and the metal plate from,' Alice was still puzzling over this conundrum. 'Who could have given them to her? And why? It would have been nice if the metal plate had also been buried with her in her tomb. That way, we could have studied it and seen for ourselves whether it could be linked in any way to the cube.'

Vijay grinned at her. He still had a surprise up his sleeve. He patted the box file in which he had found the reference to the journal.

'I told you about the file which led us to Eumenes' journal,' Vijay explained. 'This is it. For some reason, my father had catalogued a bunch of newspaper articles and other documents relating to archaeological digs around the world. I have no clue why he did this, but when I was reading the journal, something struck me about one of the newspaper articles in this file.'

He leafed through the papers in the file until he located the article he wanted. 'This is a news item from 1985. Shall I read it out to you?'

The others nodded and waited.

'Remains of altars built by Alexander the Great found,' Vijay read out the title of the article. 'Archaeologists excavating for Indus Valley ruins near the town of Dasuya in Hoshiarpur district have excavated what appear to be the mud brick foundations of a large number of massive structures. Based on the foundations, each structure's base would have been at least 17 metres square. Archaeologists have speculated that these may be the remains of the twelve altars that Alexander the Great was supposed to have built on the banks of the Beas river before commencing his long march home. For two thousand years, these altars disappeared from sight, even though for 400 years after Alexander, Indian kings were reported to have worshipped at these altars.'

He looked up at them. 'Now listen to this. While investigating one of the altars, a small circular metal plate, made from an unidentified black coloured metal, was discovered, buried under a cornerstone. The nature and origin of the plate and how it got there is a mystery since it doesn't seem to be of Greek origin. The excavation team is tight-lipped about the discovery, only revealing that the metal plaque looks ancient, much older than Alexander's time, and has mysterious symbols carved into it that appear to be hieroglyphic or pictorial in nature. The plate is being sent to the National Museum in New Delhi where it will be studied and preserved.'

Shukla smiled. He knew what Vijay was leading up to. 'So you're taking another big leap, and assuming that this mysterious metal plate is the one that Eumenes has referred to in his letter?'

'Right.' Vijay put the file back on the table. 'I don't think it is such a big leap. First, the plate seems to be much older than Alexander. Second, how did it get *under* the cornerstone of Alexander's altar? Unless Alexander himself put it there? Which is exactly what Eumenes says Alexander did.'

'I still see gaps in the logic, Vijay.' Lines creased Alice's forehead as she articulated her thoughts. 'There's a more basic assumption that even the archaeologists made: that these structures were the remains of Alexander's altars. Once again, there's no concrete evidence to substantiate this claim. What if they're just two-thousand-year-old ruins with no connection to Alexander the Great?'

Shukla frowned. 'The plaque was discovered in 1985. I've never seen it at the National Museum.'

'Suppose we call up the Museum and ask them?' Colin suggested. 'Maybe it isn't on public display. Lots of museums have stuff buried away in cartons or crates in their basements. I know the museum in Cairo does. Normally, the public aren't allowed to see stuff that is stowed away like that, but Alice here is an archaeologist. Suppose she says that she would like to take a look at it for her research?'

Alice nodded. 'Sure. I'm curious to know whether the plaque really does have a connection to the cube or not. It would be great to be able to either validate the claims in this journal or determine if this is all part of the fantasy built up around Alexander.'

'Worth a shot.' Vijay rose and made his way to the desk where his mobile phone lay.

'Perhaps I can help,' Shukla said. 'I used to have a friend who was a curator at the National Museum. He may be able to pull some strings for us.' He gave Vijay the number.

Within the next few minutes, Vijay had spoken to Shukla's friend, obtained the number of the curator of archaeology, who was also the Keeper of the Collection, and fixed up to visit the museum to study the plaque.

Vijay put the mobile phone down, his eyes shining. 'Let's see if our speculations make any sense. In any case, we're not going to be able to solve the riddle of the cube. We don't even know how Alexander's mother got hold of the thing. But, as Alice said, it will be nice to piece together an ancient mystery and see whether there is truth behind the story in the journal.'

'You are so damn right that we aren't going to solve the riddle of the cube,' Colin said, forcefully. 'The last time we set out to decipher verses, we ended up tangling with terrorists and almost got our asses blown sky-high. This was an interesting discussion but here's where it ends. We look at the metal plate, see if Eumenes was a fart or not and close the chapter there.'

Vijay smiled. 'Sure. I'm with you. I'm not going to be stubborn this time around. This cube is of no relevance to us. Whatever its secrets, they will remain buried forever.'

He didn't know how wrong he was about to be proved.

25

Evil designs

'They're on the move,' Krishnan reported.

Cooper stared at the cluster of dots on the screen. He smiled. 'They're leaving the fort. Good.' This was the opening he had been looking for. Outside the fort, they were vulnerable. 'Track them and keep me informed.'

He turned to a muscular young man standing next to him, 6 feet tall, with wavy blonde hair cut in a tousled fringe, and striking blue eyes. Riley had joined his team of killers just one year ago, but had impressed him with the way he killed – cold blooded and with precision. Unlike Cooper, Riley preferred knives, cords and his bare hands. 'I like to feel my targets when they die; the touch of a body going cold with death, the last gasp – that's what I like,' he had once explained to Cooper when questioned about his antipathy to guns.

It was this inclination of his that led him to work out rigorously and pump up his body with physique enhancing steroids to increase his physical strength. For close contact killing, you needed to be stronger than your victim. You wouldn't be very successful if your victim could overpower you.

He had hated it when he had to use guns twice in the same night, two nights ago in Greece. His orders that night had been to plant explosives in the tomb Cooper and Stavros had excavated and blow it up. But the woman archaeologist had unexpectedly turned up at the site while he was there. He had been compelled to shoot at her to prevent her from getting away, but guns had never been his first choice of weapon and he hadn't been very accurate. He had encountered the woman again on the highway when he had landed his helicopter. He had reluctantly resorted to guns a second time that night when the woman had brazenly brushed past the helicopter to make good her escape. She had lived. And fled the country. But they had caught up with her now.

'I want you to handle this personally,' Cooper told Riley. 'Find out what they know. Then eliminate all three of them. If they head towards Delhi, leave immediately and rendezvous with our team there.'

Riley nodded. This was his chance to complete what he hadn't been able to finish that night. He had a score to settle. 'Sure. I'll take care of it. You're going after the other two?' His voice had just the trace of a southern drawl, from the long years spent in Texas.

Cooper nodded. 'We've decided to bring in the woman alive. We need to learn what she knows before we take care of her.' He pointed to a red dot on another screen. 'But before that I'll take care of the other target.' He grinned at Riley. 'I'd have sent you but we'll need long distance weapons for this one.'

'Cheers.' Riley's voice was bland.

Cooper left the suite and jabbed at the elevator button. If things went according to plan, this phase of the mission would be over tonight. As usual, there would be no survivors.

26

New Delhi

Radha drove slowly as she navigated the heavy evening traffic. After leaving the offices of Titan Pharmaceuticals, she had tried calling Imran but there was no response. Reasoning that he was probably still in his meeting with Titan's CEO, she called Vijay next.

Vijay had briefed her on the discussion over the journal and told her that they were on their way to the National Museum. 'We'll drop off your dad after we finish,' he told her. She had then decided to go straight home and wait for the others. The story of the secret journal, the metal plaque and its possible relation to the ivory cube had intrigued her and she, too, was keen to know the outcome of their visit to the museum.

She parked the car outside the gate of the white-walled bungalow in South Delhi, where she lived with her father. As she entered the house, she tried Imran's number one more time. This time, he picked up the call.

'Sorry,' he began, 'my meeting started late and then dragged a bit as the CEO kept getting calls. I just finished and was about to call you. How did your meeting go?'

Radha briefed him on her conversation with Saxena.

'Hmmm. You certainly raised his hackles there. I think we'll need to keep a close watch on Saxena. There's more to him than meets the eye.' Imran proceeded to brief her on his meeting. 'Nothing spectacular to report. He said pretty much the same things that Saxena told you. Except, his tone was milder and less threatening. He assured us of their full cooperation and complete access to their records. Which I thought was interesting. If they have something to hide, they wouldn't be so open to allowing us to inspect their internal records. I think I'll ask Patterson to check their documents on the US side as well,' he signed off.

Radha decided that the others would have to eat something before heading back to the fort. It was a long drive back to Jaungarh and they would be famished by the time they reached. But before she set to work preparing dinner for the others, a quick shower would be good.

She quickly showered, changed and began cooking. When she finished, she looked at her watch. 8.30 pm. Why weren't the others here yet? Had they found something really interesting at the museum that was keeping them? For a moment, she was tempted to call. But she knew that, if Vijay hadn't called yet, it would be for a good reason.

Switching on the television, she began flipping channels. She would wait to hear all about it.

Eliminated

Imran sighed as he disconnected the call with Patterson. His initial assessment of the task force leader had been spot on. Patterson was hard-nosed, difficult to negotiate with and driven by logic. Imran, with his stellar reputation in the IPS and within the IB, had got accustomed to having his own way most of the time. And when he didn't get his way, he would break the rules to get the results he wanted. His uncanny knack of sizing up a situation or a person and the accuracy of his hunches had served him well, enabling him to deliver the results his superiors wanted, more often than not. He had never had to justify himself or explain his hunches.

Patterson was different. He wanted facts not intuition. Evidence rather than feelings. And he was not buying into

Imran's hunch that someone at Titan was involved in the incident at the outsourced medical facility.

'Nothing extraordinary in the statements you've obtained,' he had said dismissively, when Imran had briefed him on Radha's meeting with the CMO of Titan and his own meeting with the CEO. 'I've spoken to Kurt Wallace himself and the man has not only assured me of full cooperation but has convincingly argued against the involvement of anyone from his management team in the US or in India. This seems to be more of a local operation. It may be funded by a global terrorist organisation so I suggest you dig deeper and find out who or what is masterminding this, instead of chasing Titan.'

Imran had briefly toyed with the idea of telling him about Alice turning up suddenly and her association with Kurt Wallace, and trying to connect the two with the bioterrorism angle. But he dismissed the idea as quickly as it occurred to him. He had spoken to Alice and was convinced that she was telling the truth. And he didn't see any way to connect her experiences in Greece with what had happened here, even if Kurt Wallace seemed to be the common factor.

Which reminded him; Alice had provided him with a photograph of Stavros and Peter, the two co-directors whom she had accused of murdering her team members. He had run the photographs through an international database and had scored a hit.

Imran dialled Vijay's number and spoke to him briefly, giving him the information he had come across.

His car turned into the gate of his residential complex. The guard saluted smartly, and Imran responded with a smile. The guards were low paid constables with a thankless and difficult job. He had seen other senior police officers who would either ignore them or glare at them as they passed. It wasn't in Imran's nature to do either. The least, he felt, one could do for another human being was to smile and greet them, and thank them for doing their jobs.

Imran reached his apartment block and alighted, dismissing the driver with a smile. The elevator arrived at the ground floor just as he pressed the call button, and he rode it to his sixth floor apartment. The bulb fixed to the ceiling of the landing was flickering as he exited the elevator. He made a mental note to complain to maintenance and unlocked the door of his apartment.

His living room was in darkness as he entered. He switched on the light and immediately made his way to the window, grimacing at the ugly sight of the tower under construction across the road. Five floors had been constructed and the sixth floor was being built, which was level with his apartment. Prior to this he hadn't really noticed the building but now he saw the workers every day.

This was a daily routine. His housekeeper left the curtains drawn open every day and he would return in the evening and promptly draw them together to hide the sight of the tower.

His Blackberry beeped as he entered the room. What he saw on the screen of his phone made his jaw drop as he walked towards his bedroom.

Imran was shocked by the text message he had just received. So shocked that he didn't head for the window to draw the curtains. He didn't see the figure, on the sixth floor of the building being constructed across the road, rise from the shadows.

He was barely two steps from his bedroom, when the glass of the window pane shattered, there was a whistling sound and something flew into the room.

His instinct and training took over immediately and he reacted on impulse. The rocket propelled bomb had landed between him and the door to the apartment, which was still open.

Imran dived to his left through the doorway to his bedroom even as the bomb hit the floor of his living room and exploded. The blast shook the apartment and the roar reverberated through the landing outside.

The wall of the bedroom took most of the impact of the concussive force of the blast, but Imran felt a sharp pain in his chest as he lay on the floor of his bedroom. He saw blood pooling on the floor.

His blood. He had been hit. He didn't know by what. Shrapnel? Flying glass? Whatever it was, he was wounded. Badly.

Then blackness overtook him.

His Blackberry lay three feet from his outstretched, lifeless hand. The message still visible on the screen read: "Cooper passed through immigration today."

27

Night at the museum

Vijay disconnected the call and looked around at the others. 'That was Imran,' he informed them. 'He ran a check on the photographs Alice gave him. He got a match. Peter is on the international criminal database. He's known as "The Reaper". Apparently, his real name is Peter Cooper and he's responsible for scores of killings over the last thirty years or so. He's an accomplished sniper, a whiz with a gun carrying a telescopic sight and known never to miss his mark. Twenty-one countries are looking for him. How did he come to be part of your excavation?'

'I don't know.' Alice's voice was shaky. 'He was… just … there. With Stavros. They were co-directors. Appointed by the Wallace Trust. Stavros was the archaeologist. Peter was, well, more the financial and liaison guy. He knew nothing about archaeology or the dig. But that's all I know about him. After signing up, I didn't ask any questions. I was so excited about the prospect of excavating what was possibly the tomb of Olympias that all I could think of was the excavation. What about Stavros?'

Vijay shook his head. 'Nothing. He isn't listed in the database according to Imran. That doesn't mean anything, though. He could be someone who isn't on Interpol's radar or that of any other intelligence agency, for that matter.'

'Don't worry,' Colin reassured Alice, sensing her fear. 'You left this guy Cooper far behind in Greece. There's no way he can trace you all the way to India. How would he guess that you would choose to come here, of all places, instead of flying home to the US? And even if he did, Jaungarh is so far off the map that even locals don't know where it is.'

'But we're not in Jaungarh now.' Alice suddenly realised the comfort and security the fort had provided her, especially with the security system installed there. 'We're sitting ducks for him here.'

'Even if Cooper did track you down to India and Jaungarh, which is a long shot as Colin explained, how would he know that you are driving down to Delhi today?' Vijay laughed. 'I know you've been through a very rough night in Greece. But that's behind you. And Imran has issued an alert to the Indian immigration authorities. He did that as soon as he discovered the man's real identity. If Cooper passes through Indian immigration, we'll get to know. Imran even offered to put you in a safe house run by the IB, if that happens. You're safe here. Okay, here we are.'

They had reached the museum. The main gates were locked since visitors' hours were over. Vijay made a quick call to the curator, who was awaiting their arrival. A museum guard opened the gate to let the car in and locked it behind them.

'Wow, will you look at that?' Colin pointed to an enormous *rath* in an enclosure that they drove past. 'That looks really ancient.'

Vijay parked the car and they alighted. The guard came up and informed them that he would lead them to the curator.

They walked past the replica of Asoka the Great's edict from Girnar, which stood against the inner boundary wall of the museum and entered the building, which was built around an open air rotunda.

The curator's office was on the first floor. He rose to greet them as they entered.

'Dr Shukla,' the curator advanced to shake Shukla's hand. 'I'm Rajiv Sahu, the Curator – Archaeology and the Keeper of the Collection. Delighted to make your acquaintance.' He turned to Alice. 'And you must be Miss Turner.' He shook her hand. 'Delighted. Of what service can I be to you?'

Colin scowled at Vijay and mouthed, 'So we are the bodyguards?'

Vijay grinned back and introduced himself and Colin to Sahu.

'Oh yes, we spoke,' Sahu beamed at Vijay and shook Colin's hand as well, without saying anything to him.

Alice looked confused. She thought that the subject of the metal plate had been discussed and agreed upon. 'Er ... I wanted to look at the plaque which was discovered in 1985 near Dasuya. The one that is supposed to have been buried by Alexander the Great at the base of an altar he had constructed near the Beas before he turned back to return to Greece.'

'Certainly, certainly.' Sahu didn't move. 'I wasn't very clear what your interest is in that artefact. You know it isn't available for public viewing.'

'We spoke, Mr Sahu,' Vijay interjected. 'We were referred to you by Dr Dutta. You had agreed to show us the plaque.'

'I agreed to let you into the museum after visitors' hours,' Sahu responded without looking at Vijay. His eyes were still fixed on Alice. 'Which, in itself, is against government regulations. But I wasn't asking you. I was asking Miss Turner to explain her interest in the plaque. She is asking to see an artefact that is not on public display. Surely you don't think I'm going to oblige every person who claims to be an archaeologist and walks through these doors? Even if they are referred to me by Dr Dutta?'

He peered at Alice, expectantly.

'I am an archaeologist,' Alice responded heatedly. 'Do you doubt my credentials? You can look me up on the internet. One of my interests is ancient Greek history. Especially the

Hellenistic period. When I heard that you had an artefact here that could be connected with Alexander the Great, I simply had to see it.'

'I'm sure you have some sort of identification on you,' Sahu continued as if he hadn't heard her. 'Your identity card, for example? Something to back up what you have just said?'

Alice felt her cheeks flush as she rummaged in her purse and pulled out her identity card for the joint mission in Greece and handed it to Sahu. The curator studied it for a moment then handed it back to her.

'You can see the metal plate.' Sahu pulled out a key ring with a single key from his pocket. 'I'll show you where it's stored. It's on the second floor.' He eyed the others disapprovingly. 'Is everyone going with you?'

'Yes, they are,' Alice said firmly. 'Thank you very much.'

'Follow me,' Sahu instructed and marched off. He led them up the stairs and through the Arms and Armour gallery, which had glass cases containing swords, spears and all manner of ancient and medieval weapons. At one end of the gallery was a door marked "Private". Sahu unlocked the door.

A sense of anticipation gripped them. What were they going to find?

28

A new mystery

The room was dark. Vijay used his mobile phone's built in torch to search for the light switch which he now flicked on. A light dangling from the ceiling shattered the darkness with a burst of illumination and Alice gasped.

The room had shelves lined with tablets of all shapes and sizes, inscribed in scripts of all kinds, none of which were familiar to her. She realised this was a treasure trove of history.

Shukla, too, felt the same way. He looked around like a child who walks into a toy store and tries to figure out just which toy he wishes to play with first.

'Which one is the plaque that we seek?' Vijay wondered aloud.

'It is this one.' Sahu picked up a small black metallic plate, circular in shape, and showed it to them. On the face of the tablet were inscribed six symbols.

They stared at the face of the tablet. The six symbols didn't make any sense to them.

Sahu made a show of looking at his watch. 'I can give you fifteen minutes and no more. Please lock up after you finish. I will be in my office.' Without another word, he strode off towards the stairs.

For a few moments, they all stared at the seal, trying to make sense of it.

'Well?' Alice said after they had gazed upon the tablet for a while. 'Any thoughts?'

Shukla shook his head. 'I really can't see anything here that connects to the cube. I guess I was wrong.' He smiled wryly. 'Well, it doesn't hurt to hope. Or speculate. It would have been really interesting if I was right.'

'I can't see anything either. This tablet just doesn't make sense,' Vijay agreed.

'Okay, let's get out of here and head for Radha's place,' Colin rubbed his hands. 'I always look forward to her cooking.'

'Wait, let me photograph it.' Vijay held up his mobile phone and quickly took a few photographs.

They locked the room and crossed the gallery. Even in the semi darkness, the weapons displayed looked terrifying. They could imagine just how deadly they were in battle.

As they walked through the corridor leading to the stairs, there was a loud, anguished scream. It came from the direction of the curator's office. It was followed by a series of screams, piercing and charged with agony.

Trouble in the Museum

Sahu strode towards his office, feeling somewhat irritated. He had wanted to leave on time today but Dutta's unexpected call had thrown his plans into disarray. He couldn't refuse Dutta's request especially since he had promised it wouldn't take too much of Sahu's time. But the curator still didn't understand why an American archaeologist was so interested in an obscure metal plaque that had been discovered almost three decades ago. While the discovery of Alexander's altars had made the news at that time, no one had ever been able to prove that the ruins discovered were, indeed, the famed altars. The entire theory had been swiftly debunked and Alexander's altars had retained their distinction of having remained undiscovered to this day.

The media had quickly lost interest in the story, and the metal plate had been forgotten and languished in the room upstairs ever since then. He had no idea how the woman had even heard about it, but Dutta had mentioned that Shukla was a good friend, so he had had to comply.

Sahu entered his office and stopped short. There were two men in the room. Three, if he counted the dead guard who lay on the floor in a pool of his own blood, his throat slit.

A tall, blonde young man stood behind Sahu's chair, calmly wiping a large and ugly looking Bowie knife with tissues from Sahu's tissue box while the other man stood by the side of the door, holding a gun. Sahu noted that, even though the gunman had on a mask hiding his features, his nose, eyes and hands indicated that he was Caucasian.

Sahu instinctively turned to run but realised there was no escape. The gunman had moved into position behind him, barring the doorway. He was trapped here.

Riley slid the knife into a sheath at his waist and looked at his mobile phone. 'Rajiv Sahu,' he read from his phone. 'Curator of Archaeology.' He put the phone away and looked at Sahu. 'Where are your visitors?'

Sahu stared back at him, shocked speechless. Who was this man? He had walked into the museum, killed a guard and was now asking about the people whom he had just left in the tablet room.

Finally he found his voice. 'Upstairs,' he stammered, indicating the second floor with his thumb.

Riley nodded. 'Let's all sit down, shall we? I need to ask you some questions before I take care of your visitors.'

After Krishnan had reported to him that the four targets were passing through Gurgaon and heading towards Delhi, Riley had left the hotel and met up with the team based in Delhi. When he learned that his targets had stopped at the

National Museum, Riley realised that their destination was not a random choice. He had called Cooper who had instructed him to follow the targets, investigate their activity at the museum to gain any information possible, before eliminating them.

And the curator was the best person to give him that information.

'Now,' Riley said as Sahu sat down at his desk. 'Tell me what your visitors wanted.'

Sahu looked at Riley with wide eyes, terror oozing out of every pore in his body. Riley smiled. The man reeked of fear. And Riley loved that smell in his targets before he killed them. It gave him a high that no psychotropic substance could.

'One of them is an archaeologist,' Sahu blubbered.

'The American woman. I know that already.' Riley's voice was hard. He was getting impatient. 'Tell me something I don't know. Why are they here?'

He gestured to the gunman who slid beside Sahu, grabbed his wrist and slammed his hand on the desk, palm downwards, fingers splayed. Riley unsheathed his knife and examined the curator's arm as the blade hovered over it. Finally, he selected a spot on Sahu's hand and cut away a slice of flesh. Blood oozed out immediately.

Sahu let out an agonised scream which echoed down the empty corridors and galleries of the museum. The pain was unbearable. Riley chose another spot and sliced off some more flesh.

The curator screamed again and again, as if the agony would be lessened by lending it a voice.

'Now, I'm asking you once more,' Riley's voice was low and sinister. 'What did the archaeologist want from you? Why is she in the museum?'

29

Realisation

'That was Sahu's voice,' Vijay said. 'I'll go and check on him while you guys lock up.'

Vijay sprinted down the stairs and through the corridor towards Sahu's office. As he neared the office, he heard a man's voice, low, strong and deadly, over the sound of the curator's anguish-ridden screams.

'Now, I'm asking you once more,' the man said. 'What did the archaeologist want from you? Why is she in the museum?'

Vijay stopped in mid stride. A cold fear took hold of him. Someone was asking about Alice. Someone *knew* that Alice was here at the museum. Was it Cooper? How could it be? Cooper couldn't have made it through immigration without Imran knowing about it. And Imran would have alerted them immediately.

His instinct kicked in and all questions were brushed aside. A warning siren went off in his head. He had to alert the others!

Discovered

Riley heard the sound of running footsteps in the corridor outside and motioned to the gunman to investigate. The man dashed out of the room. Riley turned his attention back to the curator.

'I'm waiting,' he said. With his free hand, he grabbed the curator's uninjured arm and held the knife aloft, prepared to slice flesh off his other hand. The desk was covered with blood.

'The metal plate,' Sahu blubbered through his tears as he jerked his good arm in futility, trying to wrest it from the vice-like grip of his captor. 'It was found buried beneath the foundations of Alexander's altar!'

Riley's ears pricked up at this news. He didn't know much about history or archaeology – these weren't his areas of interest – but he did know that the mission had revolved around Greek history. And he had seen for himself the tomb in Greece. He had also seen the artefacts in the dig hut at the excavation site of the tomb when he blew it up. So he knew that, somehow, this metal plate was important.

'It wasn't a guard. I didn't get a good look at him and the corridor is too dimly lit, but I could make out that much.' The gunman who had been in the curator's office reported through Riley's earpiece. 'He went upstairs. Must be part of the target group. I'm calling the others in and going after them.'

'Do it.' Riley turned back to the curator. 'Where are they now? Where is the metal plate?'

By now Sahu was broken. He told Riley everything he wanted to know.

'Second floor. Arms and Armour room,' Riley instructed his men. 'Herd them and keep them for me. I'll be up in a minute. I want to talk to them before I kill them.'

Defence

Vijay sprinted to the end of the corridor and dashed up the staircase, two stairs at a time. The others were almost halfway down.

'Back up!' he gasped. 'We've got to get back upstairs.' He looked at Alice. 'They know you're here.'

There was no time for questions or to exchange further words. The urgency and desperation in Vijay's voice was sufficient for them to hurry back up the stairs.

A plan was forming in Vijay's mind as they retreated. He swiftly outlined it to the others as they hastened towards the galleries on the second floor. 'We don't how many of them there are,' he whispered. 'And we don't know if there's another way down to the museum entrance from here. We can't go back down the main staircase since they'll be coming after us. And we have to assume they are armed. So here's what we're going to do. We're first going to grab whatever we can from the arms and armour displays. We need to have something to defend ourselves.'

'*Beta*, we can't fight them,' Shukla said gently. 'Especially if they have guns. The swords and spears from the displays won't be of any use against guns.'

Vijay shook his head as they entered the gallery with the weapons. 'I'm not suggesting that we make a stand here. The weapons are just a precaution. I agree we can't fight them—it would be foolhardy. But we need the weapons just in case something goes wrong. Here's what we should do. It is our only chance.' He sketched out the plan and the others nodded.

Vijay and Colin lifted a small stone sculpture from among the statues lining the corridor and broke the glass on the displays that housed the weapons they had selected.

Shukla picked out an inscribed battle axe that had belonged to Nadir Shah, dated to around 1739 AD. It was 52 centimetres in length, just right in terms of size and weight for him to wield without difficulty.

Colin chose the inscribed sword of Tipu Sultan and Vijay selected a mace from Kashmir from the 18th century.

'Just like you to pick the biggest and heaviest weapon around,' Colin grinned at Vijay, his sense of humour bringing in an element of lightness even in this grim situation. 'You sure you will be able to swing it around when you most need it?'

'Let's hope I don't have to find out,' Vijay said soberly. 'What's your choice, Alice?'

Alice looked scared and confused, knowing that time was running out, yet unsure what weapon she could use. The thought that her hunters in Greece may have caught up with her had set off a wave of panic in her mind. Finally, Vijay made the choice for her, plucking out a Rajput wood and ivory spear from the late 16th century. Just 38.5 centimetres in length, it was lightweight enough for her to carry without a problem. She, too, hoped she would not have to use it.

Armed with their weapons, they took up their positions according to Vijay's plan and waited. Under the circumstances, they had little option but to hope that the plan would work.

30

Will the plan work?

The three gunmen met at the foot of the staircase leading to the second floor. Two of them had been positioned on the ground floor, guarding the two corridors that led in and out of the museum's main lobby to ensure that no one entered or left the museum.

The sound of glass breaking came to their ears and they looked up with one accord at the floor above.

The lead gunman indicated the stairs and they moved up, swiftly but quietly.

There was silence on the second floor as they reached the end of the staircase. And semi darkness. The corridor lights were switched off, as were the lights in the galleries closest to them. The only light that came to them was from the galleries on the far side of the rotunda.

They looked around, trying to make out the museum signs and work out which was the gallery that housed the arms and armour display. One of them silently pointed out a floor plan that was fixed to the wall near the staircase. The lead gunman shook his head as he took out a flashlight. He didn't have a choice and had to risk being seen by the targets. It was clear that they were dealing with a smart bunch of people, who were using the lack of light to their advantage.

He located the gallery they sought on the map and pointed it out to the other two. A thought occurred to him and he also signalled that their quarry could be armed. One could never be sure. Even though Riley had told them they were after a group of ordinary people. He had known men to lose their lives by underestimating the enemy. He wasn't about to join their numbers.

From where they stood, the three men could see the entrance to the gallery. The door was open. It was pitch dark inside.

The lead gunman signalled again. They had to find the main switch for the corridor lights. The men spread out and started examining the walls.

'Got it,' one of them whispered, his throat microphone picking up the vibrations generated from within his neck so that his whisper was barely audible in the silent museum.

He flicked a switch and the corridor lights snapped on, blinding the three men momentarily.

The lead gunman grimaced under his ski-mask. While the corridor lights would provide some illumination, however faint, in the darkened gallery, it would be difficult for them, going into a pitch black room from the lighted corridor. Hobson's choice.

The three men slowly made their way to the entrance of the gallery.

Cat and mouse

Vijay stiffened as he saw the lights go on outside. He had anticipated that the gunmen wouldn't enter a fully dark room, and the diversion to find the light switch was the only way he could think of to buy them those few precious extra seconds that would enable them to settle down.

Even though he didn't hear a thing, a shadow loomed in the doorway. *Trained killers,* he thought to himself. They were clinically efficient.

The shadow disappeared, and another one took its place, only to be replaced by a third shadow. All three melted into the near darkness of the gallery, as the gunmen stayed out of the line of the doorway and out of the light coming through it.

What now? Vijay wondered. There was no way to check if the others were implementing the plan. He would just have to count the seconds, as they had planned and hope that they were able to make it.

Almost there...

Riley listened to the gunman's voice in his earpiece and nodded. He roughly jerked Sahu to his feet. 'You're coming with me,' he said. 'We've got work to do upstairs.'

He half dragged the bleeding curator up the stairs, trying to reach the gallery where his targets were hiding, before they could escape.

Foiled!

Vijay grimaced as he saw the shadows loom on the wall. The others were silently making their way out of the room as planned. But, while the plan counted on their being able to observe their hunters entering the room, they hadn't considered the fact that they, too, would be seen leaving the room. And he didn't know if there were more men outside or even downstairs. But this was their only chance.

He waited. But no third shadow made its way through the doorway. Who was missing? And, what surprised him was that none of the three men hunting them had attempted to follow the two members of his group out of the gallery. Something was wrong.

Without warning, the lights in the gallery came on. He blinked as his eyes tried to adjust to the sudden increase in brightness. *What was happening?*

31

Trapped

Alice slunk out of the gallery, as they had planned. They had taken up their assigned positions behind different displays which occupied the room – tall cases displaying different parts of body armour, mannequins wearing the armour of emperors and kings – and waited.

They had counted on the men entering the room after switching on the corridor lights. The plan was to wait for 20 seconds after the last man entered the room, just to be sure there were no others, and then sneak out, one by one, at intervals of ten seconds.

Colin joined her after a few moments and they stood there, waiting for Shukla. Vijay had volunteered to be the last one. 'Because I've got the most powerful weapon,' he had said, quite seriously. They hadn't argued. They were short of time.

The seconds passed and Shukla didn't appear. Colin looked at Alice, worried. They didn't want to leave without either Shukla or Vijay. Colin struggled to decide what they should do. Going back inside was not an option. While none of their hunters had followed them outside, they could be waiting for them to return.

An unpleasant thought struck him. *What if Shukla had been captured already?*

The decision was taken out of his hands as Riley appeared on the landing of the second floor, dragging a bloody Sahu behind him. 'Lights in the gallery,' he ordered Sahu, as he fixed Alice and Colin with a sneering smile. Sahu obediently complied.

Alice and Colin froze where they stood. They didn't know who this man was but the sight of Sahu, his right hand covered in blood and the Bowie knife in Riley's hand was enough for them to realise one thing.

They were trapped.

The curator's fate

Vijay stared in horror at the sight before him. Alice and Colin were being shepherded through the door, along with a blood covered Sahu, by a tall, muscular man with blonde hair, who brandished an enormous Bowie knife. It was obvious that the blonde man had ambushed Alice and Colin outside the gallery; but what had he done to Sahu? Vijay now realised why Sahu had been screaming in anguish. The curator's face was now dull, the pain replaced by shock, numbing his senses.

On the other side of the room, three gunmen stood, their faces concealed by black ski-masks, covering the three prisoners.

Riley consulted his phone. 'Alice Turner. Check. Colin Baker.' He looked at Colin. 'That must be you. You're the only other white guy in the room.' He looked around. 'There were five of you at the fort. The two who were nosing around are covered. Which means there's one guy missing.' He raised his voice. 'Vijay Singh! I know you're in here. You can't hide. I'll go easy on these two if you show yourself now.'

Vijay realised two things in that instant. The first was that somehow, they had been under surveillance at the fort. He couldn't fathom how, but this man knew their names and also knew that the three of them had been together at the fort. He also seemed to know that Imran and Radha had been with them. The second was that this man's information was not perfect. He didn't know about Shukla. Vijay couldn't work out why Shukla seemed to be a blind spot, but he hoped that the linguist had realised that and would stay concealed.

He stepped out from behind the case displaying a suit of armour, dragging the mace behind him. 'I'm here,' he said, simply.

Riley beamed, satisfied with the way things were going. Then, abruptly, he turned to Sahu, grabbed him and slit his throat in one motion, dropping the curator's body to the floor, where his blood started pooling. 'We don't need him anymore,' he explained to the others.

As the others looked on, horrified, he grabbed Alice and pressed the bloody tip of his knife against her throat. 'Now,' he whispered to her. 'Where's that metal plate?'

Two of the gunmen moved closer to Vijay and Colin, aiming their guns at them. Just beyond reach of an arm or a leg, but close enough to be an effective shot at point blank range.

A small dot of red appeared on Alice's throat where the knife point pressed against her skin. She tried to speak but the words wouldn't come out.

Riley chuckled. 'Let's find out if you've got it on you.'

'Wait,' Vijay stepped forward, unable to contain himself. He could see that Alice was beside herself with fear. 'She doesn't have the metal plate. It's in a room behind that door.' He indicated the door they had locked just a few moments ago. 'I have the key.' He looked at the gunman who had his weapon trained on him.

The gunman nodded. 'Easy now,' he cautioned Vijay, his voice muffled by the ski mask. 'Any tricks and I won't miss at this range.'

Vijay slowly fished out the key ring and threw it to Riley. The blonde man half dragged, half carried Alice to the door and unlocked it. He stared at the repository of tablets and seals inside. 'Which one is it?' he snapped.

Alice showed him the plaque. Riley shoved her away roughly towards the third gunman who backed up to catch her as she stumbled towards him. The blonde man sheathed his knife then picked up the seal and looked at it.

Vijay and Colin watched with surprise as something totally unexpected happened.

32

334 BC
Macedonia

Alexander was in his apartments in the royal palace, gazing out of a window, lost in thought, when his mother entered, unannounced.

'Son,' Olympias began. 'I have a gift for you.'

Alexander turned, frowning. He had grown up with his mother's idiosyncrasies, but he still hadn't got accustomed to them. Her breaking into impromptu, ecstatic dance at unexpected moments, the inexplicable love of snakes, and entering his rooms unannounced – they still irritated him at times. But he loved her with all his heart and could never bring himself to reproach her.

His dark, intense eyes searched her hands for the gift she spoke of but they were empty, clasped before her.

'Come on, mother,' the young king protested. 'No games now. Tell me what it is. You know I love gifts.'

'Before I do, I want you to promise me something,' she replied, smiling at him. He was possibly the only person she didn't wish to manipulate or take advantage of. All she wanted was for her son to be a great man, for his glory to live forever. And she would do anything to ensure that happened.

Alexander's brow furrowed. 'Depends on what it is,' he replied.

'Oh, I think you will relish fulfilling this promise,' his mother goaded his curiosity on. 'It is about your campaign against the Persians.'

Alexander fixed her with a piercing gaze. 'Mother, you know how close that is to my heart. To avenge the humiliation the Persians heaped upon us, marching across our lands, subjugating us – that is the only goal I seek now. I will not rest until I bring the Persian Empire under Macedonian rule.'

'I know, my son,' Olympias smiled affectionately at his *pothos*. 'But why stop there? There are lands beyond Persia, to the east.' Her voice lowered to a whisper. 'The land of the eastern gods, where the Indus and other great rivers flow.'

'The Ends of the Earth! I have heard of the riches of this land, Mother,' Alexander was thoughtful now. He had heard stories of gold and precious stones in the Indus valley and of the natives paying tribute to the Persians in the form of gold dust. 'But it means spending a few more years away from home. Is it really worth it? The Persian Empire will yield all the wealth we need.'

'It is not material wealth that you will seek in those lands.' There was a twinkle in his mother's eyes. 'You were born of a god. The son of Zeus. I have told you that before. But you are still a mortal.' She paused and looked him in the eye. 'There is a myth from the land of the Indus. An ancient legend about a great secret that will make you a god. It is that secret that I am asking you to seek.'

Olympias told Alexander about her meeting with the philosopher from the eastern lands. She gave him the parchment and the metal plate that the philosopher had given her and explained the inscriptions and engravings to Alexander, just as they had been explained to her.

'But this has to be a secret mission. If your army knows what you seek, there will be trouble. They will not follow you to the ends of the earth, for they will not believe.'

When she finished, Alexander studied the parchment. 'It is my destiny,' he said at last. 'Born of a god. And I will be a god.'

33

PRESENT DAY

DAY THREE
A summons

Radha heard the doorbell ring and hurried to open the door. Was it Vijay?

A man in a safari suit stood at the doorstep, looking mournful. He looked like he bore bad news and Radha's heart sank.

'Miss Radha Shukla?' the man asked.

Radha nodded, her heart in her mouth.

'I'm Hoshiar Singh from the Intelligence Bureau.' The man flashed an identity card at her. Radha barely looked at it. She wanted to know what he was doing here at this time of the night.

'Mr Imran Kidwai is in hospital,' Hoshiar Singh continued. 'Someone tried to kill him in his apartment this evening using a rocket propelled bomb. His condition is critical. I was told to inform you in case you would like to come to the hospital with us.'

Radha gasped in shock. Imran in hospital? A bomb? She could hardly believe what she was hearing. She had just spoken to him a short while ago.

'Give me a minute,' she said and stepped inside to grab her phone. She quickly typed out a text message informing Vijay about Imran and asking him to meet her at the hospital. 'Let's go,' she told the man as she locked up the house and hurried down the garden path towards the waiting car.

An unlikely rescuer

Shukla watched from behind the display with a suit of armour belonging to the Mughal Emperor, Aurangzeb, as Alice was dragged to the room with the tablets. Like Vijay, he had realised that Riley was unaware of his presence in the group. He didn't know whether it was of any use or not, but he decided to stay hidden for now. If nothing else, when the others left, even as captives, he could get to a telephone and call Imran for help. He cursed inwardly. This was the first time in his life that he regretted not carrying a mobile phone. For years, he had refused Radha's attempts to convert him. 'I've always been accessible even when there were no mobile phones,' he would say. 'If someone needs to contact me, they know where to find me.'

Today, he realised how useful a mobile phone could have been in a situation like this. A text message would have been enough to summon help at this very moment.

Meanwhile he saw Alice being pushed away by Riley and stumbling forward. The third gunman backed up to catch her from falling, coming within a foot of the suit of armour behind which Shukla had sought refuge.

The gunman caught Alice, but only barely, almost losing his own balance in the process.

Something went off inside Shukla's head.

He sprang out from behind the armour and swung the blunt end of the axe head at the head of the gunman, as he was trying to recover his balance and catch Alice simultaneously.

The axe head connected and the gunman went down heavily, crashing into the glass of the display, dropping Alice as he fell.

Suddenly all hell broke loose.

Vijay and Colin had noticed Shukla emerge from hiding and swing the axe. While they were taken aback at this unexpected manoeuvre, they had an instant of a start on the gunmen standing next to them.

The gunmen were fully focused on their captives and reacted with surprise as their colleague crashed to the floor. They were momentarily distracted.

Vijay and Colin took advantage of the moment. Colin ducked and pirouetted on one knee, moving closer to the gunman covering him, and lashed out with his other leg. He caught the gunman in the knees. The man's legs folded under him, dropping his gun. Colin dived for the gun and struck the man on his head with the butt of the weapon, knocking him out cold.

Shukla helped Alice up and they ran for the door. As Colin tackled his captor, Vijay slipped to the floor, rolled over and swung the mace towards the gunman behind him. As the mace flew over his body, he rolled back and out of the way just in case it rebounded. The mace had eight blades mounted on a cylindrical rod and it hadn't lost its potency. It struck the gunman on his thighs, slicing through the muscle and left him writhing on the floor.

It had taken just seconds for the entire scene to unfold and Riley had no time to react. By the time he had unsheathed his knife the four captives had dashed out of the room, slamming the door of the gallery shut behind them.

Riley recovered quickly from his initial surprise and sprinted towards the door. Suddenly the gallery went dark and he cursed. Someone in the group had had the presence of mind to switch the lights off before they headed downstairs.

He slowly made his way through the darkness, bumping into a few exhibits as he walked towards the door. When he finally reached the door and opened it, he saw that the corridor outside, too, was sheathed in darkness. Through the open windows, he heard a car engine start up outside the museum.

A wave of anger washed through him and he savagely thrust the knife into the wooden balustrade of the stairwell. He would have to inform Cooper. But it wasn't concern about Cooper's response that drove his rage. Tonight's episode was a blot on his record. His men had failed him.

This would not happen again.

34

New Delhi

After their hurried getaway from the museum, Vijay raced through the streets of Central Delhi, weaving through traffic, trying to put as much distance as possible between them and the museum. None of them could dismiss from their minds the sight of the curator being murdered in cold blood before their eyes.

Finally, he relaxed slightly though his tension still showed in his tight grip on the wheel. 'Was that Cooper?' he asked Alice.

Alice numbly shook her head. She was still in a state of shock. She didn't know who the young blonde man in the room had been but she realised that her pursuers had not given up the chase. They had, somehow, followed her all the way from Greece to Delhi. And they even knew that she had taken refuge at Vijay's fort!

'We need to inform Imran. Whether Cooper is here or not, tonight's incident was not random. Someone has been tracking you, Alice,' Vijay gave voice to her thoughts. He passed his phone to Colin. 'Call Imran, will you? He's on speed dial.'

Colin nodded and swiped the screen of the smartphone to get rid of the screensaver, then typed in Vijay's password. 'You have a text message from Radha,' he reported.

'What's the message?' Vijay wondered.

Colin's jaw dropped as he read the message.

'What's wrong?' Shukla enquired from the rear passenger seat where he was seated with Alice.

'It's Imran,' Colin's voice shook with emotion. He couldn't believe what he was reading. 'His apartment was bombed this evening. He's in hospital. Radha's gone with some IB men to the hospital and she's asked us to meet her there.' He gave Vijay the hospital address and Vijay swung the car around immediately. The hospital was not far from where they were and they could be there in less than fifteen minutes.

IB or not IB?

Radha sat in the car and stared glumly at the traffic around them. A host of questions swirled around in her head. Why had Imran been targeted? Why would anyone want to kill him? Had this anything to do with his visit to Titan earlier that day? And if there was a link between the Titan visit and the attempt on Imran's life, did that mean that she, too, was a target?

She hunched her shoulders and was grateful for the fact that she was in a car with three men from the Intelligence Bureau. It made her feel somewhat safer.

'What did the doctors say about Imran?' she turned to the IB agent sitting next to her, a surly looking man with a thick moustache.

He shrugged. Hoshiar Singh, who was in the front passenger seat turned around and replied instead. 'All we know is that he has lost a lot of blood. We'll only get to know more when we reach.'

Radha fought back her tears. She had forged a very special bond with Imran last year. She had been kidnapped and almost killed and Imran had rescued her. He couldn't die. Not now.

The car came to a roundabout and took a left turn. Radha looked out of the window, still lost in her thoughts, and gave a little start. She hadn't been paying much attention to the route they were taking. They had been heading in the general direction of the hospital, from South Delhi. Preoccupied with the notion of losing Imran, she hadn't noticed when they began moving in a direction that led away from the hospital. It was only now that she realised that they were passing through Chanakyapuri, and heading towards Dhaula Kuan, a route that would lead them to Gurgaon.

She glanced at the surly agent next to her and briefly studied the two agents in front. None of them seemed to be aware that they were heading the wrong way; and if they were, they didn't seem perturbed. The car radio was on and Hoshiar Singh was humming along with a song that was playing, one of the latest Bollywood hits.

Something was wrong. An uneasy feeling took hold of her. Were these really IB agents? Or was this all part of the fallout of the visit to Titan Pharmaceuticals? She tried to recall the agent's identity card but realised that she hadn't looked at it closely. He could have been showing her his driver's licence for all she knew. She chided herself for being so careless.

But, if these people were masquerading as IB agents, then why hadn't they killed her outright? It would have been so easy at her house with no witnesses around. Why pack her into a car under the guise of taking her to see Imran? Unless the news about Imran was a ruse to draw her out. A sudden spark of hope flickered within her at this thought. Maybe Imran was fine after all. But that spark was quickly doused by the realisation of her own predicament.

Radha sank back in her seat. Maybe she was being too paranoid. But if she was right about this, then she had to ensure that the men didn't get to know about her suspicions. She glanced at the doors on either side. They were locked shut by the central locking mechanism. But that didn't mean that they couldn't be unlocked. Only, she couldn't attempt to jump out of a moving car. She'd only succeed in injuring herself and it would be too easy for them to pack her back in the car.

She realised she had just one chance at trying to get away. If that failed, they would be doubly alert and she wouldn't have a hope in hell.

Radha closed her eyes and tried to calm herself, steadying her breathing so that she didn't give anything away. She had to be patient and wait until they came to a traffic intersection where they would have to stop. That was the only opportunity she would get.

She stared ahead at the road as they continued to speed along to an unknown destination. *What was going to happen to her?*

35

At the hospital

Vijay swung into the parking lot of the hospital and screeched to a halt in a vacant spot. The four occupants of the car jumped out with one accord and dashed to the Emergency wing of the hospital. Vijay and Colin reached the reception together with Alice close behind. Shukla waved them on and brought up the rear since he couldn't run like the younger members of the group.

'Imran Kidwai,' Vijay breathlessly enquired at the reception. 'We are his friends.'

'Just a moment, please,' the receptionist responded in a clipped tone. She looked through some papers, then typed in something and peered at the computer monitor in front of her. Finally, she shook her head. 'No one by that name here,' she informed Vijay.

Colin and Vijay looked at each other. 'Are you sure?' Vijay asked incredulously. 'We were informed that he was brought here just a short while ago. A victim of a bombing. He's with the Intelligence Bureau.'

The receptionist shook her head firmly. 'I've gone through the records. There's been no bombing victim here lately. And definitely no one from the Intelligence Bureau. I'm sorry. Perhaps you have the wrong hospital.'

Shukla came up to them and heard the receptionist's words. He looked at them, a fearful expression on his face. He didn't need words to articulate his immediate fears. They were all thinking the same thing. If Imran was not in the hospital, who had met Radha and where were they taking her?

Opportunity knocks

The car had reached Dhaula Kuan. They had just passed over the Dhaula Kuan flyover and the Airport Express metro line ran alongside and above the road to the left, disappearing briefly into the Dhaula Kuan metro station before reappearing and heading towards the international airport.

The traffic was thick at the signal next to the metro station, as they came off the flyover. Vehicles of all types converged from the Ring Road, over which the flyover passed. Cars, buses and two wheelers needing to turn right at the signal, changed lanes in a haphazard manner, mingling with traffic that needed to go straight, creating a massive traffic jam that stretched almost to the foot of the flyover.

Radha stiffened imperceptibly. This was her chance. Once they got past this signal and the next, they would be on the expressway that led from Delhi to Gurgaon. With traffic rushing at high speed on that road, there would be no further opportunity for the car to slow down.

She glanced out of the window. The car next to them was squeezed in beside them, with barely a foot between the two vehicles. There was no way she could open the door and slip out.

The car moved slowly forward, the driver trying to cleave his way through the mass of vehicles moving in different directions in front of them. The gap between the cars increased slightly and Radha tensed. The traffic light had turned green and the jam was beginning to clear rapidly as vehicles began moving in their respective directions.

It was now or never she decided and surreptitiously moved her hand over the doorlock knob.

That was when her mobile phone began ringing. The three men in the car immediately turned to look at her. It was the last thing she could have asked for.

What's the truth?

'She isn't picking up her phone,' Vijay informed the others, a worried look on his face which was shared by Shukla. In that one moment, a father and a fiancé mirrored each other in a shared sense of turmoil and emotion.

'Try Imran,' Colin suggested. 'We need to inform him anyway about Peter. Perhaps he can help us with Radha's whereabouts?' He had a sinking feeling about this but he wasn't going to let that dampen his spirits – it would only pull Vijay and Shukla down even further.

Vijay nodded and dialled Imran's number. A strange and unfamiliar voice answered. 'Yes?'

'Er... I wanted to speak to Imran Kidwai,' Vijay began hesitantly.

'Who are you?' The voice was authoritative and commanding.

Vijay was stumped for a minute. The man who had answered the call seemed to know Imran. Yet, it wasn't Imran who had picked up the call. What could this mean?

'I'm... um... I'm a friend of his,' he finally managed. 'Vijay Singh.'

'Hold on,' the voice commanded and there was silence for a few moments. Then the man was back on the phone. 'Okay, you check out. You're on the US-India task force. Sorry, Vijay, but I had to check to ensure that it was really you calling. Under the circumstances, we're not taking any chances.'

Vijay's bewilderment grew. And a tinge of anxiety crept in. What were the circumstances? *Where was Imran?*

He voiced his question.

'You weren't informed?' the man sounded surprised. 'There was an attempt on Imran's life today. A rocket propelled bomb shot into his apartment from close range. The apartment was totalled. Imran is critical right now. He's undergoing surgery. We don't know if he's going to make it.'

Vijay's brain was spinning. So the news about the attack on Imran was true! His mind quickly pieced the information together. If Imran was, indeed, undergoing surgery as they spoke, and if they were at the wrong hospital, it meant that Radha had been duped. And if the people who had met Radha, pretending to be IB agents, had known about Imran being bombed, it didn't augur well for her. He was willing to bet that the fake IB agents were working for whoever had tried to kill Imran.

'Vijay,' the man said, 'are you there?'

Vijay didn't know how to respond for a moment. Then he asked, 'Who are you?'

A certain stiffness crept into the man's voice. 'I am Arjun Vaid, the Director of the IB. We've met.'

Vijay cringed. Of course he knew Vaid. Imran's boss. But how could he have known that Imran's boss was going to pick up the phone. 'I'm sorry, Mr Vaid,' he stammered, 'I didn't recognise your voice. But I really wasn't expecting...'

'That's fine,' Vaid's voice came back. 'Where are you at this moment? And is Radha with you? We aren't ruling out a link to their visit to Titan Pharmaceuticals today.'

A cold fear gripped Vijay. He and Radha had been over this many times before. When Imran had requested their participation in the task force, Vijay had initially refused. It was Radha who had persuaded him to join the task force.

'Who better than you to be a part of the task force,' she had argued. She knew about his secret and so did Colin. He had felt compelled to share it with the two most important people in his life. 'This is your chance to contribute not just to your country but to the entire world. Chances like this come once in a lifetime, if at all.'

So he had reluctantly agreed. But he hadn't bargained for Radha's desire to be a part of the task force as well. Imran had been keen on her joining but Vijay hadn't. He had argued persuasively but lost.

'It is too dangerous,' he had remonstrated.

'Oh, so it is dangerous for me but not for you,' she had retorted, her eyes flashing in her characteristic way. 'Because I'm a woman and you're a man?'

'No, it isn't that,' he had feebly protested. In his mind, he futilely despaired at the irony of her statement. It was she who had pushed him to accept! So how was he discriminating against her? But he knew better than to voice his thoughts and finally threw in the towel.

Now, he thought, it was coming back to haunt him. And his worst fears had come true. Radha had, for the first time in her life and against better wisdom from Imran – no less – participated in a field mission. And now, even Vaid didn't know where she was.

He brought Vaid up to date on what had happened. Vaid agreed with his assessment about the fake IB agents being somehow mixed up with the people who had bombed Imran's apartment.

'Don't worry,' Vaid assured him. 'We'll put an immediate trace on Radha's phone. If it is GPS enabled and the GPS is active, we'll be able to locate her in no time. And I'll ensure that you are updated about Imran's condition. God knows we all want him to make it through this. Stay where you are for now. I'm sending agents over for you. It just isn't safe for any of you for the time being.'

'Thanks,' Vijay disconnected the call and briefed the others. As he spoke, a thought crossed his mind like a flash. It was a comment that Vaid had made. Suddenly he knew how the blonde man had known about them all being together at the fort. And it also explained why the blonde man hadn't known about Shukla.

36

September, 328 BC
Samarkand, modern day Uzbekistan

The Sogdian palace was lit up with lamps and torches. An air of bustle and gaiety prevailed. The conqueror was hosting a banquet at the palace. After an unexpected rout, he had retreated to Balkh and regrouped his army. He had then sent four mobile units across the river valleys of, what is, modern day Tajikistan and one unit across modern day Uzbekistan to reunite in Samarkand. The chiefs of the rebellious tribes, along with their families, had retreated to the Sogdian rock, which was to be Alexander's next stop. For more reasons than one.

But for now, Alexander was celebrating. He was the emperor of Persia. And tomorrow, he would conquer the Rock. Nothing seemed to stand in his way.

Within the palace, the banquet was in full swing. Wine flowed like water and tables were heaped with choicest Sogdian delicacies.

Generals and soldiers, Macedonians and non-Macedonians alike, mingled in the halls and partook of the feast and drink. For a while, rivalries and politics were forgotten, the wars behind and ahead were consigned to oblivion, and bonhomie prevailed.

But not for too long.

In one part of the hall, Alexander, with Hephaestion and a group of men from his inner circle, held sway. Loud voices and shouts, punctuated by bouts of raucous laughter indicated the level of drunkenness that prevailed in that corner of the hall.

Before long, the effects of the wine had taken a stranglehold on the men and Hephaestion stepped forward.

'Silence, good men!' A few of the generals and soldiers nearby gave him their attention but he was mostly ignored in the immense din that prevailed. Someone passed a rude remark aimed at Hephaestion and Alexander burst out laughing, prompting a smile even from the subject of the joke.

Hephaestion decided to show people who was in charge. He jumped onto one of the tables laden with food, dumped the contents of two bronze serving dishes and banged them together violently several times.

The noise in the hall lowered to a murmur as the clanging of the bronze dishes attracted attention. Something was happening and people wanted to know what it was. If Alexander's lover was banging dishes on a table and the conqueror himself was in splits, it was worth taking notice.

Satisfied that he had the attention of as many people as was possible, Hephaestion gestured to one of the men sitting next to Alexander.

'Lend an ear, good men, to the verses composed by Pranichus, our local poet,' Hephaestion chuckled and jumped off the table.

Goaded by shouts of encouragement, Pranichus took Hephaestion's place on the banquet table and began reciting the verses.

This was the turning point of the night. A large section of the men in the hall laughed and joked at the verses or passed remarks among themselves as Pranichus recited them. But there was a section of men whose faces darkened and became hard as the recitation progressed.

These were the men from the old guard, the veterans who had served under Philip, Alexander's father. They had also fought by the young conqueror's side and had been instrumental on many occasions, including the battle of Gaugamela, in turning the tide in favour of the Macedonians. They did not like what they heard now.

The verses were based on a defeat suffered by Alexander's generals at Samarkand, the rout that had forced Alexander to retreat to Balkh in the winter of the previous year. In the verses, the generals were being mocked for their resounding defeat at the hands of the Bactrian tribes.

The veterans began murmuring among themselves. One of them, Clitus, who had been recently appointed Satrap of Bactria and Sogdia, was especially incensed.

'Macedonians are being humiliated before barbarians and enemies,' he said through clenched teeth, his anger growing. 'How can we stand by and watch this happen? Will no one among us stand up and be counted as a man? Shall we stay silent as they continue to mock us?'

'When there is success, Alexander is responsible. When there is defeat, it is the generals,' another veteran complained. 'This was never so in the time of Philip.'

Clitus turned on him. 'Then why do you not speak up? Stop this nonsense now! We have always had freedom of speech under Philip and even with Alexander. Surely they will see reason in our thinking?'

'They are drunk,' another man admonished. 'Too much wine has addled their brains. It is best not to interfere at this time. Remember what happened in Persepolis.' He was referring to the drunken banquet after Alexander had marched, victorious, into Persepolis, the capital of the Persian empire. During that banquet, a drunken Alexander had decided to set fire to Persepolis. And in doing so he had destroyed one of the most magnificent cities in the world of that age.

'And don't forget when Philip got drunk and tried to kill Alexander,' another veteran spoke up, referring to the occasion of Philip's wedding to Cleopatra, a Macedonian girl from high nobility. Cleopatra's uncle, Attalus, had remarked that Philip would finally produce a legitimate heir, implying that Alexander was illegitimate. And, even though Olympias herself had claimed that Alexander was not fathered by Philip but by Zeus, Alexander had been enraged. He had thrown his cup at Attalus upon which Philip stood up and drew his sword to kill Alexander. In his state of drunkenness, he had charged at Alexander only to trip and fall on his face.

But it had demonstrated the extent to which events could escalate after a night of heavy drinking. And tonight had been the same. The veterans did not want to provoke an incident.

But Clitus was determined. 'This has to stop,' he insisted. 'Now. If none of you are man enough, I will do it. I saved Alexander's life at Granicus. And don't forget that he handed half the army to me and the other half to Hephaestion after the execution of Philotas. He will not turn a deaf ear to my entreaties.'

He pushed his way through the throng and reached the banquet table where Pranichus held sway.

'Enough!' he commanded, addressing Pranichus. 'No more!'

Pranichus stopped in mid-verse and looked at Hephaestion and Alexander.

The young king stood up, swaying slightly under the influence of the copious amounts of alcohol he had consumed.

'And why should he stop?' Alexander asked of Clitus. 'He speaks the truth.'

A hush fell over the hall. This was no longer a faceoff between Clitus and Pranichus. Alexander had involved himself.

Pranichus quietly climbed off the table and retreated, as Alexander confronted Clitus, who held the conqueror's gaze.

'Sire, it has been the tradition since your father's time that credit for victories and responsibility for defeat...' Clitus began, but was cut off by Alexander.

'My father!' he spat. 'You speak of my father as if he was fair and just. Did he give me credit for the part I played in his victories? You speak of my father's traditions? The only tradition I know of is the ill will he bore me. The envy with which he regarded me. What of those? Are those the marks of a fair man?' Alexander glared at Clitus and took another swig of wine from his cup.

'Sire,' Clitus responded, 'you do no justice to your father's memory. He began the invasion of Persia and would have done what you have done today, only many years before, had his time not been cut short by an assassin's dagger.' He paused, the hurt and anger bubbling up now, reason giving way to emotion. 'You forget, sire, that you are what you are today because of your father. He laid the foundation for everything that you have achieved today. His achievements were far greater than any of yours so far. And today you believe you are such a great man that you pretend to be the child of Ammon and disown your own father, Philip!'

There was a moment of silence at his last words. It was as if the men had collectively stopped breathing at that moment.

'Villain!' Alexander responded, the wine clouding his sense of reason. 'Do you believe that you will be allowed to slander me, cause discontentment among the Macedonians, without retribution?'

But Clitus remained unfazed. 'If you cannot bear to hear men speak their mind, why do you invite free-born people to your table? It would be better if you kept the company of barbarians and slaves. They would fawn over you and kiss your Persian girdle and striped tunic!'

Alexander exploded with rage. He threw his cup at Clitus, spilling the wine on himself and the general. People scattered as Alexander went for the banquet dishes, pulling off fruit from the table and throwing it at Clitus. He looked around for a weapon but there was none within reach.

'Summon the guards!' Alexander yelled, his voice slurring. 'Call the guards! Where are my guards?'

Some of Clitus' friends grabbed the general and dragged him out of the palace, away from Alexander's fury, across the moat, where he would be safe. Once Alexander's anger had blown over, Clitus could return and join the party if it had not finished by then.

Alexander's bodyguards had arrived on the scene by now and formed a protective circle around him.

The group of friends who had rescued Clitus returned and signalled for the festivities to continue. The skirmish was over and would be forgotten by tomorrow in the haze of the hangover that would follow the night's feast.

But this night was not destined to end that way.

There was a commotion at the doorway and Clitus marched in. It was not in his nature to run away from a fight. He had stood his ground in battle and he would make a stand now.

'Ah me! In Greece an evil custom reigns!' his voice boomed across the hall as he marched towards the conqueror, reciting a passage from *Andromache*, by Euripides, his tone insolent.

Alexander, who had been making his way back to where his friends were seated, turned. On seeing Clitus, his rage was kindled again. His reaction was instant and spontaneous. He grabbed a spear from one of his guards and rushed at Clitus, running the spear right through the general.

'You are no different from Bessus!' he shouted as Clitus fell to the ground, blood spurting from where the spear had impaled him. There was a large pool of blood on the floor of the banquet hall and the men shrank back as if the blood was cursed. They had never seen Alexander like this before. It was like he was a man possessed.

As the life force drained out of Clitus with his blood, Alexander fell to his knees. Somewhere through his drink induced haze, the realisation of what he had done penetrated through. He collapsed, overcome with tears, on Clitus' lifeless body. The general's blood soaked his sandals and his cloak but he didn't care.

For the first time in his life, Alexander had killed someone for daring to challenge him and express a difference of opinion. And, in doing so, he had violated two Macedonian traditions. The first was executing someone without a trial in the presence of the army. The second was Zeus' law of hospitality which Alexander broke by killing a guest at his table. A guest who had saved his life and served the royal family with loyalty and distinction.

That night was a watershed. It was the first time Alexander had allowed his ambitions to get the better of him.

And it would not be the last.

37

PRESENT DAY

DAY THREE
Escape...

Radha acted on instinct. The moment the three faces turned towards her, she pulled up the door lock knob and slammed open the door of the car, ignoring the insistent ring of her mobile phone. The car door crashed into the fender of the car alongside, and its driver immediately stopped and got out to inspect the damage.

She ignored the screaming driver and the honking of the cars behind them, and weaved her way through the traffic, aiming for the metro station that was a few metres away.

Behind her, the aggrieved driver stomped his way to the driver's side of the offending car, only to be confronted by the muzzle of a Glock. He backed off hurriedly, his rage forgotten, doused by the cold water of fear and self preservation.

The three men in the car gave chase as Radha reached the sidewalk and sprinted up the escalator to the metro station. Drivers honked angrily at them and subsided equally fast as they saw the guns brandished by the fake IB agents.

'Train's coming!' one of the men shouted, as the yellow light of an approaching train washed over the façade of the station. They increased their speed, vaulting over cars stalled by the sight of the guns and followed Radha up the escalator.

Radha risked a glance behind her and saw that the traffic had not stopped the men. Their guns were in plain sight but they weren't shooting at her. She wondered why.

But there was no time for speculation. The train drew up at the platform and screeched to a halt as she emerged from the escalator. There was no time to be a good citizen and stand in the inordinately long queue for tickets. Radha vaulted over the row of turnstiles, disregarding the shouts of people behind her. She ran to the far end of the platform and boarded the very last coach, hoping against hope that the train would leave before the men reached the platform.

The doors of the train shut and she fearfully glanced out of the windows. Her three pursuers were still on the platform. One of them caught her eye and glared at her balefully as the train began gathering speed and moved out of the station.

Suddenly, there was a commotion, as the man glaring at her looked around him, prompted by cries from his colleagues, and sprinted away, heading for the exit. As the train sped away, Radha realised why her three captors were fleeing. Five men, all dressed casually, had dashed up the escalator, vaulted over the turnstiles and were now in hot pursuit of the fake IB agents. The newcomers also brandished handguns. She didn't know who they were, but since they were chasing her captors, they had to be the good guys.

She sank into a vacant seat and wiped her brow. Only now did she recall the phone call that she didn't answer while making her escape from the car. She pulled out the phone and shook her head when she saw the number. It was Vijay. What timing, she thought to herself and dialled the number.

Vijay picked up immediately. 'Radha, are you okay?' The concern in his voice, along with the fear for her safety, was heartwarming and made her relax immediately.

'I'm fine,' she told him and narrated what she had just undergone , including the final scene of her kidnappers fleeing the five armed men who had made a last minute appearance.

Vijay chuckled. 'That would be the IB guys Vaid sent. He had put a trace on your GPS and sent out a team to help you out. Looks like his plan worked.'

Radha smiled but her smile faded away almost immediately as she realised something. 'Imran's hospitalisation is a fabrication.'

'No it's not.' It was Vijay's turn to give her the news. 'You should be at the airport in ten minutes, tops,' he said. 'I'll head there right away. You just find a quiet spot and hunker down until we come.'

Radha grinned at Vijay's Americanism. It reminded her of the Louis L'Amour novels she used to read. It was good to smile after all that she'd been through and good to know that Vijay would be at the airport soon to pick her up.

She slipped the phone back into her jeans pocket and closed her eyes. Whether it was the stress of the evening's events or the fatigue of the day's journeys from Jaungarh to Gurgaon and Delhi, she didn't know.

All she knew was that the train seemed to have stopped and she was being shaken awake. She woke up, disoriented and stared at the men standing before her with blurry eyes.

Gradually, her vision cleared and she made out a tall Caucasian man, flanked by six men. They were all armed. The white man had a handgun pointed straight at her face. The coach was empty. All the other passengers had dispersed. Or fled.

He grinned as the realisation hit her. 'We're at the airport, my dear,' he smirked. 'Welcome to Indira Gandhi International Airport.' He mimicked the airport announcements, his accent perfectly matching those of the English announcements at the airport. 'Fasten your seatbelt, poppet. You're about to go on a long ride.'

IGI International Airport, Metro station

Vijay looked around the station, bewildered. He had arrived ten minutes ago to witness the train leaving the station, bound for Central Delhi. There was no sign of Radha on the platform. All he could see around him were passengers who had just come in from their flights, waiting for the next train to arrive.

Where was she?

He walked the length of the station once more, just in case he had missed her earlier. Though it was highly improbable that he had, he didn't want to take any chances.

He had left the others to wait for the agents promised by Vaid and rushed to the airport. The traffic had been bad, but he knew that Radha would not wander off when she knew he was coming for her. He was at his wit's end. Calling her phone wasn't helping either. It was switched off. That was another thing that bothered him. Why would she switch off her phone?

Nothing seemed to make sense. Unless she was being held captive when they had spoken. Perhaps she was pressured into lying to him about having shaken off her pursuers. It was an unpleasant thought but, given what had befallen Imran, he couldn't rule anything out.

Vijay called Colin and updated him. Colin, Alice and Shukla, accompanied by three IB agents, were on their way to the airport. The agents had arrived shortly after Vijay had left and their identities had been verified with Vaid before the others accompanied them.

The plan was for the IB agents to escort them back to Jaungarh. There had been a great deal of discussion over where exactly they could go. No place seemed to be safe at the moment. Vijay's argument, which won the moment, was that despite their adversaries knowing that Alice was at Jaungarh, they had stayed their hand until she, with the others, had moved out of the fort.

'I feel the safest place, at the moment, is the fort,' Vijay had concluded and the others had agreed with him.

Unable to come up with any ideas on how to locate Radha, Vijay dialled Imran's number again. Vaid, unable to reveal his own mobile number to Vijay, had suggested this as a contact number for the time being.

'Is everything okay?' Vaid asked as he picked up the call.

'Not really.' Vijay updated him on the situation. 'I have a request,' he added. 'Can we track the location of Radha's mobile phone once again since it is GPS enabled?'

'I'll get someone to track it right away,' Vaid responded. 'But we'll only get a location trace if her phone is on. If it is switched off, as you mentioned, then we can't do much.'

Vijay's heart sank. If Radha had, as he feared, been abducted, there was little chance that her captors would keep her phone switched on. And if they did, they would be sure to ensure that her GPS was disabled so that her location could not be tracked.

He had worked out that their attackers at the museum had used some kind of advanced technology to identify them as well as keep a tab on all them through the GPS on their smartphones. The fact that the whereabouts and identities of each of the others, except Shukla, were known to the men at the museum pointed to this. Shukla was the only one without a mobile phone and they didn't know about him. After this realisation they had all switched off the GPS on their phones.

Vijay was afraid. Whoever these men were, they were not amateurs. And if the technology at their command was the same as the one that the IB used, then they were also powerful people. It was his worst nightmare come true. He may just have lost Radha.

38

Prisoner...

Radha's eyes fluttered open and she moaned. The first thing she saw was the colour of her surroundings.

White. Pure and pristine. A white ceiling. White walls. Perhaps even a white floor. As this thought came to her, she realised that she was strapped to a bed, her wrists and ankles bound; with little leeway for any kind of movement. A drip was attached to a needle that was inserted into her left arm.

She struggled with her bonds for a few moments before realising the futility and surrendered to the reality of her situation.

Her head was heavy and her body felt like lead. Where was she? And how did she get here? She had a vague recollection, as if through a haze, of a man pointing a gun at her in a train coach. Of being shepherded off the train, onto the platform. And then there was no further recollection.

Her nasal tract still burned from the acrid fumes of the chemical which she had been forced to inhale. The strong grip at the base of her neck, forcing her face into a damp cloth, had left a bruise on the back of her neck and a dull pain to accompany it.

She now realised that she was wearing a hospital gown. Where were her jeans and the top she had been wearing in the train? Who had changed her clothes? An offensive, humiliating feeling of having been defiled by an unknown person washed over her, accompanied by a fury that suddenly exploded without warning.

It came as a shock to her as the rage consumed her and then all rational thought was swept aside as she vented her anger, screaming loudly and struggling against her bonds with an intensity and strength that she had not known herself capable of displaying.

...or guinea pig?

Dr Varun Saxena stared with great interest at the video monitor, one of a bank, in the centre's control room. He turned to his companion and nodded to him. 'You were right, Gary,' he said. 'I never knew that this drug had such a strong side-effect.'

Gary Freeman grinned. 'Hey, I hate to say "I told you so" but I did tell you so.' He jerked a thumb at the video monitor which was displaying Radha's outbreak of emotion. 'I think you'd better give her the antidote right away. That is, if you want her fully intact. The drug's effects won't wear off until another two hours and in that time she could lose a hand or two.'

On the screen, Radha still fought her bonds with undiminished intensity, apparently oblivious to the needle in her arm. The drip, along with its tubing, jerked violently as she thrashed about in futile fury.

Saxena glanced one last time at the video monitor, then picked up the intercom and issued instructions. Within moments, a nurse entered the room and injected something into the drip. The antidote was swift to act, calming Radha's exertions almost instantly.

'You may not have got this kind of a display with your regular specimens,' Freeman continued, chuckling. 'They're so full of the shit we keep injecting them with that you never know what might have interfered with the effect of the drug. It was a good thing that this one came along. Just at the right time.'

'She didn't "come along", Saxena informed him as the two men left the room. 'She was brought here by Cooper. We have to dispose of her sooner or later. Once we find out what she knows about Operation Mahabharata.'

'Really?' Freeman looked concerned. 'See, you guys keep me locked away here and I don't know what's happening in the outside world.'

'Don't have a choice,' Saxena shot back. 'We're supposed to be doing clinical trials here. Even I tiptoe my way here on the rare occasion that I visit. We can't afford this facility to be linked to Titan in any way. And the studies that you are conducting here have to be below the radar. You know that. If word leaks out, that genetic research is being carried out at this facility, it would be catastrophic. Especially if it was revealed that the head of genetics at Titan was leading the research.'

'Yeah, I know, I know. But I don't have to be happy about it,' Freeman grumbled. 'Is the op at risk?'

Saxena shrugged. 'Don't know. That's why she's here. We need to find out. She came to me, masquerading as a journalist. I didn't know it at that time. It was only when Cooper alerted us to the connection between her and the IB agent who came to meet Swaroop that we got to know that she was undercover.'

Freeman whistled. 'So she was working with an IB guy? She's also Indian intelligence?'

'We don't know yet. But that doesn't matter. The IB guy's dead...or dying at least. Cooper took care of that. And once we find out what she knows, she'll join him. Until then, Cooper's going to use her as bait. So, while we're keeping her on ice, we may as well make good use of her presence here. Good, fresh specimens are hard to come by.' He grinned unpleasantly and Freeman chuckled again.

39

The link discovered

Vijay, Colin, Alice and Shukla sat in the study at the fort. The IB men had dropped them back some time ago and then left. If they had been followed or if there were any more people stalking them, they had been careful not to make themselves obvious.

Back in the fort, Vijay felt a palpable sense of relief and security. They would be safe here. But through the journey to Jaungarh and since their return, they had all been disturbed by the lack of any news about Radha. It was like she had disappeared off the face of the planet.

Shukla sat, despondent, his face reflecting his anxiety for his daughter. 'Why isn't Vaid investigating Titan?' he asked for the umpteenth time, of no one in particular. Vijay had assured him earlier that Vaid had personally spoken to Swaroop Varma, the CEO of Titan Pharmaceuticals. The man had been shocked to receive a personal visit from the Director of the IB and seemed to have been genuinely concerned about what had happened to both Imran and Radha. He had assured full cooperation both in the investigation and the hunt for Radha, even going to the extent of offering to allow IB agents to inspect every office and outsourced facility associated with Titan in India.

'The IB is checking all leads,' Vijay said patiently. He tried to mask his anxiety for Shukla's sake. 'We just have to have faith in them. And hope that something turns up soon.'

Alice spoke up. 'I've been thinking about something the blonde guy at the museum said.' She looked at Vijay. 'Do you remember when he was counting us off? He said something about Imran and Radha.'

'He said they were "covered"', Vijay replied morosely. He should have figured at that time itself that Radha and Imran were both targets. But he knew he couldn't blame himself or anyone else for not considering this at that time. They could think of nothing else but their own fates which had hung by a very slender thread. They had been really lucky to have gotten away. Those men had been professional killers.

'Yes, that, too, but he also mentioned that they had been nosing around.' Alice looked at him warily. She knew it was a tricky time to be bringing this up. But she also had a feeling this may just be the break they were looking for.

'Yeah, I remember that,' Colin frowned, and Vijay and Shukla also nodded morosely. Colin slapped his thigh as he realised what Alice was saying. 'Good heavens! The two *are* connected!'

Vijay and Shukla still looked confused. Alice realised that their emotions were probably clouding their thinking so she explained. 'All this time we've been thinking that the involvement of Peter with my excavation and what happened to me in Greece had nothing to do with Imran's discovery of the bioterrorism lead here in India. But could it be possible that the two are actually connected?'

Shukla looked at Vijay, unsure if this was good news or bad news. Vijay didn't respond immediately. Alice could almost hear the wheels spinning in his mind as he analysed and sifted data from their conversations and the encounter at the museum. She knew Vijay well from their days together. He had an amazing knack for analysing facts, but he also relied a lot on his intuition – a killer combination. She knew that he was putting facts and instinct together right now to validate what she had said.

'You could be right,' Vijay said, finally. 'They knew about each one of us, except Dr Shukla. They have access to technology that allows them to track our movements. So they monitored Alice's presence at the fort and were able to follow us to the museum. They were also monitoring Radha and Imran's movements and knew that they had visited Titan Pharmaceuticals. That much is clear from what the blonde guy at the museum said. And both Imran and Radha have been targeted after that visit. The question is: what is the connection between the excavation in Greece and the bioterrorism angle? We know that they are after the cube. We also know now that Alexander was on a quest to find something on his journey to India. Something that Eumenes describes as the "secret of the gods".' Vijay was now thinking aloud, trying to work things out.

The others sat and listened. Colin and Alice knew Vijay well enough to know that they shouldn't interrupt when he was working things through. Shukla was distracted by his worries surrounding Radha's whereabouts and was only half listening to Vijay.

'So,' Vijay continued, 'the obvious conclusion is that this secret that Alexander was looking for is a possible source of bioterrorism. The only thing that I can think of is that it is a virus or a bacteria that can devastate populations. Something that bioterrorists can use to their advantage. What else can it be? That would also explain the cells at the facility that ran clinical trials for Titan. And the test reports that described an unknown bacteria and virus. But that raises a host of questions. Why would a bacteria or virus be called a "secret of the gods"? Why was Alexander looking for this secret? What did he do with it when he found it? Or is it something else that we are missing out on?'

There was silence as the others digested these thoughts. Vijay's conclusion seemed to be logical. The questions he had raised were also very relevant. But there didn't seem to be any clear answers. Especially to explain Alexander's quest, if the secret involved a bacteria or virus that could be used for bioterrorism.

Shukla rose. 'I think I'm going to turn in for the night,' he said glumly. What he really wanted was to be alone right now. He really wasn't interested in this discussion about Alexander and the link to bioterrorism. His daughter had been kidnapped. No one, not even the IB, knew where she was. And if there were bioterrorists involved, then her life was surely in danger. If they could bomb the apartment of a senior IB officer, what chance did Radha have as their prisoner?

Vijay nodded, understanding. He, too, was despondent, but with this latest revelation, something told him they had a fighting chance. He didn't know how or what that chance was, but he trusted his gut feeling. 'Why don't you guys get some rest?' he told Colin and Alice. 'I'm going to work on this angle a bit more and see if I can think of something that may be useful for us.'

Colin knew that his friend was acting on a hunch. He didn't argue. Instead, he patted Alice on the shoulder and rose. 'You're right,' he said to Vijay. 'See you in the morning.'

As the others left the study, Vijay walked over to the huge bay windows that overlooked the hillside the fort was built on and stared into the dark night outside.

There was a darkness in his heart that matched the surroundings of the fort. But deep down there was his natural rebellious streak that was beginning to surface. It was a trait that had served him well most of his life. It made him stubborn at times when he should have given up. On some occasions, this had led to some grief, but more often than not, he had been able to achieve what he wanted by grimly hanging on.

He hoped this was one of those times. Radha was the only precious thing left in his life. Sure, there was Colin who was a great friend, almost a brother, to Vijay. But Radha had given him the love he had never had since his parents had passed away. Even with Alice, he reflected now, it hadn't been this way. Radha's love was selfless, almost unconditional. He had never thought it possible.

And he was not going to lose her now.

40

A proposal for barter

Cooper sat back and appraised the situation. Things had gone according to plan so far, with the exception of the fiasco at the museum. Riley had reported in a while back and updated Cooper. The young man had sounded angry at having lost his quarry.

'Don't worry yourself about it,' Cooper had told him. 'Shit happens. We've got the woman now. They'll come to us. And, we have a bonus. We have the metal plate. Without it the cube would have been useless anyway.' Cooper picked up the phone. It was time to move ahead. Time to make a call.

He dialled Vijay's number. It was picked up almost immediately.

'Vijay Singh?' Cooper enquired. He didn't want to play his hand without being sure he was speaking to the right person.

'Yes. Who is this?'

'My name is Peter Cooper. You may have heard of me from your friend Alice.'

There was silence at the other end. Cooper could only imagine Vijay's shock at being called by him at this time of night. He could also visualise Vijay's hopes rising, for news of Radha. This was exactly what he wanted. The success of his plan depended on how badly Vijay wanted to acquiesce to his demands.

Cooper waited, letting the silence grow heavier.

'Where's Radha?' Vijay demanded finally, unable to take the suspense any more. 'If you have harmed her...' he left his sentence incomplete, unable to think of a suitable ending. What could he do to an unseen, unknown enemy when he didn't even know where they were hiding?

'Don't make foolish threats that you can't carry out,' Cooper advised him. 'Your fiancée is with us. She is safe. For now. And her future safety and well-being depend on how well you cooperate with us.'

There was silence again. This time Cooper didn't wait but pressed on.

'I have a proposal,' he said. 'A barter. You have something we want. And we have something you want. Why don't we exchange? Everyone's happy and all's well that ends well.'

'You want the cube?'

'Yes. And Alice Turner. Give me both and you can have your fiancée back.'

Silence again. Cooper could picture Vijay struggling with his emotions. It was a tough choice. A former girlfriend for a fiancée. The fate of both hung in Vijay's hands.

'I'm not an unreasonable man,' Cooper continued. 'I will give you until 12 noon tomorrow to think about it and let me know. Until then, you have my assurance that not one hair on your fiancée's head will be harmed. But I will expect a decision from you by then.'

He disconnected the call and stretched. It was time to hit the sack. It had been a long day. Age was catching up with him. There was a time when he had enjoyed a field job. The thrill of stalking a target, sometimes losing it, then catching up with it again was a powerful allurement. Now, the physical effort sometimes tired him out. But he had a job to do. And he was nothing if not meticulous.

Tomorrow he would call Vijay Singh again. And the fate of two women would be decided.

41

DAY FOUR
A glimmer of hope

Colin entered the study to find Vijay fast asleep, his head on the desk, resting on his arms. The desk was littered with printouts and Vijay's notebook was open, his pen resting on it. Clearly, Vijay had been busy through the night. Colin wondered what his friend had been doing and whether he had learned anything that could help them.

He walked over to Vijay and shook him gently. 'Hey, buddy, wake up.'

Vijay lifted his head off the desk and looked at Colin, bleary eyed. 'I fell asleep,' he mumbled.

'No shit. You look a mess. You better go downstairs and freshen up.'

Vijay nodded, still disoriented. Then, a thought seemed to strike him and he brightened up.

'I found something,' he informed Colin. 'Let's have breakfast and I'll tell you guys.'

Leaving Colin wondering what he had discovered during the night, Vijay hurried out of the study.

An hour later, they assembled in the study. Vijay sat at the desk, sorting out the papers and stacking them on the desk.

Three pairs of eyes gazed at Vijay expectantly, filled with curiosity.

'I did a lot of research on Alexander the Great,' he began. 'I downloaded a BBC documentary by Michael Wood and watched it – all four hours of it. I read sections of various books written about the man. You won't believe how many people have written about him. I read about the route he followed from Macedonia to India. The people he fought along the way, the stories around what he did in different cities that he passed through. And I learned a lot about the man. He was stubborn. He refused to give up in the face of all odds. And he was determined.'

'Sounds a bit like you,' Colin grinned. 'You could be describing yourself, you know.'

Vijay scowled at him but didn't respond.

Alice said nothing but in her head she was thinking the same thing. Vijay's determination, perseverance and refusal to conform to popular belief had helped him succeed in many ways. It was what had attracted her to him in the first place. A man who knew his mind. And was not afraid to follow it. But it had also been the cause of their break up.

'It seems that Alexander was driven by something at every step of the way. When he left Macedonia, it was the *pothos* – the desire, the longing – to avenge the defeat of the Greeks at the hands of the Persians. So he marched to Persia, defeated Darius and when Darius was murdered at the hands of his own nobles, he pursued them across the mountains until he caught up with them and killed them. Now, he was ruler of Persia but he didn't stop there. There was another *pothos* that drove him further eastward. All the writers I read explained this desire as an ambition to conquer the known world and march to the ends of the earth. Apparently, Alexander had been taught by Aristotle that beyond the Indus lay the great ocean and the ends of the earth.'

He paused and looked at Alice, who nodded her approval. 'Go on,' she said, 'you're doing a great job.'

'This is where it gets all mysterious,' Vijay continued, having validated his research. 'First, it appears that Alexander never told his troops when they left Greece that they were marching to the ends of the earth. It was only after they conquered Persia that he told them that they would be marching on eastwards. Once again, there seems to be a logical explanation for this. If he had told his soldiers how far from home they would be marching, they may not have followed him in the first place. But that doesn't make sense to me. Alexander was a leader par excellence. He led his men on a twenty-thousand mile journey from Macedonia to India and then back to Babylon. They marched across freezing mountain passes, baking deserts, sometimes without water or food. They followed him everywhere, without protest. The only exception was when they reached the Beas river in Punjab and they persuaded Alexander to return home saying they would march no more. These men would have followed him into the depths of the earth if he had demanded it of them.'

He looked around to see if everyone was following him. Satisfied that they were, he resumed. 'But we have a different theory from that of these writers. They didn't have access to the cube or the secret journal of Eumenes. They couldn't know that there may have been a secret quest Alexander had embarked on; a quest known only to him and his mother. But our theory provides a logical explanation of what happened.'

'I see where you are going with this,' Alice said. 'If Olympias had the cube and the parchment which she gave Alexander, she would most likely have told him to keep the quest a secret. Alexander would have disguised the quest in the garb of conquering the known world and marching to the ends of the world. But when he left Macedonia, he told his troops only about the invasion of the Persian empire and not about his plans to march to the Indus. Not because he was afraid his men wouldn't follow him but because he didn't want them to know about the "secret of the gods". And, if I'm guessing right, you also think that the rebellion at the Beas was engineered or recorded as such to disguise the fact that Alexander had accomplished his mission and wanted to go back home himself.'

'Exactly,' Vijay beamed. 'He buried the metal plate at the base of the altar near the Beas because he had achieved his quest. Remember, Eumenes says that Alexander had become a god after entering the cave guarded by a five-headed snake? And we know that Alexander had begun proclaiming himself a god right from the time he defeated the tribes in Bactria – that was why Callisthenes was put to death.'

'So what you're saying,' Colin said slowly, 'is that the parchment that Olympias gave Alexander should somehow correspond with the route that Alexander took on his way from Persia to India. That's why you were studying the route he took.'

'Bingo!' Vijay's face shone with excitement. He had reasoned this out by himself and it felt good to see that the others could follow his line of thinking. It seemed to validate his reasoning. He had already decided on his course of action and it all depended on what conclusion this discussion reached.

'So, what did you find?' Colin asked.

42

Prisoner

Radha awoke with a start. For a few moments she was disoriented. The pristine white surroundings in which she found herself were unfamiliar.

Then it all came back to her. The Airport Express. The man with the gun. Her losing consciousness. The hospital gown. The straps binding her. The uneasy, creeping realisation that her rage was about to explode. But try as she might, she couldn't remember anything after that. What had happened? And she realised she had been moved to a much smaller room than the one in which she had woken up earlier.

She looked down. She still wore the gown. But she was no longer strapped down. How long had she been unconscious?

Gingerly, she raised herself on the bed and sat up, her legs dangling over the side. She felt weak; drained, as if she had expended a lot of energy in some great physical effort.

She was suddenly aware of the pain in her wrists and ankles. She examined them one by one, wondering at the deep cuts where the nylon straps had dug into her flesh.

She got off the bed, the white marble floor cold against her bare feet. There were no slippers in the room. The walls were solid. There was a frosted glass door to the room but it was locked. She grabbed the handle, pulling and pushing, trying to open the door but to no avail. There was only one way to open the door and that was from the outside. People could enter but she couldn't leave. Not without an access card to activate the sensor fitted at the side of the door. She was well and truly a prisoner.

As her hands left the door handle, it slipped away abruptly and the door swung outwards. She stumbled backwards, alarmed, as Saxena and Freeman entered the room.

'How is our patient today?' Saxena greeted her affably.

'I am not a patient!' Radha's eyes flashed angrily. 'Why am I here?'

'I'm the one who will be asking the questions today.' Saxena indicated the bed. 'Sit.'

A feeling of nausea accompanied by a sudden weakness washed over Radha. She backed up to the bed and sat down, glad to be off her feet. For some reason her legs were feeling wobbly.

'After-effects of the psychotropic enhancer,' Freeman remarked to Saxena, observing her perceptible discomfort and correctly guessing the cause. 'Nausea and weakness.'

'Who is he?' Radha remained defiant.

'Ah, I didn't introduce you.' Saxena gestured towards Freeman. 'Dr Gary Freeman. Expert in genetics and the head of genetics at Titan Pharmaceuticals. He's been working on a top secret project for us for many years now. And he's close to a breakthrough. Now, let's get some answers. First question: what does the IB know about our mission?'

Radha looked blank. She had no idea what mission he was talking about. All she knew now was that Imran's suspicions had been confirmed. Titan Pharmaceuticals was involved in some way with the clinical trials at the destroyed medical centre. But what did a genetics expert have to do with the clinical trials?

An annoyed expression crossed Saxena's face. 'I want an answer,' he said firmly. 'Silence is not an option. We have ways, painful ways, to make you speak. I'm being gentle with you right now. Don't try my patience.'

'I don't know what you are talking about.' Radha had no desire to find out what means Saxena had at his disposal to elicit answers from her.

'I find that hard to believe. You came to my office, snooping around, posing as a journalist. You are affiliated with the Intelligence Bureau. In what capacity, I don't yet know. You had all the details about the fire at the medical facility in East Delhi. Including the cells for the patients. You clearly know a lot about us.'

Radha's face registered surprise. How did they know about her association with the IB? 'I really have no idea what you are going on about,' she protested feebly, taken aback by their level of knowledge. 'I have nothing to do with the Intelligence Bureau.'

Saxena smirked. 'Don't underestimate us,' he warned her. 'We have a second team keeping tabs on the lot of you. We know that all of you, including the IB agent, were together at Jaungarh fort. Which, of course, is owned by your fiancé.'

'Okay, I admit that I know Imran Kidwai. But I'm telling you the truth,' Radha insisted. 'We had our suspicions. We thought that Titan was mixed up in whatever was happening at the centre that got gutted. But we didn't know what it was.'

Saxena looked at Freeman then fixed Radha with a stern look. 'I really don't know whether or not to believe you. Why were you investigating us if you didn't know what we were working on?'

Radha hesitated. She felt terrible that she was telling this man everything. But she was scared. Of the pain. Of the cuts in her hands and legs. Of the terrifying feeling she had had earlier of not being in control of herself. She knew that these people were capable of anything. And they wouldn't hesitate to do anything to get what they wanted.

'We thought Titan was involved in bioterrorism. That you were creating a new type of pathogen that could be used by terrorists and dictatorial regimes,' she blurted out.

For a moment, Saxena simply stared at her. Then he burst out laughing. 'Bioterrorism!' he nudged Freeman, who chuckled back. 'A new type of pathogen!' He shook his head. 'You really don't know what our project is about, do you?' He looked at Freeman. 'I guess we really don't need her anymore. Let's ask Cooper what he wants to do with her. I'd like to use her for a few more trials before he disposes of her.'

They swept out of the room, leaving Radha alone, confused and terrified. She had no doubt about her fate. If she wasn't going to be used as a guinea pig, she was definitely going to die.

43

A part of the puzzle

'You see,' Vijay carried a sheaf of papers from the desk to the coffee table where the others were seated, 'there were two mysteries surrounding the route that Alexander took on this journey.'

He pulled out a map that traced in bold red Alexander's march across modern day Afghanistan, Pakistan and India.

'The first is here,' he indicated a region in the south of Pakistan near the coast. 'After heading down the Indus on his way back to Babylon, Alexander divided up the army. He sent part of it by sea across the Persian Gulf. And he led the other part of the army from the coast to Turbat.' He indicated the town on the map. 'Then, inexplicably, he headed south to the sea through Pasni, marching one hundred miles through the harshest terrain – the Makran desert. It took him 60 days to cross the Makran and he lost a sizeable chunk of his army there.'

'That's strange,' Shukla remarked. 'Why didn't he travel back by sea? Why divide the army?'

'And not just that,' Alice took up the narrative, since she was familiar with this story. 'From Turbat to Persepolis is pretty much a straight line.' She indicated the route on the map. 'Alexander marched through the Makran to Pasni and then headed to Persepolis. Even if there was a logical reason to divide his troops, if he was heading for Persepolis anyway by land, he didn't need to go through the desert at all. Modern writers explain this by saying that Alexander wanted to conquer the desert, especially since it had been crossed by Queen Semiramis and Cyrus the Great.'

'Maybe he just wanted to prove to his men that he was a god?' Colin hazarded a guess.

'It doesn't matter why,' Vijay replied. 'I just brought it up to show that there were two options I had to consider that could have provided evidence for a secret quest. The Makran desert was one. If Alexander was on a secret quest, he could have been looking for the location of the secret in the Makran desert. That would explain the detour.'

'But it doesn't,' Colin continued for him. 'Because, by then, he had buried the metal plate under the altar at the Beas river. Which means that he had already realised the purpose of his quest. So what's the second mystery? I'm guessing you found something there.'

Vijay grinned at him. 'The Makran adventure wasn't the only time Alexander divided his army up for no obvious reason. That was the second time he did it. The first time was here.' He showed them a town on the map. 'This is Jalalabad. From Jalalabad, he sent Hephaestion with one section of the army across the Khyber pass, into what is now Pakistan. The other part of the army was led personally by him, up this river valley and then to Pakistan through the Nawa Pass, which is further north from the Khyber pass.' He pulled out another map; this one was a map of Afghanistan. He showed them the two passes on the map. 'And get this – no one has been able to satisfactorily explain why Alexander headed north and then east. There are some authors and some websites who have provided a military explanation – saying that he had to protect his flank from the hill tribes. But the battles he fought to conquer the hill tribes were not fought in the Kunar valley. They were all fought here – on the Pakistan side of the present day border with Afghanistan. He could just as easily have crossed through the Khyber pass and then divided the army, sending one part east and another north to subdue the hill tribes. The final battle

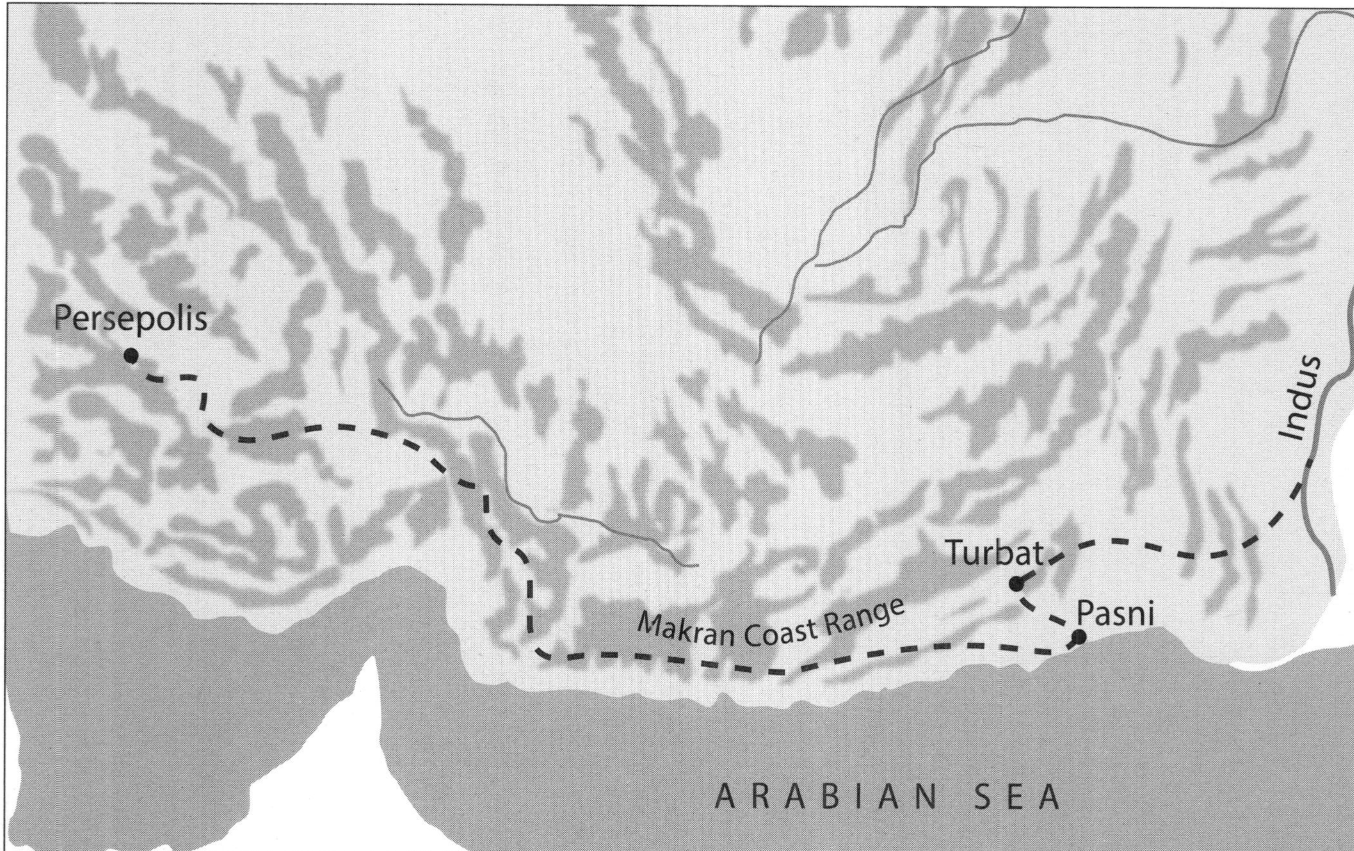
Persepolis
Indus
Turbat
Pasni
Makran Coast Range
ARABIAN SEA

with the hill tribes was fought at Pirsar, which the Greeks called Aornos. That is definitely in Pakistan and not in the Kunar valley. I'm not convinced by the military-motivated explanation of Alexander's movements.'

'The Kunar river valley,' Colin read out the name from the map. 'You think this is where the secret is hidden?'

'I don't get it.' Alice was still puzzled. 'It certainly sounds like Alexander had a reason to go to the Kunar valley and his quest could have provided that reason. But this is still speculation. What makes your explanation – our theory – more convincing than all the others?'

'This.' Vijay held up the translated journal of Eumenes. 'And the verses on the cube.' He turned to Shukla. 'Can you please translate the verses on the cube once more for us?'

Shukla nodded. He didn't know what Vijay had in mind but he did know one thing— Vijay thought this was important. At a time when his fiancée's life was in danger, Vijay would not go off on a tangent trying to solve a mystery like this if he did not think that it was useful in some way.

He picked up the cube and began reading the verses. Vijay shook his head as each verse was read, until Shukla had read out three verses. On the fourth verse, he nodded.

'That's it. That's the one.' Vijay looked at them. 'Do you see it now?'

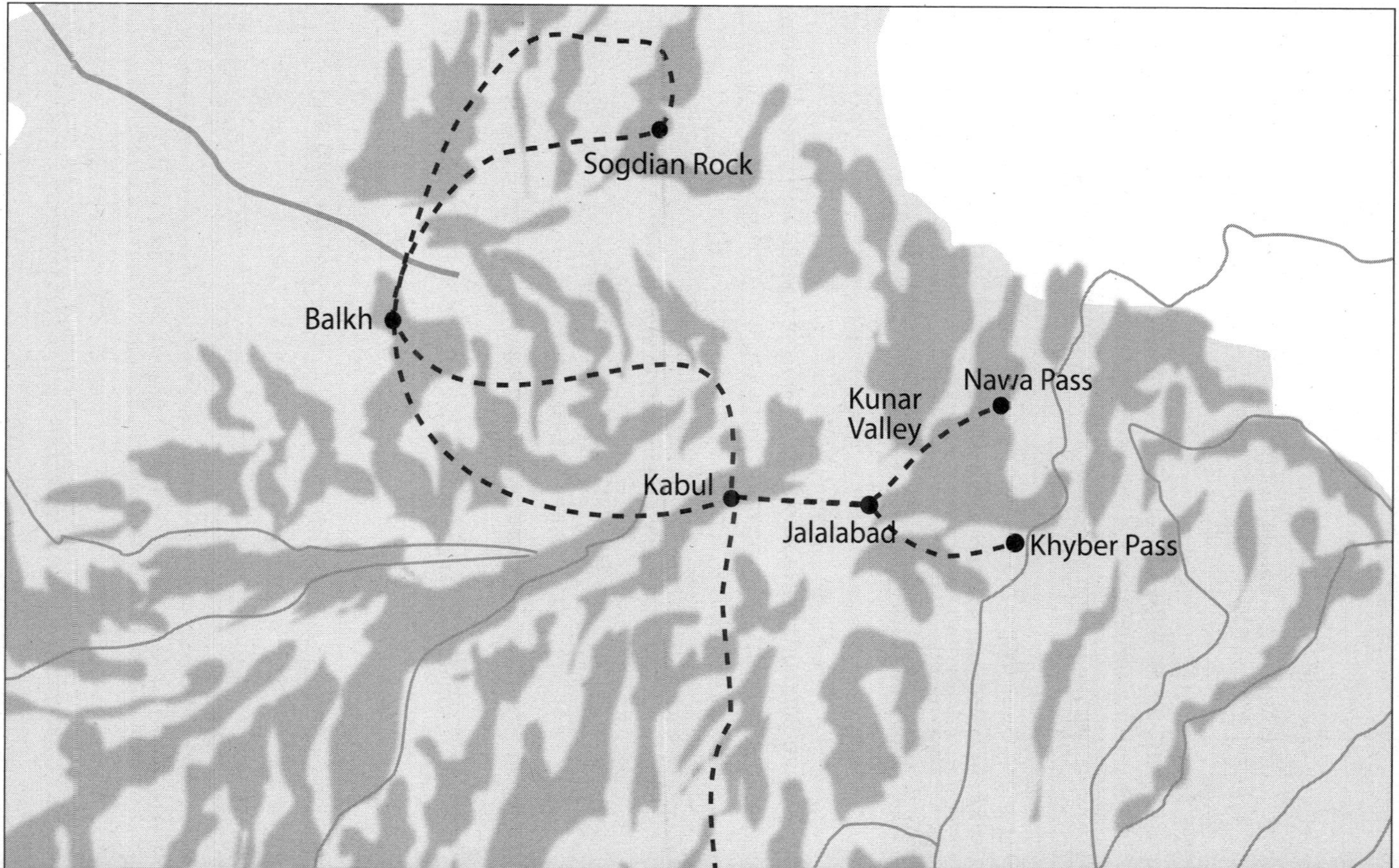

Sogdian Rock
Balkh
Kunar
Valley
Nava Pass
Kabul
Jalalabad
Khyber Pass

44

The first clue

The others stared blankly back at Vijay. They still did not understand. The verse that Shukla had just read out was:

'Then enter you the portal to
The valleys parting east and west
Choose wisely here, remember where
You march and where Surya lies.'

'Okay,' Vijay held up his hands. 'Granted it isn't that obvious. It isn't supposed to be. This was a secret quest, right? Protected by cryptic verses. Unless you know what you are looking for, you wouldn't be able to interpret any of the verses. That's how these puzzles work, right?'

'So we're looking for something that Alexander knew about,' Colin decided to give it a shot. 'If the parchment with these six verses was supposed to guide Alexander to the secret, then each of the verses should describe either one or more landmarks or locations.'

'Right,' Vijay beamed. 'I've had all night to think about this. It took me hours of thinking and research before it dawned on me.'

Colin snorted. 'Dawned on you, my ass! You were sleeping when I came up in the morning.'

Alice was studying the map closely. If what Vijay was saying was right, then there should be something on the map that fitted the description in the verse. Something that was a portal to two valleys.

It hit her like a ton of bricks. 'Jalalabad!' She looked at Vijay.

'Good work,' Vijay gave her a thumbs up sign. 'You can see on the map that Jalalabad is located at the entrance to two river valleys. One goes eastwards – that's the Kunar valley. The other goes westwards – that's the Laghman valley. Remember when we first heard the verses we all thought they seemed to be some sort of instructions or guide but we didn't know what they led to? Now we have the answer. The "portal" in the verse is Jalalabad. The verse is exhorting the reader to choose the valley in the east – where Surya or the sun lies. Radha was right.' Vijay fell silent as he mentioned Radha's name.

'And the valley to the east is the Kunar valley.' Colin nodded. 'It certainly fits together very well.'

'But what do the other verses mean?' Alice asked. 'They should also refer to locations on Alexander's route. But I can't think of any locations that match with any of the other verses.'

'Well one of them mentioned a rock which could be the Sogdian rock,' Vijay reminded her. 'If we all think hard enough and, perhaps, do a bit of research, I'm sure we can figure out the other locations. But the important thing is that the secret itself seems to lie in the Kunar valley.'

'I hate to be a wet blanket, but that is an assumption we are making.' Alice didn't look happy. 'We could be right but just because Alexander made a mysterious trip to the Kunar valley doesn't mean that he went looking for the secret there. It could have merely been one of the stops on the way and not the final destination. Without the metal plate, there is no way of saying in which order the verses should be read. And unless we know the order of the verses we really cannot say with certainty that this verse shows us the location of the secret.'

'That's where I thought you guys could lend a hand,' Vijay replied. 'I've printed out a whole lot of information based on my research. Maps, descriptions, Google Earth views – the works. If we agree that my logic makes sense until now, then perhaps if we all put our heads together we may come up with something.'

'How is this going to help Radha?' Shukla finally spoke up. While he had faith in Vijay and his judgment, he couldn't sit by quietly any more. His daughter was in deep trouble and here they were, researching an ancient puzzle. He had to reassure himself that their priorities were in order.

Vijay hesitated. He wasn't sure if he should explain. He didn't want to tell them about the call. How could he? But he realised he would have to. He owed them an explanation.

'I thought I could use this as a bargaining chip,' he said finally. 'Cooper called me last night. He wants the cube because it leads to the secret. If we can solve the riddle of the verses then I can exchange the information for Radha's safety. I hate to admit it but that's really our only hope to save Radha. If the IB hasn't been able to get a trace on her location yet, I don't know how we're going to be able to find her. Our only option is to get them to release her and this is the best way to do it.'

Shukla pondered this for a while. 'I guess you're right,' he conceded. 'Let's see if we can make any headway with this.'

They bent their thoughts to focus on the reams of information that Vijay had collated through the night. Would they be successful in finding the clues that would help them discover the information Cooper was seeking?

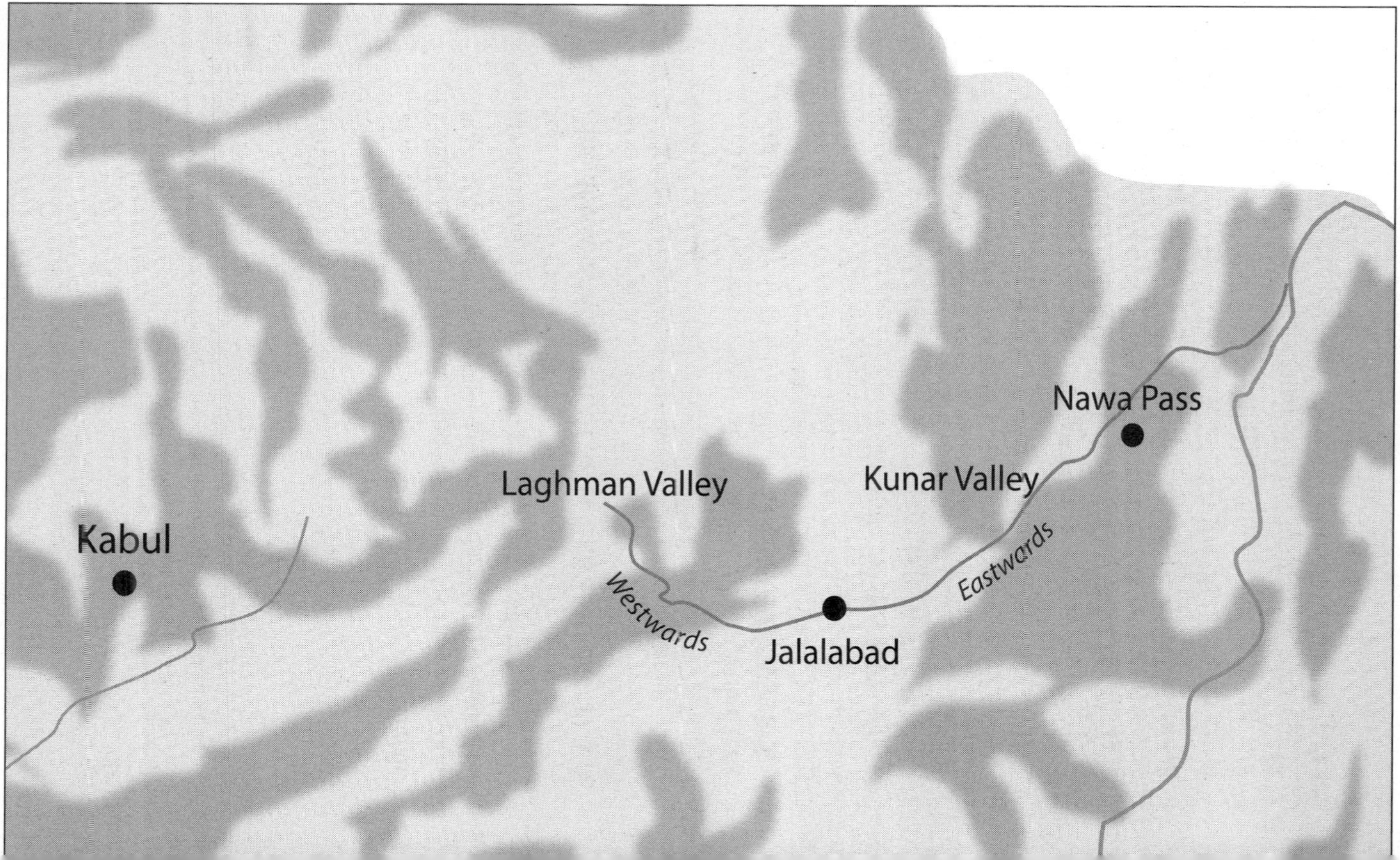
Kabul
Laghman Valley
Westwards
Jalalabad
Kunar Valley
Eastwards
Nawa Pass

45

A counter offer

Cooper looked at his watch. 12 noon. Time to call Vijay Singh. He dialled Vijay's number and listened as the phone rang without being picked up. He frowned. It didn't make sense. The man's fiancée was his prisoner. He had expected the call to be picked up with greater alacrity.

He disconnected and tried again. This time the call was picked up promptly.

'Cooper?' There was a strained edge to Vijay's voice which pleased Cooper.

'Well?' Cooper came straight to the point. 'What have you decided? Your fiancée or your ex-girlfriend. Which one will it be?'

'I have a counter offer.' Vijay's voice was stronger now, though the undercurrent of tension still percolated through.

Cooper raised his eyebrows. This was interesting. He had not anticipated this. He decided to see where this was going.

'Go on,' he commanded.

'Your primary interest is not Alice or Radha,' Vijay began. 'You want the location of the secret that Alexander the Great went searching for in the land of the Indus.' Vijay paused. 'And I can help you find that location.'

Cooper was taken aback. He recalled what Van Klueck had told him about this man and his friends. His respect for Vijay went up a couple of notches. But it also told him one thing — the man desperately wanted his fiancée back but he was also trying to protect his former girlfriend. If he had taken the trouble to invest time and effort and analyse the few clues available to him to come up with the right answer it was clear that Vijay Singh took his relationships very seriously.

It also meant, Cooper reflected, that Saxena would need to find out if Radha and her IB colleagues knew about the objective of the mission. Had Vijay Singh worked this out after she was kidnapped? Or had they known this all along? He knew it was impossible for anyone to have suspected the true nature of the secret that they were trying to unearth. That was something that only the Order would know. But this was a project that had been kept secret for decades. He could not allow the mission to be compromised any more than it already was, especially now that they were so close to fruition.

Cooper realised he had already taken too long to respond. Vijay was smart enough to have understood that he had touched the right nerve. But there was a way to turn this to his advantage. He still held a trump card.

'And just how can you help us find the location?' There was no point in denying or pretending not to understand what Vijay had just said.

There was a distinct note of triumph in Vijay's voice as he answered. 'We've deciphered one of the verses on the cube. You couldn't have done it by yourself anyway. We can decipher all five verses and tell you exactly where the secret is located.'

'That's where you are wrong,' Cooper shot back. 'We have the metal plate that Alexander buried near the Beas. With the cube and the metal plate together, it will be child's play to decipher the verses. Why do we need you?'

'Think about it. We've managed to decipher the verse without using Alexander's metal plaque. We have resources that you don't — Alice, for one and Dr Shukla for another. We can give you the answers faster than you'd get them yourself.'

Cooper considered this. There was some merit in Vijay's assertion. He had no doubt that his team would crack the verses, using the vast resources of the Order. But if he could get this done faster using Vijay's team it wouldn't hurt. And if they tried to pass on information to the IB, he would have them all eliminated. Van Klueck had anyway handed him a blank cheque on this matter.

'How do I know you are not bluffing?'

He listened intently as Vijay explained the meaning of the verse and how they had arrived at their conclusion.

Cooper made up his mind. 'Your terms?' He knew what they were but he didn't want to sound like he was caving in too easily.

'You will stop pursuing Alice and you will release Radha.'

Cooper grinned. He had been right about Vijay. He had to give it to the man. Full marks for perseverance and determination even in the face of insurmountable odds. 'Accepted but with two conditions. First, you and your team will meet me at the international airport this evening at 4 pm sharp. We will all travel together to Jalalabad tonight. We will journey to the Kunar valley tomorrow. Second, Radha stays in my custody until I have verified your claims. If you play dirty, she will be injected with the same cocktail that you know was found in the blood of the patients at the medical facility.'

There was a moment's silence as Vijay tried to control his anger at the blatant threat. 'I don't have a choice. But only I will come with you. The others will stay back here. And how do I know that you'll keep your end of the deal?'

Cooper considered this. If they were right about the location, he didn't want everyone in on the secret. He didn't really need all of them to go all the way to the Kunar valley. He had suggested that only because it gave him the opportunity to eliminate the lot of them in one fell swoop, out of their country, where no one would be the wiser. The plan would work just as well if Vijay accompanied him and the others stayed back. They could stay in touch using the satellite phones that they would anyway need in Afghanistan. Vijay would do. In any case, he believed that Vijay and his friends were harmless. It was Radha who was connected with the IB, not them. He would make certain that the others would be watched to ensure that they didn't go anywhere. He would arrange for that right after this call.

His response was curt. 'You don't. But, as you've just said, you don't have a choice. I'll see you at 4 pm sharp. Don't be late.'

46

The gamble

Vijay disconnected the call and slowly made his way back to the study. He had excused himself and rushed out to take Cooper's call in the sitting room below. He had not wanted the others, especially Alice, to hear the conversation. Vijay mulled over how he would break the news to the others. And he also wondered if, in his desperation to save Radha, he had only succeeded in getting them deeper into the clutches of Cooper and company. The only saving grace was that he would go by himself with Cooper. The others would be safe, here, in Jaungarh.

As he entered the study, he saw curiosity on the faces of the others. He knew they were wondering why he had dashed out of the study to take the call.

'It was Cooper,' Vijay was thinking every word through as he spoke. 'He had said he would call at 12 noon. We've struck a deal.' He explained his offer to Cooper, leaving out the part about Cooper's follow up on Vijay's decision regarding Alice and Radha.

There was consternation on their faces when he finished. Colin was the first to speak, almost before Vijay finished. 'Are you nuts? Going by yourself with this bunch of...of...I don't know who they are but they are dangerous! Haven't we seen enough to know that by now?'

Alice nodded. 'I don't know what you were thinking, Vijay. After what they did in Greece and their attack on us at the museum, how could you?'

Vijay was silent. How could he tell them that this was the only way out of his dilemma? How could he disclose the agonising decision he had faced, trying to balance the fates of Radha and Alice?'This was the only way to save Radha,' he said instead. 'You guys will stay out of this. Especially you, Alice. I want you all to keep working on the verses while I am with them. Any breakthroughs, let me know immediately. The faster we can solve this riddle the faster we can get Radha back.'

'You're not going alone,' Colin stood up and walked to Vijay, looking him in the eye. 'We're buddies. We do stuff together. I'm coming with you.'

Vijay knew better than to argue. And, if he was honest with himself, he knew he would be glad for Colin's company. But he had made up his mind about this. He sighed. 'I'm sorry buddy,' he said. You're going to sit out this game with the others. And I'm not open to discussion.'

Colin opened his mouth to reply but Vijay's phone rang again. It was Vaid.

'I'm sorry but we have no fresh leads on Radha,' Vaid updated him. 'We're still looking. These guys seem to be professionals. They've been operating under our radar all this time and they are experts at covering their tracks. But we'll pick up their scent sooner or later.'

'I hope so,' Vijay replied. 'I have some news for you.' He told Vaid about his deal with Cooper.

There was a guarded pause before Vaid responded. 'You're taking a big risk,' he told Vijay. 'A very big risk. You know that they won't release Radha that easily. And you are all at risk anyway. They know that all of you, including Radha, are linked to the IB. If, as we suspect, there is a bioterrorism angle to this then you pose a threat to them.'

'I don't think so,' Vijay replied. 'I think they believe that only Radha is connected to the IB. They probably attribute Imran's presence at the fort to the fact that he's connected to her and that she is my fiancée. Otherwise they would surely have made us targets as well. Even at the museum, Alice was their real target. If we hadn't been there with her, they would have left us alone.'

'I think you had better come to the office,' Vaid replied. 'We should brief Patterson. He's the head of the task force. He needs to know what's happening. And I don't think he's going to be happy that you've taken this decision without consulting him first.'

'I'll come over right away,' Vijay promised. 'I can go to the airport from there.'

'You may wish to detour to the hospital before that.' There was a note of cheer in Vaid's voice. 'Imran's out of danger. He's conscious and wants to meet you.'

Vijay put his phone away and looked at Colin, whose annoyance was writ large on his face. 'Cheer up, son,' he said. 'You're needed here.' He grinned, trying to lighten the situation. 'You claim to have more brains than I do. Well prove it, then. Help Alice and Dr Shukla work out this riddle. That's the best way you can support me.'

Colin didn't respond immediately. He was trying to come to terms with Vijay's decision. He knew his friend. Having made up his mind, there was no force on earth that could shake him. He knew he had to accept Vijay's departure without him. Finally, he nodded. 'I can't say I'm happy about this. But if this is what you want...' He paused and then embraced his friend. 'Watch your back, buddy. I won't be there to do it for you.'

Vijay nodded to the others and left the study. He knew this was a gamble. Would it pay off?

Intelligence Bureau Headquarters, New Delhi

Vijay and Vaid gazed at the image of Patterson on the monitor in the conference room. The African American's usually grim countenance was even more deeply lined today with traces of annoyance at having been woken up in the middle of the night.

'This had better be important,' he warned the two men sitting in the conference room. 'I have a meeting with the President tomorrow and I don't have too many hours of sleep left. I had just hit the sack when you guys called.'

Vaid swiftly outlined the events of the day as told to him by Vijay. As he spoke, Patterson's visage grew darker and his eyes glinted with anger. He was a man given to hard discipline as a Navy Seal and despised people who did not follow rules.

Patterson glowered at Vijay as Vaid concluded his report but didn't speak immediately. He seemed to be contemplating the information he had just been offered.

'First things first,' Patterson said after a few moments. 'I owe Kidwai an apology. He was right. There is a connection of some sort between Titan Pharmaceuticals and the events in Greece. We need to dig deeper and I'll get cracking on that in the morning. But we need to be discreet. Either Wallace himself is involved. And if he is not involved we need to be careful whom we speak to and what we disclose. This is a sensitive matter. Wallace is close to Congressmen, Senators and even the President. We can't go assuming anything.'

Vijay and Vaid nodded. They waited for Patterson to continue.

'Next,' Patterson fixed Vijay with a piercing gaze. 'Much as I admire your ability to solve riddles and puzzles, you don't have the authority to go negotiating with terrorists. Or the experience. You seem to have forgotten that you are a member of the task force. And I decide who does what in this task force. Not you. You can't go running around taking decisions like this on your own.'

He paused, as if weighing his next words. 'But now that you have,' he continued, 'we don't have much choice in the matter. But I want you to understand this. If you've done this for your woman, then you're a fool. A hopeless, optimistic fool. Your woman's dead. Sure, she may be alive now, but if you think they are going to release her once you hand over this secret to them on a silver platter, then you need to think again. You're dead and she's dead. Both of you. So, if you're doing this, it isn't for her. It is for the task force. You're doing this to ensure that whatever lies in the cavern in Afghanistan or wherever it is located, doesn't pose a threat to the world. That's what this task force was set up for. And that is your responsibility. Is that clear?'

Vijay swallowed. The truth in Patterson's words rang home. His entire being was fighting against the logic Patterson had presented but deep down he knew that the leader of the task force was right.

He fought back the tears as he replied. 'Got it. Loud and clear.'

'Now,' Patterson resumed, 'if this great secret has anything to do with bioterrorism, we can't just stand by and allow these people to get away with it. For Christ's sake, we don't even know who they are!'

'So what do you propose?' Vaid realised what Patterson meant.

'You go ahead with your deal,' Patterson instructed Vijay. 'We'll cover your back from here.'

Vijay looked puzzled. 'How are you going to do that? You don't even know where Radha is being held.'

'Listen carefully.' Patterson lowered his voice and told them. When he had finished, he fixed Vijay with a stern gaze. 'Be careful out there, boy. We don't work miracles. I almost lost a member of the task force this last week. I don't want to lose two more now.'

47

Jalalabad, Afghanistan

Vijay sat with Cooper in the Land Rover as it jolted across the streets of Jalalabad. When he had reached the airport at New Delhi, he had been hustled to a waiting Gulfstream G550 jet. They had flown from Delhi to Kabul, a flight that had taken 90 minutes, accompanied by five members of Cooper's team — burly, muscled men with scars to prove their mettle — who were all armed.

As the aircraft landed in Kabul, Vijay noticed another private jet parked on the tarmac. It was a Gulfstream 650ER, a long range jet. He wondered who it belonged to. Cooper had told him that they couldn't fly direct to Jalalabad as the airport was being used for military purposes and, at times, for United Nations aircraft. There were two wide-bodied aircraft belonging to commercial airlines, but were no other small planes around.

After clearing immigration, they had boarded a Land Rover for the 90 minute drive to Jalalabad. Vijay had not bargained for the ride he eventually got. The road itself was smooth and well-paved, having been resurfaced in 2006 by a European Union backed project. But the quality of the road only seemed to encourage Afghan drivers to challenge the contours of the landscape that the road passed through.

While he could not help but admire the bewitching scenery of the Kabul gorge, through which the road passed, more than 2000 feet above the Kabul river, death and danger dogged them the entire journey. The highway itself had only two lanes, barely wide enough to accommodate two cars abreast of each other.

On the inner lane, a bleak cliff towered above the road, almost perpendicular in its incline. The outer lane was protected by a ledge barely a foot high, beyond which lay empty space and a steep drop to the valley floor below.

Ancient Ladas — survivors of the Soviet era — rickety buses and battered Toyota taxis competed for speed and space on the road as if trying to get the most out of the drive while the road lasted; before it disintegrated once again into the potholed chain of craters that it had been after the Soviet invasion. The local cars whizzed past the Land Rover, around hairpin bends and sharp turns, passing within millimetres of each other, weaving through the traffic at top speed. The only vehicles that seemed incongruously slow were the tractor trailers carrying their burden of cargo, lumbering along the road as if time did not matter to them, in sharp contrast to the rest of the traffic.

Twice on the journey, Vijay saw evidence of the disasters that occurred daily on this highway. The first was the sight of the twisted remains of a car at the bottom of a ravine. The second was a head on crash between a container truck and a sedan. Clearly, the luckless sedan driver had not been able to whip back into his lane in time and had rammed, at high speed, into the truck. The accident caused a bottleneck on the highway and traffic crawled slowly around the mangled remains of the car and the immense bulk of the truck.

Finally, though, they had made it to Jalalabad and they were now headed to a rendezvous with their local escort who would accompany them to the Kunar valley in the morning.

The Land Rover drew up at a decrepit building, its plaster peeling and window shutters broken. It was clearly in need of maintenance and repairs. But it seemed that comfort and luxury were not priorities for these people. For the millionth time, Vijay wondered who these people were that Cooper was working for.

As they walked into the hall that occupied almost the entire ground floor of the two-storeyed building, Vijay got part of his answer. Seated on a moth-eaten, cloth upholstered sofa, that may have been a light yellow at some point in time, was a tall, distinguished looking man with a high forehead, aquiline nose and silver grey hair. His grey eyes framed by rimless spectacles seemed to size Vijay up as he entered.

On the table before him was the metal plate that Vijay had seen at the National Museum – the one that had been buried by Alexander at the base of Zeus' altar near the Beas river.

'Evening, Christian,' Cooper nodded to the man, who nodded back without smiling.

Even without speaking, the stranger conveyed a sense of authority and unbridled power. Vijay didn't know who he was, but this was undoubtedly Cooper's boss. The man behind this entire project.

He didn't know whether the stranger's presence here was good or bad. But he hoped that he would at least get some answers to the myriad questions that had plagued them so far.

'At last,' the tall man gazed upon Vijay, his grey eyes appraising him thoughtfully. He gestured to another sofa, equally battered, that stood nearby. Vijay sat down.

'My name is Christian Van Klueck,' the stranger introduced himself. 'You have not heard of me, no?'

Vijay shook his head. The name didn't ring a bell.

'It doesn't matter. I know who you are,' Van Klueck continued. He looked at Cooper. 'Good job, Cooper. Always reliable. Will you organise the men for our expedition tomorrow, while I catch up with this gentleman?'

Cooper nodded and strode off as Van Klueck turned back to Vijay, who realised that the Gulfstream jet he had seen at Kabul airport must belong to this man. Who was he? The man had a strong European accent. Probably from Germany or Austria. Someone very wealthy no doubt. And how did he know Vijay?

'You have been a thorn in our side,' Van Klueck told Vijay. Despite the nature of the statement, he didn't look upset or annoyed. 'I lost a good friend last year because of you. And the Order lost a dedicated member.' He shook his head. 'I would not forget you in a thousand years.' Again, there was no obvious malice in his tone or expression. Which made his words all the more chilling.

A cold fear crept up Vijay's spine as he heard these words.

'It doesn't matter now,' Van Klueck continued. 'That's all in the past and I don't believe in living in the past. The future awaits us. And we must focus on what lies ahead. There is so much to be gained. Of course, the past is important, no?' His gaze pierced Vijay. 'We must learn from the past and build on it to secure our future.'

Vijay had no idea what the man was talking about. To him it sounded like a lot of babble. But this man before him didn't seem to be capable of babbling. He struck Vijay as a man of precision, planning and calculated moves. Nothing impulsive.

'Cooper told me you had deciphered one of the verses,' Van Klueck continued, oblivious to Vijay's bewilderment. 'So what lies in the Kunar valley?' He leaned forward and looked into Vijay's eyes. 'Tell me.'

For the first time in this conversation, the European had referred to something that was familiar to Vijay. But even now, Vijay did not have a ready answer.

'I don't know,' he shrugged in response. 'The verse only seemed to describe the location of Jalalabad. The location of the Kunar valley was a deduction based on Alexander's route in this region.' He explained how they had concluded that there was a strong possibility that the secret lay in the Kunar valley.

Van Klueck contemplated Vijay's words. 'So you don't

know the exact location. But you do believe that this is where our search ends.'

Vijay hesitated before answering. This was the opening he had been looking for. 'It will help if I know exactly what you are looking for. Right now, we're trying to interpret the verses without knowing what they lead to. Alexander knew. If we knew, we'd probably be able to decipher the verses much faster.' He held Van Klueck's gaze with the defiance of a man who had nothing to lose. Patterson had told him that he and Radha were doomed. And if he was going to die anyway, he would get his answers before that.

Van Klueck looked thoughtful. He hadn't expected this kind of spunk from Vijay. Finally, he nodded and smiled; a cold smile that didn't reach his eyes. 'Perhaps you are right. Maybe if you know a little bit more, you could be of more use.'

Vijay waited as the European seemed to weigh in his mind what he should reveal and what should remain secret.

48

The truth about Alexander

'I think you have already figured out part of the truth about Alexander the Great,' Van Klueck said finally. 'In reality much of what we know about his life is based on facts that have been distorted, on many occasions, to reflect the inclination, philosophy or the motives of the person writing the record. As a result, it has become very difficult for us to work out exactly what is historically accurate about the man and what is glorified fiction.'

He waited for Vijay to acknowledge his remarks. After Vijay had nodded, he continued. 'And that is where artefacts like the cube are useful. They help us validate parts of the story that could be passed off as just another fantastical rendering of Alexander's exploits by an ardent admirer or sycophant.'

Vijay nodded again, remembering Alice's objections to their analysis. There was so much fluff in the records about Alexander that it was difficult to believe everything written about him.

Van Klueck held out his hand. 'The cube please.'

Vijay handed the cube to him and watched as he fitted it into the metal plate. It was a perfect fit.

'So how do *you* know which parts of the Alexander story are correct and which ones are fantasy?' Vijay was curious. What was the source of this man's knowledge and power?

'Wouldn't you like to know?' Van Klueck smirked. 'But I'll tell you something. Olympias was a member of our Order. And she knew about this cube because it was created by one of the first members of our Order. Thousands of years ago.'

Vijay was stunned. If what Van Klueck was saying was true, then the Order, whatever it was, was far more ancient than the brotherhood formed by Asoka the Great, which they had discovered last year.

Van Klueck appeared pleased to see the shock on Vijay's face. 'That's how we know that Alexander's quest in the land of the Indus was not some yarn spun by his spin doctors. We were the ones who provided him with the means of finding what he wanted.'

Vijay found a weak link in this suggestion. 'That doesn't make sense,' he shot back. 'Today, you're looking for the secret that he found. But if you had the means to find it two thousand four hundred years ago or more, as you claim, why didn't you find the secret then? Why hand it to Alexander on a platter, allow him to hide the metal plate, and then go looking for it more than two thousand years later?'

Van Klueck's face darkened. 'That's because Olympias tricked us. This secret has been protected for thousands of years before Alexander. Remember, this is the secret of the gods. The gods of the land of the Indus. The cube and the metal plate were created for the express purpose of ensuring that the secret would remain protected. And a small brotherhood of Vedic priests was created to guard over the secret. They were the only ones who had access to it. Olympias invited one of the priests to her court on the pretext of understanding more about the origins of the Order. And, somehow, she persuaded the priest to part with the location of the secret. For that transgression, the Order withdrew all protection to her after Alexander's death. She would never have suffered such a humiliating death if the Order had continued to protect her.'

'What is this Order that you belong to?' Vijay opened another line of questioning.

Van Klueck shook his head. 'I have told you enough already.

Know only that we are as old as mankind itself. There was a time when we were known and feared throughout the world. But we decided that our influence and power was better obtained by staying out of sight and out of the minds of humanity.'

He paused before continuing. 'Anyway, Alexander found the secret but things went horribly wrong and he died. You know the history. His funeral cortege was hijacked by Ptolemy and his mummy was buried in Alexandria, where it lay until the fourth century.'

'Which is when it mysteriously disappeared,' Vijay murmured, remembering his research.

'It didn't disappear,' Van Klueck assured him smugly. 'Christianity was spreading through the world. We saw the signs. Anything that was related to the pagan gods was being destroyed. And Alexander was worshipped as a god. Before long, his mausoleum would have been desecrated and his mummy destroyed. So we took matters into our own hands. We spirited the mummy away from its burial place in Alexandria and buried it in another, secret, location. No one was supposed to know about the burial place. However, unknown to the Order at that time, a map had been created. A map that was hidden away for all these centuries. Until we rediscovered it, quite by accident, a few decades ago. We excavated the mummy. Which turned out to be quite a boon for us. Over the centuries, the story behind the secret he discovered had turned into a myth. We scarcely believed it was possible. So, we tested the mummy. And we discovered that the myth was true. The secret of the gods was no myth after all. And Alexander had, indeed, discovered it. That is when we decided that we needed to find the secret. But we were missing the cube and the metal plate. We knew that the last time they had been seen was with the priest who met with Olympias. But he disappeared after his meeting with her and no one ever knew what happened to him.

When we heard about the possibility of the tomb of Olympias being discovered, we realised that there was a chance that the cube and metal plate would be found within it, buried with her.'

'So you got Cooper to join the excavation and got Stavros on your side to recover the artefacts.'

'Exactly. So now you know.'

Vijay frowned. 'This certainly plugs gaps in the information we had and explains what's been happening. I can even begin to guess at the links between the excavation and the clinical trials you have been conducting. The tests you ran on Alexander's mummy... they threw up results that needed the clinical trials to validate them, right?'

Van Klueck smiled again. 'Close. But only partially correct. The trials were necessary because the tests we ran on Alexander's mummy threw up a discovery that we were unprepared for. You see, the cube was created based on a myth from your great epic, the Mahabharata. There is a story in that epic that vividly describes what Alexander found and also explains the tests that we ran on him. In order to understand the results of those tests, we needed to run the clinical trials on living people.'

Vijay racked his brains, trying to think of a myth from the Mahabharata that would have led to clinical trials and a discovery based on medical tests conducted on the corpse of a man dead for over two thousand years. But he couldn't think of anything.

'I don't know what you're referring to,' he said finally.

'It is the myth called, "The Churning of the Ocean", in English. Or, more accurately, *Samudramanthan*.' Van Klueck's pronunciation of the Sanskrit word was perfect but Vijay barely noticed. His entire attention was taken up by the mention of one of the most famous myths from the epic.

'But... how?' he was confused. 'That myth is pure fantasy — the churning of the ocean using a mountain and Vasuki as the rope to obtain *amrita*. There's no science behind it.'

Van Klueck smiled sympathetically. 'Everyone is so accustomed to treating the Mahabharata as an epic poem or as a fantasy story, that they find it difficult to believe that there could be great science embedded in it.'

Vijay waited, trying to contain his excitement. He now knew that he was on the cusp of learning about another secret that the Mahabharata had held deep within for over two thousand years.

'Let me explain it to you.' Van Klueck leaned forward and began.

49

DAY FIVE
A glimpse into a mystery

Radha blinked in surprise at the unexpected sight of Saxena smiling at her. He had walked into her cell unannounced and told her that he would take her for a walk around the medical centre.

'I've been asked to take good care of you,' he explained to her, amiably. 'Apparently, Cooper's move in bringing you here has paid off big time. It looks like we'll be able to advance our deadlines for his part of the project. Which means that my part gets done faster as well.'

Radha ruminated over his words as he led her out of the cell and through a maze of corridors which she had never been through before. But all thoughts were banished from her mind as they emerged on a long balcony surrounding a rectangular atrium. The roof bore powerful lights that combined with the lamps on the balconies to light up the immense space. The balcony continued without a break on all four sides of the atrium. She counted eight storeys to the building.

Radha considered the immensity of the building with awe. Her movements had been restricted within a corridor leading from her cell to the toilet block. While she had seen other inmates in this prison in the communal toilets and bathrooms, she had never imagined that the building could be of this size.

'Two hundred and fifty cells,' Saxena informed her as he noticed her gaping. 'Eight floors of this facility are underground — the ones that you see before you. Two floors are above the ground. From the outside it appears to be a low rise, nondescript building. No one knows what we have in here.'

'Who is Cooper?' Radha asked, having got over her initial surprise.

'You don't know? I thought the American archaeologist would have told you. He was the co-director on her excavation project. Peter Cooper. He was planted there by us.'

This was another shock for Radha. So there was a connection between these people and Alice's experience in Greece. But what was it? And who was "us"?

A thought struck her. She recalled her conversation with Vijay when the others were enroute to the museum. He had told her about Eumenes' journal and the description of Alexander's quest for the "secret of the gods". Was that the connection between Saxena's operation and the excavations in Greece?

'So you're trying to figure out the secret that is mentioned in the riddles on the cube?' She voiced her thoughts, without mentioning the journal. If it was secret, then she didn't want Saxena knowing about it.

Saxena looked at Radha, appraising her. 'You do know more than you let on. And you're right. I am working on the greatest secret that the world has ever seen. One that will enable the Order to rule the world without anyone even realising it. We will pull the strings and people will dance like puppets at our beck and call.'

Radha was intrigued. She had to know more. What was Saxena ranting about? She decided to call his bluff. 'So you say,' she scoffed. 'All I see here are clinical trials that end in people dying. Everyone dies. What's the big secret in that? Is the Order going to rule a world of dead people? Is this a new pathogen that you've discovered that will wipe out the world's population, leaving the Order intact? Who will you rule if there's no one left?'

Saxena glared at her. 'We aren't going to kill people,' he said emphatically. 'We will give life, not take it away.'

Radha looked at him, her expression clearly indicating her disbelief. 'You want to believe you are important in the scheme of the Order. But all you're doing is conducting clinical trials that are resulting in failure.'

Saxena's face revealed his fury at her words. He was immensely proud of what he was trying to achieve. He was very close to success. He longed for the recognition that was deservedly his. The Order would not be forthcoming with any recognition until the mission was over. But he had achieved so much! And here was a woman, who knew nothing of what he was doing, disparaging his achievements! He could restrain himself no longer.

'You don't believe what I say?' he challenged Radha. 'You think this is all about a pathetic virus and clinical trials that are going nowhere? You...'

Radha interrupted him. 'I think you are blowing up your little mission into something much bigger. Something that is important. But it isn't. I don't believe a word you say.'

'Fine, then,' Saxena fumed, his compulsion for recognition and admiration getting the better of him. This woman wasn't going anywhere. And there was no way anyone would ever find her. 'Come with me. I'll prove it to you.'

He led the way to a set of elevators and pressed his access card against the card reader as he punched the button for the lowest level of the building. The high speed elevator descended with startling swiftness and they soon reached their destination.

Saxena briefly told her about the Order and how Olympias had obtained the cube and persuaded Alexander to extend his ambitions beyond conquering the Persian empire. The elevator doors opened to reveal a long, white corridor lined with doors on either side. Most were shut but some were open to reveal laboratories stacked with all kinds of equipment and devices, servers and monitors, and manned by technicians in white laboratory coats.

'This is the nerve centre of our operations here for my mission,' Saxena explained. 'Freeman's project occupies the two floors below us.' He led Radha into an office at the end of the corridor. It was furnished with a large desk and a leather chair in one corner of the room, with a stainless steel workstation attached to the opposite wall. A tall bookcase stood to one side of the desk, the shelves sagging under the weight of enormous medical tomes. On the desk was an LCD monitor, a keyboard and mouse.

'Sit down.' Saxena indicated one of the two chairs facing him across the desk as he sat on the leather chair.

Radha sat and watched Saxena fiddle with the computer keyboard and mouse.

After a while, the virologist swivelled the monitor to face her. His demeanour was that of a scientific expert about to deliver a presentation to an awestruck audience.

'You folks believed that we were manipulating pathogens for bioterrorism,' he smirked. 'That's about as far from the truth as you can possibly get. The reality is just the opposite. We don't want to kill people. We want to protect them from disease.'

'You really expect me to believe that,' Radha scoffed. 'After all the mayhem you and your people have caused, now you want me to attribute all of that to a noble cause?'

'Tch, tch,' Saxena reprimanded her. 'Every coin has two sides. You saw just one side. All that we've done, not just in the last few days but in the past decades, was essential to our success. We're on the cusp of a major scientific breakthrough; one that even modern technology has not yet been able to deliver. Yet, the secret behind this revolution in medicine has been with us for thousands of years, hidden behind a veil of riddles and myths. A veil that most people don't even know exists, leave alone being able to penetrate it.'

'I have no idea what you are talking about,' Radha confessed.

'You do read the newspapers?'

Radha shot a dark glance at Saxena but the virologist was asking the question in earnest. 'Of course, I do,' she replied.

'Very well, then, you must have read about a major issue facing the medical world today. It has been a concern that has been building for years but the media have only recently got hold of it. For years now, people have been misusing and overusing antibiotics. The result? Bacteria have evolved and built resistance to many drugs used to combat some of the deadliest diseases known to humanity. Some of these strains have even become resistant to multiple drugs. There is a very real threat that the antibiotics that have shielded mankind from life-threatening diseases ever since the discovery of penicillin will very soon be obsolete. The shield that protected us from killer diseases like tuberculosis, for example, is weakening and will soon be gone. We will be in the prehistoric ages, medically speaking; we will find ourselves in the dark ages when deadly bacterial infections were untreatable.'

Radha nodded. There had been a lot of coverage in the international media over this issue. New technologies were being researched and new breakthroughs were being sought to combat this frightening future scenario. She began to understand the motives of this group, whoever they were. 'So the clinical trials are aimed at finding that elusive breakthrough that will replace antibiotics?' She still didn't quite understand how Saxena intended combating the threat he had mentioned.

Saxena tapped a button on the keyboard next to him and a three dimensional image appeared on the screen, spinning slowly. It was an icosahedron — a twenty-sided polygon. He tapped another button and the screen split. To the right of the first image, another one appeared, also three dimensional, of irregularly shaped disks.

'The figure on the left is a retrovirus,' Saxena explained, indicating the first image.'And the one on the right is a bacterium.' He paused. 'Both are previously unknown pathogens. We obtained both from the body of Alexander the Great.'

50

328 BC
Balkh, present day Afghanistan

'What is troubling you, my dear Callisthenes?' Alexander beamed at the historian. 'Things are going the way they should. My plan is working. We have conquered Persia. Subdued the tribes of Bactria. Even vanquished the mighty Sogdian rock.' He put an arm around Callisthenes. 'And you, my dear historian; you have accomplished the great mission I sent you upon. The greatest mission of all. The one that will make me a god!' The young conqueror slid his arm off the historian's shoulders and looked at him. 'You are troubled. Of that I have no doubt. Tell me why. I must know.'

Callisthenes held Alexander's gaze but hesitated. The fate of Clitus was fresh in his mind. This was not the Alexander with whom he had set forth from Macedonia to conquer the Persian empire. That had been a young man who had decided to build upon his father's dreams and conquests. Who had the audacity and the courage to take on the mightiest empire in the world. And who had the charisma to get his troops to follow him through intense cold and starvation, and fight fatigue and thirst across thousands of miles. For *that* Alexander, Callisthenes would have willingly forfeited his life.

But the Alexander who stood before him today was different. Was it his success that had made him arrogant? First the fall of Darius, then the capture of Bessus — the murderer of Darius and claimant to the Persian throne — and finally, the conquest of the Sogdian rock and, with it, sovereignty over the

Bactrian tribes... This was enough to turn the mind of a mature man. And Alexander was still young.

Or was it the secret mission that Alexander had harboured ever since he left Macedonia? Callisthenes hadn't known about it until a few months ago, when Alexander briefed him on the assignment in the Bactrian forests and across the Oxus river. When Bessus had decided to flee across the Hindu Kush and take refuge in Bactria, this had provided Alexander with the perfect opportunity to march the entire army across the mountains and into Bactria.

With all the fighting that happened, including the first ever defeat Alexander suffered since he set off on his journey of conquest, no one had noticed Callisthenes leave the camp and disappear for days on end. Events had conspired to work in Alexander's favour.

Maybe he truly was the son of Zeus and his divine father was looking out for him. But Callisthenes felt that still did not give Alexander the right to act the way he did.

'Sire,' he began cautiously, 'you are a changed man.'

'Indeed I am,' Alexander slapped the historian's back cheerfully. As was usual nowadays, the conqueror had drunk a lot of wine and was in an exuberant mood.

And Callisthenes had seen how swiftly that mood could change to one that was dark and vengeful.

'Maybe we should talk about this some other time,' he suggested, not wanting to arouse Alexander's ire. There was no way he could provide his king with a truthful answer without annoying him.

And Callisthenes did not lie to his king. He might have overreached in his writings about the conqueror and woven fact with fantasy, all the more to increase the glory of his king. But to his king he would be honest. That was his way.

Alexander looked him in the eye. 'So,' the conqueror rubbed his chin thoughtfully. 'My historian has something to say. Something that he feels I will not like.'

Callisthenes hated it when Alexander was this perceptive, which was very often. He said nothing.

'Come on, Callisthenes,' Alexander urged. 'Do you think I have drunk too much wine? That I cannot hear what you have to say? You are my respected historian. Why, no one else has my ear the way you do! Speak up, man, and tell me what is troubling you! Come, I promise you that I will hear you out.'

Callisthenes realised that he was cornered. Any further attempt at postponing this conversation would imply an answer in the positive to all the negative thoughts Alexander had in his mind.

'Very well, my King,' Callisthenes took a deep breath. 'It is your announcement that worries me. That you wish to be worshipped as a God using the Persian rituals.'

Alexander laughed, his laughter echoing off the walls. 'And you do not agree?'

Callisthenes was silent.

Alexander looked thoughtful. 'Why do you feel it is wrong?' he asked finally. 'You are the one who has announced to the world that I am the son of Zeus-Ammon. Your book, which will write history one day, tells of the proclamation of the Oracle at Siwa about my divinity. You write of the parting of the sea.' He cocked his head and looked at Callisthenes. 'Remember? And there is more.' Alexander put a hand on Callisthenes' shoulder. 'You believe that I am a god, Callisthenes. Surely you cannot lie when you write. And if you believe that I am a god, what can you find wrong in my asking my people to worship me as one?'

Callisthenes did not respond. He realised that he did not have an answer for Alexander. Everything that his king had said was true. Except the part about Callisthenes believing in Alexander's divinity. But how could he tell the conqueror that his book was an exercise in flattery? To ensure his status in Alexander's court even after he truly became a god?

'Your silence is disturbing.' Alexander became contemplative. 'Am I to take that as assent? Or as dissent? Only you can tell me. I have heard you out as I promised.'

'What you have said, sire, is true.' Callisthenes struggled to find a way out of this mess. 'Every word is true.' He dropped his voice to a whisper. 'But, my king, the mission is not yet complete. Only when you reach the secret location and drink of the waters as instructed, will you truly become a god! Not now. Not yet.'

Alexander's eyes flashed. 'So you think I am not a god until I have followed every step of the map that my mother gave me?'

Callisthenes lowered his eyes.

Alexander correctly interpreted that as meaning that the answer to his question was "yes".

'And what of my divine birth? Does my mother lie when she says she slept with Zeus? You know I cannot be the son of that filthy scum Philip!' Alexander's fury was growing with every word he uttered. 'And the words of the Oracle at Siwa – do they mean nothing to you? Is that a lie as well?'

They were passing a wooden table with a bronze plate balanced atop the legs. Alexander bent down and flung the bronze plate down the corridor, trying to vent his rage. 'And just who are you, Callisthenes, to pass judgement on my birth and divinity? A historian, that is all! Your job is to record events as they pass. To ensure that history will know what happened. Not to pass judgement. Never forget that I am your king. Your life is in my hands. Just like the life of every subject in my kingdom. Which now stretches from Macedonia to Bactria. Is that not the power of a god? To take away life?'

Callisthenes realised that the moment to restrain the conversation was past. He knew his king only too well. Alexander had already passed a sentence on the historian. He knew he was condemned. And in the face of death, he did not wish to appear cowardly.

'The power of a god,' he said calmly to his raging king, 'is not to take away but to give life. And that is something that you have failed to do.'

Alexander's fury turned into a raging inferno. 'I am Alexander! I don't need you or your approval to be worshipped as a god,' he shouted as his anger took over his senses. 'I don't need your secret ingredients to be a god. I am a god and will be worshipped as one. Damn you and anyone who thinks otherwise! Guards!'

Callisthenes stood and looked Alexander in the eye. 'Patroclus was a far better man than you, Alexander. But still death did not spare him.'

The guards came up and held Callisthenes as Alexander smiled cruelly. 'You know,' he told the historian. 'I can see now where the pageboys got their courage to try and assassinate me. Only someone who was very close to me could have given them the motivation to rebel. And the opportunity. I wondered who it was. But now I know. It was you, Callisthenes. And tomorrow, you shall be tried for it. The penalty for treason is crucifixion. You know that well. Goodbye, my friend.'

He turned around to stalk away but Callisthenes was not done yet. Alexander froze at the last words of the historian as he was dragged away by the guards.

'You may pretend to be a god, Alexander. You may believe you are a god. But you will never be a god. You will die before you return to Macedonia! Never will you set foot in your homeland again!'

51

PRESENT DAY

DAY FIVE
Alexander's secret

'You're joking!' Radha couldn't help herself. This was stretching the limits of credibility. 'Alexander's body disappeared from Alexandria hundreds of years ago. Everyone knows that.'

'In the 4th century AD actually,' Saxena corrected her. 'To be more exact, around 391 AD. The Order stole his mummy from Alexandria and buried it in another location where it would be protected from desecration.'

'But the Order desecrated his body anyway by subjecting it to pathological tests that extracted a virus and a bacterium.' Radha realised that the Order only cared about one thing. Itself. Nothing was sacred. Nothing was out of bounds. Like the facility she was imprisoned in. She realised now, as she put the facts together, that these two pathogens were the very ones that had shown up in the tests Imran had told them about. Saxena and his team were testing the unknown pathogens on unsuspecting volunteers. Sentencing them to a sure death. And a slow one. She felt her anger rise and tried to quell it. She wasn't sure if the drugs they had given her earlier had worn off their effects. It wouldn't do to have a fit of rage at the moment. She could hurt herself badly now that she wasn't restrained.

Saxena shrugged. 'Well, it had to be done for the advancement of science,' he replied in a matter of fact tone.

'Anyway, these two organisms hold the secret that will help us build another shield against disease.'

'I still don't get it.' Radha's disbelief was evident in her tone and expression. 'You say Alexander went searching for this great secret. He found it. Yet, two years later he was dead. And all the victims of the clinical trials exhibited the same symptoms as Alexander after a few years. These organisms only bring death.'

'That's where you are wrong!' Saxena hissed, his annoyance apparent now. 'These organisms give life! What you see on the computer screen here are not the original organisms that infected him. The retrovirus is a bacteriophage. A virus that infects bacteria.'

He changed the image on the screen. 'Viruses cannot replicate by themselves. They need to hijack host cells in order to replicate. This is the virus replication process.' He indicated the diagram on the screen. 'A virus attaches itself to the target cell and then penetrates the cell wall of the host cell through either fusion with the cell membrane or translocation of the viral genetic material across the host cell membrane. Once the host cell has been penetrated, the virus uses the cellular machinery of the host cell to replicate and make functional and structural viral proteins. The newly formed viral nucleic acid and structural proteins are then brought together to form the nucleocapsid of the virus. The newly formed viruses or virions are then released through a process called cell lysis which leads to the bursting of the host cell to release the virions. This also leads to the death of the host cell.'

Another image appeared on the screen. 'The virus we are dealing with,' Saxena continued, 'is a retrovirus. Its genetic information is encoded by RNA rather than DNA. A retrovirus also contains an RNA dependent DNA polymerase, which is a reverse transcriptase, which enables the synthesis of a DNA form of the viral genome after infection of a host cell.'

He stopped as he saw the blank expression on Radha's face. It was clear that she hadn't understood a word of what he had just said. 'Okay,' he tried again. 'You understand that in all organisms, genetic information is encoded in DNA which is double stranded, right? Well, in retroviruses, genetic information is encoded by RNA which is single stranded. Normally, in any organism, when genetic information has to be duplicated during cell replication, DNA gets transcribed to RNA which then conveys the genetic information required to create proteins to replicate the DNA.'

Saxena paused to see if Radha was still with him. She nodded and he continued. 'In retrovirus replication, however, the RNA has to be converted to DNA which is why it is called reverse transcription. Which is why the reverse transcriptase protein is required – to enable this process. Once the retrovirus is internalised by the host cell, its RNA is released and reverse transcribed into single stranded DNA. This single stranded DNA is then further reverse transcribed into double stranded proviral DNA. This provirus is inserted into the genome of the host cell using another enzyme from the virus – called integrase – and then transcribed into RNA. The RNA gets translated, as is done in normal replication, to produce proteins necessary to build a new virus and virions assemble and are extruded from the host cell.'

Radha began to see why Saxena was going into so much detail. 'So a retrovirus actually becomes part of the host cell genome?'

'Exactly. That's when lifelong infection begins. Retroviruses have the ability to acquire and alter the structure of host cell sequences. They can even insert themselves into the germ line genome of the host cell and behave as a transposable or moveable element. Which means that they are pieces of DNA that can jump around in the host genome at random, altering the host genome in the process and causing mutations in the host DNA. They can activate or inactivate genes near the site of penetration into the genome. They can even rapidly alter their own genome by recombination and mutation under selective environmental stimuli. Which is why the HIV virus is so deadly. It is a retrovirus. And it can turn on DNA that is usually dormant in healthy people.'

Radha's head was spinning. She tried to make sense of all the information she had just received. 'I get it. But if a retrovirus is so deadly, how can it help build a shield against disease?'

52

Immortality

'That's the problem,' Saxena sighed. 'Viruses have a bad reputation, and rightly so. Most of them cause severe, untreatable infections. It is very, very difficult to kill a virus because they are tough little critters. Even if their host dies, they lie dormant, waiting for an opportunity to infect another host and carry on the viral cycle. They have been known to lie dormant for thousands of years without losing potency. But there's another side to viruses which is less known. You know what the microbiome is?'

Radha recalled reading about it somewhere. 'The community of microscopic organisms that coexist within people.'

'Right. It is a symbiotic existence. Friendly collaboration. The best known are the bacteria that live in our guts. In exchange for food and shelter, bacteria aid digestion and help to regulate our metabolism. But there's a little known story about symbiotic viruses that target nasty bacteria. And that's where our little retrovirus comes in. As I explained before, it is a bacteriophage. So, for example, the mucus membranes of human beings – the soft tissue in our throats and noses – are rich in bacteriophage. Which is good for us because bacteria also tend to proliferate in mucus. So, by preying on the bacteria that could cause mucus related infections, these viruses actually form a shield or a backup immune system for the hosts.'

'So the retrovirus you found inside Alexander's body keeps bacteria at bay?'

'Even better. And this is where the clinical trials have proved immensely useful. Without them we would never have made the discoveries that will lead us to success. You see, we found the virus and the bacterium in Alexander's mummy. But we didn't realise their association until we started infecting subjects separately with each one and then monitoring the results. One of the results was that the retrovirus by itself, in the absence of the bacteria, adapts rather well to the human body as a host organism. And, once it adapts to the human host environment, it proceeds to switch on genes that produce proteins that help slow down the ageing process. For example, IGF1, which is a key protein to continue building muscles. Absence of this protein leads to weakening of muscles and a poorer ability of muscles to repair and regenerate. Then, there is the key protein, telomerase, which is the topic of much debate over slowing the ageing process. There is strong evidence that the absence of telomerase is one of the major reasons why we age and die. The problem with telomerase is that its presence also leads to cells continuing to replicate without stopping – in other words, a cancer. But the presence of the retrovirus also leads to the production of BRAF, a protein that helps regulate the cycle of growth and division of healthy cells – a kind of a brake on cancer. The retrovirus also seems to somehow activate a protein called p53, which is present in a dormant form in all cells. P53 induces the expression of genes that cause cell cycle arrest and apoptosis, preventing the proliferation of malignant cells. This is easily explained, of course. The presence of a new retrovirus in the body induces greater production of Interferon, a protein that stimulates the transcription of the gene encoding p53, resulting in cellular p53 protein abundance.' He stopped and looked at Radha. 'I could go on forever. There are new genes it switches on that produce more, unknown proteins that have been proven through our research to have beneficial effects on the human body in terms of strength, regeneration and repair.'

'That is amazing,' Radha conceded. This did sound like a major medical breakthrough. 'You also mentioned that the virus infects the bacteria. Does that kill them off? Is that the virus shield you meant?'

Saxena shook his head. 'It is so much bigger than that. When we infected people with the bacteria alone, we found two things. First, the bacteria are deadly for humans. But not immediately. Once ingested, they form a biofilm in which the cells are surrounded by large expanses of matrix material. This happens to protect the bacteria from the natural immune responses of the body. At this point, the bacteria also go dormant as a result of a cell mediated immune response which contains the infection but does not eradicate it. So, for a while, there are no apparent clinical or symptomatic effects. We suspect that when the retrovirus infects the bacteria it causes changes in the bacterial genome that halt the production of these proteins that can kill a human being. Maybe even enabling the bacteria to produce proteins beneficial to humans. We don't know. For that, we need the original virus.'

'But you said that you found the virus separate from the bacteria in Alexander's mummy,' Radha pointed out. 'Isn't that the original virus?'

'No. I had said we made two discoveries as a result of the clinical trials. I've only told you about the first discovery. The second thing we found was that the bacterial genome already contained the virus in the form of a prophage. At some point in time, the retrovirus infected the bacterium but did not survive to replicate in the manner that I described earlier. Perhaps it died out for some reason, surviving only as genetic material incorporated into the genome of the bacteria – a prophage. And this is where things get interesting. Something – we still don't know what – stimulates prophage induction after the bacterial infection occurs. The retrovirus then replicates within human cells via the lysogenic cycle.'

Saxena realised that he was getting too medical with his terms and held up his hands. 'Basically what this means is that the latent form of the retrovirus – the prophage – is excised from the bacterial chromosome. This is called prophage induction. Once that happens, the virus replicates in the usual manner, commandeering human cells to create copies of itself. This is when the retroviral infection occurs. But, as I've explained earlier, this is good for the host because the retrovirus is beneficial.'

Saxena folded his arms and looked triumphantly at Radha. 'So you see how powerful this virus is? And the benefits that it can deliver to mankind? And just think – the Order will control this. The power to stop ageing. The power to combat any disease. Forget about antibiotics! We will have the power to confer immortality! The world will be at our feet, begging for this. No wonder they called it the secret of the gods!'

Radha frowned. Something didn't add up. 'If the virus is all that great, then how come Alexander died after ingesting it? Why didn't it change the genome of the bacteria as you suspect?'

'Because something went wrong when he ingested them. We didn't find the original virus. Only the prophage. I have no idea what exactly went wrong. But without the original virus, the bacteria didn't change. They stayed dormant until something triggered their pathogenicity. When that happened, he didn't stand a chance. We've seen this in our subjects. Time and again. Once the bacteria are activated, the subjects die within a few days. Sometimes they linger for a month or two. And this is why we need the original virus and the original bacteria. We need to find the place where Alexander sourced them. Once we have them we can find out how the retrovirus really works.'

'So the reason you needed to excavate the tomb of Olympias was to find the cube, which would lead you to the source of the original organisms.' Radha understood the connection now.

'Exactly. Once we have that, we have the secret in our hands.'

'So what makes you so sure that Alexander made a mistake? Maybe he didn't. Maybe these are pathogens after all. Delivering death and suffering.'

Saxena frowned. 'Two reasons. One, our clinical trials. They bear out what I have just told you. And the second is a much older, more credible reason.' He paused. 'Because the evidence is in the Mahabharata.'

Radha was taken aback. She hadn't expected this reply. Saxena smiled, evidently pleased at her reaction. 'Oh, yes,' he said. 'You've heard the myth. You just didn't know what it actually meant.'

He paused and then launched into another explanation. When he had finished, Radha sat in stunned silence. What she had just heard would turn the world on its head.

And if he was right, the world would be a slave to the Order.

53

On the trail of Alexander

Alice, Colin and Shukla looked at each other despondently. The better part of the day had passed without any further breakthrough. They had sifted through all the papers, studied the maps and photographs and discussed the four remaining verses on the cube, and the additional verse from the journal of Eumenes. All to no avail. They still had only one deciphered verse, the one from yesterday.

Earlier in the day, Vijay had briefly called them on the landline in the fort. He had told them that he had been given a satellite phone by Cooper which would enable him to keep in touch with them even in the mountains of the Kunar valley where cellphone signals would not work. The call had been brief and he hadn't been able to tell them much but he had sounded excited. And he had told them that the "secret of the gods" was the *amrita* – the secret of immortality — described in a myth from the Mahabharata. But he hadn't been able to explain in detail since the time he was allowed on the call was limited. The only thing he had communicated to them as a parting shot was an ominous plea. He was running out of time. They had to find some more answers soon.

They had hoped to have some news for Vijay by now. The thought of him surrounded by potential terrorists and confirmed murderers was too terrible to contemplate. And their lives, including Radha's, depended on the promise Vijay had made, which haunted them.

'Let's go through this again,' Alice pressed Shukla. The linguist was also weighed down by his worry about his daughter. There was still no news regarding her whereabouts.

She sifted through the papers again and frowned. There was something about one of the maps that had bothered her from the start. But she just hadn't been able to put her finger on it. What was it?

Pulling the map towards her, she studied it once more. It was a map showing Alexander's route through Afghanistan. They had gone over this several times. The verses had to correspond to locations on this route. But they hadn't been able to work out the correlations between the verses and the places Alexander had visited on his way to India.

Colin noticed her musing over the map. 'See something there?' he asked.

Alice pursed her lips. 'There's something nagging me, but I don't know what it is. Something looks really familiar.' She shook her head.

Colin adjusted the map so he could get a better look at it. 'Alexander's route,' he remarked. 'Interesting. He entered Afghanistan, headed south before turning north via Khandahar, Ghazni and Kabul. Then, he went north across the Hindu Kush mountains, circled around the Sogdian rock and returned to Balkh before turning towards Jalalabad and the Kunar valley. That looks pretty much like a very planned march across the region. I find it difficult to believe that this could have happened by accident.'

Alice stared at the map as if she couldn't believe her eyes. Something Colin had just said had set off a blinding light in her brain. She saw it now. It had been staring her in the face all this time. And she hadn't been able to figure it out.

'That's it!' She snapped her fingers as Colin gave her a curious glance.

'What's it?' he asked.

'Vijay was right all along,' Alice replied. 'I should have seen it earlier. The secret lies in the Kunar valley. That's their destination.'

Shukla looked puzzled. 'How did you reach that conclusion, Alice?'

'See here.' Alice put her finger on the map at the location of the Sogdian rock indicated on the map. 'Look at the sequence. The Sogdian rock comes before Jalalabad. We may not need the metal plate after all. It is possible that the verses in the journal of Eumenes are in geographical order and Alexander planned his route in the same order. If we can work out the locations that the first two verses refer to, then we can verify if my logic is correct.'

They bent over the map again.

After a while, Shukla looked up. 'I guess I was distracted,' he said sheepishly. 'I should have seen this before. Vijay, in his call this morning, had given us a clue. And I still didn't figure it out. But when Alice spoke about the order of the verses in the journal corresponding to the route Alexander took, it struck me.' He looked at Alice. 'I think you are right.'

He pointed to a river running across the map. 'This is the river Oxus. And I think the second verse refers to this river. The Sanskrit word used in this verse is "*chakshu*". Which means "eye". And that is how I have been translating it all this time. But, in the Mahabharata, the Oxus is referred to as the *Chakshu*. And the verse referring to the Oxus comes before the verse referring to the Sogdian rock. If the secret of the gods is the *amrita* from the Mahabharata, then it is very likely that the clues also have some reference to the Mahabharata. That would also explain the reference to Sukra who is also mentioned in the epic.'

Alice studied the map once again. 'I think you're right, Dr. Shukla,' she said. 'This makes sense. The verse is an instruction to cross the Oxus. Only a river can be "swiftly flowing".'

'And there's the first verse –the one that is not on the cube, but is mentioned in the journal,' Shukla continued. 'Now that we know that the secret is somehow linked to the Mahabharata, this verse makes sense. The line of a mighty king that was felled was the line of the Kauravas. Dhritrashtra is the mighty king referred to in this verse. The Kauravas were his sons. They were all killed. There is a hint in the last two lines about the nature of the "ruse" that led to the destruction of the Kauravas: "roll the dice". It refers to the dice rolled by Shakuni. He was the uncle of the Kauravas and the brother of Gandhari who was the wife of Dhritarashtra, the father of the hundred Kaurava brothers. Gandhari was the princess of Gandhar. And Shakuni was the prince of Gandhar. According to one version of the Mahabharata – I think it is from Andhra Pradesh – Shakuni's father, Subala, was imprisoned by Bhishma, along with the rest of his family. Shakuni watched them die as they gave up their food so he could live and avenge them. According to that legend, Subala asked Shakuni to use his bones to make the dice that were used in the Mahabharata. That was the "ruse, born of death, sworn vengeance." The dice, created by the death of Subala, and the vengeance sworn by Shakuni. Gandhar is the ancient name for Khandahar.'

They looked at the map in silence. The route Alexander took now reflected the meanings of the verses they had just discussed. From Khandahar to Kabul. From Kabul to Balkh. From Balkh, across the Oxus river, to the region of the Sogdian rock and then back to Kabul before moving on to Jalalabad.

'We still don't know what the "saltless sea" refers to,' Colin wondered. 'Something important seems to be there according to the verse. The "kernel of the quest".'

'It has to be something north or west of the Oxus river,' Shukla mused. 'But it somehow doesn't make sense. Who

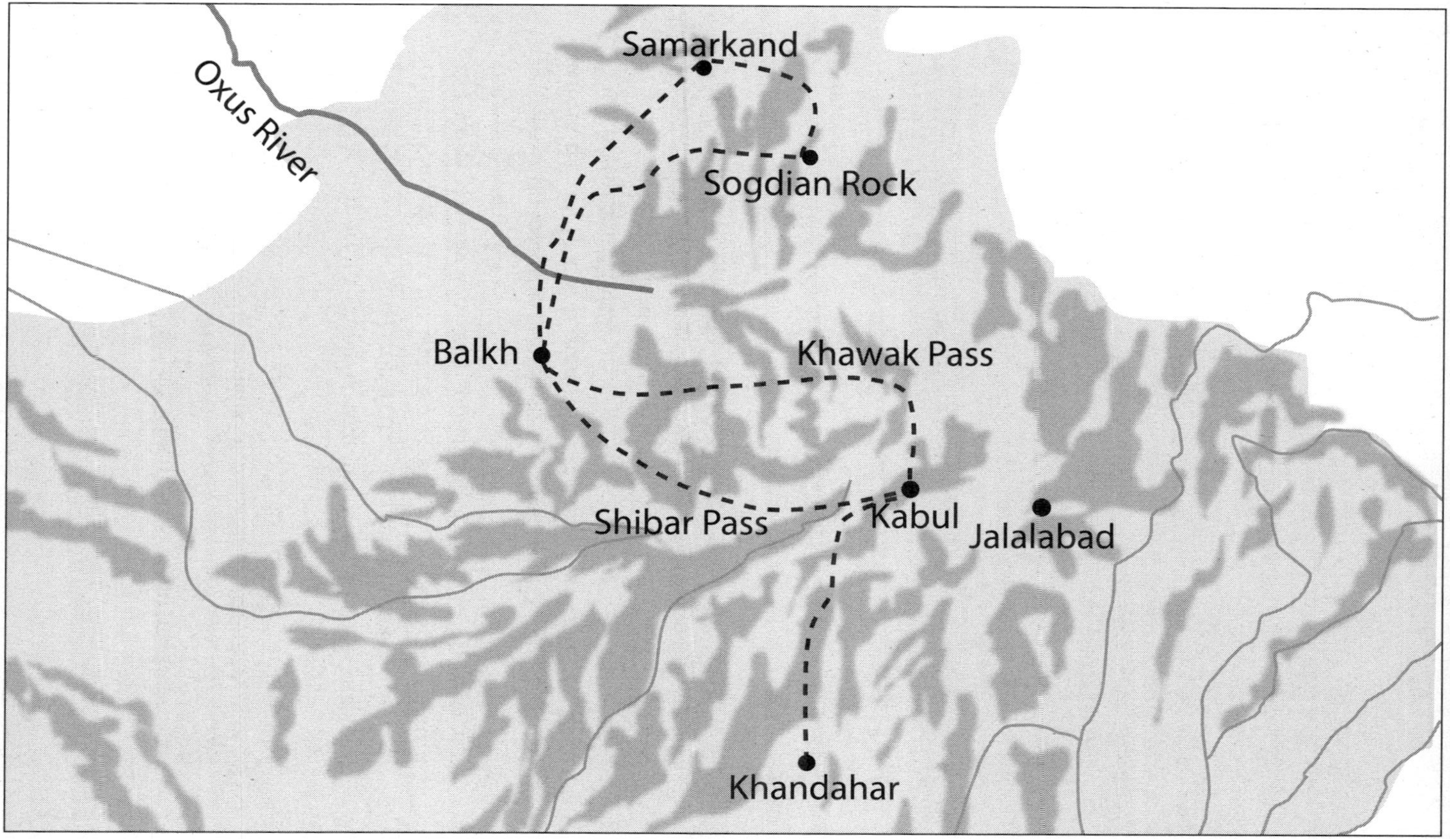
Oxus River
Samarkand
Sogdian Rock
Balkh
Khawak Pass
Shibar Pass
Kabul
Jalalabad
Khandahar

are the "three brothers"? And what is the arrowhead? Not to mention the "serpent's seal".'

'Alexander had the benefit of a ready-made map,' Colin huffed. 'And here we are trying to guess at the meaning of obscure riddles.'

'The important thing is that we've established that the Kunar valley is the final stop in this journey,' Shukla concluded. 'Which means that the last two verses refer to locations within the valley. Finally, we have something for Vijay.' There was a note of hope in his voice.

As if on cue, the phone on the desk rang. Colin sprinted across the study and picked it up. It was Vijay. Colin updated Vijay on their analysis.

'It certainly sounds logical,' Vijay agreed. 'Thank everyone for me, Colin. I've got to go now. They are waiting to set off. Now we've got something to go on.'

54

Jalalabad, Afghanistan

Van Klueck looked at Vijay enquiringly as he disconnected the call. He had been present during both calls, watching and listening, when Vijay had called home. There was no way Vijay could do anything but what he was supposed to do – communicate with the rest of his team to solve the riddle.

'The Kunar valley is the final stop.' Vijay briefed Van Klueck on his conversation with Colin. 'The verse about day and night and the staff and the one about the fiery gaze of the serpent both have to refer to locations in the Kunar valley.'

Van Klueck looked at Cooper who was standing by. 'What does our guide say?'

'He isn't sure about the reference to Shiva's staff in the mountains,' Cooper replied in an even tone. 'But he also says that he isn't a local from the valley. He's from Jalalabad. We'll have to ask around at the villages in the valley. It is a 90 minute drive to Asadabad from here. The road's in good shape. It was laid just a few years ago as part of a USAID project to link Kabul to the border with Pakistan. I say we go take a look.'

'I don't think we need to go all the way to Asadabad,' Van Klueck mused. 'There must be a path leaving the road and going into the mountains. How else would Alexander have found the location?'

Vijay agreed with him silently. Eumenes and Alexander had made it to the location in pitch darkness, with only the light of torches to aid them, according to the secret journal. The only way they could have accomplished this was if there was a means of going deeper into the mountains surrounding the valley that could be traversed on foot and without too much difficulty or the need for climbing gear.

But he said nothing. He didn't want them to know about the secret journal. Instead, he watched as Van Klueck assented to leave and Cooper went about hustling his men in preparation for the trip.

A piece still missing

Colin scowled at the printout of the verses on the ivory cube. It had given up most of its secrets. But one verse describing a location on Alexander's route still remained to be deciphered. The one about the three brothers and the serpent's seal.

'I'm not satisfied,' he said. 'If all the verses on the cube are equally important, we can't ignore this one. Without this missing piece, the puzzle is just not complete. No matter what they find in the Kunar valley, it won't give them what they are looking for. And this refers to the "kernel of the quest". If the secret is located in the Kunar valley, then what is the kernel? That should really be the most important part, shouldn't it?'

Alice's brow furrowed with concentration as she puzzled over the verse. 'This one is really obscure. We've worked out the bit about the Oxus river. But nothing else in this verse seems to make sense.'

Shukla sat silently, his face expressionless. They could only guess at the maelstrom in his mind.

'There's only one way to crack this,' Colin said finally. 'I'm going to do what Vijay usually does in a situation like this. Search the internet till kingdom come. Something's got to turn up.'

The Kunar Valley, Afghanistan

Vijay, seated in the leading Land Rover, looked back at the fleet of Land Rovers following behind. There were six SUVs, packed with men armed to the teeth. He had observed that, apart from their guide who was a local Afghan, all the other men were Caucasians. Probably mercenaries from Europe and the US, he assumed. Or part of a private army belonging to the Order. Either way, the muscle power available to the Order was a scary thought.

This road was nothing like the one from Kabul to Jalalabad. The gorges and the steep drops were missing. So far, the road had followed the course of the Kunar river, running alongside it through a flat valley with fields stretched on either side. While the valley narrowed in places, it was reasonably broad until now.

On their right, the road was bounded by the Kunar river as it snaked through the valley. Further south, Vijay could see the Safed Koh mountains which bordered the North West Frontier Province of Pakistan.

To their left rose the Hindu Kush mountains, the backbone of Afghanistan, lofty and intimidating. Somewhere in those mountains lay the secret of the gods.

Vijay recalled his research on Alexander. After Darius, the Persian emperor, had been defeated by Alexander, he had been murdered by one of his nobles, Bessus, and left to die in ignominy. Bessus had taken the name Artaxerxes V and fled across the Hindu Kush mountains to Bactria, thinking Alexander would not pursue him there. But Alexander had crossed the Hindu Kush through the Khawak Pass, disregarding the perils of the journey. His troops had run short of supplies during the march. They were forced to kill their pack animals and eat raw meat to survive. But Alexander finally caught up with Bessus, who was eventually tortured and killed.

Alexander had then gone on towards the Sogdian rock. And somewhere there, Callisthenes had left the army to embark on his clandestine mission to the region of the Sogdian rock and the other location indicated in one of the verses that they had yet to decipher. What had he collected from there and brought back for Alexander? Would they find the answers in the Kunar valley?

55

A prisoner's thoughts

Radha sat in her cell on the floor, hugging her knees. What Saxena had disclosed to her earlier in the day had numbed her. And no one apart from her knew about it. She was convinced that nothing could stop the Order from completing its mission and achieving its goals.

What was most galling for her was the fact that she could do nothing about it. It was eating her up. She wanted to get out and tell the world about what was really happening, why the clinical trials had been established. But she also knew that Saxena had revealed the Order's plans to her only because there was no way out of here for her. She was locked in a cell she couldn't open from inside. There was 24X7 CCTV coverage of her cell through the cameras installed in the corridor outside. Any unusual movement would be noticed immediately. A male guard came in at regular intervals to check on her. And, even if she managed to somehow overpower the guard and get out of the cell, she had seen the facility outside. It was buried underground. She had seen no exit doors.

She had to face the cold truth. There was no way out of here. The only way she would get out of here was if someone broke into this place and rescued her.

Which was highly unlikely because no one knew where she was.

Search for the signposts

The elevation had been increasing steadily since their departure from Jalalabad. The valley had narrowed considerably now. The fields on either side had disappeared and the road now wound through the foothills of the Hindu Kush, still clinging to the river on its right.

They had enquired at several villages they passed but had found no clue to the signposts that were supposed to guide them to the location they sought.

They were now entering dangerous territory. Occasionally the boom of rocketfire came to their ears. The war in Afghanistan had an active battlefield in this valley. Even two thousand years after Alexander, the bloodshed here had not abated. Cooper had assured Van Klueck that the local units of the Taliban had been informed about their presence in the valley.

'They won't be firing missiles our way today,' he had told Van Klueck. So far, that promise had seemed to hold true. Vijay hoped that it would remain this way until they returned to Jalalabad.

Another village consisting of mud huts loomed up ahead. The convoy stopped and the local guide hopped out to make his usual enquiries.

This time, he seemed to have unearthed something. They could see him smiling broadly and making gestures towards the mountains.

Presently, he loped towards the lead SUV in which Van Klueck was seated along with Cooper and Vijay. Cooper got out and exchanged words with him then turned to Van Klueck.

'Around a kilometre from here, according to the villagers, there's a track leading into the mountains. A two hour trek will bring us to some rock formations and rock inscriptions from an ancient era. Our guide says we should find our signposts there.'

Van Klueck shot a glance at the guide. 'How do we know he isn't feeding us a tall tale? When we get up there we'll probably only find scratches on the rocks left by cavemen forty thousand years ago.'

Cooper grinned. 'I checked that with him. He's coming with us. And he knows the consequences if we don't find what we're looking for.'

'Very well, then. Let's go.'

The convoy set off again.

An escape plan

The seed of a thought had germinated in Radha's mind. It had been triggered by the realisation that only someone breaking through the defences of the facility from the outside could find her. And that was not impossible, provided someone knew where to look.

Suppose she could find a way to get a message out of here? Anwar had done that with Imran. The unpleasant memory of Anwar's fate accompanied this thought and she pushed it away with a queasy feeling.

She knew she was doomed anyway. They were holding her only as a bargaining chip for Vijay to help them. Once their purposes were served, she would be killed. Or worse, used as another subject in their awful experiments. She remembered Saxena's remarks about Freeman's project. What were they doing that involved genetics?

It didn't matter for now. The important thing was to get to the IT section and see if she could somehow send out a message.

Radha resolved she would at least try. She knew the consequences of failure. But she couldn't just sit by and watch as Saxena and his team went about their mission with no one the wiser.

A glimmer of hope

Colin sat at the laptop and rubbed his weary eyes. Darkness was falling outside and he had been at work for several hours now. He stood up and walked to the window, looking at the lights of the little village at the foot of the hill.

He had managed to work out one part of the verse. Or at least he thought he had. But that hadn't helped in any way.

After a lot of thinking and discussion with the others, reinforced by research on the internet, he had concluded that the "saltless sea" referred to the Aral Sea, a lake which was fed by the Oxus river, known today as the Amu Darya.

Even though the Aral Sea was a pale shadow of what it was 60 years ago, it had seemed to be a promising candidate. First, it was the nearest sea to the Oxus river. Second, one would need to cross the Oxus to reach the Aral sea, if one was coming from Balkh. Third, the Aral Sea was originally a freshwater sea. It had only turned salty over the decades, as the water of the rivers feeding it was diverted, and the sea itself shrank to a fraction of its former size. This had led to an increased concentration of toxins and salt in the water.

But while the Aral Sea appeared to meet at least three conditions for being the sea referred to in the verse, he had drawn a blank beyond that. Searches for the three brothers linked to the Oxus river or the Aral Sea had unearthed nothing.

He had begun to doubt Shukla's translation of the "eye". Suppose it was an eye after all and not a reference to a river? That would lead to a new conundrum: what was meant by a "swiftly flowing eye"?

Colin sighed. This wasn't as easy as he had thought. He wondered how Vijay was doing. There had been no news from him.

He sat down again at the laptop. Time was running out. For him. And for Vijay and Radha.

56

In the mountains

Van Klueck perched on a boulder and watched his team search the surroundings for the signposts. Daylight had begun to fade but they carried powerful portable searchlights which illuminated the mountainside and the rocks around them.

The trek had lasted the promised two hours. It was here that their guide had called a halt and indicated that this was the location where they should begin looking for the signs indicated in the verse.

Their surroundings did seem to correspond to at least a part of the verse. They were now high above the Kunar river. Van Klueck estimated that they were now at least 2000 feet from the valley floor, on a sort of ridge. And the verse had referred to a ridge above the river.

As he sat there, he reflected on what accomplishing his goals here would mean. A step up in the Order. Closer to the top. Maybe even part of the closed group that ran the Order. His family had been members of the Order for centuries. They had served with loyalty, even in their freewheeling pirate days. But the Van Kluecks had come a long way since then. They were wealthier. More powerful. More respectable. And they had moved up the ranks of the Order over the years.

Today, he was within grasping reach of the ultimate prize in the Order; a position that would seat him at the same table as the man who ran it. The one with the original bloodline. A bloodline that had started with the Order and propagated through thousands of years, unbroken and pure.

As he looked on, the searchlights cut through the growing gloom, highlighting the men in stark relief. His gaze settled on Vijay. He didn't understand the man. Didn't he know that his fiancée and he were doomed? He certainly wasn't stupid. Yet, he seemed to show a dogged persistence in the face of even the longest odds. Could he have a backup plan? But Van Klueck knew that Vijay was unarmed. He shook his head. It didn't matter. The man was good at solving puzzles and cracking riddles. And today, he was helping them of his own volition. The European couldn't ask for more.

Vijay moved through the dusk, accompanied by two armed men with searchlights. He tried not to dwell on his fate and focused on the rocks and the mountainside. The villagers and the guide had been right about the inscriptions and drawings. The boulders around abounded in crudely inscribed artwork and script. But nothing yet corresponded to the description in the verse.

Moving to another section of the mountain, he noticed a deep alcove in the mountainside, more like a short passageway a few feet in length that ended in a wall of rock. The entrance was rectangular, and just above the entrance, was a square aperture that seemed to have been carved through the rock. But it was too small for anyone to crawl through. He wondered what the purpose of the aperture was since it certainly wasn't a means of accessing the alcove, even if the entrance was sealed. He indicated to his guards to train their searchlights on the rock face at the rear end of the alcove, which was shrouded in darkness.

Vijay found himself looking at a hunting scene carved into the rockface that was enclosed in the natural alcove. Two archers with drawn bows were hunting an indeterminate animal, probably a deer, and there was a smaller animal at the side of one of the hunters. It could have been a dog, though it was difficult to say since the drawings were very crudely sketched.

His first reaction was similar to Van Klueck's response earlier. These seemed to be crude cave drawings, thousands of years old, carved by people who were living in caves and hunting for sustenance. How could any of these rock drawings have any bearing on their quest?

Vijay was in the process of drawing away from the artwork when something caught his eye.

He had missed an element of the painting. High above the scene he had just studied, cut into the rock, were a five pointed star and a circle surrounded by small linear cuts radiating outwards. He realised what he was looking at.

'It's here,' he called out. 'The first signpost.' He gazed at the drawing. Where was Sukra in this picture? The son of the rishi Bhrigu? Was he one of the hunters depicted here?

Van Klueck hastened up to check on Vijay's discovery, accompanied by the rest of his men.

'Day and night meet,' Vijay explained. 'The sun and the star, representing day and night respectively. Together in the same painting. This is it.'

'Hmmm.' Van Klueck peered at the artwork. 'I think you're right. But now, how do we find Shiva's staff?'

Vijay's excitement at the discovery subsided. He didn't have an answer.

57

Step one

Radha decided it was time to go for it. She didn't want to wait until it was too late. She took a deep breath and pressed the call button that she used to summon the guard whenever she wanted to use the toilet or take a shower. There was a large common bathroom on the floor with enough cubicles to accommodate all residents of the floor together. The toilets were located adjacent to the bathroom.

True to routine, the guard showed up, carrying a small cane which worked like a taser. It carried an electric charge, which could be used to stun, or merely to hurt and shock. The guard had never used it on Radha but she had seen him use it on other inmates. He clearly derived pleasure from seeing his victims squirm, especially the women. While Radha was uncomfortable with her plan, she felt no sympathy for the guard and what she was planning to do to him.

Radha hurried down the corridor, acting as if she was in a hurry. The guard increased his stride and speed to keep up with her. Out of the corner of her eye she glanced back and saw a big grin on his face. The man was clearly twisted. It only made her resolve stronger to carry out her plan.

She reached the row of toilets; each one was a small cubicle with a door that swung open outwards. As she unlatched the door, she contemplated it thoughtfully. It was quite flimsy, made of layered particle board. Would it serve her purpose?

There was only one way to find out. She entered the cubicle. There was no latch on the inside. It was assumed that people would have their privacy.

She waited. Her plan hinged on so many factors that were determined by chance that she was not even sure if it would work. She drove the thought out of her mind and willed it to happen.

The minutes passed.

Nothing.

There was silence inside the cubicle.

And outside.

She steeled herself. Patience.

Still, nothing.

Then just as she was about to give up, she heard the guard approach the door.

She stood up. This was the moment of truth. She had to be able to estimate the correct moment to strike.

Guessing that the guard was standing within striking distance, she lunged at the door, throwing her full weight behind her charge.

The door swung open violently, with great force, striking the guard in the face. He teetered backwards with the momentum of the assault, lost his balance and toppled over.

The momentum of her lunge carried Radha forward, causing her to trip over him as he lay on the floor, clutching his nose.

But he was quick to recover. Realising what Radha was trying to do, he attempted to sit up, though blood was streaming down his face from a broken nose. His right hand clutched the electric cane, ready to use it on her.

For a split second, Radha panicked. Her plan had failed. She had counted on knocking him out.

Then, her steely resolve took over. She recalled what she had learned in the close combat training sessions she had undergone on joining the task force. Using her hips as a lever, she swung one leg hard at the guard. Her heel caught him on the side of his head with the same impact as a karate roundhouse kick.

The guard went down again.

She grabbed his electric cane and studied it. As she had thought, it was a modified version of a taser. There were different shock levels. She set it to stun and pressed it against his body.

The guard jerked a couple of times and then went still. But he still wasn't knocked out, just incapacitated. She had no idea how long it would take him to recover. She had to make the best of that time.

Radha realised she was breathing heavily and sweating. She had made it so far.

The tougher part was yet to come.

The search for Shiva's staff

Vijay sat and racked his brains. They had been right about the verse. It had referred to the Kunar valley. They had found the ridge above the river. They had found the day meeting the night.

But where was Sukra? How would they find Shiva's staff?

'I'm going to call the others,' he told Van Klueck as he dialled the fort's landline number on the satellite phone.

'Better make it snappy,' the European shot back. It was getting dark now and, though they had carried equipment and provisions to spend the night out in conditions like this, he was keen to complete the quest and get it over with.

The phone rang a couple of times and then a tired voice answered. 'Yes?' It was Colin.

'Hey, I need help.' Vijay swiftly outlined the situation to Colin. 'Are the others there? Can we spend some time trying to work this out?'

'I don't know where they are,' was the answer. 'But let's see if you and I can work this out. You say there's a picture of a hunting scene and above the hunt there's a star and the sun.'

'Right. And according to the verse, day and night meet and Sukra shows the way to Shiva's staff. But I can't see anything that corresponds to Sukra.'

'Hmmm. That's a tricky one. Okay, describe the painting to me in detail once again. Every little detail, mind you.'

Vijay described the alcove in the mountainside and the artwork on the rockface.

'Nuts,' Colin complained. 'We thought that all the pieces of the picture would be there. Day, night, Sukra. One happy family. All pointing towards a trident. It never is that easy, is it?'

Vijay listened as Colin prattled on, knowing that this was his friend's way of thinking and analysing.

'So, if the picture isn't showing you the way, something else has to.'

'Yes, but what?'

'It's a long shot, but you could try this. While we were talking, I googled Sukra. Guess what I came up with?'

58

Radha's adventure begins

Radha picked herself up from the floor, holding onto the taser. She had decided to carry it with her. The guard's access card would come in handy too, so she purloined it. There wasn't anything else of much use in his pockets.

There was no knowing when he'd come to so she decided not to waste too much time and head out of the toilet immediately. Once he regained consciousness he was sure to raise an alarm and then all hell would break loose.

She wondered what would happen then. Nothing pleasant as far as she was concerned, of that she was sure. But she would cross that bridge when she came to it.

The elevator was her next stop. There was nothing on these floors. The nerve centre of the facility was located in the basements.

The lowest three basement levels, she reminded herself. Eight floors of prison cells were anyway below ground level.

She had not seen an IT room in the level Saxena had shown her earlier. It had to be on one of the levels occupied by Freeman's project.

But she couldn't go wandering around those floors in a hospital gown. She would be instantly recognised as one of the inmates. The problem was she didn't have a change of clothes and there was no way of knowing where her own clothes were, if they had been retained at all.

She thought for a minute, mulling over an idea that was forming in her mind. She wasn't too convinced of it but it seemed to be the only choice she had.

The elevator doors opened. She held her breath, electric cane at the ready in case someone stepped out.

But the elevator was unoccupied. She jumped in and pressed the button for the floor she had visited earlier, using the guard's access card to enable the elevator.

The elevator rode noiselessly and swiftly down the shaft and reached the floor she had chosen.

The doors slid open silently.

Radha stood for a moment, her heart in her mouth. She had determined to stay the course but every fibre in her being was telling her to shut the doors and return to her cell.

But there was no turning back now. She was too far gone. The attack on the guard would not go unnoticed. Or without retribution.

Radha took a deep breath and stepped out of the elevator.

Waiting for the magic...

Vijay disconnected the call. What Colin had told him certainly made sense. He could think of no other course of action. All he could do was hope that they were both correct about this.

Van Klueck looked at Vijay enquiringly as he joined the others.

'We have to wait,' Vijay told him, and explained what Colin had worked out on the call. 'Just a short while more. The sun has almost set. We need to look towards the northwest.'

Cooper looked sceptical. 'Are you sure this is gonna work? Sounds like a lot of mumbo jumbo to me.'

'There's as much science in what you're going to see in a short while as there is in the secret of the gods,' Vijay shot back.

The sun dipped below the horizon and darkness descended on the mountains. A heavy silence hung in the air as the men waited and watched.

For several minutes there was nothing.

Vijay was sweating. Why wasn't it happening?

In the hospital

Imran lay in his hospital bed and grimaced. Not so much from the pain but from the thought that he was lying here when he should be out there joining in the search for Radha. And hunting down the people who tried to kill him.

Vijay had dropped by yesterday to see him and had updated him on all that had happened. Imran had been glad to see Vijay. And Vijay had reciprocated.

'We all thought you were going to die,' Vijay told Imran. 'Thank heavens you pulled through.'

'Just about,' Imran had smiled back weakly. The shrapnel had missed his vital organs and major arteries, which saved him. His quick presence of mind in diving into the next room the moment the glass pane in the window shattered had saved his life. His injuries had led to blood loss and weakness but he would live to fight another day. *Literally,* Imran thought grimly.

He had been shocked to hear about Radha and the fact that they had been unable to find any trace of her even two days after her kidnapping. It was like her captors had vanished with her into thin air.

Imran's immediate response after Vijay had left was to call Vaid and demand that he be linked to the search for Radha and the activities of the task force, from his hospital room.

Vaid had reluctantly agreed, knowing that there was no arguing with Imran. And he could empathise — if Imran couldn't be out there in the field, he wanted to be able to monitor it from his room. After all, he was the head of the task force in India.

As a result, Imran's room now resembled a mini IT centre, with stacks of equipment, routers, servers and cables snaking everywhere. Three flat screen monitors were positioned at different angles, with live feed from different locations where teams were working on the case. One monitor connected him directly to Patterson.

Imran had spent the whole day talking to the teams, trying to understand what they had been doing, analysing leads. But there was nothing to go on.

Absolutely nothing.

It was as if Radha had ceased to exist.

59

A helping hand

Radha made her way towards the room where Saxena had brought her earlier in the day. She moved quietly, trying to be as unobtrusive as possible. So far, her luck held. Like before, most of the doors opening off the corridor were shut. And, where the doors were open, the men inside the laboratories were too busy with their work to notice what was happening in the corridor.

As she proceeded down the corridor, she couldn't help glancing through the small glass windows set in the doors that were closed. They, too, led to laboratories where men wearing surgical masks and gloves were busy at work.

She noticed that there weren't any women here. Only men. She wondered why. But that wasn't important right now. There was a ball of nervous fear deep down in her stomach. It gnawed at her, accentuating her doubts.

Radha had observed Saxena closely on her various encounters with him. She had reached the conclusion that he was a bully. And, like most bullies, he was most comfortable when he possessed power over other people. His ability to rule their lives, determine whether they were happy or sad, if they lived or died, was what gave him his smug confidence. She was hoping that, like most bullies, deep down he was a coward. It was clear to her that his attitude and behaviour stemmed from deep rooted complexes and insecurities. She had pinned her hopes on the fact that, if confronted with someone who had power over him, he would buckle and capitulate.

She could only hope that she was right. If she wasn't…

Radha moved on, hoping that Saxena was in his office.

To her relief, he was there, seated before the computer monitor and scribbling furiously in a notebook.

Radha hesitated for a moment, unsure. But she was here now. There was no going back. And time was running out. The CCTV cameras were sure to have captured her movements. Somebody was sure to have noticed her make her way here. She had to act fast.

She slid into the room, shutting the door behind her and locking it from inside, as Saxena looked up in surprise.

His surprise turned to shock and then anger as he realised what was happening.

'Quiet.' Radha tapped the electric cane on the desk before Saxena could react.

The virologist looked at the cane, recognising the instrument. He shrank back instinctively. Radha smiled. She had been right about this man. He was a bully to his core. And now he was afraid.

'You know you won't get away with this,' Saxena warned her, his eyes darting nervously between the cane and Radha as he spoke. 'How long do you think it will be before security comes looking for you?'

'Long enough for me to do what I need to do,' Radha shot back. 'Open your internet browser.' She brandished the electric cane menacingly as she spoke.

'You wouldn't dare.' Saxena stared at her.

'Try me.' Radha knew that her chances of escape were slim. And Saxena would pay her back in full for what she was doing now. But she had to get word out about this facility. Her fate was sealed anyway. This was her only chance of sending out a message to the outside world. She wouldn't get another opportunity.

Saxena saw the determination on her face. A strange feeling overcame him. He was accustomed to being the one in charge, the one who could punish or reward. And he always enjoyed that feeling. Now, the tables were turned. And he didn't like it one bit. He felt nauseous. And cold. It was the same feeling he had had when he was in school and was caught smoking in the boys' room. The punishment that had followed that transgression had been burned into his memory. After that incident, he had ensured that he always had the upper hand. That he would always be the one meting out the punishment.

And today, after all those years, he was back in the boys' room. And someone with a cane stood before him. Someone with the ability to hurt and humiliate him.

After many years Saxena felt the taste of fear again. This was not a fair fight. And he could not stand the thought of getting hurt again, both mentally and physically. 'Fine. I'll cooperate. But you can't send out emails from here. This is a secure facility. No emails. No phones. We'll have to go upstairs. To the ground floor.'

'Fine. Let's move.' Radha motioned towards the door.

They moved out of the office together, Radha staying close to Saxena, ready to use the electric cane if required.

To her surprise, instead of turning left towards the elevator she had come by, Saxena turned right — towards the large white doors at the end of the corridor. Radha had assumed that these doors led to a stairway but she was wrong.

Saxena swiped his access card and the doors opened to reveal another elevator landing. This facility was larger than Radha had realised. But she wasn't surprised, given the work they were doing here.

They boarded the elevator and Saxena swiped his card once again and chose the ground floor. The elevator shot up.

As the elevator rose, Radha realised that it was programmed to skip the eight floors where the inmates were housed. The employees working in the labs did not have access to those floors.

The elevator stopped and the doors opened. To her left

and right were white doors, blocking the corridor at both ends. Saxena turned to the right and Radha followed him.

'What is behind that door?' she asked, indicating the door that lay behind them.

'That's the door to the main clinic and the reception,' Saxena replied gruffly. He looked at her thoughtfully. 'You may want to change your mind about sending a message. It would be pretty easy to overpower me with that thing,' he indicated the electric cane, 'and use my access card to open those doors to your freedom.'

Radha was overcome with anguish. She knew that Saxena was taunting her. She was so close to freedom. All that lay between her and the outside world were a set of doors. But she knew there was no way she would be able to get away by herself. Already the alarm must have been raised and people would be scanning the CCTV monitors to see where she was.

Today, she didn't have a choice. There was a much bigger picture to think of than her own fate. With the Order controlling the lifespan of humans, they would have ultimate power. The world would be a slave to them. Without even knowing it. She could not allow it. She would not allow it.

Her best bet lay with sticking to her plan. She was almost there.

'Keep going,' she said to Saxena instead.

Saxena led her into an office and opened up the web browser on the laptop that sat on the desk. 'Go ahead,' he gestured to the laptop as the browser was launched on the screen.

Radha looked around. She couldn't take the chance of having Saxena stand by as she typed out the email. She would have to put the electric cane down and that would leave her exposed. But there didn't seem to be anything in the room that could be of use to her.

She made a quick decision. 'Sit there.' She pointed to the chair at the desk. Saxena sat down calmly and watched her unplug the laptop from its power cable and back up to the door. He knew what she was going to do.

'Before you go,' he said, 'know that when this is over and you are back in your cell, I will personally ensure that you live the rest of your life in pain. I promise you that.'

Deep down, at her core, Radha was horror-stricken. She knew that Saxena would make good on his promise. But she had resigned herself to her fate when she had decided on this plan. She had to go through with it.

Backing out of the room, she latched it from outside and quickly began accessing her email account. Saxena was sure to raise the alarm from inside the room even if her escape from her cell had gone undetected until now. She had minutes, if not seconds, to complete her task.

She swiftly typed out her email message, addressing it to as many people as possible. There was no telling when they would see it. She could only hope that it was sooner rather than later.

The email client confirmed that the message had been sent. She put the laptop down and slumped to the floor, overwhelmed by the feelings of terror and apprehension that she had kept at bay all this time.

Struggling with her emotions, she pulled herself back together. There was no sign of the security guards yet. Perhaps she could still try to make a break.

She rose and headed towards the white doors beyond which Saxena had indicated that her freedom lay.

So far so good.

Just a few feet more.

Just then, her worst fears came true. The doors to freedom suddenly turned into the doors to hell. They slammed open and three armed guards burst through, running through the corridor towards her, drawing their weapons as they ran.

Radha realised that the game was up. She would never see the outside world again.

60

Sukra points the way

Vijay stared at the north western sky with a fixed gaze, trying to will the phenomenon to happen as Colin had described it.

Van Klueck, behind him, made an impatient sound. Cooper stood by, his face impassive. He had already expressed his apprehensions about this.

The last light of the sun disappeared, and the reign of night began.

'You know,' Van Klueck began, then froze.

Vijay, too, saw it.

It had begun.

'Keep a watch,' he instructed the others excitedly. 'Make a note of the exact point where it will be visible.' He glanced back quickly to ensure that no one was standing in front of the rock drawing in the small alcove.

As they looked on, against the canvas of the night sky, clearly visible at this altitude, a bright point of light appeared. It was brilliant against the other stars that twinkled weakly in its glow.

The moment that the drop of light freed itself from the clutches of daylight that had seemed to hold it prisoner, a dagger of light illuminated the five pointed star carved into the rock face in the alcove.

'That's it!' Vijay yelled. 'That's Sukra. Or Venus, as the planet is known in the western world. And the tip of the mountain right below it is where we will find Shiva's staff! It isn't far from here.' He now understood the purpose of the aperture above the

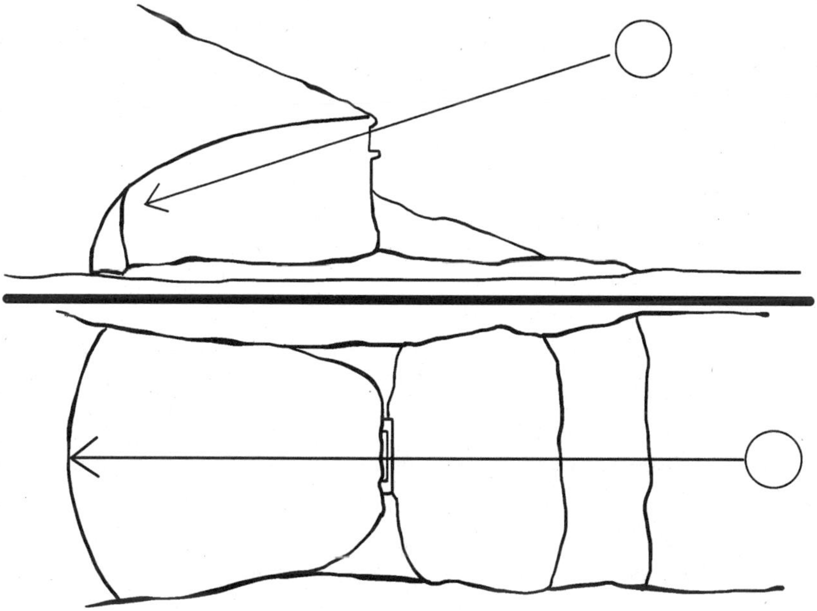

Venus shining through the lightbox onto the rockface at the back of the alcove.

alcove entrance. It was a lightbox, designed to allow the light of the planet to shine upon the five pointed star carved into the back of the alcove.

There was silence among the men as they began hiking towards the point that Vijay had indicated. Cooper gave the alcove a second glance as if he couldn't believe what he had just witnessed.

No wonder Alexander came here at night, Vijay thought to himself. It wasn't just to keep the mission a secret from his troops. His main motive would have been to be able to see the planet Venus light up the location of Shiva's staff.

The powerful searchlights lit up the mountainside as they followed a natural path towards their destination.

As they came closer to the point, Vijay wondered what they would find there.

Will she make it?

As the guards charged down the corridor, the guard in the lead skidded to a halt and took aim, firing off a volley of bullets at Radha.

Radha felt as if a stick of dynamite had gone off in her chest and she reeled. She felt like she was thrown back at least five feet and her legs gave out from under her. As she slumped to the floor, everything around her seemed to go into slow motion as adrenaline was released and her synapses began firing faster. It was akin to a high speed camera producing a slow motion effect. Waves of paresthesia surged through her body as she lay on the floor, her right lung constricting and her breaths agonisingly short and painful. Each breath felt like there was a knife being turned in her right lung. Even through the pain she could feel another sensation: warm blood pouring out of the bullet wounds, soaking her hospital gown which was sticking to her body. She wanted to think but she was in a state of shock and thoughts would not come to her numbed mind.

The shooting had stopped and there were shouts all around her. She vaguely recognised Saxena's voice. He seemed to be angry and reprimanding someone. The words were indistinct. A white film seemed to cover everything around her and her vision began to fade as she began to go into hypo-volemic shock.

Then, everything went black.

61

Shiva's staff

Vijay stood and gazed in awe. They were standing at the very spot where Venus had emerged. The mountain formed a ridge at this point.

Carved into this ridge in bold relief, clearly revealed in the light of the searchlights, was a twenty foot tall *trishul*.

Shiva's staff.

Or, as Eumenes had put it, in the Greek context, Poseidon's staff.

Whether it was the sight of the staff that transfixed the group or the fact that they were so close to their destination, no one moved for a few moments.

Van Klueck was the first to break the spell. 'Right. Where's our last stop then? The five headed snake.' He looked at Vijay as if to say 'this is why you are here. Tell me.'

Vijay tried to remember what Eumenes had written in the journal. Alexander had not found it difficult to locate the snake after passing the trident. So the unusual rock formation must be nearby.

What had Eumenes said?

'Let's spread out and search in a radius of one kilometre around here,' Vijay instructed. From what he recalled, Eumenes had mentioned that a fairly long time had elapsed before they could locate the serpent rock. It could lie in any direction.

The men spread out in groups of three and began searching. They all knew what they were looking for. And once they found that, the secret of the gods would be within their grasp.

The missing link

Colin sat and stared at the laptop. He wasn't accustomed to this. Vijay was usually the researcher. For everything they had done together, including the company they founded and the project that had made them rich, it had been Vijay who had done all the research. Colin was good at analysis and reasoning and operations while Vijay was the thinker between the two. They complemented each other well.

But now, when the chips were down, he was struggling to do what Vijay would always accomplish so effortlessly.

He sighed and ran his hands through his hair, just as Alice walked in.

'Anything yet?' she asked. Colin had updated her and Shukla on his conversation with Vijay and the discussion about Venus.

'I haven't heard back from Vijay, so I'm assuming that the Venus connection was spot on. But I still haven't been able to crack the last verse. The one about the eye and the three brothers. I've googled everything possible. But nothing seems to work.'

Alice looked at the map that Colin had brought up on screen.

'If we're right about the Aral Sea,' she said, 'then the "three brothers" will be somewhere to its south. We know that because Alexander didn't go beyond the Aral Sea. And if we look to the south, we have two countries here. Uzbekistan and Kazakhstan.'

'Right.' A new energy took hold of Colin. 'I didn't try searching using the countries as keywords.'

'Give it a shot,' Alice encouraged him. 'Let's see.'

Colin typed in "three brothers Uzbekistan" and browsed through the entries the search engine threw up. He went through the first six pages then looked at Alice despondently.

'How do we even know that Google is going to know the three brothers? After all, the cube was made thousands of years ago.'

'Try Kazakhstan,' Alice prodded him gently. 'Let's try everything.'

Colin nodded and typed "three brothers Kazakhstan".

Again, there was nothing relevant on the first page. He clicked to the second page.

Nothing again.

The third page.

He froze. He could sense Alice drawing in her breath as she stood next to him.

On the screen, were a series of photographs with the title caption reading : "Images for Three Brothers Kazakhstan".

62

A sliver of hope

Imran listened as Patterson spoke. This was their second call since Imran had had the equipment installed in his hospital room. They were discussing possible options in the current situation. Imran's initial feelings about Patterson were giving way to a grudging admiration for the man's intellect and strategic ability. While he still thought that Patterson was a bit of a Neanderthal when it came to interpersonal relations, he couldn't argue with any of the strategic points that he was making today.

Of course, there were parts of Patterson's plan that Imran didn't feel happy about. The part about assuming that Radha was lost, for example. Patterson insisted that they should not hope. While Imran felt that they should not give up hope that they would eventually locate and rescue her.

'In war, you don't win by hoping. You win by doing,' the big African American had boomed over the flat screen monitor. 'As far as Radha is concerned, if we get a lead, any indication of her location, we'll double our efforts to find her. But, for now, there's nothing we can do. On the other hand, there's still plenty we can do for the other aspects of this case. We should focus on that instead of sitting and hoping and praying. If she lives, that's great. We don't lose a member of the task force. But let's not count on it.'

There were other parts of the plan, too, that Imran was not comfortable with. But he agreed that they didn't have a choice. The risk was too great. It was all or nothing.

'Right, then. You sleep well tonight. Tomorrow's a big day. One way or the other. Hopefully we'll come out tops,' Patterson signed off.

Imran sighed as he watched the screen fade to black. Then he remembered his phone. An email message had come in while he was speaking to Patterson. He wondered who it was.

His eyes widened as he saw the name of the sender even before he opened the message.

Imran couldn't believe his eyes. It was Radha! She was alive! She had sent him a message. Somehow, from somewhere, she had managed to find a way to let them know that they should not lose hope.

Throwing off the covers, he winced as he made his way out of bed and changed out of his hospital gown and into his own clothes, dialling his office as he did so.

'Arjun, pick me up right away. I'm forwarding you an email. I want a location trace immediately. Do it now.'

The source

An hour had passed and there was no sign of the five-headed serpent that was to lead them to the secret. But there was a renewed energy in the group, goaded on by Van Klueck, now that they were within striking distance of their goal.

Cooper's satellite phone rang. He moved off to the side and spoke in low tones. Vijay strained to hear what he was saying but he could only catch a few words. 'Do whatever...ensure...I will...' But the man sounded concerned. He spoke briefly but rapidly to the caller and then pocketed the phone again.

Vijay didn't know about the other men but he was beginning to tire. The continuous exertion at this altitude was affecting him. He decided to rest for a while. It wouldn't matter if it took them an additional fifteen minutes to find the damn serpent.

As he lowered himself to the ground, he heard Van Klueck's voice. It was overflowing with excitement. 'Over here!'

All thoughts of resting were forgotten as Vijay joined the others in rushing to where Van Klueck stood. Outlined by the searchlights was a massive rocky outcrop, at least fifteen feet high. It looked like a wave but it was easy to see how it could be interpreted to be a five-headed serpent. Vijay reflected on how ancient the rock formation must have been. At some point in time, he thought, it must have actually resembled a serpent, for the verse to indicate its shape. Thousands of years of erosion had still not changed the basic shape of the formation. He now realised how old the cube was. Much older than they had thought.

'Look for the entrance to the cave,' Van Klueck commanded and the group fanned out, searching.

It didn't take long to find the narrow fissure through which only one man could squeeze at a time.

'You go first,' Van Klueck grinned at Vijay. 'Let us know if it is safe to come in.'

Vijay shook his head as he grabbed a searchlight from one of Cooper's men and made his way through the fissure.

He found himself in a narrow passage through the rock, which abruptly ended in a flight of steps cut into the interior of the mountain. He shone the light down the steps. They went down for quite a distance, deep into the heart of the mountain.

'It looks fine,' he shouted back. 'There are steps here which go down at least five hundred feet. You won't hear me once I've gone down them!'

Without waiting for an answer, he started down the stairs. He was equally keen to see what lay at the bottom. There had been so much mystery around the secret and now that he knew what the secret of the gods actually was, he wanted to see for himself where it all began. Was it really as it had been described in the Mahabharata?

As he made his way down, the light around him was augmented as the others followed him. He continued down the steps until he finally reached the bottom.

He flashed the light around. He was in an enormous cavern. Words failed him as he took in the immensity of the space. It was as if the cavern stretched through the interiors of the entire Hindu Kush range. Its walls were not visible.

The only thing that he could see was what stretched before him, occupying most of the cavern.

The source of the myth. The origin of the secret.

And it was exactly as it had been described in the Mahabharata. He was standing in the presence of what had been the basis of the creation of one of the greatest myths of all time.

63

The search starts

Imran pressed his hands over his stitches as the car sped towards the airport. An hour had gone by since he had received the message from Radha. While the geographical origin of the message was being traced, Imran had fast tracked a request for an aircraft to be available within 30 minutes to fly him and a commando team to the source of the message. Ten minutes ago, the location had been identified as a medical facility which was an hour's drive from Jaipur. Strangely, though, this facility was not listed as a contracted centre for clinical trials by Titan Pharmaceuticals.

As long as the search had remained academic, with no leads and only endless discussions on how best to find Radha, Imran had accepted his confinement to a hospital bed. Now that her location was known, there was no way he would stay back. He had to be a part of the rescue team. He had done it before and he wanted to do it again. And he had developed a very special bond with Radha. He would have fought tooth and nail if anyone had even suggested that he watch from his hospital bed as they attempted her rescue.

They would be in Jaipur in less than an hour. From the airport, they would proceed by helicopter to their destination.

Imran had also run a check with Titan Pharmaceuticals to ascertain the whereabouts of their senior management. Some of them were travelling but only one man was officially listed as being on tour to Jaipur, where he was speaking at a medical convention.

The Chief Medical Officer, Dr Varun Saxena. This had to be more than a coincidence.

Imran's face was set in stone as they arrived at the airport and were hustled towards the waiting aircraft.

He was going to get Radha back safe and sound.

Time to go

Saxena and Freeman watched as Radha's inert body was carried out of the room to a waiting ambulance. Her motionless body was attached to a drip, a feeder tube and an oxygen mask.

'You must be really desperate,' Freeman remarked as the orderlies disappeared with Radha's body. 'She's dead. No one could survive those bullets. The blood loss alone will kill her if the shock hasn't already. You will never get her to the facility in time to replenish her blood. And if any of her vital organs have been hit, you don't stand a chance of reviving her.'

Saxena's face was grim. 'Those bloody guards. They weren't supposed to shoot her. She's a hostage for god's sake! You don't shoot hostages until you're good and ready for it.'

'Hey, come on, they were only doing their job,' Freeman protested. 'How were they to know she was a hostage? Security saw her movements on the CCTV, they investigated, found a guard tased silly in the toilets on her floor. And then you were locked in by her. You raised the alarm. When the guards saw her on the ground floor, all they knew was an inmate had escaped and had put you in peril. So they did what they're supposed to. Remember? "No survivors, no witnesses"? That's what they did. Don't castigate them for doing their job.'

'They are bloody idiots,' Saxena muttered. 'They've just complicated matters. But I'm not desperate. Even if she dies, Vijay Singh won't get to know. I've informed Cooper. He'll handle it.'

Freeman was curious. 'So why did you inject her with the cocktail of the virus and bacterium? If the bullets don't kill her, that will. We know that. There isn't a single specimen who has survived that trial. And you've given her an extra large dose.'

Saxena shook his head. 'I thought this was a great opportunity for us to experiment. We've never had a healthy subject with a mortal wound, who has been subjected to the dose. Let's see what happens. Worst case, she'll die anyway. But it might just turn out to be interesting. Remember what we found in Alexander's mummy?'

Freeman nodded. 'I do. Another six months and you will see the results of my experiments.' He shrugged. 'I guess it doesn't hurt.'

Saxena looked around. 'Let's get out of here. In a way, I'm glad I was around when she sent the email. At least we had time to clean up and evacuate this place. The servers are being wiped right now so the IB won't get their hands on any data. There's no way they're going to be able to link this facility to Titan. Though I've left a little something for the IB to see.'

Freeman nodded. He knew what Saxena was referring to. 'Pity we have to leave all the specimens here, though.'

'Doesn't matter,' Saxena replied. 'We have all their histories and test results with us. We can always start again with different specimens, using the results we already have. And we may not need the specimens anyway. If Cooper succeeds in getting samples of the source, we are done.'

They beamed at each other, clearly pleased. Either way, the mission was going to be a success. Nothing stood in their way now.

64

Ocean of milk

Vijay stared at the sight that greeted his eyes. Before him stretched a vast body of water. So vast that its edges could not be seen except for the shore that was nearest to him. The lake seemed to occupy almost the entire cavern from what he could see.

But it was not the discovery of the lake that stunned him. Van Klueck had told him about it and he had been prepared to find a large body of water. What took his breath away was the appearance of the lake.

As far as he could see, the surface of the lake reflected silver-white in the colour of the search light. As the others joined him and stood gazing at the lake, as overwhelmed as he was by this sight, the searchlights revealed the endless stretch of silver-white water, calm and still, with not a ripple.

'No wonder they called it the Ocean of Milk,' Van Klueck muttered at Vijay's side. 'And now we know why.'

But there were more surprises in this immense cavern. As the searchlights played along the wall that supported the stairway an array of metal pipes and stone channels came into view. A large stone channel ran along the wall, coming from the direction of the lake, ending at a large stone basin. The other pipes and channels connected a number of small stone basins to each other and to a large metallic contraption that towered above them. The metal used for the pipes and the device was black. The searchlights did not detect the slightest sign of rust in the metal. To him, the entire apparatus looked rather like the brewing vats he had seen in some of the micro-breweries in the US.

A shout came from one of the men. 'There's something moving here!'

The searchlights were all aimed in the direction the man indicated. Everyone stood still. For a while nothing moved.

Then, something wavered at the edges of the light. A large, circular form. To everyone's surprise, a huge tortoise ambled into the pool of light created by the searchlights. It was a large specimen, at least twenty feet in length. Vijay couldn't believe his eyes. The creature moved slowly across the pool of light and disappeared into the darkness on the other side.

'Okay, get to work,' Van Klueck ordered. 'I want samples collected and secured in the next ten minutes. Then we get out of here.'

Vijay walked to the shore of the lake and studied the silvery surface. It was impossible to believe that this was the very body of water that was described in the myth. Except that he now knew the real reason for the colour of the water. This was the source of the bacteria that the Order had found in the mummy of Alexander the Great. He had drunk from this very lake on that fateful night two thousand three hundred years ago.

But why had he died? Why hadn't it worked for him?

'Time to go,' Van Klueck's sharp voice intruded on his thoughts. 'Everyone out.' He turned to Vijay. 'You had better have the meaning of the final verse for me by the time we get back to Jalalabad.'

The riddle solved

Colin and Alice sat in the study, waiting for Vijay to call. There was no way for them to contact him since Vijay had not been permitted to share the satellite phone number. Shukla had retired to his room, ostensibly to sleep. Though Colin wasn't sure how much sleep he would get, since there was still no news of Radha.

The phone rang, the sound shattering the silence of the night. Colin scrambled to pick up the call, activating the speaker so Alice could also participate in the call.

'Hi Vijay,' he greeted his friend. 'Alice is here, too.'

'Guys, I hope you have something for me. Anything.'

'We do.' Colin couldn't keep the pride out of his voice. 'The last location you need is the Ustyurt plateau which straddles Kazakhstan and Uzbekistan. The place mentioned in the verse is a natural formation called the Three Brothers, which is in the Kazakh part of the plateau. It's in the boondocks of Kazakhstan. Quite painful to get there. Alice and I researched the whole darn thing for three quarters of an hour.'

'Excellent!And the arrowhead? The one that "shows the way"?'

Colin told Vijay what he had discovered via the internet.

'Sounds logical. Amazing but definitely possible. I would bet on this anytime.'

'So would I. But, frankly, I have no idea what you will find there. I couldn't crack the meaning of the "kernel of the quest".'

'I know what it is. It is the virus. The plateau is the source of the virus. We found the source of the bacteria in the Kunar valley. That's where the *amrita* was manufactured. So the only thing that's missing is the original version of the virus. And since the virus is the key ingredient for the *amrita*, it has to be the kernel of the quest.' Vijay told them about what he had seen in the Kunar valley.

'So now only the verse that mentions the stuff that Callisthenes collected from Bactria remains to be deciphered,' Alice observed. 'Do you want us to research that as well?'

There was a pause and muffled conversation. Then Vijay came back on the line. Apparently he had been consulting with

Van Klueck. 'No need,' Vijay replied. 'They're working on it. Now that they know what the verse is about and they know where to find the stuff that the verse mentions, they will do it themselves. Thanks, guys. You've been a ton of help.' Vijay signed off and disconnected the call.

Colin looked glumly at Alice. 'He didn't mention Radha even once.'

Alice pondered this. 'You're right. He didn't sound like he was happy that he was now in a position to negotiate her release.'

'Not that he would have been successful if he tried,' Colin reasoned. 'But it sounded to me like he's given up on the chances of getting her back.'

They sat together in silence, wondering what Vijay must be going through. He was alone in the company of people who had kidnapped his fiancée. And if he believed there was no hope for her, it was time to get seriously worried.

65

Jaipur, Rajasthan

Imran sat in the Mi-26 heavy lift helicopter, one of two that had been requisitioned from the Jaipur airforce base. The Mi-26 is the world's fastest heavy lift military transport helicopter, which made it ideal for this mission. The two choppers were now being used to transport the commandos to the location that had been targeted by tracing the cell phone Radha had used to contact him.

They had just flown over the outskirts of Jaipur, leaving the lights of the city behind them, and were now passing over large patches of darkness punctuated by small patches of light. Against the night sky, he could make out the silhouette of the other helicopter, its bright red warning lights flashing with a steady rhythm.

Approximately ten minutes after leaving the city, Imran saw a large patch of light come into view dead ahead. It was the compound of the medical facility which was their target. As soon as they had pinpointed the location, an alert had gone out to the Jaipur police to set up roadblocks around the compound. But so far, the police had not reported anyone trying to leave the medical centre.

Imran was worried. That could mean only two things. Either Varun Saxena was not at the facility or he had left before the roadblocks were set up. Either way, he feared that the CMO of Titan had escaped the dragnet.

The immense helicopters began to descend as they reached the target location. There was a large driveway that led to the main entrance of the facility. It was in this driveway that they planned to land.

As the helicopters touched down, their hatches were opened and the commandos spilled out, securing the perimeter of the compound, taking up strategic positions. The main body of the commandos began stealthily advancing towards the building, followed by Imran. There didn't seem to be an armed force within the building that would resist the operation but they did not know what to expect either.

The lights were out in the reception. The building looked deserted and silent. No one was around. Not even a night guard.

The commandos activated their night vision goggles and entered the building. Light switches were located. But there was no one here. The commandos swarmed through the two storeys of the building. There was nothing to be found. The place had evidently been evacuated.

'Go through the CCTV archive. If they haven't wiped it clean you may find some clues there,' Imran instructed Arjun. His deputy left with the rest of the IB team to check the archives while Imran continued his inspection of the ground floor. When he reached the elevator, he recalled the discovery of the basement in the last medical centre they had searched in Delhi.

Imran checked the elevator and discovered the buttons for three basement floors. They could only be accessed using a card based security system. This time, he had come prepared. The electronics expert on his team carried a handheld master programmer that could override the elevator's security system and allow them access to all the floors.

His earphone buzzed. It was Arjun. 'Sir, there's something you need to see.'

'I'm coming now,' Imran told him. He turned to the commandant of the commando team. 'Sweep all floors once you gain access. Report to me when you are done. I want to know what's down there.'

Before long, he was standing next to Arjun in the security centre.

'Sir, there is something very strange here,' Arjun remarked before playing the video clip that he wanted Imran to see. 'The archives have been wiped clean. There are no recordings here except for one. I don't understand it. Why would they wipe out everything and leave just one short clip??'

'Let's see it.' Imran's face was hard. He had a bad feeling about this. In his book, if only one clip had been saved from erasure, it was for a purpose. He waited apprehensively as the clip began playing.

The video clip showed Radha sitting on the floor pounding away at a laptop.

Imran was immediately alert and a sinking feeling overcame him. This was not good.After a few seconds, Radha put the laptop down and rose. She looked around cautiously and then moved away. As she moved, Arjun pointed to a flurry of action at the edge of the screen. There was no audio on the clip but the three guards with their guns raised were clearly shooting at Radha. Imran watched in horror as Radha collapsed in a pool of blood. There was blood all over the floor, pouring out of her bullet wounds.

The clip abruptly ended there.

Imran stood rooted to the spot. He was numb. He had just watched Radha die.

66

DAY SIX

Samudramanthan

Vijay sat in Van Klueck's luxuriously appointed Gulfstream jet. They were flying to Aktau International Airport in Kazakhstan, from where they would be transported by helicopter to the location described by Colin. An armed escort was standing by, awaiting their arrival. It seemed that the Order was able to mobilise men and weapons almost anywhere they wished.

It was still dark outside. Van Klueck had insisted on leaving immediately. He had wanted them to be over the plateau before the sun rose. While they now knew what they were looking for, they still did not know the time of the day when the shadow would be cast to reveal the hidden entrance to the source of the virus. It was safest, he reasoned, to be there at dawn, just in case.

An advance team had already left from Aktau, traversing the distance of almost 400 kilometres in a 4-wheel drive, a journey that would take almost half a day on the sand and clay tracks that led to their destination. Their job was to scour the area, secure it and await the arrival of the main team.

A thought struck Vijay. The cavern with the lake in the Kunar valley had borne out what Van Klueck had told him earlier. But he still could not reconcile what he had seen with the myth from the Mahabharata.

He voiced his thoughts to Van Klueck.

Russia
Russia
Kazakhstan
Aral Sea
Aktau
USTYURT plateau
Caspian Sea
Uzbekistan
Syr Darya River
Amu Darya River (Oxus)
Turkmenistan
Tajikistan
China
Iran
Afghanistan
Pakistan

'Of course the Mahabharata explains what we found,' Van Klueck sniffed. 'You just need to interpret the verses correctly.' He stood up and walked to a cabinet, pulled out a thick book and returned to his seat, placing the book on the table. 'Do you understand Sanskrit?'

Vijay shook his head.

'Of course not. Like most Indians.' Van Klueck couldn't hide the disdain in his voice. 'I am fluent in the language,' he continued. 'So let me explain it to you.'

He opened the book and flipped through the pages. 'This is a volume of the *Adi Parva*, the first book of the Mahabharata. This is the book that contains the myth of the *Samudramanthan* or, as it is popularly but erroneously called, The Churning of the Ocean.'

For the first time Vijay realised that the European's diction while speaking Sanskrit was almost perfect. It carried little of the usual accent that most Westerners had while speaking the language. He must have learned it at a very early age and then practised it through the years, in order to be fluent while speaking and reading, Vijay mused.

'Ah here we are,' Van Klueck put his finger on the page. 'There are a few shlokas in the *Adi Parva* that tell us about what happened thousands of years ago. The traditional interpretation, however, has overshadowed the original meaning of the shlokas and the true nature of the event was lost over time. In fact, the English name given to this tale is itself a misnomer. It is true that *Samudramanthan* can be interpreted to mean "churning the ocean". But the root of *manthan* is *manth* or *math*. Which can have multiple meanings in English. Churn is just one of those meanings. *Math* can also mean stir, agitate or mix. So, if we were to disregard the traditional interpretation of the title itself, it could mean either "stirring the ocean" or "mixing the ocean". Which, as you will see, is more appropriate to describe exactly what happened. And the apparatus we found by the side of the lake is where the mixing happened. The water from the lake must have been pumped via the stone channel along the wall and the stone basins were used to collect and channel the rest of the ingredients into the mixer. It is possible that the device used to pump the water created the illusion of the lake water being churned, hence the popular interpretation of the root *math* to mean "churning". Let me elucidate further.'

He peered at the book, switching on the overhead light as he did so. 'Let's take this shloka:

देवैरसुरसंघै श्च मथ्यतां कलशोदधिः
भविष्यत्यमृतं तत्र मथ्यमाने महोदधौ॥12॥

The traditional meaning of this shloka is: "after churning the great ocean by the Gods and the Danavas, the water of the sea will become an urn of nectar". But if you replace the word "churning" with "stirring" or "mixing", using the root *math*, the entire meaning changes. You can now interpret this as: the Gods and the Danavas mixed or stirred the water of the sea and it became an urn of nectar.'

He moved to the next shloka and read it out.

सर्वौषधीः समावाप्य सर्वरत्नानि चैव हि।
मन्थध्वमुदधिं देवा वेत्स्यध्वममृतं ततः॥१३॥

Here, the traditional meaning is: "(After) acquiring all the medicinal plants and jewels, O gods, churn the ocean then you will gain the nectar". Again, replace "churn" with "mix" or "stir" and you can see where the verse on the cube describing the plants and fruits becomes relevant.'

Vijay couldn't believe what he was hearing. Here was a myth that he had heard dozens of times while growing up and Van Klueck was giving him a totally different interpretation from the one he had learned.

'Now, here's a shloka that directly addresses what we found in the Kunar valley:

ततस्तेन सुराः सार्धं समुद्रमुपतस्थिरे।
तमूचुरमृतार्थाय निर्मथिष्यामहे जलम्॥८॥

The traditional meaning of this shloka is: "Then the Gods and the Danavas stood on the bank of the ocean and said for the sake of nectar we will churn the water". Here, interestingly, *samudram* can be interpreted to mean "gathering together of waters". The reference is clearly to a large body of water. Which is what we found, isn't it? So, this shloka can actually mean: "then the Gods and the Danavas stood on the bank where there was a gathering of waters and said for the sake of nectar we will stir or mix the water"'.

He flipped a few pages and indicated another verse. 'Here's where the science comes in. Of course, you need a radically different mindset, an open mind, to interpret this shloka correctly:

तत्र नानाजलचरा विनिष्पिष्टा महाद्रिणा।
विलयं समुपाजग्मुः शतशो लवणाम्भसि॥१९॥

Traditionally, this has been interpreted to mean: "Then, smashed by the great mountain, various aquatic animals proceeded together towards their destruction and were reborn a hundred times in the salt water". The translation of the word *jalacara* to mean "aquatic animals" is erroneous. This word means "water-goer or living in water" and can refer to any organism in the water. Including the bacteria that inhabit the lake we found. Note also that the word *vinispishta* can mean "ground down, crushed into powder". Finally, again, there is a reference to a salt water body. *Ambhasi* is water and *lavanam* means salty, so here we are again, talking about a body of salt water which perfectly describes the lake we found. So, the new translation goes like this: "the marine organisms, or bacteria, in the salt water were destroyed and reborn a hundred times". A rather good depiction of what happens when the retrovirus infects the bacteria and changes their genome – a rebirth of sorts, wouldn't you say?'

'Mr Van Klueck,' the pilot's voice came over the speakers. 'We're beginning our descent into Aktau. Landing in 30 minutes.'

Van Klueck shut the book and looked at him appraisingly. 'There's more of this. Much more. But do you see how the Mahabharata actually tells us that a scientific event took place thousands of years ago? And it wasn't an ocean or sea, but a large, saline body of water that provided the basis for this event. Which you have now seen with your own eyes.'

Vijay nodded. Words failed him. He was only just beginning to grasp the immense hidden meaning behind the shlokas which superficially told the tale of a fantastic event.

67

The best laid plans of mice and men

Patterson scowled at the camera. This was going to be an all-nighter for him. Imran had returned from Jaipur and was back in his hospital room. His stitches were hurting and he was exhausted from his exertions, having been up all night. The travel to Jaipur and back hadn't helped since he was still weak from blood loss and the surgery.

Imran had briefed Patterson about Radha. The big man had taken the news stoically. This was war and he had lost team mates before. There would be time to mourn later. There was still much to be done.

But he wasn't happy with the news that Colin had given them.

'Why did they have to choose Kazakhstan of all places?' he growled. 'We just withdrew from our military base in Kyrgyztan. There are no other American bases in Central Asia. As long as they were in Afghanistan, we could have provided Vijay some support through our drone bases there and gotten him out of there without too much of a problem. We still have troops there. Kazakhstan is going to be difficult. That's a crazy region. Any flight from Afghanistan will have to cross Uzbek and Kazakh airspace. And we can't use choppers from the Afghan bases – they won't have the range. I don't see any of these countries agreeing at short notice to allow our fighter jets to enter their airspace.'

'Does that mean that Vijay's going to be completely on his own?' Imran wondered aloud.

Patterson shrugged. 'I'm going to do my damndest to ensure that we can still back him up. That is not my main worry. I'll work every contact I have in Washington to be able to do it. But I'm not sure if we have enough time for that. If they're going to be at the final location by dawn tomorrow, local Kazakh time, that gives me only a few hours. That's it then. I'd better get going.'

'All the best.' Imran signed off and switched off the monitor. A hollow feeling took hold of him. He had already lost Radha. And Patterson didn't sound very confident about being able to help Vijay. Imran knew the odds. And, though he fought it, he couldn't shrug off the feeling that he was going to lose a second friend today.

The Three Brothers

Vijay stared out of the helicopter as they passed over the Ustyurt plateau. Far below stretched a flat highland plain, carpeted with sand. Very little vegetation could be seen in the pre-dawn light and no sources of water were visible as far as the eye could see. This was desolation at its keenest.

From the desert sand rose giant terraces, chalk escarpments that seemed to reach out in an attempt to touch the intruders flying overhead. The jagged, ruptured cliffs were at least 300 metres high and flaunted different colours, from pristine white to blue and pink. It was like gazing down on another planet while orbiting it.

Was this where the source of the virus was located? They would find out soon.

As if on cue, the pilot turned around and informed them that the rock formation known as the Three Brothers was in sight.

'Look out for the arrowhead,' Van Klueck instructed. 'I want every eye on the ground.'

To Vijay's immense surprise, the flat highlands they were flying over had huge arrows seemingly carved into them. He was reminded of the Nazca figures carved on the ground, stretching for miles. But here, apart from the arrows, there were no other shapes visible.

The arrows themselves comprised a U–shaped bag from which two arrows with clearly defined tips stuck out.

Vijay now understood the meaning of the verse. He also understood why Van Klueck had wanted to be here before sunrise.

The Three Brothers formation now loomed ahead of them, majestic and eerie at the same time. The three upright columns of sheer rock rose proudly from a bed of chalk that climbed steeply like a gargantuan chalk dune submerging their nether regions. The columns were bare, bereft of any vegetation, their eastern side set on fire by the new born sun.

Vijay could not take his eyes off the spectacular creation of nature which surpassed the desolate beauty of the plateau that he had witnessed so far. If there ever was a composition of nature that could give eternal life, this seemed to be an appropriate place to find it.

'The Three Brothers,' Van Klueck murmured, somewhat pointlessly, also taken up by the beauty of the rock formation. Then he snapped back issuing instructions with military precision.

Far below, on the ground, an SUV could be seen, with little ant-like figures around it – the advance team.

And then Vijay saw it. Another set of arrow heads. Carved into the stone of the plateau just like the others they had passed on the way. It was pointing towards the Three Brothers, unlike the other arrowheads on the plateau which all pointed northwards.

The arrowhead that points the way.

But which one was the arrowhead referred to by the verse? Each one was pointing at the rock formation but at different parts of the rock.

'Which one is it?' Cooper shouted above the roar of the helicopter rotors.

'The shadows will touch the one that will lead us to the Seal!' Van Klueck shouted back. 'Look, they are retreating already.'

He was right. The long shadows cast by the early morning sun shining on the rock were shrinking, drawing back towards the rock formation like a bride drawing in her train.

'We can't hover here indefinitely!' Cooper yelled. 'We have just enough fuel to make the journey back to Aktau!'

'They're marking the arrowheads!' Van Klueck responded. 'We'll go down now.'

The helicopters began their descent as the advance team on the ground started scurrying around the various arrowheads. Vijay understood what was happening. With the advent of daylight, the advance team were planting white flags on the perimeter of each arrowhead. When the shadow of the rock formation struck the correct arrow, they would know by the shadow cast on the white flags as it retreated towards its creator.

The choppers landed in a storm of dust and sand, the sound of the rotors dying out to give way to a silence that was deafening.

It was a beautiful sight. All around them was a vast stony desert plain in the centre of which stood the rock formation called the Three Brothers. In the distance, the cliffs began changing hues as the sun rose higher in the sky.

'This doesn't make sense,' Vijay said. 'Both arrowheads are in shadow right now. As the shadow of the rock recedes, it will touch the tips of both arrowheads. They are pointing in the same direction!'

'Patience,' Van Klueck said. 'Remember, the cube was made by the Order. There is a purpose to everything we do. If the verse says we will find the location in this manner, I believe we will.'

The group waited as the shadow of the triple headed rock continued to recede. Which one of the two arrowheads was the one they sought?

68

The Serpent Seal

The armed men gave a shout in unison as the shrinking shadow passed over the tips of the two arrowheads and then lingered over the tip of the one that was to the extreme right. It pointed to the shortest of the Three Brothers.

Vijay now realised the truth behind Van Klueck's words. He had been incredulous until now. But the receding shadow, while passing over the arrowheads, had itself become an arrowhead pointing away from the rock. By some strange natural positioning of the rock and the sun, the tips of the arrowhead-shaped shadow and the carved arrowhead on the plateau now met.

Van Klueck shot a triumphant glance at Vijay, who nodded in acknowledgement. 'Let's go.' The European started forward as the others hauled large trunks from the helicopter and followed him in the direction of the arrow.

As they approached the smallest peak, Vijay felt a thrill of anticipation. What would the Serpent Seal reveal itself to be?

Cooper looked back at the arrowhead. He was clearly calculating something in his head. 'The arrow is sloped upwards,' he said finally. 'Which means the point at which we need to dig is on the slope. I think it should be about there.' He indicated a spot on the steep face of the rock formation.

Instructions were given and five men stepped forward. One of the trunks was opened and equipment was pulled out. A discussion began among the five men, with repeated glances towards the rock. Not being a climber, Vijay didn't understand

the discussion but he could make out enough to know that they were trying to decide what equipment to use.

As he looked on, one of the men picked up a cylindrical device and aimed one end at the summit of the shortest of the three peaks. A grappling hook shot out and soared over the top of the rock, trailing a climbing rope behind it. Vijay realised it was some kind of a compressed air cannon that shot the hook at the rock. The hook landed with a clank on the summit. Another man pulled on the climbing rope, which slid forward a few inches, then became taut, indicating that the hook had found a hold in the rock.

Another device was unpacked and attached to the rope. Vijay didn't know what it was until one of the men slipped on a harness and attached the device to it. He pressed a button and the motorised winch pulled him rapidly up the rope.

'You're looking for either an opening in the rock or a seal with the sign of the Order,' Cooper instructed the climber, speaking into his throat microphone. The climber, like all the other men in the group excepting Vijay and Van Klueck, was equipped with a throat microphone and a tiny earpiece for communication.

The winch continued to pull the man up the slope until, at around seventy feet, he stopped and proceeded to attach the rope to the rock so that he was not dangling in mid air.

'He's found the seal,' Cooper informed Van Klueck. 'It is intact.'

Van Klueck nodded. 'I thought as much. Now we know what killed Alexander.' Vijay looked at him enquiringly but Van Klueck did not elaborate on his cryptic statement.

The men got busy unpacking the rest of the trunks. There were portable generators, power drills, jackhammers, electric hole making machines and manual implements like shovels, spades and pickaxes, along with enormous hammers for breaking rocks.

The other four men now used similar devices to shoot grappling hooks at the summit of the rock and climbed up to join the lead climber, who lowered a rope which was tied around his waist. A bag containing the equipment was tied to the rope and hauled up by the climbers, thick cables snaking out of the power tools, connected to the generators on the ground.

'You'll have to break the seal,' Cooper told the men on the slope. 'No need to be gentle about it. We'll close the opening later.'

The generators were started up, the noise echoing over the vast, stony plateau, scaring a few rabbits and birds out of their nesting places. The climbers began attacking the rock, using the drills and the hammers to break the seal. From this distance, Vijay could not see what the seal looked like. But he realised it was well camouflaged. No one would have known that there was a seal hidden somewhere on the rock formation.

Finally, there was a shout from the climbers, a loud crack and pieces of rock tumbled down the slope. The seal was broken.

A square, black opening yawned in the rock, dark against the white slope in which it was set. It didn't look very big and, as the lead climber hoisted himself into the opening, Vijay realised that it couldn't be larger than three feet on each side. Just enough to fit one man at a time.

The power equipment was lowered along with the five winches, as the climbers entered the orifice one by one. They carried the manual implements with them.

'It's a horizontal tunnel leading through the rock,' Cooper reported to Van Klueck. 'Narrow, so they're on their hands and knees.' After a while, it seemed the men had stopped and Cooper listened intently to his earpiece. He turned to Van Klueck. 'They're in a chamber. There are stairs leading down from there. We should join them now. Once they descend, we're going to lose contact with them.'

'Let's go,' Van Klueck motioned to the men to follow him, as he strode to the base of the rock and grasped one of the winches. 'Time to see what the old haunts of the Order looked like.'

Almost there

Vijay winched himself up, sandwiched between two guards. He didn't really have to do much; the winch did all the work. The guard in front of him disappeared into the opening which was just large enough to accommodate one man. Vijay followed him, the light from his helmet lamp illuminating the guard's posterior.

The tunnel ran horizontally through the rock. It was not uncomfortably narrow. There was space on either side and above Vijay, provided he didn't raise his head too high. The floor and walls of the tunnel were polished smooth.

After stretching for around thirty feet or so, the tunnel opened out into a large chamber. Vijay clambered out and joined Van Klueck and the men who had gone before him and watched as the rest of the group emerged from the passage.

'Lights,' Van Klueck ordered and powerful portable searchlights were switched on, illuminating a stairway that descended into deep darkness, the bottom of which could not be penetrated by the searchlights.

On Cooper's signal, an advance team of four men made their way down the stairs. Cooper monitored their movements through his earpiece as they relayed back reports on their movements.

The group waited silently, patiently, in the chamber as the minutes passed. Finally, after what Vijay reckoned was at least twenty minutes, Cooper nodded to Van Klueck. 'All clear,' he said.

Van Klueck nodded back and the rest of the company began the descent down the stairway.

69

Nectar and jewels

Vijay stepped off the final stair and looked around in wonder. The searchlights revealed a large hall, cut out of the rock. This was no cavern, natural or man-made. The chamber they now stood in had clean geometrical lines. It was rectangular, with smooth polished walls. A number of doorways, leading into darkness, lined the walls on either side. At the far end, set in the wall facing the group, was a rectangular stone that seemed to protrude from the wall.

Under instructions from Van Klueck and Cooper, the group split up into smaller units and spread out to explore what lay beyond the open doorways. Vijay, accompanied at all times by two guards, followed Van Klueck as he moved from room to room.

In the first room urns that were one foot in height stood on shelves that lined the walls. There were at least one hundred urns, all made of the same black metal that the metallic plate had been forged from.

A single word, written in the Devanagari script came into view as the searchlights swept the higher reaches of the walls.

'*Rasakunda.*' Vijay read out the inscription. But he didn't know what it meant.

Van Klueck saw his puzzled expression and chuckled. 'These are vessels that contained a special kind of potion which is described as nectar in the Mahabharata,' he explained condescendingly. 'The potion had the ability to impart great strength to whoever drank it. In the Mahabharata, when Bhima is poisoned by Duryodhana and descends to the kingdom of the

Nagas, he is given this potion to recover and build his strength. According to the epic, Bhima drank eight jars of the nectar, each of which was said to provide the strength of a thousand elephants.'

'You mean these are the same jars that were described in the Mahabharata?' Vijay could hardly believe what he was hearing. He had already learned that the Mahabharata was based on actual events that occurred thousands of years ago. He had seen evidence of that. But to encounter actual objects from the ancient epic was another thing.

Van Klueck shrugged. 'Maybe not the same jars. But that's what the inscription says.' He turned to Cooper. 'After all these centuries, the urns will be empty. The nectar would have evaporated. The water must have contained the retrovirus. That's the only explanation for the sudden strength the nectar conferred on whoever drank it. There may be some residue which contains the virus. Collect enough samples.'

Cooper nodded and bags were produced. Vijay hadn't noticed, but each one of them had a collapsible nylon bag fastened to his waist. The men proceeded to examine the urns and selectively collect some of them in the bags.

Van Klueck strode out and entered the room on the opposite side of the chamber. This room had walls lined with jewels that glittered in the beam of the searchlights. The European nodded. 'Everything is as it should be,' he said, more to himself than to Vijay. 'That's what the shloka meant.'

Vijay understood what Van Klueck was muttering about. One of the shlokas he had interpreted for Vijay on the flight to Kazakhstan had mentioned medicinal plants and jewels. The reference to medicinal plants had been quite clear – it meant the plants which Callisthenes had been assigned to collect from the forests of Bactria. But at that time, Vijay hadn't understood the reference to the jewels. Now, he realised that the jewels were right here. With the virus.

Van Klueck had muttered something about knowing what had killed Alexander, when the seal on the rock was being broken.

Vijay now knew what that remark had meant. He, too, knew why Alexander had died despite drinking the *amrita*.

The final barrier

'It is a door,' Van Klueck announced after a quick inspection of the stone slab that protruded from the wall opposite the entrance to the chamber. The group had swiftly explored the smaller chambers on either side of the main one. But apart from the vessels in the first chamber and the jewels in the second one, they had not found anything of significance apart from some inscriptions on a wall of one of the rooms. It seemed that whoever had occupied this place had cleared it out before sealing it, leaving only the urns and the jewels behind. It was difficult to fathom why those hadn't been transported away but there was no time to analyse or speculate. Van Klueck was in a hurry to get a more reliable sample of the virus. And he was convinced that it lay behind the stone door.

However, despite this conclusion, there seemed to be no way of opening the door.

'Break it open,' Van Klueck commanded, unable to wait any longer.

The massive rock-breaking hammers were produced and three men set to work on the rock.

There was evidently something important behind the rock, for it would not yield easily. The three men laboured for half an hour before cracks began appearing in the rock. All the while, splinters from their efforts flew around the chamber. The other men had to shield their faces with their hands to avoid being hit in the face by the shards that rocketed out of the stone. The men attacking the rock now stepped back and were replaced by three others, to provide fresh energy to complete the task.

After another half an hour of back breaking work, the stone door finally splintered into smaller pieces and disintegrated.

A yawning black hole was revealed.

What was hidden beyond that opening?

70

327 BC

PRESENT DAY AFGHANISTAN

From Man to God

Eumenes held aloft the torch as Alexander squinted at the parchment his mother had given him before he had embarked on his campaign of conquest to the East. She had told him that it had been given to her by a philosopher from the very lands his army was now camped in. But it was not the source of the parchment that had interested him. It was the tale of the myth — the secret of the gods — that had driven him to lead his army across Asia and into the land of the Indus.

He stared at the dark landscape around him, trying to identify the meaning of the verses on the parchment, as explained to him by his mother, with the topography of the land.

'It should be here, somewhere,' he muttered, half to himself, half to Eumenes. 'We just passed Poseidon's staff.'

Eumenes nodded. 'Shall we proceed further? Perhaps it is ahead?'

Alexander grunted. They had been searching for almost an hour now, their task made more difficult by the darkness and the unevenness of the rocky ground upon which they walked. But Alexander had needed to carry out his search under cover of the darkness. That was the only way to find Poseidon's trident.

He had cleverly motivated his army to march this far and was not going to allow anything to come in the way of his success.Initially, he had told his soldiers that they were fighting for glory. For Macedonian glory. Avenging their humiliation at the hands of the Persians. They would fight the Persians and defeat them. Alexander would rule Persia. This had resonated well with his troops, especially the battle hardened veterans who had served under his father, Philip II. They could see in his plans, an extension of Philip's ambitions and his conquests. Alexander, to them, was a true son to his father.

Over the last few years, they had routed Darius, killed the nobles who had betrayed the Persian monarch and established Alexander as the ruler of Persia. And then, at Balkh, as the troops contemplated returning home, Alexander had dropped the bombshell. They were marching on to Asia. He had goaded them on with stories of conquest of the world, marching to its ends and establishing Macedonian supremacy in the lands of the Indus. His men, flushed with their victories and the seeming invincibility of their king and his army, had rallied around him.

Now, he was within sight of the true reason he was here. The secret of the gods. Dividing his army into two parts, he had led one section up the Kunar valley, following the instructions on the parchment. Callisthenes had already completed his part of the mission, in which he had complied with some of the instructions on the parchment, while Alexander had led his army against the Sogdian rock and subdued the Bactrian tribes.

Alexander now had all he needed according to the instructions on the parchment. He and Eumenes had slipped away from the camp tonight, searching for the final signs that would lead them to the location of the secret.

Slowly, cautiously, they moved forward, skirting the rock formations that rose around them like silent sepulchres in the night, towering above them. Far below, unseen to them, hidden by the mountains and the cloak of darkness, the river flowed on. It had seen conquerors come and go and was oblivious to the presence of even this king, who would be one of the greatest conquerors of all time.

Eumenes glanced around anxiously. Alexander had refused to bring along any of his guards, trusting his sword and his skill as a soldier. 'Who will attack the man who has conquered the world?' he had scoffed at Eumenes when the latter had suggested that they be accompanied by a host of soldiers. But Eumenes did not share Alexander's confidence. Alexander had made no secret of his desire to subdue the hill tribes of this area, arguing that they posed a threat to the flanks of the army. Eumenes knew that this was a cover up for the secret mission they had undertaken tonight. But the local tribes had fled at their approach, retreating to their stronghold at Aornos, a few miles away across the pass that would lead them to the east. Who could tell whether a disgruntled tribesman was skulking in the shelter of the rocks and the trees, waiting for an opportune moment to assassinate the ruler of the civilised world?

'There!' Alexander's hoarse whisper intruded on his general's thoughts.

Eumenes strained to see what Alexander had noticed. Another strange shaped rock formation loomed ahead of them. But this one was different. It seemed to have been massively eroded in layers on either side, giving it the appearance of an immense wave breaking over their heads, stretching to the sky above.

A massive wave. Or a snake with five heads. Which matched the verse on the parchment.

Alexander hastened towards the snake shaped rock, Eumenes scrambling after him, trying to keep pace with his king.

Presently, they stood before the rock. It was much taller than it had seemed when they first saw it, stretching around fifteen feet above their heads.

Eumenes held the torch close to the rock, trying to detect any means of entry to the underground cavern that, according to the parchment, lay beneath the rock.

Alexander found it. It was a narrow fissure, hidden behind a fold in the rock. Unless one knew it was here, it would have been impossible to see it, even in broad daylight.

'Wait here,' Alexander commanded, as he took the torch from Eumenes. 'I will be back soon.'

Eumenes started to protest, but was silenced immediately. 'This is a sacred place,' Alexander told him. 'Fit only for a god. I shall go on ahead by myself.'

The young conqueror disappeared into the fissure, leaving Eumenes alone in the darkness. But the general was not worried about his own safety now. Neither of them knew what lay beyond that fissure. They only had the word of a stranger to go by. What if this was a trick, a ploy to kill Alexander?

Time passed, slowly, agonisingly and Eumenes sat down on the hard, stony ground, awaiting the return of his king.

Finally, after what seemed like eternity, Alexander emerged from the fissure. His armour was wet, and his face shone.

'It is done,' he said, handing the torch back to Eumenes. 'Now, I am finally a god!'

71

PRESENT DAY

DAY SIX
The Kernel of the Quest

The now open portal gave way to empty space, every pore of which was filled with a blackness that threatened to ooze out of the doorway and overwhelm the small chamber they stood in.

There was a collective gasp as the searchlights played on the impenetrable wall of darkness that formed a hidden cavern beyond the stone doorway.

On the floor of the cavern was a roiling mass of snakes of all kinds, in all possible sizes. There were cobras and rat snakes, which were easily identifiable. There were others that were barely one foot in length. There were black snakes, along with green, grey and rust coloured ones.

Only Van Klueck was unmoved. Vijay glanced at him and saw, to his surprise, that the European had a grim, satisfied look on his face. He seemed to have anticipated this.

'Gather them up,' the European commanded. 'I want two of each type of snake. Get your hands on as many as possible.'

The men hesitated. There were possibly non-poisonous snakes in there. But most of the snakes seemed to be poisonous.

Cooper barked out orders and whipped out a gun. 'I want every man in there now! You have guns. Get in there and get the samples! Shoot if required, there are enough of them! Work as a team of two and watch each other's back!'

The men looked at each other and, hesitatingly, moved into

the cavern. Ten men stood at the doorway, holding searchlights to illuminate the floor and make it easier for their comrades.

The mass of snakes roiled even more as the men crossed the threshold. Their bags were now held in one hand, a gun in the other as the men moved gingerly through the snakes, trying not to step on them.

There were immediate casualties. One man stepped on a cobra which struck with lightning swiftness. The man collapsed on the floor while the others continued their march. Another unfortunate man stumbled on a pile of snakes while trying to avoid treading on a cobra. He was immediately attacked by a coiled, hissing mass of snakes and went down with a scream as he was bitten multiple times.

The others ventured carefully among the serpents, trying to learn from the mistakes their colleagues had made. Working in twos, they cautiously picked up snakes using their rifle barrels and slipped them into the bags. It was a painstakingly slow operation but there were no further losses.

Vijay stood and watched apprehensively. He was not worried about the fate of the men in the cavern. He was more concerned about what would happen next. To him. And to Radha.

The men in the cavern began making their way back as he looked on. He observed that, as long as the men were able to find spaces among the snakes where they could tread without disturbing the creatures, they were safe. By and large, though the snakes seemed to resent the intrusion, they left the men alone.

Finally, the last pair stumbled past the broken stone doorway, into the main chamber. Their foreheads were beaded with perspiration and their clothes were sticking to their bodies. It was cool down here but the pressure of the task they had undertaken had drenched them in sweat.

'Good.' Van Klueck smiled appreciatively. 'We now have the virus. Our operation here is over.'

Vijay frowned. He didn't understand what Van Klueck meant. They had collected snakes. Where was the virus?

But the European was speaking again. 'Let's move.' He fixed Vijay with a stony stare. 'And now, I guess it is, as the Americans say, "payback time". You gave us enough grief last year. I think it is time we put a stop to that. In any case, you know too much about us and this operation. So you'll understand when I tell you that we're not taking you with us. You're staying here.'

Vijay's heart sank. Even though he had always known that this was a possibility, he had hoped that the European would keep his promise. He should have known better. Especially after he had learned what they were after.

But there was still one last hope he clung to. It was not for himself.

'But you will let Radha go?' he ventured.

Cooper grinned. 'We would if we could.'

'She's dead,' Van Klueck informed him in his usual matter of fact manner. 'She tried to escape and was shot by our guards.' He turned to the men who were looking on. 'Let's get moving!'

Vijay stood, rooted to the spot. He felt numb. His mind felt like a vacuum had sucked all his thoughts out, leaving a large empty hole. A deep, dark void. His legs gave way under him and he slumped to the floor, his back bent, his face buried in his hands.

He had lost loved ones before. His parents. His uncle. But somehow, nothing had hit him as hard as the loss of Radha. Patterson had prepared him for this. But how can you ever be prepared for losing someone who you love more than life itself?

Dimly, through a mist, he sensed, rather than heard, people moving around. Someone was saying something to him. A searchlight was thrust into his hand. But the dark depression in his mind had engulfed him. Mind and body. The loss was overpowering. Nothing else registered.

The men moved on, back up the staircase. Cooper had handed Vijay a searchlight. 'We aren't cruel,' he grinned. 'We'll leave you with some light. At least as long as the batteries last.'

Vijay sat, hunched over, staring at nothing, as Van Klueck and Cooper disappeared up the stairway.

He was too far submerged in shock for a critical question to enter his mind.

How long would it be before the snakes discovered the open doorway and entered the chamber?

Nowhere to run

Vijay didn't know how long he had sat there in a stupor. He was jerked out of it by a loud rumble that shook the chamber and caused the shards of stone from the broken doorway to shiver on the floor.

For a moment he was disoriented. Then, he recovered and remembered where he was. The keen pain of his loss had settled into a dull ache. He had his faculties back.

In the light of the searchlight, he saw thick swirls of dust cascade down the stairway. He realised what had happened. Van Klueck and his team had emerged from the rock and blown up the opening of the tunnel, sealing it and sending boulders and dust surging down the stairway.

He was trapped.

But there was worse happening. He heard scraping sounds around him. There was hissing on the fringes of the searchlight, emanating from the darkness that reigned beyond the reach of the light beam.

Vijay trained the searchlight on the floor of the chamber and froze in horror.

The snakes had discovered the chamber and were making their way in.

72

Firepower

Van Klueck watched the last of his men winch their way down the slope and join the others who had descended earlier. The captured snakes and the urns had been safely stowed away in the helicopters. The men were now busy packing the climbing and digging equipment in the trunks and loading them onto the helicopters.

'Birds on the horizon,' one of the men said suddenly.

All eyes turned to the direction the man had indicated. The stowing of equipment and loading of trunks paused.

Two distant specks were visible over the flat badlands that stretched to the west. They were rapidly getting bigger.

Choppers. Heading in their direction.

Cooper began rushing the men. He didn't know who was in those helicopters but they definitely weren't friends. No one among their allies knew about this part of the mission. If there were helicopters arriving, it was not good news.

'Go, go, go!' he yelled, spurring the men to work faster. They caught the urgency in his tone and accelerated their pace, sprinting where they were ambling earlier and dumping stuff in the trunks rather than carefully packing them.

The choppers grew in size and the staccato sound of their rotors came to their ears. They were fast helicopters and were rapidly covering the distance between them and the rock.

Cooper realised they would not have time to load all the equipment.'We have to leave the stuff here,' he told Van Kluek, who nodded his assent.

The men dropped the trunks and began boarding their own choppers.

Cooper squinted at the horizon where the two helicopters were now big enough to be discernible with the naked eye.

'Bad news,' he told Van Klueck. 'Kazakh airforce. Eurocopter EC725s.'

Van Klueck nodded. 'Let's fly. And hope they have only the machine guns and cannons. No rocket launchers.'

Cooper hopped into the chopper and the two helicopters lifted off.

The Kazakh airforce choppers were closing in fast. Van Klueck's helicopters weren't built for speed. His troops were in an Mi-26, the largest heavy lift helicopter in the world, capable of accommodating upto 82 passengers, and just right for the 60 men Van Klueck had needed for this mission. It also had a range of 432 nautical miles, which was ideal for the distance they had to travel on this mission. His own helicopter was an Agusta Westland AW139M, built for upto 15 passengers with a range of 537 nautical miles.

The Kazakh choppers, on the other hand, were smaller. They had a top speed of 324 kilometres per hour, just faster than the Agusta at 306 kilometers per hour and much faster than the ponderous Mi-26 at 295 kilometres per hour. Moreover, they were probably on a reconnaissance mission and weren't carrying troops unlike the choppers belonging to the Order. That made the Kazakh choppers lighter. And faster.

'We aren't going to make it,' Cooper said grimly.

'Get the rocket launchers out,' Van Klueck commanded. 'They won't be expecting armed resistance. We have to get them off our tail.'

Cooper issued the command. There were two rocket launchers stowed in the rear of the cabin of the Agusta chopper, which were hastily unpacked and readied for an assault. Two men stood by ready to fire them.

The unsuspecting Kazakh choppers drew closer.

'Wait,' Van Klueck instructed. 'We don't know if they have rocket launchers. Let them come into range. We have only one shot. Make it count.'

Exploring

Vijay stood up, warily, wondering what he should do. He was trapped down here with hundreds of snakes. The only way out had been destroyed by Van Klueck.

A thought struck him. It didn't offer much hope but it was something to go on. If this chamber was associated with the Mahabharata then it had been built thousands of years ago. The snakes couldn't be that old. They would have to feed in order to breed and replenish their population.

That meant that there must be some means of getting to the surface. Openings in the rock that would allow the snakes to crawl out of their home and feed on the fauna that inhabited the plateau. The air down here seemed to be fresh even after being sealed for centuries. Maybe one of those openings would be large enough for him to crawl through? It was worth exploring. He had no other hope of survival.

But first, he wanted to complete a task that had been on his mind all along. He hadn't been able to do it while Van Klueck and his men had been around. He entered the room where he remembered one wall bore inscriptions and shone the searchlight on the carvings. They were strangely shaped inscriptions, unlike anything he had ever seen before. Holding the searchlight with one hand, he took out his smartphone and clicked a few photographs of the inscriptions before making his way back to the main chamber.

Now, to find his way out of this mess.

He picked up a shovel that lay on the floor, along with other spades, shovels and pickaxes that the men had carried here with them and left behind when they departed. It might come in useful.

There was only one problem. He would have to wade through the sea of snakes that stretched before him.

73

Nailbiting tension

'They're going to attack the choppers,' Patterson announced. He was on a tele-link with Imran, who was still in his hospital bed but wired to the rest of the world through the equipment in his room.

Patterson had burned the telephone lines in Washington, reaching out to his network in the defence forces and Congress. He had gone all the way up to the President of the US. He had a team mate in the field and he wasn't about to abandon him. It was not his way.

Finally, through diplomatic and defence channels, he had broken through to the Kazakh defence ministry and impressed up on them the urgency of the situation. However, Patterson was constrained by the fact that much of what he knew was classified information and could not be shared with a former Soviet state. It had been extremely difficult to convince the Kazakhs of the dire need to send combat troops or commandos to ground zero in the Ustyurt plateau. They had finally agreed to send a two chopper mission to reconnoitre the plateau and report back.

The entire operation was being monitored by the Kazakh air command and the video link was shared with Patterson and Imran.

They had watched as the cameras on board the Kazakh choppers had zoomed in on the two helicopters on the ground, clearly capturing the reactions of the men who had first speeded up the loading of their choppers, then abandoned the effort and taken flight.

Then, they looked on as one of the choppers on the ground took off and headed eastwards in an obvious attempt to flee the scene while the other one hovered, as if unable to make up its mind about what it wanted to do.

That was when Patterson realised that the chopper, an Agusta Westland AW139M, was planning to attack the oncoming helicopters. While the Agusta was fitted only with machine guns, if they were waiting to attack, then he was sure they were carrying rocket launchers on board.

The Kazakh air command had realised the same thing. Patterson and Imran could hear excited gibbering and commands being shouted out as people scrambled to warn their pilots and to take counter measures. They had not been expecting armed resistance. While no one really knew who these people were, they had not been expected to possess any kind of fire power. And the EC725 choppers were armed only with machine guns and a 20mm cannon.

Patterson and Imran watched in horror as the tell-tale muzzles of two rocket launchers appeared through one of the large sliding cabin doors of the AW139M.

Dogfight

The rocket launchers were fired but, warned by the air command, both Kazakh choppers had anticipated the attack and took quick evasive action. The projectiles soared through space and curved downwards directly towards the Three Brothers.

Van Klueck's men were already reloading the rocket launchers when the rockets hit the rock formation midway up its slope and exploded just below the two larger peaks. The roar was deafening but the men in the Agusta chopper weren't interested in what was happening below.

They were targeting the Kazakh helicopters.

They fired again.

A discovery

There seemed to be no boundaries to the cavern. The darkness stretched around him on all sides as Vijay continued to tiptoe around the snakes.

He was worried. Until now, he had managed to sidestep, step over and evade snakes slithering past him. They had largely ignored him, except in a few cases where he had heard warning hisses as he passed by. How long would his luck hold out?

Flashing the searchlight around him, he wondered how far he had come. The darkness had cloaked the entrance to the cavern like a thick black curtain drawn across a window to block out sunlight. A more worrisome question arose in his mind. How long would his searchlight last?

But he had to keep going. He had no other choice. To stop now would be suicide.

Abruptly, the ground beneath shook, and a shudder ran through the cavern. From the invisible roof and walls of the cavern, a long moan issued forth.

He stopped and stood still. Something had happened. No, something was happening. The ground continued to tremble and the snakes had begun dispersing. They were slithering away from him, moving at speeds that he would not have thought them capable of.

It was like they were fleeing something. But what?

It dawned on him that if he followed the fleeing snakes, they might lead him to a means of escape. Unless whatever they were running away from caught up with him first.

He started after the snakes, even as they glided past him, between his legs, at his sides and sometimes even over his feet. They seemed oblivious to his presence and only intent on one thing — getting away.

Vijay continued moving forward. The snakes seemed to disappear into the darkness faster than he could follow them.

Suddenly he stopped in his tracks. He couldn't believe what he was seeing. Not more than fifteen or twenty feet ahead, and to his right, were stone stairs. His hopes soared. He hurriedly moved forward, anxious to get to the stairs.

It was an ill-timed move. Two cobras were gliding by just as he stepped forward. One of them came under his foot and reared up hissing, ready to strike.

Vijay jumped back just as the snake struck, missing him by millimetres, but landed on a cobra which was languorously making its way in the same direction. The snake gathered its coils in preparation to strike.

Whether the fall broke something in the searchlight or the batteries chose that moment to run out of charge, Vijay would never know. The light died out and the cavern was flooded with darkness.

All around he could hear the slithering of the snakes. But he had no idea which direction the stone staircase lay.

74

Strike one

The second round of rockets fared no better than the first round. Once more, the Kazakh pilots were quick in their anticipation and managed to evade them.

Van Klueck was getting annoyed. 'Damn it, have you guys gone cross-eyed?' he admonished his gunners. 'We can't get out of here until we get them off our tail!' He looked out towards the east where his second helicopter was rapidly diminishing in size.

One of the Kazakh choppers came straight at them now, machine guns blazing. Van Klueck knew what was coming next. Either the 20mm cannon or a 68mm rocket launcher, if the chopper had an axial pod fitted.

'Now,' he shouted.

One of the gunners took aim and fired the rocket launcher for the third time.

This time, it found its mark.

The chopper exploded in a ball of fire and plummeted towards the Three Brothers, striking the shortest peak and then tumbling down the slope, coming to rest on the plateau, a blazing wreck.

Trapped

For a few moments, Vijay stood still, unable to decide his next move. The slithering and scraping had become louder since the light died out. He didn't know whether it was his heightened sense of hearing that was his body's way of trying to compensate for the loss of vision, or whether the snakes were getting more perturbed. But it scared him. A wave of panic threatened to flood and overwhelm him.

He forced himself to think. He took a few steps forward and felt around in the darkness.

Nothing there.

He tried retracing his steps. That didn't work either.

Vijay began to despair. When the stairway had come into view, he had thought he had a chance, however slim, of making it out of this place.

Suppressing the fear and terror that was rising within him, he tried to concentrate on the noise of the snakes around him. Could he make out in which direction they were heading?

Big brother

'Missile warning!' the chopper pilot called out. 'Incoming! ECM initiated!'

'The pinnacles!' Van Klueck yelled. 'Use the pinnacles! And then let's get the hell out of here!' He realised what had happened. The Kazakh air force must have been monitoring their helicopters. He hadn't expected them to react so fast. They must have spotted his intention to attack the helicopters well in time. There was no other explanation for the speed with which they had been able to mobilise their fighter planes.

'MiG 29s!' his pilot called out as he took the chopper into a deep dive aiming to put the Three Brothers between them and the incoming air–to–air heat seeking missile. The Agusta had a Missile Approach Warning System, which had alerted the pilot to the missile. But the chopper also had a Counter Measures Dispensing System which used Electronic Counter Measures to throw the missile off course.

Van Klueck saw the flares light up over the Three Brothers and realised that his pilot was taking no chances. In addition to the ECM, he was also deploying flare decoys and probably also special material expendable decoys that oxidise in air to produce an infrared signature that the missiles would home in on.

The chopper swooped in low, with the Three Brothers forming a protective cover, and gunned ahead at full throttle towards the east. The border with Uzbekistan was not far and the Kazakh jets would not undertake any aggressive manoeuvres near the border.

The mission was going to be a success.

Stairway to heaven

Vijay crouched low, his eyes shut to enhance the sense of being sightless, listening to the snakes. He tried to still his breathing so that it would not interfere with the sounds the reptiles were making as they continued their exodus.

Snakes slipped past him, some of them touching his feet as they went. He tried to combine his sense of touch and hearing to judge the direction he should take. After a few minutes he decided to move forward. He first slid one foot along the floor and then the next, so that he would not step on or trip over any snakes.

Another thought struck him. Where did the stairway lead to? He shook his head. He should have thought of this before. He looked upwards. Far above him, through the darkness, he saw a small bright point of light. An opening to the outside world.

His hopes restored, he painstakingly made his way forward, his arms outstretched and his eyes shut. Despite the overwhelming darkness, he had to fight his urge to open his eyes. It was an uncomfortable feeling.

Suddenly, his shovel, which was held outstretched before him, hit something hard. He moved quickly forward and his hands brushed against rock. He felt around in the darkness and made out the shape of one stair. Then another. He could have cried with joy. He had made it. But there was no time to celebrate. He had to get out of here. Whatever had spooked the snakes, it was not worth waiting to find out.

He put the shovel down, clambered onto the lowest stair and began working his way upwards. The shovel would have to be left behind. It was a dangerous climb. The stairs were carved into the rock and were not more than three feet in width. To his left was the wall of the cavern. On his right was empty space and a drop to the floor of the cavern. One slip was all it would take. He shuddered and clung to the rock wall on his left as he made his way upwards.

It was a long climb and the stairway seemed to go on forever. Sweat drenched his clothes and his hands were raw from brushing blindly against the rock wall as he tried to find a grip to ensure he wouldn't slip. His thighs were beginning to cramp from the long, slow climb. But he wasn't going to give up.

Vijay now realised where he was. Inside one of the Three Brothers. This was a stairway carved within one of the huge pinnacles that rose from the sloping bedrock of the rock formation. Which one it was he couldn't guess – it couldn't be the shortest one since the entrance was below that one. But it didn't really matter. He didn't stop to think about what he would do when he reached the summit. He would tackle the problem of climbing down the rock when he reached there. For now, all he wanted was to be out of the darkness, out of this cave and in the open.

Slowly but surely, the opening above him grew bigger. And brighter. He redoubled his efforts and tried to increase his pace. He was close. Very close.

The light from the opening had begun to illuminate the staircase and he could see the dim shapes of each stair.

A surge of hope washed over him. There couldn't be more than another forty or fifty feet to go. He was going to make it!

He hurried up the next few stairs.

Then, all hell seemed to break loose. The summit of the pinnacle above him exploded with a thunderous sound. Bright light suddenly shone down on the stairway and masses of rock rained down.

He held his hands over his head, trying to shield his face, abandoning the security of the wall as he tried to fend off the falling rocks, some of which were the size of footballs. Rocks pelted down, striking him on his hands, his chest, his legs, and rolled off the edge of the stairway and into the chasm.

Almost simultaneously, there was another explosion, this one more like the detonation of an explosive device. The tower of rock enclosing the stairway shuddered. Vijay staggered back under the assault of the rocks. A couple of large rocks hit him in the chest and hips, drawing blood. Intense pain shot through his thigh as another rock struck his leg.

He heard the roar of jet aircraft and the beat of helicopter rotors overhead. His right leg slipped off the stairway. Arms flailing, he tried to regain his balance. For a moment, he teetered on the stairway. He flung his arms at the rock wall in a desperate attempt to stay on the staircase.

Then, gravity took over and he was treading air as he toppled into the chasm.

75

Frustrated and foiled

Patterson and Imran watched the scene on their monitors. They had looked on, horrified, as the first helicopter was brought down. As the second helicopter took evasive action, they lost sight of the Agusta chopper. But, within seconds, they saw the missile streaking through the sky, heading eastward, its infrared homing device searching for the heat signature of the Agusta.

When the rocket launchers were spotted sticking out of the Agusta, the Kazakhs had scrambled a couple of MiG 29s to back up the helicopters.

Then, as the remaining Kazakh helicopter resurfaced, buoyed by the appearance of the Kazakh jets and the fact that the Agusta was on the run, they saw the Agusta fleeing eastward, leaving a trail of flares.

Patterson let fly a string of expletives. 'The bloody idiots! They should have listened when I told them to send in troops backed by the airforce. These guys are well equipped. They've got ECM and dispensable decoys to counter the missiles.'

They watched as the missiles headed for the decoys. One of the missiles slammed into the centre pinnacle, pulverising the rock, sending debris flying down the slope. When it had passed, the pinnacle was a good fifty feet shorter than it had been earlier.

The second missile crashed into the rock formation at the base of the pinnacle, where it reared up from the bedrock, one hundred feet above the surface of the plateau.

The two men had to be content to be silent observers as the Agusta made good its getaway. The roar of the jets was reassuring but couldn't mask the fact that the enemy had escaped.

The jaws of death

As Vijay tumbled over the edge of the stairway, he grabbed desperately at the stairs with both hands. One hand got some purchase for a split second. Then it slipped off as he made another grab at the stone stairs.

This time, he managed to get a better hold with one hand and he wildly lunged with his other hand to get a grip on the rock.

But he knew this couldn't last long. His fingers were raw and aching from the bruising climb up. His hip had a gash where the large rock had struck him and there was intense pain in his thigh.

He had only managed to postpone the inevitable for a few moments.

As if to reinforce his thoughts, the stairway shuddered and he heard a series of loud cracks.

Vijay looked down at the chasm below. Something was happening. The shuddering grew more violent and cracks began appearing in the staircase.

He now knew why the snakes had been fleeing the cavern. They were simply following what their sixth sense told them. All animals possessed the unique ability, not shared by humans, to sense disaster. And the snakes had known what he hadn't at that time.

The pinnacle was collapsing.

The Two Brothers

The helicopter pilot made a pass over the rock. He had been instructed to search for a member of the task force who had been a prisoner of the group that had shot down his comrade. Even though it was highly possible that the man he had been sent to rescue was still held captive in one of the two helicopters which had got away, he decided to sweep the area. Just in case.

But there was nothing to be seen, apart from the plumes of black smoke rising to the sky from the wreckage of the downed Kazakh chopper and the missile that had crashed into the pinnacle.

It was futile. The man was either dead. Or gone. Either way, his mission was unsuccessful. And he had lost two comrades. They had been good men.

Sighing, he turned the helicopter around to fly back westward, towards the airforce base.

His co-pilot let out a sudden shout. He had been peering curiously into the wrecked pinnacle and had spotted a man clinging on to the rock.

The pilot quickly activated the external hydraulic hoist system as he positioned the chopper directly over the pinnacle.

Will he make it?

As the rock walls of the pinnacle, and the stairway itself, started to splinter, Vijay heard the sound of the helicopter's rotors directly above his head.

He glanced up and saw a hoist swinging down towards him.

The stairway lurched as it began to disintegrate.

The hoist inched its way down to Vijay. He held on grimly.

Just a few more inches.

Almost there.

Now.

With a thunderous roar, the walls of the pinnacle collapsed and the stairway shattered, leaving Vijay holding onto large rocks suspended in mid-air.

Vijay felt the hoist touch his shoulders and he grabbed at it. Around him, the pinnacle was imploding in a huge cloud of dust that enveloped him. He coughed as he tried to maintain his grip on the hoist and his eyes burned.

Then, he was being winched up and strong hands were pulling him on board the chopper. The door of the cabin shut and the helicopter rose, carrying Vijay to safety.

76

Intelligence Bureau Headquarters, New Delhi

'It seems we grossly underestimated the enemy,' Patterson concluded. The task force was completing a review of the operations which had led to the events on the Ustyurt plateau and Vijay's close shave with death.

Vijay had been flown back to India earlier in the day after receiving medical attention at the Kazakh airforce base. He was fortunate to have escaped without broken bones or any serious injuries. He had rested briefly before heading to Delhi with Colin and Shukla to attend the meeting which had been called by Patterson. At the fort, though, Vijay and Shukla had remained closeted in their rooms until it was time to depart. Neither of them was inclined to meet anyone.

At the IB office, seated in the conference room, they had discussed the entire sequence of events starting with the excavation in Greece to the events in Kazakhstan and the failed mission to rescue Radha. There was silence for a few moments after this last discussion. The team had lost a member. She had gone down displaying courage and determination, putting the objectives of the task force before her own life.

Imran had left his hospital bed for this meeting. He had insisted on attending in person. On the US side, Royson had joined the meeting along with Percy Galipos, the genetics expert on the task force.

Patterson looked dispirited. The last twenty-four hours had been harrowing for all of them. And, despite their best efforts, the enemy had given them the slip.

'The firepower they displayed in Kazakhstan was unprecedented,' he continued. 'And in Afghanistan, as Vijay has informed us, they were able to stave off the Taliban until their mission was complete. We still don't know what the Order is or who their members are. There doesn't seem to be any reference to them in recorded history. Somehow, they have been able to keep their presence hidden over the centuries. We now have some names. But nothing more. The only thing we can be sure of is that they are powerful and have immense resources at their command. They have tentacles in the highest offices of government in many countries including your country and mine.'

'And they are ancient,' Vijay joined in. 'Very ancient. If what Van Klueck said was true, it was the Order who had created the cavern thousands of years ago. And the Order had something to do with the preparation of the *amrita*.' Something struck him. 'Will you excuse me? I need to make a call. I just thought of something.'

Patterson nodded and Vijay left the room. He was back in a few minutes. His face was flushed with excitement.

The others looked enquiringly at him. It was obvious that he had something to tell them.

'It was something you said,' Vijay began, addressing Patterson. 'You called them the enemy. That's when a bell went off in my head. You see, there *is* a recorded reference to them in history.' He pulled out a small notebook. 'I just called Alice and asked her to reference a diary which was given to us last year. It belonged to a German called Bruno Beger. You know the story.'

Everybody nodded. Those who had not been a part of the adventure had been briefed about it.

'Well, in that diary, there was an entry that was a translation of a document written by Surasen, a courtier of Asoka the Great. I will read out the first paragraph for you:

'I, Surasen, do hereby put down a record of my discovery as part of the secret library of the Nine Unknown Men, the glorious brotherhood created by our beloved Emperor Asoka the Great, Devanampiya Piyadasi. I will not say what this discovery is, for the Emperor forbids any record describing what I have found in case it falls into the hands of the enemy; for this is the reason the brotherhood of the Nine was founded.'

He shut the notebook and looked at the others. 'I am convinced that the Order is the "enemy" that Asoka was trying to hide the discovery from. And he succeeded for over two thousand years. If we have to learn who these people are, we have to delve into our mythology. It is clear that their origins were in India and they have evolved since then into a global organisation.'

'Now that you mention Surasen's account, I remember the phone tap recording that Blake played for us when I first met him. That conversation also mentioned that Murphy would report to a member of the Order in India,' Imran reminisced. 'We're dealing with an invisible monster. No intelligence agency in the world knows about the existence of the Order. Yet, they have the resources and power that we have witnessed.'

'And now, they're going to relentlessly pursue us,' Shukla said sombrely. 'They know who we are. Where we live. And what we do. They will come for us. They have exposed themselves to us. And they will try and rectify that mistake. None of us are safe.'

'True,' Patterson admitted. 'But they don't know about the task force. Don't forget that we, too, have resources at our command. We may have lost the battle but the war has just begun. This time, we were unprepared. Now that we know a bit about them, we can prepare ourselves better.'

He looked at Vijay. 'And you say that this entire mission of the Order was inspired by a myth from the Mahabharata?'

Vijay nodded.

'Tell us about it.'

Vijay thought for a moment. Where was he to begin? 'I won't go into the details of the shlokas from the Mahabharata which narrate the myth,' he said, 'but Van Klueck read and translated some shlokas for me. The myth is called the *Samudramanthan*.' He looked at Shukla. 'I think you're the best person to explain what the myth is about.

Shukla hesitated then nodded. 'I'm sure everyone on our side knows the myth but I will summarise it for our friends in the US. According to the Mahabharata, the Devas – the gods – and the Asuras or Danavas – the demons – joined forces to churn the ocean of milk for *amrita* – the nectar that would confer immortality on whoever drank it. They used Vasuki, a serpent as the churning rope and Mount Mandara as the churning stick. Eventually, after years of churning, the Ocean of Milk yielded the *amrita*, among other things.'

Galipos frowned. 'I've heard that myth,' he said. 'What's the connection with the bacteria and the virus you told us about?'

'According to the translation I heard from Van Klueck,' Vijay replied, 'the shlokas tell a story that is quite different from the conventional interpretation of the verses. Thousands of years ago, there was a search for a potion that would confer immortality when consumed. In the cavern in the Hindu Kush, there is an immense underground lake which is inhabited by the bacteria we discovered at Aryan Laboratories. The bacterium is an extremophile, able to live in very salty environments. The lake is saltier than the oceans of this world. And the bacterial colony in the lake gives it a silvery white colour – the water looks like milk. Hence the reference to the Ocean of Milk in the myth.'

'Like halophilic Archaea,' Royson muttered. Seeing Patterson frowning, he hastily added, 'the red blooms in the Dead Sea.'

'So, these bacteria in their natural state produce toxins which are fatal for humans,' Vijay continued. 'But, apparently, all those centuries ago, someone discovered the existence of a retrovirus that infects bacteria.'

'A bacteriophage,' Royson interjected, helpfully.

'Exactly. Thank you. I had forgotten the term. The interesting thing about this retrovirus is that, once it infected these extremophile bacteria, it would alter their DNA and change the proteins they produced. The toxins were replaced by proteins that are beneficial or neutral to humans. However, since viruses cannot survive in salt water, and the bacteria cannot survive outside the salt water, the infection had to take place using certain herbs and plants and small quantities of crushed jewels. I don't know how but this somehow neutralised the effects of the salt water on the virus. This is the *manthan* referred to in the Mahabharata. It is not a reference to churning but a description of all the ingredients being mixed together. Once the infection process was complete, the *amrita* was ready for consumption.'

'You said the Order collected the snakes as samples from the cavern,' Patterson remarked. 'I take that to mean that they believe the virus infects the snakes.'

Vijay shrugged. 'I have no idea. They didn't say anything to me. But I thought the same thing at that time. I don't understand it though. How can snakes carry a virus that infects humans?'

'It may be possible,' Royson spoke up before anyone else could comment. 'Not something that we can dismiss outright, at least. A couple of years ago, a study by the University of California, San Francisco discovered a virus belonging to a family called Arenaviruses. These infect mammals, usually rodents. While there is no evidence that this particular virus can pass from snakes to humans, one of the genes in the virus group is very similar to the family of viruses that includes the Ebola virus, which is a haemorrhagic virus which infects humans. This discovery was pretty much unprecedented. Who's to know if there aren't other viruses out there that can infect snakes and humans? And this would be the best way to preserve a virus for thousands of years. In a live host.'

'And the plants were the ones that the verses referred to?' Imran asked.

Vijay nodded. 'Van Klueck told me, when we reached Kazakhstan, that his team had found the plants that were described in the verse. I remembered bits of their names and looked them up before leaving the fort for this meeting. The plant with the violet fruit is called,' he referred to his notebook again, '*Prangos pabularia Lindl.* That's the Latin name. Apparently it is so localised to selected provinces of Uzbekistan that it doesn't even have an English name. The other plant, with dark purple fruit is *Prunus sogdiana Vassilez.* In English, it is called the Sogdian plum. The older branches of the plant are dark grey and the younger branches are brownish green. The flowers are white or have a purple base – hence "clothed in grey and white and green or brown". This is also found in selected provinces of Uzbekistan and Kyrgystan. And, when I researched these on the internet, both plants are found together in only two provinces of Uzbekistan: Tashkent and Surkhondaryo. And, believe it or not, Surkhondaryo approximates to the region where the Sogdian rock must have been. The Rock itself has never been found. But Alexander's route went through that province before heading southwards again.'

'And this potion conferred immortality?' Royson asked.

'According to the myth, yes.'

'Can you tell us about the *amrita?*' Royson asked. 'From a scientific perspective, of course. I know you've told us that the search involved finding the original bacterium and the retrovirus, the prophage of which we found in the subjects of the clinical trials. But I'm curious to know more about exactly what happens when the potion is consumed. Did they share that with you?'

Vijay nodded. 'I don't remember all the scientific terms,' he admitted. 'But I can tell you what I remember. Essentially, the retrovirus adapts to the human body and makes it the host for replication, inserting its DNA into the human genome for this purpose. In doing so, it switches on certain genes which produce proteins that combat ageing and diseases associated with ageing.'

'Interesting,' Galipos remarked. 'Do you remember any details about the genetics or the proteins?'

Vijay frowned, trying to remember. 'Let's see. Van Klueck said that there are several reasons for ageing. For example, shortening of telomeres which results in cell loss and shrinking tissue. He said that telomeres are at the tips of chromosomes.'

Galipos intervened discreetly. 'A chromosome is a giant coiled DNA molecule. At the end of each chromosome there is a repeated sequence which is meaningless from a genetic point of view. This is a telomere. It is like the aglet at the end of a shoelace, protecting it from fraying. Every time a chromosome is copied, a little bit of the telomere gets left out. You can see how, after lots of copying, the telomere gets so short that any further replication will start leaving out meaningful genes. That is when a cell stops dividing. Interestingly, apart from growing old and leading to cell loss, cells that stop dividing but don't die have been shown to have malignant effects on healthy cells.'

'Yes,' Vijay agreed. 'So, one of the genes that gets switched on is the one that controls the production of telomerase which enables repair of the telomeres. So cells keep replicating and there is no cell loss, which reverses the ageing process.'

Galipos nodded. 'Interesting. But the production of telomerase would also lead to unlimited cell division and replication – essentially a tumour. Or, by another name, cancer. So how does that help?'

'That's the interesting part. Apparently, the virus also influences the production of a protein that leads cells to commit suicide. This protein targets senescent and malignant cells. Effectively killing off any cancerous growth in the body.'

Galipos whistled. 'That sounds like p53. A protein that leads to cell cycle arrest and apoptosis or a signal to a cell to kill itself. It targets cells with genetic damage, which is essentially what cancer cells are, and induces apoptosis in those cells. So the virus also ensures control of runaway cells. Very interesting.'

'There are other genes which he mentioned, which produce proteins that provide a check on diseases like cardiovascular diseases, diabetes, hypertension and even Alzheimer's. These genes improve the functioning of muscle groups in the body or cause enhanced regeneration of tissues. All activated by the retrovirus. But I don't remember them all now. Of course, Van Klueck also said that the reason they were conducting clinical trials was because they wanted to understand exactly how the virus works. And that's why they needed the original virus. The prophage just wouldn't work the same way. But he was very confident about the results.'

'Sounds like a miracle cure,' Colin observed.

'It does,' Roydon said emphatically. 'No wonder they wanted to get their hands on this…this mixture.' He shook his head, as if he still couldn't believe what he was hearing.

'You'll pardon my saying this,' Colin said. 'I know there are respected scientists in this room and I don't have any expertise to be judgmental about this. But, quite honestly, this all sounds very far-fetched to me. I mean a miracle virus that leads to the production of anti-ageing proteins and changes the nature of bacteria as well as targets cancer cells. It is a bit hard to believe. More like science fiction, really.'

'Not really.' Defence of the argument came from an unlikely source. Patterson had entered the fray. 'There's a lot about the human genome and viruses that we still haven't discovered. There are new discoveries being made every day. Take, for example, the Adeno-associated virus type 2 or AAV2, which infects humans but is not known to cause sickness. In several studies using mice, it has been demonstrated that AAV2 kills 100 per cent of breast cancer cells in the laboratory by activating proteins called caspases, which are essential for the cell's natural death. Cancer cells infected with AAV2 also produced more Ki-67, a protein that activates the immune system, and c-Myc, a protein that helps to increase cell growth as well as induce apoptosis.'

'Moreover,' Royson added, '8 per cent of the human genome consists of virus genes and their remains. From evolving primates who were infected with retroviruses hundreds of thousands of years ago. And we know of viruses that turn on DNA that is usually dormant in people – the HIV virus, for example. It is very possible that the retrovirus produces proteins that attach to DNA to switch on genes that we don't really know anything about. The human genome is still a big mystery. It has been mapped, but we're still trying to figure out what large parts of it do. For a long time, an enormous part of the genome – over 90 per cent of it – was termed "junk DNA" because it doesn't code for proteins. Today that tag is being discarded as new discoveries come to light.'

Galipos took up the narrative now. 'That's right. The ENCODE project suggests that almost 70 per cent of DNA is being copied into RNA rather than the miniscule numbers suggested earlier. It is entirely possible that there could be millions of genes out there. We just don't know. Recent studies at Harvard University have shown that, for one genetic class –lincRNAs – more than 83 per cent are likely to contain transposable elements. These are called "jumping genes" because they can hop around within the genome. And many of these "jumping genes" are actually descendants of ancient retroviruses that have been passed down the generations along with the rest of the genes. It is thought that many of these retrovirus remnants may be involved in switching genes on and off. So the idea of a retrovirus entering the human body and switching on new genes that we don't know about is hardly farfetched.'

'So why did Alexander die after drinking the *amrita*?' Colin persisted. 'If he found this miracle cure and consumed it, he should have lived forever.' He shuddered. 'God knows I am thankful he didn't, though.'

'I'll tell you why,' Vijay responded. 'It was Callisthenes.'

'What?' Galipos looked confused.

Colin chuckled. 'A Greek historian who was executed by Alexander.' He looked at Vijay. 'So what did Callisthenes do?'

Vijay shook his head. 'It wasn't what he did. It was what he didn't do. When we reached the Three Brothers, the Serpent Seal was unbroken. It had been untouched ever since that chamber had been originally sealed. Callisthenes never entered the chamber. And he would never have got past the door to the cavern even if he had managed to climb the rock and break the seal. He got the plants and fruit that were required. But he didn't get the virus.'

Colin whistled. 'So he planned to let Alexander die? I mean the verses are very clear. If you don't follow the instructions, you don't stand a chance. Not surprising, considering what we know about the virus now.'

'Not really,' Vijay replied. 'I don't think Callisthenes planned it. I think he just realised that there was no way he could climb that rock and break the seal. He probably thought that whatever lay behind the seal wasn't all that important. And he didn't want to tell Alexander about it. Not surprising, considering how intolerant Alexander had grown by then.'

There was silence for a while as everyone digested this. A myth from the Mahabharata had led a conqueror to his death. The world may have been a very different place had Alexander not died just short of his thirty-third birthday.

'What's the status with Titan?' Vijay asked. When Imran had discovered the eight hidden floors with the patients from the clinical trials still locked in them, he had swiftly organised a medical evacuation of all the patients to Jaipur. From Jaipur itself, he had called Patterson and briefed him on the discovery.

'We spoke to Wallace,' Patterson replied wearily. 'He was shocked to hear about the medical facility. But he also pointed out, quite rightly, that the premises did not belong to Titan. Neither was the Jaipur facility associated with Titan in any way. Kidwai has been working on tracing the owners.'

'They're absconding,' Imran reported, taking up the narrative. 'We've put out a red alert but they've covered their tracks pretty well. This was a well planned operation. They had planned for emergencies like being discovered.'

'Do you believe Wallace?' Colin asked. 'He's been popping up in the strangest places. Too many coincidences for me to swallow. Just look at it. He funded the Olympias tomb excavation. His trust hired Stavros and Peter, who turned out to be thugs. He's the Chairman of Titan Pharmaceuticals. And we did find that one medical centre affilitated with his company is involved in shady medical experiments. Even if that centre was outsourced, there's got to be some link here!'

There was silence for a few moments. Then Patterson spoke up. 'I don't dispute the facts you have stated,' he began, 'but there's no evidence. Wallace is the non-executive Chairman of Titan. Which means he doesn't sign off on day-to-day decisions made by the company. Even if those decisions involve contracting with outsourced vendors who conduct clinical trials. It is within the realm of possibility that he didn't even know that the Delhi centre was working for the Order. And the

Jaipur centre has no connection with Titan anyway. It is good enough reason for Wallace to point out that there may be a link between the two centres that Titan has nothing to do with.'

'What about the excavation?' Colin demanded, unwilling to give up. He had been very fond of Radha and was searching for someone who could be blamed for her death.

Patterson shook his head. 'Negative again. Patterson's trust is run by a man called Seymour Parker. Parker authorises all appointments. Not Wallace. He'd never heard of Stavros or Cooper. We checked Parker's background and he's clear. Cooper's papers were forged. Damn good forgery too. Near CIA quality. These guys are professionals. Even if I were to go with you and doubt Parker, there's no hard evidence that they acted wilfully in whatever they did. They're in the clear.'

'But you're going to keep an eye on them, aren't you?' Colin wasn't willing to give up.

'We have to tread carefully here,' Patterson replied. 'As a task force, we haven't built enough credibility to push our case. The first time we've seen action, we've failed. That's right. We've failed. There's no other way to describe what's happened. No matter what the reasons or the extenuating factors, the outcome is beyond dispute. Who's going to believe us if we accuse anyone? Who's going to agree to spy on people we want to keep under surveillance?'

'We can't just stand by and let them get away,' Colin protested.

'Is that your emotion talking or is that based on facts?' Patterson countered. 'I think the same way you do. The members of the task force are paramount for me. Damn everyone else. But I'm not going to be swayed by emotion. And facts tell me that we cannot accuse anyone at this point in time. If we collect the evidence, I'll be the first one baying for their blood. But not now.'

There was silence again. Colin bit back a retort and accepted the reality of Patterson's words. It was bitter but he was right.

There was no argument that could stand against what he had just said.

'What about Saxena?' Vijay wanted to know.

'No evidence,' Patterson responded. 'We can't connect Saxena to the centre. No witnesses to prove that he was even there.'

'You mean he's going to walk scot-free?' Vijay was incredulous. 'After Imran here survived an assassination attempt and Radha was killed by them?' He choked on his words as he mentioned Radha's name. 'Isn't it obvious that he is involved in this?'

'We can't arrest him,' Imran said gently. 'You and I suspect him. But without evidence, there's nothing we can do. We're going to watch him like a hawk. He's going to trip sooner or later. And then we'll nab him.'

'We have to follow due process,' Patterson explained. 'Anything we do, anyone we charge, we have to make it stick in a court of law.'

Vijay was silent. His bitterness showed on his face.

'Right, then. I think I've got all I need for a report to the US and Indian governments,' Patterson summed up. 'It wasn't an ideal start for the task force. Our enemy got away. And they have the virus. We have work to do. It won't take them long to isolate the virus, sequence it and then create the solution they are trying to develop. We have to stop them. But we don't have much to go on. Let's get to work and see what we can dig up. There has to be a trail. History may have overlooked the Order but would not have ignored it altogether.'

The others nodded. There would be no rest. They had to find the Order. And stop it. Before it was too late.

Patterson nodded and everyone stood up to leave. He looked pointedly at Vijay. 'Stay.'

Vijay hung back as the others left the room. Patterson, too, was by himself now. The big man looked down and then back at Vijay.

'I can't pretend that I know how you feel,' he said. 'But I promise you, I can empathise. I have lost buddies on the battlefield. Boys I grew up with, hung out with, guzzled beer with...' He shook his head. 'If there's one thing I've learned about war, it is this. Don't hope. War doesn't bring hope. It takes hope away. It is peace that brings hope. And that is what we must work towards. I'm sorry about Radha. I really am. But you have to move on. I suppose you harbour thoughts about avenging her death. It is natural. But I want you to suppress those thoughts. We have to work to defeat the Order. If we don't there will be anarchy. This is war, my boy. This is not about Radha. It is about the future of the world. So hang in there.'

Vijay stood for a while, silently. 'I understand.' he looked Patterson in the eye. 'Saxena, Van Klueck and the others; they can't walk free just because we don't have the evidence. If we can't collect the evidence then we have to do more. And I will work to bring the Order down. Not just to feel that I've exacted revenge. They must also be stopped from taking away the loved ones of others. Like the people who were the subjects of the clinical trials. We will stop the Order. God knows how we're going to do it. But I know we will find a way. Whatever it takes.'

Patterson nodded. *Whatever it takes.*

How many lives had been claimed already? And how many more would be claimed before this was over?

Thoughts of revenge

As Vijay left the conference room, he was surprised to find Shukla barring his way. The linguist's eyes were bright and there was a hard determination in his face that was difficult to ignore.

Vijay stood in silence, facing Shukla. He knew that the older man wanted to speak to him in private. The others had left. It was just the two of them.

Shukla waited a few moments before he spoke, as if he was trying to control his emotions.

'I have not seen my daughter's body,' he said finally, emphasising each word. 'Do you know how precious a daughter is for her father?' Vijay could see him choking back the tears and he felt a strange feeling rise within him to reciprocate. 'A daughter is her father's life. He feels pain when she feels pain. He cries when she cries. He wants to give her every bit of happiness that she wants, even if it is beyond him.' He paused, visibly composing himself again. 'She was all that I lived for. And now...now, she is gone!'

Shukla's restraint broke down and tears flowed down his cheeks. He was unable to control his emotions any more.

Vijay stood there, his own emotions a maelstrom in his mind. Shukla's words had reminded him of what he, too, had lost. A selfless human being who loved him for what he was, blemishes and all.

He gripped Shukla's arms and looked into his eyes. 'I will bring her back,' he assured Shukla. 'I couldn't do anything to help her. I couldn't save her.' The words tumbled out and he knew that his emotions were dictating them but he didn't want to control himself now. 'I promise you will see her again. I will bring her back. I don't know how, but I will hunt them down and find her body. And I will ensure that they pay for what they have done.'

Vijay was conscious that he was contradicting everything he had told Patterson just a few moments ago. But he didn't care. He didn't want to care. He wasn't a hero. He wasn't here to save the world. It was all very nice and noble to talk about ensuring that others wouldn't lose their loved ones. But what about him? What about Radha? There was no going back for her.

He embraced the old man who broke down openly now.

Two men stood in the semi-dark ante room of the conference hall, sharing their grief. In that moment, for that moment, they were one in their thoughts and feelings.

EPILOGUE

A disturbing call

Vijay sat in the study of the fort, nursing a whisky. He was alone. Colin had left that night for the US. He had gone to the airport straight from the task force meeting. Alice had gone with him. They had been booked on the same flight. Patterson had made arrangements to ensure that Alice would be under protection in the US. He hadn't disclosed what those arrangements were and no one had asked. It was better that way.

For the first time in his life, Vijay felt truly alone. When his parents had died, his uncle had been there. When his uncle was murdered, he had Colin by his side. And, later, Radha.

Now, there was no one. It was true, he mused, that one came into the world alone and left the same way. For some reason, his thoughts were dark and depressing. He couldn't stop thinking about death. He didn't find it surprising, considering how often death had visited his loved ones and taken them away.

He set his glass down on the desk. If nothing else, he would busy himself so that his thoughts would not overwhelm him. It would be better to spend time going through the cartons in the room on the fifth floor until he was too tired to continue. He would then retire for the night.

The jangling of the phone intruded on his thoughts. He frowned. Who could it be? He glanced at his watch. It was 11 pm. A bit late for a social call.

It was an unfamiliar number. He decided to answer it. 'Yes?'

'Vijay Singh?'

He frowned. It wasn't a wrong number after all. But the voice was unfamiliar.

'Speaking.'

'You don't know me.' The voice was hesitant. A bit tremulous. As if the speaker wasn't sure he should be calling Vijay in the first place. It was guarded. Cautious.

'Who is this?'

'I'm a friend of Pratap Singh,' came the reply. 'A very close friend.'

Vijay sat up. His father's name was Pratap Singh. 'What's your name?'

'I… can we meet?'

'I need to know who you are.'

'We need to meet.' The speaker was more forceful now. The hesitancy was gone. 'I need to tell you something. Your father gave me something before he died.' The speaker corrected himself. 'Before the car crash.'

'What was it?'

'I can't… not over the phone. We need to meet.'

'And why have you waited fifteen years to contact me?'

'I didn't need to. Now, I do.'

Vijay considered this. What need could have driven this mysterious caller to call him after fifteen years?

'How do I know you aren't a fraud? Making up this story about knowing my father?'

'Check your email.'

'Hold on.' Vijay pulled his laptop towards him and switched it on. He quickly checked his email. There was, indeed, an email sent just a few minutes ago. From an email address that he was not familiar with. He clicked on the email.

And froze. He couldn't believe what he was seeing on the screen. It now made sense. The file among his father's papers. The newspaper clippings and articles. The research on archaeological excavations. He was shocked. But he had to know more.

'Are you there?' the caller enquired, a bit anxiously.

Vijay shook himself out of his reverie. 'I'm here,' he responded. 'When can we meet?'

'Six months from now. Starbucks. Cyber Hub, Gurgaon. I'll call you two days prior and give you a time.'

'Why wait so long to meet if it is urgent?' Vijay couldn't understand.

'I need time to prepare,' was the terse reply.

The call disconnected. Vijay put his phone down and sat thinking. His mind spun. Who was this mysterious caller? He clearly had an urgent need to meet. So why wait for six months? His explanation didn't make sense. What preparation did he have to do? And what was he going to reveal to Vijay when they did meet? There were too many questions that were unanswered.

Six months from today this puzzle would unravel.

He would have to wait.

To be continued...

AUTHOR'S NOTE

Dear Reader,

Thank you for your interest in this book.

This book is the first in a series. Unlike my previous novel, *The Mahabharata Secret*, the story that unfolds in this book doesn't end here but continues beyond.

Now that you have read it, I am sure that there are questions that remain unanswered for you and explanations that you believe should be forthcoming. There may have been facts and situations and even characters that you did not quite understand while reading this book. This is deliberate and intended, since the story continues even after this book ends. Please be assured that your questions will be answered and any confusions or doubts will be cleared as the series proceeds to the culmination of the story.

I am hoping that the suspense and the doubts will keep you enthralled and that you will find your answers once the story ends. It is, therefore, my earnest request, that you be patient and wait for the next few books for all your questions to be answered.

I promise you, it will be worth the wait.

In the meanwhile, there are several facts that merit explanation within this book itself and I believe I owe it to the reader to explain them. Here they are.

From the Science Files

A lot of scientific research has gone into this book and, while I have tried to simplify the science as far as possible, I am conscious that a fair amount of jargon and technical description has been inevitable. I would like to present a straightforward explanation of the scientific facts that does not interfere with the unfolding of the story, so here we go.

PCR testing: Polymerase Chain Reaction is a method to analyse a short sequence of DNA. PCR amplifies (reproduces or replicates) sections of DNA or RNA. A DNA polymerase is used for the replication. As PCR progresses the DNA generated is itself used as a template for replication, setting in motion a chain reaction which produces many copies of the DNA.

Stingray: this is a new surveillance technology, a portable device, that enables the tracking of cell phone signals inside vehicles, houses and insulated buildings. The Stingray trackers work by mimicking cell phone towers and mop up phone data like text messages, emails and even cell site information. This can allow the user of the device to pinpoint the location of cell phones, which numbers are called, who people spend their time with etc.

Virus replication: All cells replicate through division, creating identical copies of the DNA that rests in their nucleus. A virus cannot replicate on its own. It needs a host, which could be any living creature, including bacteria. A normal virus replicates by translating its DNA to RNA (ribonucleic acid). The RNA is nothing but a set of instructions, like a computer program, to assemble proteins. Those proteins help to create a new virus. So, the virus infects a host cell, and the replication machinery in the host cell helps to translate the virus DNA into virus RNA, which creates virus proteins to manufacture a new virus. The baby viruses then accumulate and burst through the cell, killing it, and infect new cells, starting the process all over again. Scary, isn't it?

Provirus: the genetic code of a virus while it is contained within the DNA of a host.

Bacteriophage: are viruses which infect bacteria and use bacterial cells for replication as described above.

Virion: infectious virus particle

Retrovirus replication: A retrovirus is more cunning, more complex. They contain strands of RNA, not DNA. So, when they infect a host cell, their RNA has to be translated into DNA first. This is done using a protein called reverse transcriptase. Once the virus DNA is created, it is inserted into the DNA of the host cell. Yes! The virus becomes a part of the host, which is why a significant part of human DNA is inherited from retroviruses. Believe it or not, we are partly virus, when it comes to our DNA! The virus DNA is then translated into virus RNA, which creates virus proteins which are used to assemble a new virus. This is how the retrovirus described in this book works. When it infects the bacteria in the lake, it changes their DNA (by inserting its own DNA into the bacterial DNA). This changes the nature of the proteins that the bacteria produce – and this actually happens in real life.

Beneficial viruses: when the retrovirus infects human cells, it also turns on genes that were previously inactive. This is absolutely true. The examples given in the book are real. There are discoveries being made every day about how viruses affect our DNA and genes. Genes are basically like computer programs – only these programs produce proteins that have many functions in the body. All the proteins mentioned in the book, like p53, are real proteins. And all their functions are real. Viruses can activate genes which are dormant. This can lead to production of proteins which can have all kinds of effects on our bodies, without us even knowing about it. This is why genetics is a hot topic nowadays. Genetic treatments of medical conditions can be more effective than any medication existing today. There are proteins that benefit us in many ways. The protein p53, described in the book, really does kill cancer cells. And there are many genes that produce proteins that can help control cancer, diabetes, Alzheimers disease and cardiovascular disease just as I have described in the book. Mutations in these genes or the switching off of these genes result in these diseases afflicting us. If there was a way (like the virus) that could ensure that these genes functioned to produce the proteins that would benefit us, we could really slow down ageing. There is a lot of research going into this even as I write and, who knows, in twenty years, we could have a solution!

Prophage induction: Viruses can reproduce in two ways. The first is via the lytic cycle, in which a virus takes over a host cell and uses the cellular machinery of the host to reproduce. Copies of the virus fill the cell to bursting, which kills the cell and releases viruses to infect more cells. The second is via the lysogenic cycle. The virus is a prophage, and its genetic material gets integrated into the host's genome. The virus then lies dormant within the host until it enters the lytic stage in which the virus reproduces. Prophage induction is the mechanism by which these dormant viruses are induced to replicate by entering the lytic stage. Induction requires a stimulus that leads to excision of the prophage from the bacterial chromosome and replication.

Telomeres and ageing: Telomerase, the protein I mention in the book, is the subject of a Nobel prize. It has been demonstrated that telomerase helps to ensure that the telomeres do not shorten to the extent that cells stop dividing or die out. There is a heated debate on in the scientific community today on the benefits of telomerase. The debate centres around the possibility of cancer emerging from the presence of telomerase.

When we are embryos in our mothers' wombs, telomerase is active, since cell division is important for the embryo's growth. Once we are born, however, the gene that leads to the production of telomerase gets switched off and our telomeres start shortening from the day of our birth. We are destined to die. But this is also nature's way of ensuring that cells don't go haywire and keep replicating – which is the definition of a cancer. So, telomerase is a double edged sword. While it slows ageing, it also leads to death by cancer.

Our knowledge of genes and pathogens, while extensive, is by no means complete. Every day, research throws up new discoveries about the manner in which cells function, genes work or pathogens infect their hosts (both human and non-human). Many of the scientific facts in this book are based on discoveries which have been made only within the last two or three years.

The Venus phenomenon: described in Chapter 60 of this book is a real phenomenon. A similar phenomenon takes place at Bryn Celli Ddu, in Wales, where Venus shines into a passageway in exactly the manner described in this book. This phenomenon is well researched and described, with a scientific explanation, in the book *Uriel's Machine* by Christopher Knight & Robert Lomas. I have not heard of this phenomenon in the Hindu Kush, so that is fiction, but the phenomenon itself is not fictional at all. The concept of the lightbox is borrowed from a similar mound at Newgrange, Ireland, where the sun (rather than Venus) shines into a passageway to illuminate the rock wall within. This phenomenon is also described in the same book.

From the History Files

While a lot has been said about Olympias, Eumenes and Callisthenes in the book, there are other historical figures who have been mentioned. I thought I'd shed a little more light on them.

Perdiccas: he was the Regent for Alexander's entire Empire for several years after Alexander died. However, many of Alexander's generals conspired against him and he was eventually assassinated. His principal ally was Eumenes.

Antipater: was trusted by both Philip and Alexander. He ruled on Alexander's behalf, controlling Greece and Macedonia, while Alexander campaigned in Asia.

Polyperchon: allied himself with Antipater and became the Regent for Greece and Macedonia after Antipater's death. Eventually, Cassander defeated him to seize control of the empire.

Cassander: was Antipater's son.

Ptolemy: was appointed governor of Egypt after Alexander's death. He was responsible for instigating the rebellion against Perdiccas, and later Antigonus. He took on the title of Pharoah and started the Ptolemy dynasty.

Antigonus: was originally governor of Phrygia. He fell out with Perdiccas and fought Eumenes for Syria and Persia. He was defeated twice by Eumenes before capturing him by cunning and finally executing him.

Clitus: was a real life figure and the events described in the book leading to his death are based on *The Death of Clitus* by Elizabeth Carney of Clemson University and Plutarch's *Life of Alexander.*

If you would like to read more without going through all the books, articles, videos and websites that I reviewed, here are two sources that will succinctly give you a perspective on Alexander and Olympias, as well as the role of Alexander's generals in the succession wars that followed Alexander's death:

Alexander: http://www.ancient.eu.com/Alexander_the_Great/

Olympias: http://www.historytoday.com/robin-waterfield/olympias-olympias-funeral-games

From the Mythology files

Samudramanthan: everyone knows the myth. The two sources that I used as a basis for this book are *The Mahabharata of Vyasa* by Kisari Mohan Ganguli (a translation into English prose of the original Sanskrit text) and *Samudramanthana* by San Sarin, which contains the original Sanskrit shlokas with the traditional interpretation of each shloka since it is a critical study of the original Sanskrit text.

Both, the interpretation of the *Samudramanthan* and the science I have presented are plausible scenarios. The translation I have provided and the scientific hypothesis I have presented have been verified and validated by experts in the Sanskrit language and the medical field as plausible and convincing. Could this have actually happened? It is not impossible. Check out my website (www.christophercdoyle.com) or my Facebook page (www.facebook.com/authorchristophercdoyle) for more explanations and information on the science behind this book. If you wish to write to me or if you have questions about the science, you can email me at contact@christophercdoyle.com.